─────────────────── ★ ───────────────────

"This time, Martin, why don't you tell me the truth?"

Martin looked defiant.

"I swear I had nothing to do with Trace's death."

"If that's so, then why are you lying?" Chief Moeller turned to Caroline.

"Talk some sense into your son, Cari. I'd hate to have his baby grow up without a father."

Jake stalked out of the room. Caroline looked hard at Martin, her face giving away none of the fear she felt for his safety.

"I don't know what's going on inside your head," she said. "But you'd better get your priorities straightened out right now."

Martin pounded his fist on the table. "I'm doing my best to protect Nikki and the baby!"

"From what, Martin? What could hurt them worse than if you're arrested?" Caroline drew a deep breath to calm herself. "The chief is not a stupid man. He wouldn't have pulled you into the station if he didn't have something that linked you to Trace. Circumstantial or not, it could be enough to land you in prison...."

─────────────────── ★ ───────────────────

Previously published Worldwide Mystery titles by
MARY WELK

A MERRY LITTLE MURDER
THE RUNE STONE MURDERS
TO KILL A KING

MARY WELK

The Scarecrow
Murders

W☉RLDWIDE.®

TORONTO • NEW YORK • LONDON
AMSTERDAM • PARIS • SYDNEY • HAMBURG
STOCKHOLM • ATHENS • TOKYO • MILAN
MADRID • WARSAW • BUDAPEST • AUCKLAND

Recycling programs
for this product may
not exist in your area.

THE SCARECROW MURDERS

A Worldwide Mystery/December 2013

First published by Hilliard & Harris.

ISBN-13: 978-0-373-26875-7

Printed in U.S.A.

ONE

"RUN, MARTIN! RUN!"

Nikki Rhodes megaphoned her plea through cupped hands tinged blue by a cold October wind. The practical side of her brain ridiculed the effort even as her lips formed the words. Daybreak had revealed a battery of clouds stacked like black casino chips on the outskirts of town. They'd lingered on the horizon until twenty minutes ago when, as if pushed by some invisible croupier's hand, they'd spilled into the skies above Bruck University, announcing their arrival with a smattering of thin raindrops. The dribble quickly turned into a torrent that pummeled the auditorium and matted the yellow grass behind it.

Now, with the temperature dipping towards the freezing point, the rain had become a crystal curtain of sleet. It battered Nikki's cries into icy whispers that spiraled out of control in the gusting wind.

Given the ferocity of the storm, common sense insisted Martin could neither see nor hear her. Despite what she knew to be true, Nikki's heart rebelled at the thought of defeat. The man she loved was fighting for his life only sixty yards away. Somehow she had to let him know she was there for him.

She called out again, this time expending every inch of breath available in her hundred-and-twenty pound frame.

"Please, Martin! Ru-unn!"

This second appeal was barely born before a slap shot of arctic air splintered the words into shards of sound that boomeranged back into Nikki's face. Fragmented syllables ricocheted inside the hood of her yellow vinyl slicker and echoed in her ears like the muffled chant of a ghost choir. She shivered, spooked by the eerie mimicry of the wind.

"Run, Mar-tinnnn! You can make it, boy!"

Nikki darted a look at the grandfather-like figure roaring encouragement over her left shoulder. Raindrops bounced off the bill of Carl Atwater's Bruck U. baseball cap and trickled down his drooping mustache and Santa Claus beard. They burrowed into the red and black checkerboard of his size 54 jacket, pinged off the fat metal buttons marching soldier-like down his stomach, and splashed to the ground in ever-growing puddles around his scuffed boots.

The veteran professor of history seemed oblivious to the sudden downpour that had turned a merely gray day into a cold and miserable one. The brutal wind reddened his face beyond its usual weathered look, but his eyes never wavered from the trio of mud-spattered bodies dashing across the field behind Hildegard Hall. He exhorted the lead runner with a series of deafening war whoops, emphasizing his demands for speed with a clenched fist raised high to punch tight little circles at the charcoal sky.

Watching him bob up and down on the balls of his feet, raindrops sprinkling the air with each thrust of his arm, a picture came to Nikki's mind of a fat old sheepdog shaking off the residue of a Saturday night bath. It was a comforting image, if not a lasting one.

"Aw, come on, Martin. Wake up and move your feet!"

Nikki's dark eyes narrowed. Her mellow sheepdog had vanished, melted in the rain like the Wicked Witch of the West. In its place stood an oversized pit bull complete with bared fangs and a bad dude attitude.

"Stop it, Professor!" She waggled a half-frozen finger

under Atwater's nose. "One more word of criticism out of you, and I swear I'll…I'll…"

Biting back words that would have shocked her mother, Nikki drew in her breath and finished the sentence with a frustrated shake of her head. The professor responded in what the young woman considered to be typical male fashion. His eyebrows rose in stunned surprise, then fused into a frown mirroring his inner confusion. He seemed baffled as to the reason for her anger. He also appeared hurt by the vehemence in her voice.

Nikki chose to ignore the look of mystified pain. Atwater deserved to be told off, and not only because he'd criticized Martin. This entire mess was his fault. If he hadn't egged him on, her husband would be safe at home now instead of running for his life from a pack of thugs. But his mentor's devious plot had appealed to the macho side of Martin's character. Testosterone had triumphed over common sense, and her own dire warnings had been in vain. Martin was about to die, and for no good reason at all.

Nikki's Greek blood boiled, her fear for Martin's safety preempted by an overwhelming desire to throttle the chairman of the history department.

The professor seemed to read at least a part of her thoughts. He leaned forward, his damp beard brushing the hood of her slicker. "Don't you worry. Martin's going to come out of this in one piece."

"Yeah, sure."

The burning sensation in the pit of her stomach spread upward to her throat as Nikki stared out over the field. The sleet and driving rain distorted her view, but she could see that the gap between her husband and the two men chasing him was steadily closing. The taller of Martin's pursuers appeared to be less than a yard behind him and slightly to his right. A shorter, huskier fellow was closing from the left, a step ahead of his partner and at a better angle to intercept his prey. It was like watching a pyramid collapse, the tip slowly crumbling to be buried by the rubble at the bottom.

Without warning, the shorter man launched himself into the air. His momentum propelled him several feet forward directly into Martin's path. He fell to the earth with a bone-jarring thud, then twisted to the right, arms outstretched, and grabbed his victim by the ankle.

Nikki reached out blindly and clutched the arm of her mother-in-law. Her fingernails dug a trench in the other woman's wrist as she watched her husband struggle to escape. Martin was still on his feet, stumbling forward and dragging his attacker with him across the slick grass. Covered in mud, the man held on until the second pursuer caught up with them. This fellow slammed into Martin's back, seized him by the shoulders, and unceremoniously hauled him backwards.

"Uh, oh," groaned the professor. "I think he's a goner."

Nikki's lips trembled. She squeezed her eyes shut, unable to watch her husband's premature demise at the hands of the two thugs.

"It's over," she whimpered. "They've made me a widow."

Caroline Rhodes smothered a yelp as her daughter-in-law's nails triggered yet another spasm of pain in her wrist.

"Look on the bright side," she muttered through clenched teeth. "Martin may be dead meat, but you'll look smashing dressed in black."

TWO

OCTOBER TOOK ITS cue from March, tiptoeing past September in lamblike fashion and bestowing two weeks of tropical heat on the Midwest. City dwellers and townsfolk alike celebrated their good fortune, but none more so than the citizens of little Rhineburg, Illinois.

The year thus far had not been kind to the farmers of Rhineburg. A winter of record snowfall preceded an unusually wet spring. A hot, dry summer followed, stunting the late sown corn in the fields surrounding the town. Then September arrived, and with it, the worst weather of all.

Labor Day had barely drawn to a close when a strong current of air swept up from the Gulf, pushing moisture northward along the Mississippi River. Along with the wind came a pigeon-gray layer of haze. Smoke-like, it thickened into inky smudges on the far edges of the sky before creeping relentlessly toward Rhineburg. On reaching the outskirts of town, the smudges billowed into an army of ebony-edged clouds. They smothered the sun and cast deep shadows on the green fields below. Even the livestock took shelter when the angry black giants flexed their muscles in a day long display of electric sound and light. Abandoned by the wind, the clouds then hunkered down over Rhineburg to spew daily doses of rain upon the land.

The little community held its breath as the endless storms of September threatened to turn Rhineburg's farms into marshland. Prayers for relief were answered when October made its welcome appearance. Fifteen days of uninterrupted heat worked miracles on the soggy soil. By the end of the month, the big green and yellow combines were able to crawl unimpeded across cornfields baked crusty brown in the sun.

Like all good things, even a prolonged summer must eventually come to an end. October meant the year was dying off; no one could deny the growing evidence of autumn encroaching on the land. In the forest surrounding Bruck University, the ancient oaks stretched their stubby-fingered leaves to the sky for one last suntan before surrendering them, bronzed and withered, to the wind. The sturdy maples decorating the town square likewise changed color, blushing watermelon red in early October, then darkening to garnet and maroon as the month wore on.

Rhineburg's trees weren't alone in showing off their foliage. Chrysanthemums cast deep shades of purple, gold, and russet across backyard gardens once rich with roses, while black-eyed susans fought off death with one last blaze of color. Overshadowed by their taller cousins, tangerine marigolds vied with mounds of snowy white alyssum for last-man-standing rights. The alyssum won out when the marigolds shifted tactics. Nodding their shriveled heads in the autumn sun, they scattered their black-tipped souls to the soil in hopes of a springtime resurrection.

The most obvious sign of autumn came on the sixteenth day of the month when the winds abruptly shifted from southwest to northeast. The crisp breeze was welcomed at first. But then, like an outlaw on the run, a cold Canadian front sneaked across the border and took up residence in the upper Midwest. Temperatures plunged into the thirties at night, and thoughts of summer vanished entirely when the town awoke to the first true frost of the season on October 22nd.

With winter right around the corner, Rhineburgers began to prepare in earnest for the cold months ahead. Yards were raked, gardens mulched, and fences mended to withstand the coming snows. Tree limbs were pruned, the wood cut into cords and stacked behind sheds and under overhangs. All across town, men readied storm windows, furnaces, and snow blowers while their wives searched closets for last winter's boots.

And then, in the first flush of holiday decorating, scarecrows began popping up on the lawns of Rhineburg. Other decorations followed—skeletons, ghosts, and assorted odd-looking goblins adorned most homes by the last Saturday of the month—but none were as colorful or entertaining as the town's many scarecrows. Some were attired in the plaid shirts, overalls, and beat up old hats traditionally worn by their truck garden cousins. Others appeared as wicked old witches or black-caped vampires. Most, though, were dressed to represent the families whose homes they guarded. Old hunting jackets and army fatigues vied with football uniforms, hospital scrubs, and cast-off sweat suits as proper apparel for scarecrows. Nothing was sacrosanct in the way of costumes, the only rule being an unspoken one: political and religious themes were strictly verboten.

But Halloween wasn't the only thing on people's minds on the final weekend in October. Football fever was in the air, and hardly anyone was exempt from its effects. The object of the town's affection was a small but hardy group of young men called the Mighty Maniacs of Rhineburg High School. Undefeated and on a roll, the team was headed for the playoffs ranked first in their class. Chances were good the beloved Maniacs would earn the first state championship to grace the town records.

Chances were not so good for the slightly older fellows taking the field across town. The Big Bad Bruins of Bruck

University were finding it hard to live up to their name. Undersized, under-skilled, and under-coached, the 3B's looked more like teddy bears than grizzlies as they piled up loss after loss in their inaugural season. The team's quarterback suffered from late-throwitis, while the running backs inevitably got squashed at the line of scrimmage. The Bruins were no better at defense. More often than not, opponents slipped through the hands of the tacklers like greased pigs at a county fair.

The only thing the team excelled at was turning over the ball. Fumbles and picked off passes led to opposition victories, a fact not left unnoticed by the fans. The hapless 3B's were quickly nicknamed the "Freebies" in recognition of their skill at giving away games.

No one in Rhineburg expected the Freebies to win on the last Saturday of the month. Their track record aside, the team's best receiver was on the bench, suspended from play after an arrest for drunk driving. With little hope of victory, only a handful of die-hard fans showed up for the game. Half of them left when the first drops of rain hit the field.

As a result, there were few people left in the stands when Martin Rhodes made his last ditch attempt to score the winning touchdown. Those who saw him escape his pursuers and dash for the goal line never guessed they were watching a prelude to murder.

THREE

"HE BROKE LOOSE!" Nikki screamed. "He's still on his feet! Oh, lord! I thought for sure they were going to kill him."

Or at least break his legs, Caroline Rhodes thought sourly as she pried Nikki's fingers from her arm. She glanced at the semicircular indentations left by her daughter-in-law's nails. Blushing pink against the remains of her suntan, the tiny claw marks banded her wrist like a speckled tattoo. A demented falcon desperate for a place to perch couldn't have done a better job.

"Martin will be all right, dear," she said in the soothing nurse voice she reserved for ER patients under the age of twelve. "Look at how he's running. He has those fellows totally confused."

"He has me confused, too," the professor grumbled. "What the hell is he doing?"

"Why, I...I don't know, Carl." Caroline peered through the downpour sheeting sideways across her line of vision. Martin had become a dim blur in the distance, his figure all but obscured by the wind-blown rain.

"He can't see the end zone," Nikki cried. "He's running in the wrong direction!"

Caroline squinted across the open land lying between the auditorium and the pine forest marking Bruck's northern border. She saw nothing until the wind suddenly veered to the west. A gap opened in the clouds, and the rain abruptly slowed to a steady drizzle. Although the ground was shrouded in a thick mist, Martin's body and upper legs were now visible a mere twenty yards away from the goal line. He was dashing about like a squirrel on the close-cropped grass, zigzagging right, then left, then right again. Water splashed about his knees and squirted like miniature fountains from the spongy soil as he twisted and turned, sometimes running towards them, sometimes running away.

"This way, Martin! Over here!" Nikki bounced up and down, shouting and waving her arms.

"They're all mixed up," Carl gloated. "They can't make up their minds which way he's going."

Caroline wasn't sure Martin knew which way he was going, either, but she crossed her fingers and hoped for the best. She could tell the taller of the two men was annoyed with her son's tactics. He'd slowed his steps, following Martin's zigzag pattern with his eyes but not his feet. When he finally made a move, it was clear he intended to outflank his quarry. His muddy shoes dug into the soft earth and sent chunks of dirt skittering across the grass as he swerved to flush Martin towards his partner.

The impact of his fall had not affected the shorter man's desire to continue the chase. Scrambling to catch up with Martin, his legs spun beneath his boxy torso like the wheels of the little-train-that-could. He increased his speed even further when he recognized his teammate's strategy.

Martin's maneuvers had earned him little more than time. He was tiring fast, his breath coming in short gasps and his knees barely reaching his waist as he sprinted over the lawn. His stalkers, meanwhile, seemed to be running on an endless supply of energy. They were only an arm's length behind him now, and they were gaining precious inches with every step.

Despite the odds, Martin still had one thing going for

him. He was a born fighter, a never-say-die kind of guy. He wouldn't go down easily with victory so close at hand. For a fleeting moment Caroline considered his survival to be a distinct possibility.

"Another three yards and he's home free." She glanced over at her daughter-in-law. "Don't worry, Nikki. Martin's going to be…"

"Ooow! What a hit!"

Carl's anguished comment and the accompanying moans of those behind him startled Caroline into silence. She turned in time to see her son fall to the ground, his body crumbling under the combined weight of the opposing school's two finest defensive backs. When the referee whistled the play dead and the game over, Martin's arms were fully extended from the pile, his hands still gripping his precious cargo.

Unfortunately, the tip of the football lay two inches short of the goal line.

FOUR

"I STILL DON'T understand why the two of you are angry with me."

Professor Atwater swept the last beads of water off a row of bleacher seats and motioned Caroline to come sit beside him.

"I'm not angry, Carl. I'm annoyed. Nikki is the one who's angry."

"Oh, right! You're pacing up and down in front of me like a caged lion, but you're not angry. Either I'm entirely out of touch with the emotions of modern women, or you're into some new form of aerobic exercise. Which one is it, Cari?"

Caroline stopped pacing and pointed a finger at the professor. "Don't get snippy with me. You know you're to blame for Martin joining the football team. You're always looking for ways to outsmart Garrison Hurst, and now you've recruited my son to help you."

"I recruited your son? I did that?" Carl's bushy white eyebrows almost merged with his hairline as his eyes widened in disbelief. "As I recall, it was Garrison Hurst who finagled your boy into joining this sorry lot of underachievers. Our dearly beloved president wants the Big Bad Bruins to win, and who better to help them achieve victory than a college track star like Martin."

"We've had this argument before. I still say you were up to something when you urged Martin to sign on with the team." Caroline tugged the hood of her parka tighter about her face. The rain had stopped for the moment, but the wind still chilled her bones. "Ed would roll over in his grave if he knew Martin was playing with the Bruins."

"You're changing the subject again. But as long as you're at it, please explain why you, of all people, object to your son playing football. I thought you loved the game."

"I do love it," Caroline insisted. "But Ed had too many buddies who'd wrecked their knees playing football. He didn't want to see Martin hurt. He refused to let him play the game on a competitive level."

"And you feel obliged to follow Ed's wishes, even though he passed away almost two years ago."

Caroline glared at the professor. "This has nothing to do with carrying a torch for my dead husband. It seems insane for Martin to take up a sport he's not physically conditioned to play. He's a runner, not a football player."

"And your point is?"

"Martin doesn't have the neck muscles to take a hit to the head, and he certainly doesn't need to break a leg at this point in time. Another couple of months and he'll graduate with his PhD. He's training to be a history teacher, not a professional football player."

"I understand your concern," Atwater said. "But try seeing things from Martin's viewpoint. He's always dreamed of playing college football. Most young men do, you know."

"I might feel differently about his decision if he'd made it on his own. But, as you well know, Garrison Hurst blackmailed my son into joining the Bruins. And you went along with it."

"I did nothing of the kind! I simply said, for once, our beloved President was speaking the truth. He told Martin he'd better his odds to land a job at Bruck if he did this, and he was right. There are a lot of football fans on the faculty. Martin could use their support when he applies for a position at the university."

Caroline turned her back on the professor and stared out over the empty field. She felt as dreary as the weather. Her pounding headache hadn't dulled despite two aspirin she'd swallowed earlier. Cold, wet, and miserable, she was in no mood to continue the argument.

"I suppose you're right. Still, I'm constantly amazed at the shenanigans going on here at Bruck. They're enough to make even a Chicago politician blush. The very existence of this football team is a good example of the power of clout."

"You know I was against the Bruins from the start. It takes a lot of money to support a football program, money Bruck doesn't have. I can't tell you how many times I stood up in meetings and opposed the formation of a team. Unfortunately, Hurst has the Board of Directors and half of the faculty eating out of his hand. He painted them such a rosy picture." Carl shook his head. "Our president has visions of grandeur, Notre Dame style."

"A chip off the old Rockne, huh?"

Carl smiled, pleased to see Caroline was calming down. "Of course, it didn't help when Mayor Schoen jumped into the fray. He was more than happy to suggest the university build a new stadium for the team."

"At least it was voted down."

"A new stadium, yes. But not repairs to the old one. Teddy Schoen is a clever fellow, Cari. He knew the Board would never agree to the construction costs. He was only laying the groundwork for his proposal to renovate the present structure."

"I'm not a fan of the mayor, but I can't fault his motives on this one. The renovations are providing jobs for a whole lot of people."

"Work's been slow down at the quarry. Nowadays, there's not much of a demand for rhyolite."

The professor was referring to the pink stone indigenous to the area. The older university buildings were built of rhyolite from the quarry outside of Rhineburg, as were the police station and the town hall. While Caroline still found it difficult to take a pink police station seriously, the rosy hue of the university buildings at sunrise and sunset delighted her senses.

"This deal's been good for the town," Carl continued. "But it's costing the university a bundle. Like with all construction jobs, the estimate was a bit lower than the actual cost. And to make matters worse, the work won't be done in time for the Homecoming game next Saturday."

"You mean the Bruins are going to play here again? I thought the contractor promised a finished stadium by Halloween."

Caroline glanced at the makeshift field laid out behind the auditorium. Despite their best efforts, the university groundskeepers could do little to amend the stony soil between the two goal posts. More than one player had ended up in St. Anne's ER with a twisted ankle due to a rock emerging from the ground at an unpropitious moment.

"They fell behind schedule due to the weather last month. The outside walls are complete, as is most of the inside refurbishing. But the plumbing is only half installed. The way I understand it, the 3B's can play in the stadium on Saturday, but the fans are going to have to use portable johns stationed outside."

"The alumni are not going to be happy."

"I'm sure they won't be. Still, it may cut down on the amount of booze consumed during the game. Less liquor means fewer trips to the john."

"Hurst is going to catch hell from precisely the people he's trying to please."

A rumble of thunder sounded in the distance. Caroline glanced up at the sky where black clouds were once again massing in the west.

"Looks like we're in for another bout of rain," she said.

"Yes, it's definitely time to go home."

"I want to check out my son's war wounds before I head back to the dorm. Nikki said she'd be waiting with the car in front of the gym."

"I'll walk over there with you," Carl said as he levered himself upright. He checked his watch. "The team's post-game lecture should be over by now. If we want to catch up with the lovebirds, we'll have to take a shortcut through the auditorium."

Caroline's mood darkened again as her thoughts turned to Martin and his wife.

"Nikki's worried. She's afraid Martin will get hurt, maybe even disabled, playing for this team. The Big Bad Bruins have big, bad problems."

"They are pretty lousy. Here it is, the last weekend in October, and the 3B's haven't won a game yet."

"I'm not talking about their play on the field, Carl. There's something very wrong with the Bruins. Half of the players don't like each other, and practically no one likes the coach. It's every man for himself on this team."

"You mean they don't support each other."

"Not at all. Martin told Nikki he feels like his blockers intentionally allow the tacklers to get to him in practice. He thinks they resent him because he was brought in late and given a featured role on the team."

"He did replace a local favorite." Carl scratched his beard, his expression thoughtful. "Trace Golden was the darling of Rhineburg High School when he played for the

Maniacs last year. Everyone in town thought the 'Golden Boy' was headed for a Division I college. Unfortunately, his bad boy reputation impressed the scouts far more than his field skills."

"According to Nikki, Trace is a real troublemaker. He's always mouthing off, trying to show up the other guys. His temper has worsened since he was benched two weeks ago. He's begun to pick fights in the locker room."

"And the coach can't control him?"

"Trace's dad is on Bruck's Board of Directors. Mr. Golden was instrumental in hiring Wade Wilkins."

"Ah, yes. I'd forgotten about Trace Sr."

"But there's more to it," said Caroline. "Wilkins encourages what he calls 'a competitive edge' in his men. He purposely pits players against each other after every game. He picks on different guys to criticize, then he blames them publicly for the team's failures. Apparently he believes shame drives individual effort."

"Doesn't sound right to me. Coaches usually preach unity and team spirit."

"Good coaches do."

Caroline fell silent as they approached Hildegard Hall. Called Hildy for short, the auditorium was one of the original buildings on campus. It had been completely rehabbed in the eighties and now boasted comfortable theater seating and a professionally equipped stage. A two-story extension had been added to the back of the building. The extension housed an area large enough to build and store props. Warehouse-sized double doors on the back wall opened onto a driveway bordering the temporary football field. A smaller door was set into one of the large ones. Caroline and Carl entered the auditorium through this entrance.

Inside the prop room the thumping beat of pop music competed with the buzz and whine of hand tools pressed into service by students constructing floats for the Halloween Homecoming parade. Carl was entranced by the flurry of activity. He paused to examine a ten-foot tall skeleton perched on a flatbed padded and painted to resemble a football.

Caroline glanced impatiently at her watch when the professor stopped a second time to admire an enormous plywood pumpkin. She'd have to hurry if she hoped to catch up with Martin and Nikki. Since Carl was now deep in conversation with two paint-spattered students, she left him in the prop room, dodged through a doorway leading to the stage, and began looking for a quick way out of the building.

Caroline had never been backstage in Hildy Hall, but her daughter Kerry, a theater major at Northern Illinois, had once told her all stages were basically alike. Walk far enough to either side and you were bound to find a way around the various curtains. The trick worked. In less than a minute she was standing on the apron of the stage gazing down into the orchestra pit. A short flight of stairs extended from the apron to the auditorium proper. Caroline descended the steps and headed towards a lighted exit sign a few feet away.

Caroline opened the steel fire door and stepped out onto a narrow strip of cement dividing the auditorium from the gymnasium. The locker room entrance to the gym was a dozen yards south of where she stood. Beyond this entrance was a second one leading directly into the main lobby. Both doors were closed, and no sounds of life drifted from the front of the building. Caroline figured she'd probably missed the team.

She hesitated, wondering if she should wait for Carl, then thought better of it. Absorbed in the construction of the floats, he'd probably forgotten all about tracking down

Martin. She decided to follow her original plan and search for Nikki's car.

The narrow sidewalk reminded Caroline of the gangways between homes in the older sections of Chicago. Wide enough only for a single lane of foot traffic, it was cracked and broken and steeped in shadows cast by the tall buildings on either side. The path led to a blacktop parking lot serving both Hildy Hall and the gymnasium. Nikki would be waiting there—if she was still waiting.

Caroline increased her pace. She was approaching the locker room entrance when the door crashed open and two Bruins came barreling out of the gym. The players were locked in a boxer's embrace, arms entwined and heads tucked low, their fists pounding at ribs, then heads, then ribs again. Banging into the auditorium wall, they rolled to the ground still trading punches. Sharp, angry grunts escaped their lips with every blow.

Caroline held her ground as a dozen or more husky young men streamed out of the gym. Crammed shoulder to shoulder on the narrow sidewalk, they craned their necks to get a view of the fight. None of the Bruins seemed anxious to separate their teammates. Instead, they watched in wary silence as the pair on the ground continued to scuffle.

"That's enough! Cut it out!"

Carl Atwater swept past Caroline and elbowed his way through the mass of bodies blocking the path. He grabbed one of the combatants by the shoulder, hauled him up, and pushed him towards his companions. Then he extended a hand to the man on the ground. Caroline drew in her breath as she saw a bloodied Martin rise to his feet.

"What the hell's going on here, Coach?"

Caroline shifted her attention from Martin to Carl. The professor was staring at the open gym door where a man leaned against the doorjamb, his muscular arms folded across his equally muscular chest. Wade Wilkins was forty years younger, six inches taller, and a good deal more composed than the professor. Dressed in beige Dockers and a Bruck U. polo shirt, he looked like a model for a health club ad with his broad shoulders, narrow hips, and deeply tanned skin. His narrow face was crowned by a thatch of thick brown hair streaked blond by the sun and cut stylishly on the sides and long in the back.

The only thing marring the coach's good looks were his eyes. They were the color of dirty seaweed flecked with specks of amber, and they were set deep in his face beneath heavy lids and jutting brows. Like the eyes of a cobra, they had a hypnotizing effect on Caroline when they flicked in her direction. Staring back into their muddy green depths, she felt the hairs rise on the back of her neck.

FIVE

"WHO WANTS TO KNOW?"

Wilkins's voice was deep and challenging. He elevated one eyebrow and stared at Carl with an amused smile.

"I'm Professor Carl Atwater, chairman of the history department here at Bruck." Carl waved a hand in the direction of the players. "Some of these young men are my students."

"Oh? Well, they're not in class now, Professor, so there's no need for you to worry about them."

"I worry about any Bruck student who feels he has to settle an argument with a fist fight, Mr. Wilkins. I'm sure President Hurst feels the same way."

Wilkins's lips curved downward. "The boys were a little upset over the loss today, Professor. Some of them felt like Mr. Rhodes didn't try hard enough."

Martin took a step forward. Carl stopped him with an outstretched arm.

"Football is a team sport, Mr. Wilkins. Players have to help each other if they want to win."

"The boys know how to work together, don't you, fellas?"

Wilkins scanned the players, his smile broader now. Some of the boys ducked their heads. Others shuffled their feet and stared anywhere but at the coach. A couple of Bruins nodded in vague assent, but even those young men appeared uncomfortable with the situation.

Wilkins ignored Carl as he continued to address the

team. "Okay, guys. I want everybody out of the gym in five minutes. Rest up tomorrow because starting Monday, we'll be practicing an extra hour each day. We're going to christen the new stadium with a victory in the Homecoming game."

Having said his piece, Wilkins turned his back on the Bruins and walked into the locker room. His apparent dismissal of the professor along with the players didn't sit well with Atwater. Carl's jaw muscles twitched spasmodically, a sure sign he was livid with anger.

Caroline was in no mood to soothe her friend's feelings. Martin's injuries worried her. She wanted to rush over to her son, but she held back, determined not to embarrass him in front of his teammates. She waited impatiently as the players shuffled back into the gym.

One young man stopped and placed a hand on Martin's shoulder.

"You better wait here, Marty. I'll grab your bag for you."

Martin wiped a trickle of blood from his lip. "Thanks, Al. I'll be out front with my wife."

"You ain't no Mohammed Ali," said Al, a crooked smile erasing the look of gravity in his eyes. "But you can give as good as you get. And that's all you gotta do."

He gave Martin the thumbs up sign, then turned and disappeared into the gym.

"Have you got a handkerchief, Professor? I don't want Nikki to see me with my face all bloody. Mom doesn't matter," Martin added with a wry grin. "She's used to seeing carved up characters in the ER."

"I'd prefer my son not be one of them," Caroline said testily. She glanced at the oversized red and black bandanna the professor had pulled from his pocket and rolled her eyes. "You have to be kidding, Carl."

"So I've got a big nose," Carl grumbled. "What's the

big deal? Those teensy-weensy things they sell in the dime
store were made for Lilliputians, not real men."

"Not real men who play football, you mean."

"Let's not get into it again, Mom." Martin threw her
a warning look. "It's going to be hard enough explaining the fight to Nikki without having to defend myself
to you, too."

"The boy has a point, Caroline. One woman at a time
is enough."

Caroline wrinkled her nose at the professor before turning her back on the two men.

"I'm going to go look for Nikki. Feel free to join us at
the car when you're done mopping up the blood."

She walked away feeling more light-hearted about Martin's condition. A visual once over had convinced her his
injuries were minor. His nose was swollen and slightly
out of kilter, but his breathing was unobstructed. And he
was moving about easily, which meant he probably hadn't
fractured any ribs. The inch long laceration on his cheek,
though, would require a few stitches.

As for Martin's role as a football player, she was more
than willing to stand back and let Nikki tackle the subject after the matter of the fight had been cleared up. Her
daughter-in-law had disapproved of Martin's decision from
the start. Nevertheless, she'd reined in her emotions until
today. The game had taken a definite toll on Nikki. It
would be some time before she recovered from the fright
of seeing a bruised and battered Martin limp off the field
after his disastrous last run.

A light rain had begun to fall by the time the three
of them reached the front of the building. They got into
Nikki's car, Caroline and Carl climbing into the back and
Martin sitting up front with his wife. Nikki looked over
at him and shook her head.

"I guess you didn't break a leg, but you sure messed up your face."

"It didn't happen on the field." Martin kept the bandanna pressed to his puffy nose and aimed his eyes straight ahead. "I had a little trouble with one of the guys after the game."

Nikki leaned over and placed her hand under Martin's chin. He didn't resist as she gently turned his face towards her. Tears sparkled on her cheeks when she saw the ugly gash and the dark bruises forming under his eyes.

"It was that sonofabitch Trace Golden, wasn't it? He did this to you, right?"

The rap, rap of knuckles hitting the car door saved Martin from the start of another argument with Nikki. He shook off her hand and turned to roll down the window.

"Hey, man. What are you carrying in this thing? Lead weights?"

Martin reached out and grabbed his gym bag. "Thanks for bringing it, Al. You want a lift over to the dorm?"

"Naw. A walk in the rain will feel good after sitting in the locker room listening to Wilkins. It might even ease my burning desire to choke the living daylights out of the guy." Al waggled his fingers at Nikki. "Your husband played real good today, Mrs. Rhodes. Don't let nobody tell you he could of done better."

"Thank you." Nikki smiled weakly. "And thanks for bringing Marty's bag."

"Don't mention it, ma'am. And now you better get going. Marty here looks like he could use a little nylon to tie up the hole on his cheek." Al slapped the car door with the palm of his hand. "See you Monday, buddy."

Caroline watched the young man stroll off towards the dormitories.

"He seems like a nice enough fellow. What's he majoring in?"

"I don't know," Martin replied. "Al transferred to Bruck from a community college. He didn't play football there, but he was a punter back in high school. He's the team's field goal kicker. Unfortunately, we haven't given him many chances to show his stuff."

"The Bruins will give him plenty of opportunities next Saturday," Carl assured them all. "By the way, I heard all ticket holders will receive miniature pumpkins, compliments of President Hurst, when they pass through the gates of the stadium. Hurst thinks the pumpkins will add a nice touch to the Homecoming game."

Nikki glanced over her shoulder and rolled her eyes at Caroline. Martin simply shook his head.

"You sure know how to pick up a guy's spirits, Professor. I'll bet those pumpkins will come flying out of the stands every time we fumble the ball."

"As long as they hit the opposing team, it's okay," replied Carl.

"Enough already with pumpkins and football." Caroline tapped Nikki on the arm. "It's time to get over to the ER and patch up your husband's wounds."

"Mom's right," said Nikki as she switched on the engine. "Time to get a move on. But getting back to the fight, Martin, I'd like to know what started it."

"Later, Nikki. I don't feel up to talking about it right now."

"Oh, really?" Nikki threw him a hard look, her eyes cold enough to freeze the hottest regions of hell. "Well, you better start feeling up to it, because I don't intend to wait any longer. I want the truth from you, and I want it now."

Ultimatums had never gone down well with Caroline's son. This time was no different than any other. Martin slouched down in his seat and stared out the window, his mouth clamped shut beneath the big red bandanna covering his nose. Nikki assumed her own stubborn posture, occasionally glaring at Martin as she guided the car around Bruck Green and drove towards St. Anne's.

In the backseat, Carl made mental guesses as to which one would break down first. Caroline, who knew both of these young people quite well, simply closed her eyes and waited.

SIX

CARL EXCHANGED PLACES with Nikki in the tiny ER waiting room.

"He's ready to talk," he said as he settled himself on the faded herringbone couch opposite the doorway. "You better go catch him before they wheel him away to X-ray." He watched the girl walk out of the room, her back stiff and her chin held high. "She's still in a huff, isn't she?"

"That's the understatement of the year." Caroline rubbed her tired eyes. "This day is getting longer by the minute. What I wouldn't give for a cup of hot chocolate and a warm bed right now."

"There's nothing I can do about the bed, Cari. But I can supply the hot chocolate." Carl reached into his pocket and pulled out a handful of change. "There's a vending machine down the corridor. I'll go get you a cup."

Caroline waved him back to his seat. "Forget it. Nikki and I already tried. The machine's broken. So tell me, what did Martin have to say for himself?"

"Before I give you all the gory details, I want to know why you didn't go in there with your son. You do work in the ER."

"As Martin has so often pointed out to me, he's no longer a child. He's a grown man who can take care of himself."

"Come off it. You're a born worrier when it comes to your children."

Caroline arched her eyebrows in a "what, me?" look.

Her lips twisted in a sardonic little smile. "Why should I worry about Martin? Outside of a little cut and a broken nose, he's doing pretty good for a guy who took a beating from his teammate after being trampled by two linemen twice his size."

"Show a little compassion, Cari."

"Compassion? Forget it, Carl. I refuse to baby the boy. Martin decided to follow your advice. Now he's paying the price."

"Must we fight?"

"Not if I can help it. You asked me to explain why I didn't go into the ER with Martin, and I did. It seems to me, Nikki is the one who needs a little support right now. The poor girl is a nervous wreck."

"The season's almost over. Martin's only got to make it through a few more games."

Caroline shot Carl a look of annoyance. He pretended not to notice as he rummaged through his pockets for a piece of gum. Finding nothing there but his house keys, he gave up the effort and returned his attention to the woman drumming her fingers on the arm of the chair across from him.

"You're going to break a nail," he warned her.

"I'll survive. Now quit stalling and tell me what the fight was about."

"I promised Martin…"

"Out with it, man. You know I'm not going to give up until I know the whole story."

"I suppose you're right," sighed the professor. "It's impossible keeping a secret from you."

"This is not the Spanish Inquisition, Carl. You don't have to act as if I'm torturing you."

"All right, already!" The professor threw up his hands

in surrender. "But don't tell Martin I blabbed. The fight between Golden and your son was over Nikki."

Caroline looked at him in disbelief. "Nikki? What's she got to do with it?"

"Coach Wilkins picked on Martin today for his post-game victim. He criticized him for dodging around on the field trying to lose his tacklers. He said if Martin had only run straight ahead, he would have scored the touchdown."

"I doubt it. The only thing a straight path would have accomplished was a quicker end to the game. So what else did Wilkins have to say?"

"He implied Martin wasn't putting out a hundred per-cent. He accused him of having ties to the administration. Said it was the only reason he was on the team."

"Martin's no slacker. Whatever he does, he gives it his all."

"Wilkins was baiting him, Cari. He was trying to get Martin's goat. Then Trace Golden chimed in. He made a crude remark about Nikki and—how do I put this?— her ability to please her husband. He accused Martin of spending more time romancing his wife than practicing running routes."

"I'm sure young Mr. Golden didn't phrase it in those words," Caroline said, her voice shaking with anger. "I can see why Martin threw a punch at him."

"Apparently Wilkins made no move to stop the fight. It went on for several minutes in the locker room before they slammed into the door and ended up outside. We only caught the last of it."

"I'm glad you talked Martin into opening up. Nikki would have found out about it one way or another. It's bet-ter she hears it from her husband than from someone else."

"So I told Martin. Nikki works in the post office. Lord knows, the P.O. is the center of gossip in town. News of the fight will get around fast. By Monday, everyone in Rhineburg will have heard a bigger and better version of the story."

"So let them talk. It won't bother me at all." Nikki swept into the room followed by her husband. She pointed at the seat next to Caroline. "Go sit by your mother, dear. You can fill her in on all the gory details while I go get the car." She grabbed her slicker off the coatrack and disappeared out the door before Martin could protest.

"How's the nose doing?"

"It's broken, but at least the bleeding's stopped. I feel all stuffed up, Mom," Martin complained as he lowered himself gingerly into a chair. "Like I have a bad head cold. Worse, though, every bone in my body hurts. Especially my ribs."

"Stop on the way home and pick up a bag of ice," Caroline said. "Ice packs will relieve some of your muscle pain. And don't try to blow your nose. It'll only start bleeding again."

Martin waved a sheaf of papers at his mother. "They gave me discharge instructions. It's all written down here."

"Old habits die hard, Martin. By the way, why wasn't your name in the program? I saw your number listed there, but it was next to Trace Golden's name."

"Coach says the programs were printed before the season started. My name's not listed because I joined the team late. I've substituted for Trace ever since his suspension took effect, so I'm wearing his uniform." Martin scowled. "Another reason why Golden's on my case. He says the scouts are going to think I'm him. He's afraid I'll ruin his great reputation as a receiver."

"Why does Golden care what the scouts think?" asked Carl. "Is he planning to switch schools?"

"He's hoping to impress them so he can move up to a

better program. He's convinced he's Division I material, but as far as I know, no other team has shown interest in him."

Carl snorted. "I'd be thrilled if that little weasel did transfer. He's one hundred percent trouble. And speaking of trouble, did either one of you see those flyers they were handing out at the game?" Carl reached into his pocket and pulled out a crumpled five-by-seven piece of paper. "I stuffed it in my jacket without reading it. But then I was talking to some of the kids who were building floats in the back of the auditorium. They were wondering if the school was actually going to sponsor a rodeo the night before the Homecoming game."

"A rodeo?" Caroline took the flyer from Carl and quickly scanned the cramped printing. She shook her head as she handed the paper to Martin. "President Hurst is going to have to plead temporary insanity in order to explain this one."

"What's wrong with holding a rodeo as part of the Homecoming celebration?" said Martin. "It sounds like it should be fun."

"Check the fine print, my boy." Carl pointed to the bottom of the page. "The part stating where this rodeo's going to take place."

"The Moore Sisters' Rodeo and Wild West Show to be presented Friday, November 1st, 6 p.m., in the Joseph Bruck Memorial Stadium." Martin's eyes widened as he realized what he'd read. "Holy shit! A herd of bucking bulls is going to tear up the grass in our new stadium the day before the Homecoming game! Is Hurst crazy, or what?" Martin stood up and grabbed his jacket. "One thing's for sure, Coach Wilkins doesn't know about this. If he did, he'd have raised a stink by now. I've got to go tell him."

"I can't believe you'd want to face him again. Not after the way he treated you today."

"Believe it or not, Mom, I enjoy playing football, and I want the Bruins to win next Saturday. No rinky-dink rodeo is going to ruin our field. Not if I have anything to say about it."

Caroline watched her son storm out of the waiting room. "Time to get the flak gear out of storage. I sense trouble ahead."

Atwater shrugged his shoulders. "Well, you know what they say, Cari. A man's gotta do what a man's gotta do."

SEVEN

"HELL, NO! No rodeo! Hell, no! No rodeo!"

Dressed in their cleanest uniforms and carrying signs proclaiming their cause, the Big Bad Bruins paraded in front of Bruck Hall where the Board of Directors was meeting in closed session with Garrison Hurst. Wade Wilkins's demands that the rodeo be canceled had fallen on deaf ears when he'd called the president late Saturday evening. Trace Golden Sr., though, had been more receptive to the coach's complaints. Golden had contacted the other trustees and set up the Sunday meeting to discuss what he called "a grave matter involving the fate of the Bruin football team."

What the matter really involved was the fate of Trace Golden Jr. As president of the Rhineburg 1st National Bank with branches in Newberry, Wilhampton, and towns farther south, Trace Sr. had connections with powerful people throughout the state. Those people had connections of their own, some of them being with coaches from Division I colleges. Trace Sr. was determined to see his son better himself. Since the boy was officially off suspension on Monday, he'd be playing at his usual receiver's spot in the Halloween Homecoming game. Golden had purchased a large block of stadium tickets and was hosting a party at his home after the game. The guests included several men whose influence extended beyond the Board Room of their respective alma maters. As ex-jocks themselves, their opinions were treated with respect by the heads of various athletic departments.

Hope sprung eternal in the breast of Trace Golden Sr. He was not about to see it dashed by a few crummy female rodeo riders.

"Well, this is a first for our beloved president. A protest movement taking place right outside his office." Carl Atwater rubbed his palms together in unabashed delight. "I wish I could be a fly on the wall in there. I'd love to hear how he's going to wiggle out of this one."

The look Caroline gave the professor would have wilted a lesser man's confidence. Carl, though, was twenty-five years older than she, and a veteran teacher to boot. He'd spent a lifetime learning to ignore the dirty looks of students whose mediocre efforts hadn't earned them A's in his class. Caroline's glare was mild compared to what he was used to. He brushed it off without comment.

"I see Martin decided to march with the team." He pointed with his chin to where his star pupil walked side by side with his fellow Bruins. "Good decision on his part."

This time Caroline did more than glare. She punched the professor in the arm. Hard.

"You're insane, Carl. Totally insane."

She turned her back on both Atwater and the protesters and made her way through a crowd of students gathered on the sidewalk outside the Hall. Dodging even more students coming down Circle Road from the dormitories, she crossed the street and headed for a bench placed strategically on Bruck Green beneath the spreading branches of an ancient oak. Carl followed hard on her heels.

"I've been called stubborn in the past, even hardheaded. But no one's ever considered me insane."

"Well, you are insane, and you're driving me down the same path," Caroline growled. She sat down hard on the bench, then eased her back away from the wooden cross bars as a jolt of pain traveled up her spine. "Now look what you've done! You've made me crack my tailbone."

The professor rolled his eyes. "Why am I to blame for everything that goes wrong in your life? Maybe if you approached the act of sitting down in a more ladylike manner..."

"Now, children. Let's not fight."

Madeline "Maddy" Moeller strode across the leaf-strewn grass from the direction of St. Anne's Hospital. Her pumpkin colored hair, newly permed at the Dip-N-Do Bath and Beauty Salon, floated in loose ringlets around her elfin face and her brown eyes glowed with mischief. Plopping down on the bench next to Caroline, she threw both arms over her head and sucked in a lungful of cool air.

"What a lovely afternoon. Sure makes up for yesterday, doesn't it? Bruck Green looks like a picture postcard with all these trees—whatever they are—tossing red and yellow leaves everywhere."

"They're mainly oaks and maples, Maddy, although you might find a few birches over toward the hospital. And they don't 'toss' leaves, they 'drop' them."

"Right, Professor. Of course."

Maddy dismissed Carl's botany lesson with a casual wave of her hand. Her attention had shifted from the beauty of nature to the parading players and their increasingly loud chants.

"What a shame," she sighed. "If only they could play with as much energy as they yell, they might be a halfway decent team."

"They've been taking lessons from the cheerleaders," said Caroline. She glanced over her shoulder at the wide expanse of land separating Bruck University from the hospital complex. "Where's Jake? I thought as Chief of Police he'd be here keeping an eye on the demonstrators."

"No way," replied Maddy with a vigorous shake of her curls. "He's leaving this mess to Bruck's security department. My husband is much too busy hunting down the little monsters who egged Meyer's Bakery last night to worry about a campus demonstration."

"Might be hard to track down whoever did it," Carl mused.

"The Halloween pranks are starting early this year. But Jake has no intention of letting them get out of hand. He's pulled a half dozen young men into the station, every one of them accompanied by at least one parent."

"Reading them the riot act, is he?"

"You've got it, Caroline. Of course, none of those boys will confess to the egging. Nevertheless, Jake will put a little fear of the law into them. He's a regular bear when it comes to vandalism. Absolutely hates it." Maddy shielded her eyes with one hand and squinted at the mob outside Bruck Hall. "Speaking of bears, or in this case, Bruins, I think I see your son standing under the portico, Cari. He appears to be tossing something at the students."

Caroline craned her neck to look over the heads of the young people packed cheek by jowl in the street.

"Good grief," she muttered. "Martin's throwing Bruin pennants into the crowd. He's probably trying to drum up support for the team."

"Another smart move on his part," said Carl approvingly. "He'll have the entire faculty behind him when he applies for a job."

Caroline viewed the matter with a more jaundiced eye.

"I fail to see your point, Carl. Picketing the President's office will hardly increase Martin's chance for meaningful employment at Bruck."

"Ah, but there you're wrong," insisted the professor. "The president's circle of friends will back Martin because he did what Hurst asked and joined the Bruins. Those of us who hate the president's guts will back him because he stood up today and showed Hurst he's no pushover. And the football fans on both sides will back him because he played his heart out on the field."

"Odd as it seems, Professor Atwater's explanation makes sense." Maddy patted Caroline's knee. "Don't worry so much about Martin. He'll survive the season, and once he graduates, he'll never have to play football again."

"He'd better not! I wasn't thrilled when Martin joined the Bruins. The one I'm truly worried about, though, is Nikki. She called me last night after Martin went off with his teammates to plan today's demonstration. She's afraid things will get out of hand if Hurst doesn't agree to the Bruins' demands."

"What does she think they'll do if they don't get their way? Burn down Bruck Hall?"

"Nothing quite so dramatic, Maddy. But they're talking about going on strike against the university. Apparently they're ready to cancel the Homecoming game if the rodeo goes on as planned."

"Hurst won't let them cancel," Carl said confidently. "He's counting heavily on the game to draw people back to Bruck. The university's sent out tons of letters to former graduates inviting them 'home' for the weekend. Garrison will announce the creation of a new alumni fund during the half time celebration."

"An alumni fund? Whatever for?" asked Maddy.

"The exact purpose of it is anyone's guess," said the professor. "I've been told Hurst plans to use a portion of whatever is raised as seed money for a promotional campaign."

"You mean as in advertising the school to potential students."

"Potential students and potential donors, Cari. You know as well as I do, the president isn't content with the status quo. He'd like to enlarge the business department, perhaps even house it in a separate facility along with a computer center. He needs money, much of it in the form of donations. For many schools, donations hinge on the success of their athletic departments."

"So Hurst needs to impress the alumni next weekend," said Maddy.

"He sure does. He won't allow the game to be canceled. He might even excuse the team from classes this week if extra practice is what's needed for them to pull their act together."

Caroline glanced at her watch. "It's later than I thought. I was hoping the meeting would end before I had to leave for work, but I guess…"

"Hold on," said Maddy. She pointed to Bruck Hall. "President Hurst is coming out onto the porch. It looks like he's about to make an announcement."

The three friends crossed the street and edged their way through the mass of students standing on the sidewalk. They reached the Hall's front lawn as Hurst reentered the building. It didn't matter they hadn't caught his speech. The joyful reaction of the team and their supporters told them all they needed to know.

Carl was particularly gleeful over Hurst's apparent capitulation in the face of the Bruins' protest.

"You see, ladies? I was right. There will definitely be no rodeo performing in the stadium Friday evening."

"I wouldn't bet on it, mister."

The man standing next to Carl turned and glared at the three of them. Tall and lanky with a weathered look to his face, he was dressed in worn jeans and a denim jacket accented by a sheepskin collar. His eyes were the color of burnt charcoal, and they blazed with ill-concealed fury beneath the brim of a sweat-stained Stetson.

"There are still things in this world called contracts."

Not waiting for a reply, the man turned and blended into the crowd milling about in the street. Caroline tracked his Stetson as it bobbed above the heads of the students.

"Five will get you ten, he's from the Moore Sisters' Rodeo," said Maddy.

"And ten will get you twenty, he's hotfooting it over to the nearest telephone right now to report in to his boss." Caroline turned to Carl. "You'd better tell the team not to throw away their signs. I have a feeling they'll be needing them in the next few days."

EIGHT

"I HEAR YOU pulled another princess shift tonight. What's the matter, Cari? Getting too old to work eight hours?"

"Watch it, buster." Caroline poked Dr. Chan Daley in the ribs with the tip of a crutch. "Keep up the 'old' stuff and you'll be needing a pair of these."

Daley feigned an injury, tucking one hand protectively under his armpit. "Oh, oh! Another case of nurse abuse. I'm going to have to report you to administration, Ms. Rhodes."

"Yeah, right," said Caroline as she extended the leg of the crutch another notch. "There we go. The perfect length for young Mr. Appleby. Next time he tries to rescue a kite from a tree, maybe he'll use a ladder."

"Or call his dad," Chan said with a smile. "Six-year-olds have no business climbing twenty-foot tall trees. He's lucky all he broke was his ankle. But getting back to the previous subject, why is it you're only working four hours tonight? Is it my deodorant, or am I too ugly to be around?"

Caroline leaned nearer to Chan and peered at his face. Then she sniffed the air, wrinkled her nose, and drew back a step.

"I don't know about your deodorant, but your after-shave is something else. As for your ugly mug…well, let's just say I'm delighted to see it here at St. Anne's. You're a welcome addition to our ER."

"Yeah, yeah. I've heard that line before."

"I mean it, Chan. I'm thrilled you decided to leave Chicago and move to Rhineburg. We needed another good doc in the department. You were the perfect choice."

Caroline wasn't trying to make points with Daley. She'd worked alongside him for years at Ascension Medical Center in the Chicago suburb of Niles. He was a bright, good-humored man, an excellent physician whom she both liked and respected.

"Well, when you get kicked out of one hospital…"

"Oh, come off it. You weren't kicked out of Ascension. Roger was being his usual horrid self when he refused to renew your contract. You were a threat to his ambitions."

The Roger she spoke of was Dr. Roger MacGuffy, a former ER Director at Ascension and a petty tyrant with visions of grandeur. When Chan hadn't backed his move to become Chief of Staff, MacGuffy had cooked up a reason to dismiss him. No one quite understood what "incompatibility with the goals of the department" meant, but it was enough of a charge to send the good doctor packing.

The son of a Chinese woman exiled from her homeland by war and an Irish playwright with dubious political leanings, Chan had inherited the stoical nature of his maternal ancestors along with the silver-tongued eloquence of his father. He'd publicly accepted his dismissal as one more speed bump in the highway of life. Privately, though, he'd made his feelings known to administration. After seventeen years of unblemished service in the ER, he felt he had a right to complain. His letter to the CEO condemning the Director's political maneuvering had little effect on the internal struggle for power at Ascension, but it satisfied his conscience.

He'd ended up at St. Anne's for two reasons. Number one, he'd been recommended for the job by an old friend with connections at the hospital. Number two, his wife had been born and raised in Rhineburg.

A descendent of Chinese immigrants who'd helped build the railroad running through town, Lian Daley was a lady of grace, style, and inordinate beauty. It always amazed Caroline that Chan, a bantam rooster of a man with a Fu Manchu mustache, a chopped off ponytail, and Harry Carey-type glasses, had captured the heart of such a woman. It was clearly a case of Beauty and the Beast.

"Let's forget about the past," Chan said, grimacing as he spoke. "I'd much rather talk about you and all these four-hour shifts you've been working lately. What'd you do? Win the lottery?"

"Don't I wish! Let me go discharge Tommy Appleby. When I come back, I'll fill you in on the change in my career status."

True to her word, Caroline returned a few minutes later sans patient and crutches.

"I've been playing housemother to Bruck U.'s nursing students," she said as she sat down next to Daley. "Their dormitory is attached to the hospital."

"You live with the students?"

"I have a small apartment on the senior wing. It's small, but cozy. The job's not bad, either. My main duty is to keep a lid on the students' extra-curricular activities: late-night parties, alcohol, etc."

"Ah, yes. The indiscretions of youth."

"Actually, they're a pretty good lot. I've only had to crack down on them once or twice since school started. Although with Halloween coming up, I expect they may get more rambunctious."

"I hope the position pays well."

"I don't receive a salary," said Caroline. "But I do get free room and board. The 'board' part is no big deal as I only eat breakfast in the hospital. Still, it's nice to know there's food for the asking if I'm hungry."

"So you're not getting rich on your night job. Then why the princess act?"

Caroline grinned at Chan's use of the term "princess". It was a common enough designation for a nurse, male or female, who worked a half rather than a whole shift. The word never seemed to apply to ER nurses, though. Working four hours could be as tiring as working eight when the room was busy.

"I'm filling in as team nurse for the Bruins."

"What?" Chan rocked back in his chair and stared wide-eyed at Caroline. "I don't believe it."

"Well, you better, because it's true. I've attended every game, home and away. If it looks like a player is truly hurt, I go down on the field and assist the trainer."

"You've got to be kidding. You've been ranting and raving for weeks about your son playing football, and here you are, aiding and abetting him."

"I am not," exclaimed Caroline. "The university asked Paul Wakely to take the job, but he refused. He recommended me instead. I'm getting a nice chunk of pay for the work, and it doesn't interfere with my schedule here at St. Anne's."

"Paul was smart. He's busy enough being director of the ER without sticking his head in another noose. Do you have to show up for practices, too?"

"No. If anyone's injured during practice, the trainer sends him here."

"So you get to keep an eye on Martin."

"I try not to be too obvious, but yes, I do watch how he's doing. At least if he gets hurt, I can make sure some moron doesn't send him right back into the game."

"It doesn't sound like you think highly of the Freebies' trainer."

"You too, huh?" Caroline shook her head. "You don't

have to tell me they're bad—I know the team stinks—but please don't call them the Freebies. It's a real sore point in my family. As for the trainer, Kurt Zumwald's a local guy with a pretty good reputation in the community. This is the first time he's worked with football players, but he seems to know his stuff."

"Then who's the moron you mentioned?"

"Wade Wilkins, the coach. He's a hard-nosed type who doesn't seem to understand a minor injury can lead to a major one. He's been known to disagree with Zumwald's decision to pull a player."

"Does he give you trouble, too?"

"No. Luckily, I've never had to converse with him. I tell Kurt what I think about a player's injuries, and he takes it from there. But I saw Wilkins in action yesterday. I'll tell you something, Chan. He's not the kind of coach I'd have hired if I was Garrison Hurst."

She told Daley about the fight outside the locker room and Wilkins's unwillingness to stop it.

"There's something about the man that scares me. He's almost masochistic."

"He doesn't sound like a pleasant guy. I wonder if he can last at Bruck. Given the team's record, I wouldn't be surprised if the school fired him at the end of the season."

"He needs to win the Homecoming game. If he can do it, Hurst may forgive him for the other losses."

"The president will definitely be in an expansive mood if the game pulls in some money. Lian says Bruck needs a shot in the arm financially. The new alumni fund could provide it."

"What makes Lian think the school's in trouble?"

"Well, money's all they talk about at the board meetings."

"Do you mean to tell me Lian is on Bruck's Board of

Directors?" This was news to Caroline. She wondered why she hadn't heard of it before.

"Lian graduated from Bruck. One of the first things she did after we moved to Rhineburg was visit her old stomping grounds. Would you believe, some of her professors are still there."

Caroline didn't doubt it. Carl had been a fixture at Bruck for decades, and she supposed the same could be said for other members of the staff.

"How'd she get roped into sitting on the Board?"

Chan answered her question with one of his own. "Do you know how persuasive Alexsa Stromberg Morgan can be?"

Caroline smiled. Did she ever! Alexsa was the unofficial matriarch of Rhineburg. Still going strong at ninety-one, she was the keeper of the town's secrets, a woman who knew something about everyone in Rhineburg, but rarely shared her knowledge. Originally Caroline's nemesis, she was now her good friend.

"Alexsa talked her into it, didn't she?"

"Oh, yeah! Mrs. Morgan is the most senior member of the Board. We weren't in Rhineburg a week when she invited Lian to her home for tea. Unbeknownst to my wife, Alexsa had also invited the other directors from Bruck. Lian never had a fighting chance."

"I can believe it."

"They ganged up on her, Cari. She says she was flattered by the invitation to join them, but she had no intention of doing it at first. Then the other board members left, and Alexsa went into her arm twisting routine. She reminded Lian of the bad old days when women had a hard time getting into medical school. She knew all about the professor at Bruck who paved the way for my wife's acceptance into Northwestern."

"In other words, Alexsa pushed all the right guilt buttons."

"It wasn't hard to do. Lian's often mentioned Dr. Bradley and his influence on her life. She wants to give something back to the university. This is one way of doing it. And as a psychiatrist, she thinks it might be interesting to observe the inside workings of academia."

"It's an entirely different setting than the one she knew at Ascension."

"In some ways, different. In other ways, it's the same. The struggle for power goes on everywhere. Only the names change."

"And sometimes the methods." Caroline didn't mention the word "murder", but it sprang to mind when she recalled her previous hospital. Power. Greed. Survival. The three seemed to go hand in hand. They always led to trouble and, all too often, death.

She shook off memories of the past summer when she'd filled in for a friend in the ER of Ascension Hospital in Niles, Illinois. A death there had resulted in the arrest of her best friend and her own involvement in the investigation.

"It's been way too easy a shift," she said as she contemplated the empty ER.

"Don't look a gift horse in the mouth," warned Chan. "Save your energy for Halloween when all the little kiddies come in throwing up from too much candy."

"Aren't you a prophet of doom."

"Better a prophet than a princess."

Caroline threw Chan a dirty look before turning her attention to her replacement, a new grad fresh off orientation who'd signed on for the twelve-hour night shift in the ER. Ellen Healy was an eager young thing who listened to Caroline's report on the state of the department and then waved her out the door at exactly seven o'clock.

After a brief stopover in her apartment for a change of clothes, Caroline was on the move again. Her destination was the Blue Cat Lounge, a tavern cum eatery on the outskirts of town where she was to dine with Carl, Jake, and Maddy. She anticipated an evening of pleasant conversation with her three closest friends. What she didn't anticipate was a full-blown, no-holds-barred brawl that would land all four of them back in the ER.

NINE

"A TOAST TO Garrison Hurst. For the first time in his life, he's done the right thing."

Carl Atwater lifted his stein of beer and clinked it against Jake's glass. The two men grinned at each other, bonding in their dislike of Bruck's president.

"Now if he'd only aim for a repeat performance and leave town," Jake sighed. "I would personally pay for his train ticket."

Caroline caught Maddy's eye. The police chief's wife raised one impeccably lined brow. The look on her face said she'd heard this complaint many times before.

"I suppose he's on your back about next weekend," said Carl.

"Big time. He's making us jump through hoops over this Homecoming game."

Jake launched into a vivid description of Garrison Hurst's demands for added security on Saturday. He interjected his biting commentary with a personal opinion on the president's sanity and the legality of his many requests.

Caroline leaned back in her chair and only half listened to what was being said. She was more interested in the two men talking across the table than in the conversation itself. The pair had disparate views on many things, Carl being an academic who relished thinking outside the lines, and Jake being a strict law and order man whose purpose in life was to keep the lines straight. Despite their different philosophies, they were good friends who enjoyed each other's company.

Carl was older and heavier than Jake, but his energy matched that of the policeman. He was a curious person in love with the past who'd written a series of books chronicling the history of small town America. His nonfiction accounts sold well, and he could have lived on the royalties if he'd wanted. Instead, he chose to teach his favorite subject at Rhineburg's Bruck University.

As chairman of the history department, Carl went nose to nose with Garrison Hurst on a weekly basis. The two had divergent views on education, and their heated exchanges during faculty meetings had become something of a legend on campus. Carl's success as a writer only added fuel to the fires of jealousy burning deep inside his rival. Hurst did everything in his power to discredit the professor both professionally and in his private life. In retaliation, Carl became the president's worst nightmare, a personal nemesis who counteracted his every move.

Theirs was a feud neither man was willing to end.

The conservative Jake Moeller shared Carl's view of Hurst as a tyrannical businessman, who ran the university like a department store, shaping the curriculum to appeal to the masses. Like the professor, Jake had served in the Army before attending college. While Carl returned from World War II with a greater resect for individual freedom, Jake returned from Viet Nam with a greater respect for public restraint. As he saw it, a classical education imposed a certain discipline on the mind, which in turn cultivated a sense of law and order in society. Hurst's juggling of the curriculum was, to Jake's way of thinking, nothing more than a form of pandering to political correctness. His role as Rhineburg's Chief of Police prevented him from publicly criticizing Garrison Hurst. Privately, though, he reacted with glee every time Carl managed to upset the president's apple cart.

"The man is a total idiot," the policeman said for the umpteenth time. "I can't believe he's a college president."

"He must be doing something right," Maddy murmured. "After all, the university hasn't gone belly-up under his management."

She glanced around the table, taking in the horrified looks on the faces of Jake and the professor.

"Don't get me wrong," she added hurriedly. "I'm not a fan of Garrison Hurst. He's much too egotistical for my liking. But you have to give the devil his due. Bruck seems to be flourishing under his administration."

"I wonder if it really is," said Caroline. "According to someone in the know, the school's in financial trouble."

Three pairs of eyes stared at her. Three sets of eyebrows soared skyward.

"And what did you hear?" asked a curious Carl.

Caroline told them about Lian Daley accepting a seat on the Board of Directors.

"According to Lian, all the Board talks about is money. She said the school needs a shot in the arm financially."

"So that's why Hurst is so gung-ho over the idea of an alumni fund." Carl pounded the table with his fist. "I knew something was up! All this talk about building a computer center is nothing but a lot of hot air. Hurst needs outside money to keep the school running."

"There you go, jumping to conclusions again. Nobody said the school was going under."

"Don't you bet on it, Cari," Carl replied darkly. "Garrison probably overextended Bruck's credit when he pushed through the stadium repairs. He sunk a lot of money into football."

"Speaking of the Bruins," said Maddy, "I think the entire team just walked in."

Judging by the sudden rise in the decibel level, Caroline guessed her friend was correct. She peered over Carl's shoulder at the young men jostling each other as they flocked toward the far end of the room. She groaned when she saw her son among them.

"Solidarity is all well and good. But does Martin have to stand so close to Trace Golden?"

Carl twisted in his chair to get a better view of the team. "Looks like they've buried the hatchet, Cari. Hopefully it'll stay buried."

They watched as a waiter walked by carrying three pitchers of a dark colored brew. He placed them on the team's tables and whipped out his order pad.

Jake pushed back his chair and stood up.

"Some of those boys look mighty young to be drinking. I think I'll step over there and check out those pitchers."

"If I recall the rules correctly," said Caroline, "alcoholic beverages are prohibited during the playing season."

Jake motioned with his head to Carl.

"Why don't you join me, Professor?"

"Don't mind if I do." Carl lumbered to his feet. "Go ahead and order dessert, ladies. We'll be back in a minute."

"No dessert for me," said Maddy when they'd gone. "Anything for you, Caroline?"

Caroline shook her head. Dessert was the last thing on her mind as she watched the two men approach the team. Carl moved left, stopping at the last table to speak with several of the younger players. Jake took the right side and walked over to where Trace Golden was sitting.

Trace didn't appear fazed by the arrival of Chief Moeller. He leaned back and grinned up at Jake, then pointed at one of the pitchers. Jake shook his head at the young man before turning his attention to the others at the table. He slapped one Bruin on the back, shook hands with another, then nodded at Carl. The two of them strolled back to where Caroline and Maddy were waiting.

"Nothing but cola in their glasses," Carl reported. "They're having a celebration party complete with pizza."

"I think Trace is carrying a flask," said Jake. "I was pretty sure I smelled alcohol on his breath, but unless he walks out of here and gets behind the wheel of a car, I can't do anything about it."

"The boy's under twenty-one, isn't he?"

"Yes, Maddy, he is. But in case you forgot, the Blue Cat Lounge lies outside the limits of Rhineburg. Even if it were in my territory, I'm not carrying a breathalyzer kit. I can call the state police if I want to make a scene, but what's the point? They've got better things to do than shake down a punk like Trace. Anyway, he knows I'm on to him now. He'll probably toss his flask out the nearest window."

A silence fell over the group as a frustrated Jake downed the last of his beer. Maddy locked eyes with Caroline, then broke the tension with a whistle so piercing it elicited the immediate response of the entire waitstaff.

"Another round of beer," Maddy told one of the boys who came running over to their table. As he scurried off to do her bidding, she placed her right hand gently on Jake's arm.

"Now you listen to me, Jake Moeller. I refuse to let a little creep like Trace Golden ruin our evening. Forget about him and Garrison Hurst and all the other annoying people you've run into today. Instead, you tell me who those folks are over there."

Maddy pointed to the door where a woman dressed in jeans and a heavy parka had entered the lounge. Accompanying her was a tall man wearing a denim jacket and a worn Stetson hat.

"He looks like the fellow who showed up at the demonstration. The one who talked to us right after Hurst made his announcement to the players."

"I think you're right, Cari." Carl scratched his beard. "If we were correct in surmising his role as a representative of the rodeo, then the woman with him is probably one of the infamous Moore sisters."

The four of them watched as the couple made their way to the bar. They ordered food, then sat talking quietly, glancing from time to time around the room.

"I wonder what they're up to."

"Well, Professor, we won't find out if we don't ask." Maddy stood up with a grin. "I think I'll go over and welcome those folks to Rhineburg."

"Now, Maddy..."

Maddy brushed off her husband's warning with a shake of her curls.

"Don't be such a stick in the mud," she said as she walked towards the bar.

Jake threw up his hands in despair, but he was a perfect gentleman when Maddy returned to the table with the two strangers.

"Jake, Carl, Caroline. This is Donna Moore of the Moore Sisters' Rodeo and Wild West Show. And this handsome fellow," she said, pointing to Moore's companion, "is Ben Halloway, Donna's assistant."

Jake pulled up a couple of chairs as everyone shook hands. Moore's grip was as strong as Halloway's, but her hand didn't linger like his when he greeted Carl.

"I've seen you before, haven't I."

It was more of a statement than a question. The professor answered in the same matter-of-fact tone.

"We met earlier today during the demonstration outside Bruck Hall. I made some foolish comment about there being no rodeo on Friday, and you corrected me."

"Yeah, I remember." Halloway dropped Carl's hand. While he didn't actually smile, the lines on his weathered face rearranged themselves into something less than a frown. "I didn't mean to be rude. I hope you'll forgive me if I overreacted to what that fella said."

"That 'fella', as you call him, was Bruck University's president, Garrison Hurst. I take it you haven't met him yet."

"Not yet, but one of these days…"

"I'm the one who worked out the deal for the rodeo with Mr. Hurst." Donna Moore silenced Halloway with a warning look. "Ben's our contact man for the farmers in this area."

A good deal shorter than Halloway, Moore was a lean woman in her early forties with close-cropped auburn hair and eyes the color of hazelnuts. She was small-boned, but her upper arms stretched the fabric of her knit shirt. Caroline guessed she'd earned those muscles working with horses.

Moore turned to Jake. "Your wife tells me you're the local sheriff."

"Actually, I'm the Chief of Police for the town of Rhineburg."

"Then you must be aware of what happened today at Bruck."

"I heard about it. I must tell you, Miss Moore, I don't have any authority over what goes on at the university, even though it does lie within the town's limits. Bruck has its own security force. They only call on me in extreme situations."

"What about parade permits? Permission to picket on the university grounds?"

"You'll have to talk to Michael Bruck. He's in charge of policing the campus, and he can answer all of your questions."

"I'm not sure the issue of parade permits has ever come up before," said Carl. "Today's demonstration was the first I can recall in over thirty years."

Moore swiveled in her chair, her eyes narrowing as she took in the professor's white hair, beard, and mustache. Apparently satisfied he wasn't Saint Nick in disguise, she asked in a gracious voice, "Do you work at Bruck, Mr. Atwater?"

"I teach in the history department."

"Ah! Then you know Mr. Hurst."

"Not in the biblical sense of the word, Miss Moore. But yes, you could say I'm well acquainted with the man."

Moore ignored the professor's attempt at humor.

"Do you know if he makes a habit of breaking contracts?"

"The president does whatever he thinks is best for the university. I don't always agree with him on what's best, but then I don't have a Board of Directors behind me."

"So the board members support his move to cancel the rodeo."

"Yes, they do," Carl stated flatly. "They were all present when the decision was made."

"Hmm." Moore glanced over at Halloway. "It looks like we may have to make a statement of our own. Something that will encourage Mr. Hurst and his backers to rethink their position."

"Can't you move the rodeo to another site?" Caroline asked. "You must understand how difficult it would be to play the Homecoming game on a field torn up by horses and cattle."

A young woman wearing a pale blue apron with a brighter blue cat imprinted on it approached their table. She took a plate heaped with a burger, fries, and coleslaw from the tray she carried and set it down in front of Halloway.

"Your football game is no concern of mine," Moore said as she accepted her own meal from the waitress. "We intend to hold the rodeo as planned in the place agreed upon. We have a binding contract with the university signed by President Hurst. If he refuses to honor the contract, I'll go to court and get an injunction to shut down the stadium."

"So if you don't get to play, nobody gets to play."

"That's right, Chief," Moore said emphatically. She bit into her burger, ignoring the looks of consternation on the faces around her.

"There must be another way to settle this matter," Caroline said. "What if…"

"Hey, lady. Are you the one in charge of the rodeo?"

Trace Golden strode across the room and positioned himself just out of Jake's reach. Accompanying him were a half dozen well-muscled Bruins.

"Who wants to know?"

Moore took a sip of her beer before glancing up at the boys. She gave them the once over, then laughed.

"I'll bet you're the reason I'm here in Rhineburg tonight. You guys are football players, aren't you?"

Several Bruck students sitting at the bar cracked up. Their muffled laughter carried over to the team members.

"You got something to say?" Trace scowled at the group, daring them to speak. One of the bolder males slid off his barstool and pointed a finger at Trace.

"Tell them the truth, Golden. You guys are nothing but a bunch of Freebies."

Golden's fist materialized in the other student's face. The punch came so fast, the young man had no chance to defend himself. He staggered backwards and collapsed against the bar.

"Hey, man! You had no call to hit him!" said one of the boy's buddies as he moved in to protect him.

"Oh, yeah?"

Golden's next punch caught the second fellow smack dab in the breadbasket. He doubled up in agony, joining his companion on the floor.

At that point, all hell broke loose. Half a dozen young men leaped off their barstools and started swinging. The Bruins retaliated in kind.

"Cut it out!" yelled Jake. A stein of beer flew past his ear and he jumped to his feet, wiping foam off his cheek with one hand and grabbing for the nearest combatant with the other.

"Better duck, ladies," said Carl as he pushed back from the table.

The fight quickly spread from the bar to the back end of the room with every able-bodied man in the place taking part. Fists and food flew in equal proportions as the Big Bad Bruins took on all comers. What they lacked in numbers, the team members made up for in muscle. The floor was soon littered with students crippled by the hard right fist of an angry football player.

Urging on the men were several dozen females who had taken refuge atop the bar. They clung to each other in mock terror and shrieked encouragement to their boyfriends, occasionally swinging an empty beer bottle at one or another of the fighters.

Caroline and Maddy didn't wait to see who won the battle. They dove under the table, careful to take their beer steins with them. Down on all fours, they stared at each other.

"If I'd known those two were going to cause this much trouble, I'd never have invited them to join us," grumbled Maddy.

Grinning, Caroline treated her friend to her best Stan Laurel imitation.

"Well, Ollie, here's another fine mess you've gotten us into!"

TEN

"HOLD STILL, JAKE. Like it or not, this cut has to be cleaned." Dressed in green scrubs borrowed from the OR, Caroline swabbed the Chief's forehead with saline and an antiseptic soap. "When was your last tetanus shot?"

Jake groaned. "Please, Caroline. No shots. I can't stand needles."

"He had one a couple of years ago," Maddy said. She patted her husband's arm. "Lie still, dear, and let Cari do her work. As soon as Dr. Daley sews you up, I'll bail you out of here."

Jake groaned again, but he did settle down.

"Damn kids," he growled. "When I get my hands on Trace Golden…"

"He was one of the first ones out the back door when the state police arrived. His feet were flying so fast, he almost outran his shadow." Maddy smiled wistfully. "If only he could duplicate those moves on the football field."

"Don't mention the word football," said Caroline.

She was still seething over Martin's part in the brawl. Although he claimed he was only trying to separate the fighters, she figured he'd gotten in a few good punches himself. He now had a swollen lip and chipped tooth to match his broken nose, lacerated cheek, and black eyes. Recalling his battered face served to raise her blood pressure another notch. She took out her annoyance on Jake Moeller's wound.

"Hey! Let up on me, will you?" Jake swatted her hand away from his face. "It hurts!"

"Sorry, Jake. My brain kind of wandered for a moment."

Caroline covered the cut with gauze, then pulled a suture kit out of the overhead cabinet and placed it on the Mayo stand parked next to Jake's cart.

"Chan will be here in a few minutes. I'll leave you two to talk while I check on the rest of our patients."

She waggled her fingers at Maddy before closing the curtain on the tiny examining room. Someone had set up folding chairs under the big clock hanging in the center of the ER. She glanced over at the chairs and saw row after row of beer-and-blood-stained students waiting to be examined. Cut lips and grazed faces accounted for most of the injuries, but a few of the walking wounded sported ice packs wrapped around swollen ankles and bruised hands.

"This crew livened up the place."

Ellen Healy, the nurse who'd replaced Caroline earlier in the evening, pushed an empty wheelchair out of the way and walked over to the desk.

"Before they came in, it was only me, Mrs. Graham, and her gallbladder. The three of us, all alone in an empty ER."

"Me and Mrs. Graham. Sounds like the title of a love song," Caroline said with a smile.

"A love song about a diseased gallbladder? Somehow I doubt it'll hit the top twenty." Ellen transferred two charts to a rack near Chan's end of the desk. "I feel sorry for the state cop. He's definitely going to be up to his ears in paperwork tonight."

Caroline looked over to where Carl stood talking to an officer.

"Professor Atwater owns the Blue Cat Lounge. Poor guy. The place was a shambles by the time the fight ended."

"How awful," said Ellen. "My boyfriend and I love the Blue Cat. The food's good, and the bands are always great."

The Blue Cat Lounge was more of a hobby than a business for Carl. Run by his trusted manager, Shiloh, it was a hangout for Rhineburg's student population. The building itself was an eyesore with its mismatched shingle roof, peeling paint, and grimy windows. Its seedy roadhouse appearance, along with the crooked neon cat flashing blue above the door, purposely discouraged tourists from entering. The locals knew better: the Blue Cat Lounge housed a better than average restaurant graced on the weekends by some of the best jazz musicians in the Midwest.

Caroline watched Carl escort the officer down the hall to the ER entrance. The two men shook hands before the policeman triggered the electric eye on the sliding glass doors and walked out to his car.

Caroline joined her friend in the corridor.

"I told Captain Reese I'm not going to press charges against any of the students," said Carl.

"You're being very generous, Carl. I don't know if I'd be as forgiving if the Blue Cat belonged to me."

"It has nothing to do with forgiveness. Call it looking out for my own interests."

"Are you worried about bad publicity? I hardly think a few arrests will slow your flow of patrons."

"You don't understand," Carl said gruffly. "Garrison Hurst could decree the Cat off-limits to students. He could put us out of business permanently."

Such a complication hadn't occurred to Caroline.

"No one knows this yet, but come January, Shiloh will officially own the Cat. I'm turning over the deed to him."

"I'm surprised. But knowing you, I guess I shouldn't be."

"Shiloh's worked hard to build the business while all

I've done is sit back and reap the rewards. He deserves to own the place."

"What did Captain Reese think of your decision not to prosecute?"

"He wasn't happy. But since things calmed down once the cops arrived, and nobody resisted arrest, he agreed not to charge anyone if I promised to report the matter to the university authorities."

Carl had assured the Captain he'd call both the president and the head of campus security.

"I have every one of those boys' names down on paper. It'll be a cold day in hell before they're allowed back inside the Cat."

"So, like it or not, Hurst will hear about the fight."

"But not from me. I called Michael Bruck, and he's on his way over here now. I'll give him a copy of my list. He can have the honor of presenting it to the president."

"Ah! The head Archangel himself is coming to St. Anne's."

In charge of university security, Michael, Gabriel, and Rafael Bruck had gained their nickname for obvious reasons. The brothers were triplets in their early thirties, direct descendants of the university's founder, Joseph Bruck. All three were devilishly handsome with hair the color of stone ground mustard and eyes of Prussian blue. They were also intelligent and as fit as boxers in training. Together, they kept a tight rein on the few troublemakers attending Bruck U.

"I think that's him coming up the driveway." Carl peered through the glass ER doors at a car pulling into the lighted parking lot. "Yes, it's Michael."

"I'll go check on Jake while you two discuss strategy," Caroline said with a sad smile. She reached out and squeezed Carl's arm. "Life does get complicated, doesn't it?"

Rhineburg's Chief of Police was receiving his discharge instructions from Ellen when Caroline returned to the room.

"Feeling any better, Jake?"

"There's only one thing that will make me feel better," the big man said as he signed his release form. "Getting my hands on Trace Golden."

"Oh, stop it," scolded Maddy. "Don't get your shorts in a knot over Golden. Leave him to the state police."

"Umm…maybe you two ought to speak with Carl before you leave. I think he has something to tell you."

Jake looked at Caroline suspiciously. "Now what's the professor gone and done?"

"Go talk to him, okay? I don't have time to explain."

Caroline turned and fled into the medication room. She knew Jake's views on law and order, and she wasn't about to boost his blood pressure with a report on Carl's decision. Let the two men argue it out between them.

In the next half an hour, Caroline transported a dozen patients to and from X-ray. Between trips, she filled out discharge papers at the desk. On one of these occasions she noticed a particular chart in the "In" rack.

"Ben Halloway? What's he doing here, Ellen?"

"You know him?"

"I met him for the first time tonight. No, actually I met him this morning, but then I didn't know his name." Caroline saw a look of confusion on Ellen's face. "Forget it. I'll bring him in."

She grabbed the chart and walked to the waiting room where she found Halloway sitting with Donna Moore.

"Didn't expect to see you two again so soon."

"We didn't expect to see you at all." Moore helped Halloway to his feet. "Ben tripped over some boy's leg as we were making our escape from the restaurant. He took a header out the door and landed on the split rail fence. I think he might have injured his ribs."

"I've busted a couple of 'em in the past riding broncs." Ben rubbed his right side gingerly. "But I never broke one fallin' over no fence before."

"Let's get you on a cart and check you out."

Caroline led the pair into the ER where she showed them to a curtained off area. She handed Ben a gown.

"Strip from the waist up and put this on. I'll be back in a minute to take your blood pressure and check your lungs."

She was typing the order for Halloway's chest X-ray into the computer when Wade Wilkins strode into the room.

"Can I help…"

"Where are my boys?"

Wilkins's voice was as cold as the afternoon's wind. Caroline looked into his eyes and mentally shivered. This man was trouble.

"They're sitting right over there."

She pointed to the rows of chairs under the clock. Wilkins glanced at the boys, then peeled off his jacket and tossed it on the desk. One of the sleeves flopped over the computer screen, hit the keyboard delete button, and promptly erased the order for Halloway's X-ray. Caroline pushed the coat to the floor and aimed a silent curse at the coach's back.

The players fell silent as Wilkins approached. It was pretty obvious he wasn't happy with them.

"What the hell have you guys been up to?" he said loudly. "Don't you know we have a game on Saturday?"

"Hey, there! Keep your voice down." Ellen frowned at the coach. "This is an Emergency Room, not a football field."

Wilkins's head snapped to the side. He glared at Ellen over his shoulder. Once again he reminded Caroline of a snake with his hooded eyes and icy stare.

"You think I take orders from skinny little girls in scrub suits? You go about your business, lady, and leave my men to me."

Ellen's face turned a deep shade of red. She took a step forward, but Caroline quickly restrained her.

"Don't do it," she said as she reached for the phone. She punched in the code for security and followed it with the ER's extension number. "Let the uniforms handle this moron."

Wilkins was still carrying on at the top of his voice when, less than a minute later, two white-shirted security officers entered the ER. Caroline cocked her thumb in the direction of the door.

"He's persona non grata in here. Get him out, will you?"

The two men nodded in unison. Hired as much for their muscle as for their ability to guide lost souls through the hospital's labyrinth of corridors, the pair knew exactly how to handle rowdy customers like Wilkins. They approached the coach from the rear, one man on his right side and the other on his left. The senior officer murmured something in Wilkins's ear. Then, taking him by the elbows, the guards sandwiched him between their bodies and hustled him towards the glass exit doors.

After an initial yelp of protest, Wilkins went along quietly.

"I love it!" crowed Ellen. "He saw how big those guys were, and he completely caved in."

"All talk and no substance," said Caroline. "All bullies are alike."

"And that fellow is quite a bully."

Caroline spun around. Donna Moore was standing

outside Ben's cubicle, her face the color of whipped egg whites. She was staring at the doors leading to the parking lot as if she expected to see Wilkins come charging back in.

"I'm sorry you had to witness that little scene, Miss Moore. Unfortunately, we sometimes have no choice but to physically remove people from the building."

Moore held up a hand.

"You don't owe me any explanations, Mrs. Rhodes. What I said before is true. He's a real bully." She pointed to the Bruins sitting silently in their chairs. "Ben and I heard him shouting at those boys. I take it he's their coach."

"Yes, he is."

"Would you mind telling me his name?"

"His name?"

"I'll have to deal with him in the coming days," explained Moore. "It would be easier if I could address him by a title other than 'bully'."

Caroline mentally applauded the spunky little rodeo owner. A moment ago Moore's face had registered shock. Now she was cracking jokes as if nothing at all had happened. She'd regained her composure quickly, a sure sign of inner strength.

Thinking about her request, Caroline saw no reason not to honor it. Moore could easily get Wilkins's name from any one of the players sitting in the room. And the coach had been a visitor, not a patient, in the ER. As far as she was concerned, the rules of confidentiality didn't apply to the tyrant of the football field.

"His name is Wilkins. Wade Wilkins."

Moore's left eyebrow arched in amusement.

"Wade Wilkins. Such a memorable name for such a forgettable creature."

"And so very athletic sounding," added Ellen with a grin.

"Oh, yes, dear. *Very* athletic."

Donna Moore winked at Caroline before disappearing once more behind the examining room curtain.

ELEVEN

MONDAY AFTERNOON SAW a repeat performance of the Bruin picket line. This time the protest extended beyond Bruck Hall to include all of the campus buildings. Ignoring the security guards stationed along the way, the sign-carrying students paraded down Circle Road shouting slogans and calling out to friends who waved bright red Bruin banners from dorm and classroom windows.

The previous night's fight had drawn supporters for the team in the form of girlfriends, drinking buddies, and otherwise unoccupied football fanatics. A few of the fans were fathers of team members, while others were elderly male alumni. With nothing more exciting ahead of them than another day of retirement, the alums had donned their faded Bruck sweaters and joined the ranks of the protesters with a vigor belying their mean age of eighty-two.

The reason for the renewed attack on the university was an early morning meeting between Donna Moore and Garrison Hurst. Faced with the prospect of a lawsuit, the president quickly backpedaled on his decision to abort the rodeo. He called a special meeting of the faculty. In the presence of Miss Moore, he announced that all events previously noted in the weekend program would go on as scheduled. He then named several student athletes whose inability to contain their exuberance at the Blue Cat Lounge had earned them a one-week suspension from football. Last but not least, he proclaimed the Blue Cat off-limits to the entire student body.

"It's not fair," grumbled Martin as he sat waiting in the ER for a wound check on his two-day-old laceration. "It's not Professor Atwater's fault Trace Golden can't control his temper. Trace started the fight. He should be the one who's punished, not the professor."

"Life isn't always fair," said Caroline. She picked up her son's chart. "Any allergies I should note?"

Martin snorted in disgust. "You know I'm not allergic to anything. Why even ask?"

"I thought you might be having a reaction to football. After all, you're not out on the picket line with the others."

She batted her eyelashes at Martin before putting a check mark in the "no" box.

"Very funny. I still feel as strongly about the game as ever. But Trace is out there with his friends right now. I don't want to mix it up with him again."

"Is Trace the one who gave you the chipped tooth?"

"You're jumping to conclusions again, Mom. There were a lot of punches being thrown last night. God only knows who hit me."

"I'll bet Nikki wasn't pleased when she saw the way you looked."

"She was asleep when I got home. But she wasn't exactly jumping for joy this morning. I got the silent treatment along with my orange juice."

Caroline shook her head. "Few wives take kindly to a battered face at the breakfast table. It's a fact of life you should have learned by now, Martin."

"I'm not giving up football, Mom, no matter how hard you and Nikki push."

"Then how about giving up fighting? Nikki's anxious enough when you're on the field without you giving her more cause for worry."

"I promise you, from now on I'm staying away from Trace Golden."

"Tell that to Nikki, not me." Caroline stood up and tucked her son's chart under one arm. "And Martin, make sure you keep your promise."

TWELVE

By THREE O'CLOCK a second picket line had formed outside Bruck Hall. This one was composed of students infuriated by the ban placed on the Blue Cat Lounge. Hastily drawn signs featuring the tavern's logo competed with Bruin placards for the attention of Garrison Hurst. Several of the blue felines were pictured chomping away on human hearts inscribed with the letters "G.H." The deeds of the cats matched the sentiments of the protesters; scrawled across the tops of the signs were angry inscriptions vilifying the university's head honcho.

Caroline felt a twinge of pity for the beleaguered president when she pulled out of the hospital parking lot. Students ranged up and down the road circling Bruck Green. The younger ones appeared in a holiday mood, the boys roughhousing with each other and the girls feigning disgust at their antics. Those who'd reached the magic drinking age were not quite as rowdy. Faced with losing their favorite watering hole, they circled the Hall like a pack of snarling wolves awaiting dinner.

Driving slowly behind a particularly noisy band of students, Caroline nosed the Jeep up the road, her foot tapping the brake in rhythm to the ebb and flow of the crowd. Ahead and to her right lay Bruck Hall. She looked over at the building, expecting to find a sizable contingent of police patrolling the grounds. Much to her surprise, the only officers present were Michael Bruck and two of his cohorts. The security men appeared unfazed by the raucous

chants of the protesters. They stood shoulder to shoulder
in front of the main entrance, smiling and talking with the
students lounging on the steps.

Amazing, thought Caroline. She wondered if President
Hurst was as calm and cool as the human blockade guard-
ing the Hall. He was currently locked in his office con-
ferring with the Board of Directors. He might not be able
to see what was happening outside, but there was no way
the noise wasn't reaching his ears.

News traveled fast in Rhineburg, but thanks to Chan
Daley, Caroline was one of the first to know about the
board meeting. Lian had called Chan to say she'd be late
getting home. The ER doc had laughed when she suggested the conference could go on for hours. Caroline,
with her knowledge of university politics, knew better.
A few well-placed calls confirmed the presence of both
the Archangels and Jake Moeller at Bruck Hall. Mayor
Schoen was also in attendance along with Wade Wilkins,
Donna Moore, and a host of legal eagles. Oddly enough,
the principal of Rhineburg High School had been invited
to the meeting, too.

Whatever decision they came to, the Board was bound
to displease someone. The only question was, who would
it be?

Caroline left the university behind as she turned onto
the highway leading into town. Traffic was at a minimum,
and she pulled off at the Rhineburg exit exactly six minutes later. She eased up on the gas pedal when she reached
Wilhelm Road, content to cruise at a more leisurely pace
as she admired the scarecrow population along Rhineburg's main drag. Time wasn't a factor for Caroline. The
post office would be open for at least another hour, which
meant she could have a good long talk with Nikki before
her acting-postmaster daughter-in-law closed up shop.

Caroline studied the splendid Victorians lining both sides of the street. Built by the richer residents of Rhineburg many decades before, several of the old houses sported signs advertising shops catering mainly to tourists. Others had been converted into mini-restaurants and bed-and-breakfasts. All of the buildings had been repainted in the multi-color scheme that entitled them to be designated "painted ladies".

Jake and Maddy owned one of the Victorians on Wilhelm. Built in the Queen Anne style, the front part of the house had been redesigned to host an upscale antique shop while the back section remained the couple's living quarters. Mad Moeller's Antiques featured unique remnants of the past and was known throughout the state for its owner's honest deals.

Caroline found a parking spot alongside the town square. The post office, a chunky two-story structure formed from blocks of pink rhyolite, squatted on the corner of Wilhelm and Kaiser across from the little park. The building's rose-colored walls took on the hue of ripe strawberries in the slanting light of mid afternoon.

Unfortunately, the cheerful glow of the building's exterior was not reflected on the face of the woman working inside.

"Keep on frowning and you'll never win the Miss Congeniality award."

"I'm not in a very good mood today."

Nikki chose an envelope from a pile stacked on the counter and branded it with an inked cancellation stamp. The sound of the rubber stamp hitting the countertop echoed through the empty post office.

"Really? Who would have guessed."

Caroline eyed her daughter-in-law as the girl slammed the stamp down on a second and then a third letter. Pale as a gardenia with dark circles under her eyes, Nikki was dressed in black from the neck down.

"Nice outfit you're wearing. Goes well with the color of the ink."

Nikki's hand froze in mid-air. Then the stamp descended like a sledgehammer, battering the offending envelope and sending it skittering across the counter.

"I like black. It fits my mood."

"It's not a bad look if you're going to a funeral."

Nikki looked up at Caroline. Instantly, her eyes went from desert dry to slick with tears.

"Oh, mom. Everything's going wrong at the same time!"

Caroline pushed through the wooden gate separating the customers' side of the post office from the actual work area. She gathered a weeping Nikki in her arms and, with a pat on the shoulder and a few soothing words, guided her towards a back room that doubled as a mini-kitchen and office. When she had the girl safely seated at the table, she filled two chipped mugs with water and popped them into the microwave, then took a canister of tea and several packets of sugar from the cabinet above the sink. She placed them on the table along with two spoons and a half dozen Halloween napkins.

"I don't know where you keep your tissues." Caroline handed Nikki a square of orange paper decorated with the grinning face of a witch. "Scratchy or not, you'll have to make do with a napkin."

The microwave beeped, announcing the completion of its task. Caroline withdrew the two mugs and carried them to the table.

"If I didn't know better," she said as she dunked a packet of Earl Grey tea in her cup, "I'd say you were pregnant."

Nikki's eyes widened. "Is it so obvious?"

"To another woman, it is. But I'll bet Martin hasn't guessed the truth yet."

"I haven't told him." Nikki ducked her head. "We didn't intend to have a baby until he was out of school and working."

"You don't think he'll be happy with the news?"

"I'm not sure. He talks about all the things we should do before we settle down. He wants to travel during the summer months when he's off from work. And he thinks we should buy a house before we start a family."

"And what about you? What do you want from life?"

Nikki was quick to answer.

"I want this baby. I don't care about seeing the world, or living in a big house. I want to stay in Rhineburg, and I want Martin to get a job at Bruck. But," she added, "I don't know if any of these things are possible."

Caroline let her gaze wander to the mug cradled in her hands. If only the fortunetellers were right and you could read the future in tea leaves. How nice it would be if you could know what would happen tomorrow. But life was totally unpredictable. To paraphrase Frank Sinatra, you could be riding high one day and shot down the next.

"I wish I could say Martin will be hired by the university and you'll never, ever have to leave Rhineburg. But you know as well as I do President Hurst holds all the cards in that department. Even with a formal selection process in place, I assume the president has the final say on who teaches at Bruck and who doesn't." Caroline reached over the table and patted Nikki's hand. "As for that little life inside of you, babies don't always come at the most convenient times. I know Ed and I were totally unprepared for parenthood when I became pregnant for the first time."

"Martin wasn't planned?"

Caroline laughed at the surprise on Nikki's face.

"No way! We were very young and just starting out together. You could say we were both in shock when the rabbit died."

Nikki smiled at her mother-in-law's use of that old expression.

"Nine months is a long time," Caroline continued. "Even if you have it all planned out, things can happen during a pregnancy to throw you off stride. Jobs, family obligations, all of that can interfere with your 'perfect timing'. None of us knows what the future holds, so don't count on there always being a right time to have children."

Nikki was saved from responding by the jangle of the front door bell.

"Sounds like I've got a customer. I'll be right back."

Caroline leaned back in her chair and grinned up at the ceiling. A grandmother! Wow! There hadn't been a baby in the family for so long that she'd almost forgotten what it was like to hold one. She wondered if it would be a boy or a girl. Doesn't matter, she told herself, as long as he or she is healthy. But a little girl would be fun. She could buy her fancy little dresses and her first pair of shoes, and when she got older...

Nikki motioned to her from the doorway.

"Mom? Would you come out here, please?"

All thoughts of the baby flew out of Caroline's head when she saw the expression on her daughter-in-law's face. She scrambled to her feet.

"What's wrong? Is it Martin?"

Nikki shook her head and ducked back into the main part of the post office.

"There's someone here who'd like to talk to you," she whispered when Caroline appeared behind the counter. She pointed to the far corner of the room where a woman stood reading one of the "Wanted" posters tacked to the wall. "She says her name is Donna Moore and she met you yesterday at the Blue Cat Lounge. Is she with that rodeo?"

"She's the owner. I wonder what she wants with me." Caroline pushed past the gate. "Nice to see you again, Ms. Moore. How's Mr. Halloway feeling?"

Moore turned and extended her hand. "Ben's pretty sore, but he'll recover. And please, call me Donna."

"Cracked ribs can be painful. I know. I broke one of my own a few years ago."

Moore shrugged. "Ben's a tough guy. He can handle a little pain." She looked around the room. "Is there somewhere we can talk? Somewhere with chairs? Seems like I've been on my feet all day."

"Feel free to use the back room," said Nikki. She glanced at her watch. "I'm closing up soon, but until then..."

"Thank you. I won't keep Mrs. Rhodes long." Moore shot Nikki a smile. "Why don't you join us? You don't look all that busy, and after all, this is your post office."

Nikki didn't need a second invitation. Curiosity ran in her blood the same as it did in Caroline's. She happily abandoned the pile of letters still on the counter.

"I've come to talk to you about the rodeo," said Moore when the three women were seated around the table. "More to the point, I've come to ask for your help."

"Our help?" Caroline exchanged a look of bewilderment with Nikki. "I'm afraid I don't understand."

"You will once I explain." Moore ran a hand through her shaggy hair. "I'm joint owner of the Moore Sisters Rodeo Company along with my sister, Allison. Our dad was a rodeo rider in his younger days. When his father died, he moved back to Iowa to run the family farm. He always loved rodeo, though, and he got back into it as a stock contractor in the early seventies. When he died six years ago, Allison and I took over the business."

"What exactly does your company do?" Nikki asked as she poured a cup of tea for Moore.

"We're a member of the Professional Rodeo Stock Contractors Association. We provide the animals used in events like bull riding or calf roping. We also set up the arena and the bucking chutes, and we provide the announcers, the timers, and the bullfighters."

"Bullfighters?"

"Rodeo clowns to you," Moore said with a smile. "Ben is one of the best bullfighters in the business. He's saved many a rider from getting hurt."

Caroline shook her finger at Nikki.

"Don't you dare say a word to Martin about bullfighting, or the next thing we know, he'll be out of football and into rodeo."

Nikki laughed. "Over my dead body!"

"Martin's your son, isn't he, Mrs. Rhodes?"

"He's my son and Nikki's husband. But apparently you know that already."

Moore had the decency to look sheepish.

"I spent some time today doing research here in Rhineburg. I learned quite a bit about you and your family."

Caroline wasn't sure she liked the idea of Moore poking her nose into the Rhodes family history.

"Why are you interested in us?"

"Let me tell you a little more about my business before I get into that. Besides providing the stock and setting up the arena, we open the rodeo with a Wild West act that can't be beat. Then we close the show on a patriotic note with a dozen riders carrying American flags against a backdrop of fireworks. It's quite something to see."

"I imagine it is."

Caroline rocked back in her chair and stared warily at her guest. Moore was leading up to something, but for the life of her, she couldn't figure out what it was.

"There's more than meets the eye to staging a rodeo. It has to be sanctioned by the local rodeo association and advertised to prospective contestants. The prize money comes partly from fees paid by the contestants, but you have to line up sponsors for the rest of it. And of course, you need to hire a reputable stock contractor. When I came here in May to discuss the event with President Hurst and Mayor Schoen…"

"Hold on a minute. Are you telling me that all this was arranged last spring?"

"Why, of course." Moore appeared surprised by the question. "I thought that was common knowledge in Rhineburg. Mayor Schoen assured me that the town was fully behind the rodeo."

"The first I heard about it was Saturday afternoon when I read the flyer." Caroline looked at Nikki. "How about you?"

"I was in the dark the same as you. But you have to remember, Mom, you were in Chicago all summer, and Martin and I were in West Virginia researching the professor's next book. We probably missed the town meetings."

Nikki's explanation made sense. Still, they'd been back in Rhineburg for almost two months. It seemed strange that none of their friends had mentioned the rodeo.

"I was told by Mayor Schoen that the committee had rounded up several business sponsors, including a car dealer who'd agreed to underwrite all of the advertising expenses."

"Now isn't that interesting."

The only dealership in the area belonged to Bill Morgan, son of Alexsa Stromberg Morgan. Bill was wealthy enough to come up with a hefty donation, but once again, Caroline thought the Rhineburg grapevine would have been buzzing with the news.

"We'd already contracted for a show in Iowa this coming weekend when I received an email from my uncle asking us to come to Rhineburg."

"Your uncle?"

"He owns the feed and seed store here in town. The rodeo was his idea. He suggested it to Mayor Schoen who then talked it over with Garrison Hurst. The two of them decided a rodeo would make a great fundraiser, so they formed some kind of partnership. As I understand it, the profits are to be split equally between the town and the university."

Ms. Moore was a veritable fountain of information. Caroline listened closely as Donna rattled on about the planning for the rodeo. She wondered how well the woman had judged the personalities of the two men she was dealing with. Both could be downright devious when it came to money, and neither one of them was above a little trickery if they could sweeten their own personal pot.

"I hope you worked out an iron-clad contract," she said.

"I thought I did. But it seems there's a loophole in the wording, and President Hurst is making the most of it." Moore shifted in her chair. "I took on this job as a favor to my uncle. Dad loved rodeo, but to tell you the truth, he was a lousy businessman. When he died, Allison and I were forced to sell half our acreage to pay off his loans. We would have lost the entire farm if Uncle Otto hadn't baled us out."

"You owe him a debt of gratitude then. I suppose that's why you agreed to come to Rhineburg even though you had another job lined up."

"Yes. We also agreed to take a cut on our usual fee.

We're barely making anything on this rodeo, but we could afford to do it because of the wording of the contract. The university agreed to let us use the football field. That freed up the majority of our arena panels and chutes for the Iowa rodeo. What we have left is sufficient for use in the stadium."

"But you don't have enough equipment to put on a performance outside the stadium."

"Our main problem is seating. Sometimes we contract for rodeos where there is no available stadium or outdoor seating. That's the case in Iowa. We're providing that town with all the temporary bleachers we own. If I have to come up with more bleachers for this show, I'll to have to rent them from another source. Along with the portable johns they want me to provide, I could end up losing a bundle of money on this deal."

"Portable johns? Is that part of your usual package?"

"No. Relief stations are the responsibility of the event committee. But since the rodeo was supposed to be held in the stadium, restrooms weren't thought to be a problem. Even though the contract doesn't specifically include portable toilets, President Hurst claims I'm liable for all the necessary equipment to run a rodeo. His lawyers say that includes johns."

"That's silly," exclaimed Caroline. "Carl told me the plumbing isn't completely hooked up in the stadium. But he said the university was renting portable potties for the homecoming game. If they're already on site, why can't they be used for the rodeo?"

"Hurst says he's only paying for their use on Saturday. He refuses to pay for Friday."

Nikki rolled her eyes. "That guy is such a cheapskate!"

"Cheapskate or not, Hurst has me over a barrel. The contract states the rodeo is to be held in the 'completed' stadium. I never questioned the use of that word when I signed the papers, but now it's come back to haunt me. The stadium isn't complete, at least in the legal sense, without plumbing. According to the lawyers, Hurst has a right to break the contract unless I agree to stage the rodeo some place other than in the stadium."

"So that's why the Rhineburg High School principal was at the Board meeting today. The school's football field is equipped with bleachers."

"You're quick to catch on, Mrs. Rhodes," said Moore approvingly. "And yes, Mr. Jackson was at the meeting. Apparently there's a rack of portable bleachers on Bruck's temporary football field. Hurst figured the bleachers could be moved to the high school to complement their seating."

"But the Rhineburg football team is scheduled to play a home game this Friday evening."

"Unfortunately, you're right. Jackson nearly went through the roof when Hurst suggested he move the game to the other team's field. He refused to even consider the idea."

"He wouldn't at this point in the season," said Nikki. "The Mighty Maniacs are on a roll. Everyone in Rhineburg is talking about their chances to win a state championship."

Which was probably why the rodeo was getting so little attention on the local grapevine. Compared to the Mighty Maniacs, bucking broncos were small potatoes.

"Let's get back to the reason for your visit here today." Caroline could sympathize with Moore's problem, but she still didn't see how it affected her. "You said you needed my help."

Moore bobbed her head. "I told you that Alison and I were close to our Uncle Otto."

"You mentioned it."

"Otto's told us about the interesting things that have

happened in Rhineburg since you moved here. Murders and such."

Caroline didn't like what she was hearing. "There's been some trouble, that's for sure. But none of it was my doing."

"Still, you were involved in solving those crimes, Mrs. Rhodes. Because of that, people respect you. You're an influential woman in this town."

"I wouldn't say that. And I still don't see…"

Moore held up her hand.

"You will in a moment. First, let me tell you one other thing about the rodeo. There will be no men competing in it. The contestants will all be members of the Professional Women's Rodeo Association."

"Women contestants?" Nikki raised her eyebrows. "I thought they only participated in barrel racing."

"In a lot of rodeos, that's all they get to do. But the PWRA sanctions bull and bronc riding for women, along with calf roping events and the usual barrel races. Allison and I are strong supporters of women's rights in rodeo. When I first met with Hurst and Mayor Schoen, I suggested they sponsor an all-female rodeo sanctioned by the PWRA."

"Do women rodeo riders get the same kind of prize money as men?" asked Caroline.

"Not usually. Women have to fight for respect even when they're involved in the same events as their male counterparts."

"That doesn't seem fair," said Nikki.

Moore shrugged her shoulders.

"Fair or not, that's the reality of rodeo. For the most part, it's a male-dominated sport."

"This is all very fascinating," said Caroline. "But you still haven't explained what you want from me."

"Please, Mrs. Rhodes, be patient with me. I want you

to know about my meeting with President Hurst earlier
this morning. He was ready to break our contract, but I
threatened him with a lawsuit if he did."

"I'll bet that got his attention," said Nikki.

"It did at the time. That man backpedaled so fast, he left
skid marks on the floor. I walked out of his office believ-
ing the rodeo was going on as originally planned. Then at
noon I got a call from his secretary." Moore picked up a
napkin and twisted it into a ball. "I was told to show up at
the university at one-thirty for a meeting with the Board
of Directors. That's when Hurst's lawyers informed me of
the 'completed' stipulation in the contract."

"Not a good thing."

"No, Mrs. Rhodes. Not a good thing at all. I personally recruited some fine contestants for this rodeo. Several of them are already on their way here to help promote
the event. What am I supposed to do? Put up signs on the
highway saying 'turn back now—rodeo cancelled'? Then
there's the little matter of my livestock. They're due to arrive in Rhineburg later today."

"Why so early?" asked Caroline.

"We've made arrangements for a pre-show parade
through Rhineburg tomorrow evening."

"Tomorrow's Halloween. Everyone will be out on the
streets."

"Yes. We thought a parade would add a nice touch to
the holiday. Then on Wednesday, we'll be appearing at the
car dealership that's sponsoring the rodeo."

"You may have a problem contacting all the contestants,
but surely you're in touch with the people transporting your
livestock. It's not too late to turn them back. And the way I
see it, you won't lose any money if the rodeo is canceled."

"Money isn't everything, Mrs. Rhodes. What matters
here is my reputation as a contractor."

"People won't hold this against you."

Moore threw the napkin down on the table in disgust.

"Would you hire someone who can't deliver on her promises? Would you agree to ride in a rodeo organized by that person?"

"Surely the contestants will understand."

"Understanding doesn't put a paycheck in your pocket. Those women gave up other opportunities to perform here in Rhineburg. I promised them a rodeo, and that's exactly what I plan to deliver."

Moore appeared adamant in her decision to fight the university. Her stubbornness didn't surprise Caroline. Only the strong survived near bankruptcy. Growing a business demanded even more guts.

"The university and I are in a standoff of sorts. My lawyer says Hurst can't legally stop the rodeo if I agree to pay for the portable johns on Friday."

"And that's because Bruck has already ordered them for Saturday."

"Yes. The physical presence of toilets, portable or not, will prove that the stadium is 'complete' in the sense that it's usable. Hurst can't claim it's not usable on Friday if the same johns he's using on Saturday are in place Friday evening."

"The university could argue that there's a distinction between 'complete' and 'usable'."

"Any fair-minded judge would see through that ruse."

"You'd be willing to go to court over this?" Caroline hadn't expected Moore to go that far.

"My lawyer will get an injunction against the Homecoming game if Hurst and the Board don't agree to my use of the stadium."

"Wow! Now you're getting down and dirty," said Nikki.

"Sometimes down and dirty is necessary," replied

Moore. "But there's a way to avoid court action. And that's where you come in, Mrs. Rhodes."

Caroline crossed her arms over her chest and eyed Moore warily.

"Something tells me I'm not going to like this."

"Uncle Otto thinks the women in this town are pretty strong willed."

"Only the strong survive. Even in Rhineburg."

Moore brushed off Caroline's comment with a wave of her hand.

"I mean, they'd stand up for their rights against their husbands if need be."

"What are you getting at?"

"I want you to lead as many women as possible in a protest against the university. If they show some backbone and let the men know they're behind the rodeo, Hurst and the Board might back down on their decision."

Caroline laughed out loud.

"You mean a picket line? You want us to march down Circle Road next to the students?"

"The students and their fathers. And a lot of other men in town."

Nikki looked confused.

"Seems like I've missed something," she said. "The last I heard, only the football team was picketing."

Caroline explained about the ban on the Blue Cat and the general uprising on campus.

"I saw a few retirees mixed in with the crowd, but I wouldn't call it a huge turnout."

"You wait," said Donna. "According to Uncle Otto, Mayor Schoen has called for a mass demonstration to-night in support of the team. Practically every man in town has agreed to be there."

"You've got to be kidding."

Caroline couldn't imagine old Mr. Meyer abandoning his bakery to march around Bruck Hall. But then, he wouldn't need to close his shop. The efficient Mrs. Meyer would keep the donuts flowing until his return.

Unless, of course, she was on a picket line, too.

Caroline pushed her chair back from the table and stood up.

"I'm sorry, Miss Moore, but I'm not going to get in the middle of a fight between you and the university."

"But this is a matter of women's rights," Moore insisted. "The rodeo will be run by women and worked by women. You must see how important it is for women to support it."

"First of all," said Caroline, "I don't have any influence in this town. My opinion on the rodeo wouldn't matter to anyone in Rhineburg. Secondly, I have no desire to speak out against the university's decision. My son is on the football team, and I know how important Saturday's game is to the Bruins. There's no way they could play on a field that's been torn up by horses and cattle."

"I wish you would reconsider."

"I'm sorry, Miss Moore, but I can't." Caroline turned to Nikki. "I'll give you a call tomorrow morning. In the meantime, think about what I said earlier. You need to talk to Martin."

Nikki smiled at her mother-in-law, but made no move to accompany her to the door. Instead, she offered Moore another cup of tea that the woman eagerly accepted. By the time Caroline had slipped into her coat and dug out her car keys, Nikki and Donna were chatting away like long lost friends.

The scene struck Caroline as just a little too cozy. Given Nikki's feelings about football and Moore's willingness to use people, she suspected the two of them would begin plotting a partnership the minute she left the post office.

The results of such an entanglement could prove disastrous for all.

Unfortunately, there was nothing Caroline could do about it.

THIRTEEN

THE WEEK BEFORE Halloween, Rhineburg's scarecrow menagerie escaped the confines of town and cloned itself on the grounds of Bruck University. These campus specimens were more shabbily dressed than their country cousins, wearing castoff blue jeans, faded sweatshirts, and frayed baseball caps. Their spines stiffened by broomsticks, they resembled a ragtag army hastily assembled on the school's impeccably manicured grounds to stand guard over the halls of academia.

Despite their uniform appearance, the scarecrows were not all alike. Some of them stood with their noses buried in books that would later be found missing from the library. Others bore placards advocating everything from better food in the cafeteria to single room dorms for seniors. A few could even be seen stretched out on the ground on blankets as if catching the last warm rays of the year.

The most creatively designed of the lot were the straw athletes playing tag football on the grass outside the gym. These rugged fellows were garbed in grimy T-shirts and shorts and sported muscles that would have put Charles Atlas to shame.

The professors of Bruck University were not to be denied their part in the fun. A troupe of tuxedoed scarecrows appeared in the cul-de-sacs west of Circle Road the weekend before Halloween. Dancing across the lawns of faculty members in top hats and tails, they resembled a chorus line of Fred Astair look-alikes minus the famous Ginger.

Caroline admired this last group as she walked briskly down the sidewalk that snaked in and out of the cul-de-sacs. The scarecrows affected her mood in a way nothing else had since she'd left the post office. Nikki's alliance with Donna Moore bothered her, as did the fact that Martin knew nothing about the baby. The combination of events could spell trouble for the young couple, trouble she had no power to avert.

Annoyed with both her daughter-in-law and her own sense of helplessness, she'd returned to the dormitory out of sorts and ill at ease. She'd exchanged her uniform for jeans and a sweater, then wandered about the tiny apartment straightening things that didn't need straightening. Her stomach rebelled at the thought of food, and restlessness finally forced her out into the cool night air. A brisk walk along Circle Road was the first step towards numbing her worries. The tuxedoed strawmen provided her with a final escape.

A smile tugged at her lips now as she stopped to stare at the scarecrows. It felt good to smile, even better to close her eyes and inhale the smoky scent of a leaf pile burning in a nearby yard. Her spirits buoyed by the sights and smells of the season, she continued down the sidewalk with a lighter heart.

Her thoughts still on the scarecrows, Caroline was unprepared for the uproar that greeted her when she turned the corner on the last of the cul-de-sacs. She was still some distance from the university, but not so far away that she couldn't hear the sound of dozens of feminine voices raised in anger. Shading her eyes from the glare of a street lamp, she peered through the night shadows towards the campus. The curving road obstructed her view, but judging by the frenzied squeals coming from the direction of Bruck Hall, she figured the entire female population of Rhineburg had descended on Garrison Hurst's office.

Her curiosity thoroughly piqued, Caroline abandoned the sidewalk and cut across Bruck Green. A winding trail led through a stand of ancient oaks and ended at a point directly opposite the Hall. What she saw when she emerged from the forest was enough to send her shrinking back into its shadows.

Caught in the beams of ground level floodlights, the administration building with its pink rhyolite walls and twin towers rising fore and aft resembled a sun sugar castle under siege. Men of all ages were camped on the grass bordering the walkway. The Bruins and their supporters had claimed the area nearest the staircase where the wrought iron lanterns bracketing the portico shed some light on their cardboard signs. Behind them on lawn chairs lounged several dozen older men, probably team members' relatives. Wiser than their sons, brothers, and cousins, these fellows were content to sit back and swill beer while the younger guys did the hard work of protesting.

Farther back still stood a hundred or more students obviously disgruntled over the ban on the Blue Cat. This group was composed of both males and females, and they were the rowdiest of all the demonstrators. The girls yelled as loudly as the boys, but they seemed to be wavering in their dedication to the cause. Already a few of them had wandered into the street where the women of Rhineburg had formed their own impressive picket line.

The ladies of the town had not only shown up in large numbers to support their cowgirl sisters, but they had also garbed themselves for the occasion. Denim jeans and skirts along with cowboy boots, red neckerchiefs, and felt brimmed hats seemed to be *dernier cri* in picket line apparel. What the women lacked in style, they made up for in enthusiasm. Caroline suspected that many of them would be hoarse tomorrow as a result of their exuberant shouting.

"Isn't this the craziest thing you've ever seen?"

Caroline whirled around and smacked right into the broad chest of Chief of Police Jake Moeller.

"Good lord, Jake! You almost gave me a heart attack."

"Scared you good, did I?" Jake grinned as Caroline gingerly rubbed the tip of her nose with one finger. "That's what you get for hiding in the shadows like a peeping Tom."

"Better here in the shadows than out on the street with that gang," declared Caroline.

"Afraid they'll shanghai you into marching with them?"

"Maddy would certainly try."

"Maddy? Don't tell me my wife is here." Jake's smile vanished as he surveyed the line of women parading outside Bruck Hall. "She promised me she wouldn't do anything stupid tonight."

"Maybe she doesn't see what she's doing as stupid," Caroline said mildly. "A wife doesn't always have to agree with her husband, you know."

"I ought to haul that woman down to the station and lock her up. It's the only way to keep her out of trouble."

"Aw, come on, Jake. Maddy's in no kind of danger. Look who she's with."

Caroline pointed to the head of the line where Maddy walked arm in arm with Agatha Hagendorf, proprietor of the Rhineburg Boarding House and Home for Gentle Women. The tiny Mrs. Hagendorf had exchanged her usual black dress for a denim skirt and a sheepskin jacket. A cowboy hat trimmed with bright red roses covered her blue rinsed curls.

"Agatha will keep her in line. And if that doesn't ease your fears, look who's right behind them."

Hard on the heels of Agatha and Maddy marched Eleanor Naumann and Bertha Meyer. Best friends since childhood, the two were like Jack Spratt and his famous wife. Eleanor's angular frame boasted a flat chest sandwiched between long bony arms that ended in squared off hands the size of bookends. She had the type of face one attributed to a horse, with a high, broad forehead, narrow chin, and nostrils that flared with every breath. Her eyes were her one saving grace. Blue as cornflowers, they reflected a gentle nature confirmed by Eleanor's ready smile.

Bertha, on the other hand, resembled one of those sugary delicacies displayed in her husband's bakery. She was a diminutive woman in height while amply proportioned in every other way. Her face was round and plump as a bismarck punctuated by twin dots of licorice for eyes. Her head was capped by a crown of short fluffy hair the color of vanilla frosting. Below a set of double chins, her figure rolled downward in ever broadening stages with an imposing bosom topping a torso aptly described as butterball in shape.

"They do seem to be enjoying themselves, don't they?"

"At least Maddy had the good sense to wear a warm coat," said Caroline. "Check out Sue Walker. She looks like she's freezing in that thin skirt and jacket."

Sue's red cotton skirt blossomed over several layers of stiff crinoline. The white roses and blue piping decorating the hem were repeated on the wide lapels of a snug-fitting red cotton jacket open at the throat to reveal a white blouse. The outfit was beautiful, but highly impractical given the weather.

"That's her latest square dancing dress," said Jake. "Tom Walker's a real control freak, but he does let Sue go to the Saturday night dances down at the VFW hall."

"He 'lets' her go? You mean she has to ask his permission to leave the house?"

"I said he's a control freak. Actually, Tom goes with her to the dances. It gives him an opportunity to jaw with the other guys at the bar. He never sets foot on the dance floor." Jake pointed to the far end of the picket line. "Speaking of freezing, I'll bet the cold is getting to your daughter-in-law."

Caroline groaned when she caught sight of Nikki.

"I should have known she'd be here," she said in disgust.

Dressed in her bright yellow slicker, Nikki stood out from her companions like a dandelion in a bed of roses. The vinyl slicker didn't rate as cold weather gear, so Nikki must have had something other than warmth in mind when she'd chosen to wear it. Caroline could only guess at her daughter-in-law's motives.

She glanced over at the Hall where the Bruins were holding their ground near the staircase. Rafael Bruck had replaced his brother Michael on the cold stone steps. He was speaking to a delegation of players led by Trace Golden, and he didn't look at all happy. Golden was practically in his face, standing toe-to-toe with the security man and gesturing wildly at the windows of Hurst's office.

Raf didn't budge an inch. Caroline saw him point to the lawn before lifting a walkie-talkie to his lips. Within seconds, two burly officers emerged from the Hall, their expressions less friendly than Raf's. Trace backed down the steps before they could lay a hand on him, but Caroline could tell he was angry. He shook his fist at the Chief of Security as his buddies led him away.

Martin was not among the players surrounding Golden, nor was he with the rest of the team. Caroline scanned the crowd on the lawn. She picked out a few familiar faces, but none of them belonged to her son. She was about to

give up the search when she saw a flicker of movement
in the shrubbery near the west corner of the Hall. Martin stepped out of the shadows of a long-needled pine and
stood exposed in the glare of a floodlight. He stared at the
demonstrators in the street, his eyes riveted on one figure in particular.

Caroline could tell by the set of his jaw that Martin was
furious. The picket line that Nikki had helped organize
now stretched in an oval from Bruck Hall on the west to
the science building on the east. Nikki was approaching
the curve of the oval opposite from where Martin stood. If
she saw her husband at all, she gave no sign of it. Her appearance was entirely carefree as she tossed her head and
laughed at a comment made by one of the other women.

It dawned on Caroline what her daughter-in-law was up
to. Nikki was using her yellow slicker to attract her husband's attention much like a matador used his red cape
on a bull. Martin would have had to be blind not to notice
his wife as she walked past him waving a sign that read
"Rodeo Riders Have Rights."

"Martin looks pretty upset."

Caroline's voice was tight with worry, but Jake didn't
pick up on the vibes.

"Can't say I blame him," grumbled the unhappy policeman. "A woman ought to be more supportive of her
husband."

Caroline let the comment slide. She knew that Jake's
reaction had more to do with Maddy's presence on campus
than with Nikki's endorsement of the rodeo. Jake viewed
Maddy's involvement in the picket line as a betrayal of his
position as Chief of Police. Martin probably saw his wife's
actions in the same light. Instead of backing the Bruins'
protest, Nikki was rooting for the enemy.

Caroline stepped out of the shadows and pushed her way

through the demonstrators on the street. She was only a few feet away from Nikki when the young woman walked past her husband. Martin reacted exactly as his mother suspected he would. Like an enraged bovine, he charged into the picket line and snatched the sign from his wife's hands.

"Give that back!" Nikki shouted. "You have no right…"

"You're my wife, and that gives me the right!"

Martin tore the sign in half and threw it on the ground.

Oh, oh, thought Caroline. Bad move on your part, my boy.

"Stop it, you two," she said, stepping between them like a referee at a wrestling match. She glared at Martin, then gave Nikki the same disapproving look. "You're acting like a pair of fools."

The long oval picket line had shrunk into a compact circle with the battling couple forming a bull's-eye in the center. Caroline looked around and saw Maddy and her picketing partner occupying a front row position directly behind Nikki. Maddy gave her the thumbs up, but Agatha was too busy marveling over Martin's feisty wife to take notice of the elder Mrs. Rhodes. Behind Martin stood Eleanor Naumann and Bertha Meyer. Arms locked across their chests, the two old friends looked ready to tackle the young man if he tried any more of his shenanigans.

Outside the ring of females another circle had formed. This one was composed of Bruin football players and their male supporters. Martin's friend Al sidled over to a spot behind Eleanor and quietly wormed his way between her and Bertha. Standing behind Al and to his right was a grinning Trace Golden.

"Could we have a little privacy here?" Martin scowled at the women of Rhineburg, but the ladies scowled right back. "I'm not asking for heaven," he shouted when not one of them budged. "I only want to speak to my wife."

"Maybe she doesn't want to speak to you," a woman in the back row yelled.

"Yeah, you sign ripper! Maybe she wants an apology instead!"

"Let's see some action, Jackson!"

"Down on your knees, slimeball!"

Slimeball? Even Caroline thought that was going a little too far.

"Okay, now," she said loudly. "Let's all calm down." She raised her hands and motioned everyone back. "Why don't you all go back to your picket lines and give the three of us a little time alone."

Martin wheeled on her. "The three of us? What's that all about, Mother?"

"We need to talk, Martin."

"*We* don't need to talk. Nikki and *I* need to talk."

"Not until you apologize," said Nikki. She jabbed Martin in the chest with her forefinger. "You had no right to tear up that sign."

Martin swept aside his wife's hand. "*You* had no right to go behind my back and hook up with those lunatics from the rodeo."

"You tell her, Marty." Football fan Tom Walker had left his beer can on the Hall's front lawn and, along with his drinking buddies, had joined the Bruins in the street. Emboldened by liquor-induced memories of his youth, he breached the inner circle and clapped Martin on the shoulder. "Now that's the way to handle a woman!"

"Oh, yeah?"

A snarling Sue Walker laid down the yoke of subservience she'd worn since day one of her marriage. She straightened her back, pushed past Nikki, and confronted her beer-guzzling husband.

"Let me show you how we women handle a man."

Sue brought her cardboard sign down hard on Tom's head, then whacked him in the stomach for good measure. She continued to beat on him with the sign as, more stunned than in pain, he yelped and fell back into the arms of his comrades.

General mayhem ensued after that. The ladies of Rhineburg charged the outer circle like a modern day version of the Light Brigade. The younger males quickly scattered out of reach. Their older compatriots were not quite as nimble. Gripping their signs like lances, the enraged women poked at the behinds of the fleeing men.

The ladies showed no mercy as they drove their husbands, brothers, and assorted male relatives back towards Bruck Hall. Like hounds nipping at the tail of a fox, they chased the men onto the lawn and cornered them at the staircase. While most of the women continued to flail away with their signs, a small guerrilla force veered off from the group and headed for the beer coolers. It took them less than a minute to empty every can of its golden liquid.

Back on the street, Martin and Nikki were still glaring at each other like two boxers at a pre-fight press conference. Martin's teammates had straggled back to the scene and planted their oversized frames behind their fellow Bruin. Nikki had her own backup in the form of several dozen young women. Attuned to the inequities in the male/female relationship, the girls had abandoned their boyfriends and thrown their support to one of their own. A shouting match quickly erupted between the two groups.

"Quiet down, all of you!" Caroline commanded as insults piled up faster than the snow on Kilimanjaro. She laid a hand on her son's arm. "We need to get away from here, Martin."

Martin was beyond all semblance of his usual self. His face was taut with emotion, and when he looked at Caroline, the hostility in his eyes unnerved her.

"If there's anything I don't need right now, it's you interfering in my life."

Her unease turned to anger, and Caroline exploded.

"Like you interfered in my life a year ago? Remember how you blackmailed me into moving to Rhineburg? Made me sell the house and leave the neighborhood I loved? I'd call that interference of the first class, Martin."

"I'd call it saving my mother's sanity!"

"Oh? Well, let me tell you something, young man. What's good for the goose is good for the gander."

"And what the hell is that supposed to mean?"

"Martin! Mom! Stop it," cried Nikki as she pushed between them. She looked from one to the other, then covered her face with her hands and burst into tears.

Martin stared at his wife, the anger slowly receding from his eyes. His shoulders sagged and his face took on a wearied, almost sorrowful look.

"Please go home, Mom," he said quietly. "This is none of your business."

"That's where you're wrong, Martin." Her son may have calmed down, but the same could not be said for Caroline. Fueled by Nikki's tears, her temper flared to new heights. She gathered the girl in her arms and held her tight. "Anything that affects my grandchild is my business."

Martin reacted like he'd been sucker punched. His head snapped back, his eyes widening in surprise as he drew in a deep breath. The air rushing over his vocal cords seemed to catch in the back of his throat and choke him. The sound that emerged was the low guttural groan of a man in pain.

"You're pregnant?"

The question was barely audible, but Nikki shuddered so violently one would have thought the words had been shouted in her ear. She buried her head deeper in Caroline's coat.

Martin took a step backward, distancing himself from his wife. A myriad of emotions played havoc with his features, his face registering first shock, then embarrassment, and finally, deep-seeded anger.

"You sure are good with secrets, Nikki," he said bitterly. "First this rodeo business, and now a baby. I guess I'm the last person to hear anything around here."

Shaking his head in disgust, he pushed past his teammates and jogged off towards the gym.

That was the last anyone saw of him that night.

FOURTEEN

"I'M A LOUSY mother," Caroline said later that night as she walked with Carl down a quiet Circle Road. "I knew I shouldn't mention the baby, but I totally lost it when Nikki started to cry."

"You were frustrated," said Carl. "It's understandable."

"But not forgivable."

"Martin loves you. He'll get over his anger."

"I'm not so sure of that. You didn't see his face when he walked away."

Carl slowed his steps and gazed up at the sky.

"It's a good night for viewing the stars. No clouds to obscure them."

Familiar with the professor's philosophical thought processes, Caroline asked, "Is that a celestial observation, or a commentary on life."

"A little of both," said Carl. "I think human beings are much like stars. We're born in an explosion of energy and fueled through life by our own internal fire. Some of us stand out like the brightest stars in the sky. Others glow with less intensity. Regardless of how much light we cast, we all have one thing in common: like the stars, we're consistent. We shine with the same amount of radiance whether the sky is clear or cloudy."

"You're saying that Martin's the same man tonight that he was this morning?"

"He's basically a decent fellow who cares deeply for his family. One argument with you won't change that."

"I hope you're right."

"I am right. What fuels Martin's fire is a deep love for Nikki. He won't stay angry with you because he simply *can't* stay angry with her. Don't let a few troublesome clouds distort your view of your son, Cari. Martin still shines the same as ever, and so do you."

"I think I lost a bit of my luster tonight."

Carl laughed. "Apologies are great cloud erasers. If you feel bad about what you said, go talk to Martin. Tell him you're sorry and be done with it."

"It's too late to do that tonight. I'll stop by school in the morning and apologize then."

It was eleven-thirty, long past bedtime for either one of them. Despite the late hour, Caroline felt not in the least bit sleepy. She knew she was functioning on nervous energy alone, but that didn't worry her as much as the nagging fear tearing at her heart. The apprehension she'd felt since her visit to the post office had now deepened into a real sense of foreboding. It was something even Carl couldn't help her shake off.

When Nikki refused to go home after the fight, Caroline left her with the other women and walked over to Carl's little bungalow in the southernmost cul-de-sac bordering Circle Road. Carl was watching football, and for a while, the Monday night game between the Steelers and the Buccaneers took her mind off the scene outside Bruck Hall. All semblance of normalcy ended when Jake Moeller pounded on the front door.

"Keep an eye on her," Jake pleaded as Maddy trounced into the living room. "The rodeo people have arrived, and all hell's breaking loose."

The words were barely out of his mouth before Jake was out the door and running towards the Hall. A furious Maddy filled in the details for her friends.

"Donna Moore and her sister Allison arrived on campus a few minutes ago. They were leading a caravan of trucks loaded with livestock and equipment for the rodeo."

"Oh, oh," said Caroline. "I'll bet that upset the Bruins and their supporters."

"It sure as hell did," said Maddy with a grin. "But we women surrounded the trucks and wouldn't let the boys near them. We guided them back to the field behind the auditorium where they're setting up temporary pens for the animals even as we speak."

"They can do that?" asked Carl.

"It's in their contract," Maddy replied. "The horses and the calves will be quartered on neighboring farms until the night of the rodeo, but the bulls will stay here on campus."

"I hope the Moore sisters intend to post a few guards near the pens," said Carl. "I'd hate to see one of those animals get loose on the grounds."

"They aren't stupid," said Maddy indignantly. "They'll be posting guards all right, but more for the protection of the animals than the students. Heaven only knows what those football players might try to do."

"Does Hurst know they're here?" asked Caroline.

"Oh, yes. He made an announcement to the crowd a few minutes before the trucks arrived. The university lawyers are still in discussion with the firm representing the Moores. They'll be allowed to use the area behind the auditorium until, as Hurst put it, 'the conflict regarding the rodeo is settled to everyone's satisfaction'."

Carl grunted but said nothing. Caroline took up the questioning.

"So why is Jake so upset?"

"We women naturally followed the trucks over to the auditorium. So did the Bruins and their gang. Actually, almost everyone ended up there sooner or later. The security men did their best to hold back the crowd, but Rafael Bruck had to ask Jake for help. Jake radioed to his people, and they're on their way here now. Jake insisted I stay with you two rather than walk the picket line. It seems perfectly silly to me, but you know how ornery Jake can get when he's forced to work for Garrison Hurst."

Caroline suspected that Jake's mood had more to do with Maddy's safety than with his grudge against the president. She had the good sense not to say that, though.

"You might as well relax and watch the game with us," said Carl. "Jake will be back soon enough."

As it was, it was over an hour before the big policeman returned to the house.

"The campus is buttoned up tighter than a scarecrow's shirt," said Jake as he eased his tall frame into a chair. "The Archangels can handle it from here on."

"Any arrests?" asked Carl.

Jake shook his head.

"Trace Golden must have had a hot date. He vanished even before the trucks arrived. Without their hot-tempered leader, the Bruins faded fast. For the most part, everyone kept away from the rodeo folks." Jake took a pull at the bottle of beer handed to him by Carl. "And it made sense to stay away. Those bucking bulls are mean-looking critters."

"I wouldn't want to tangle with one," said Carl.

Jake grinned. "I wouldn't either. Once the pens were up and the bulls inside, people started wandering away. I think they wanted nothing more than a warm bed by then."

Caroline could tell Maddy's dander was up by the way she fidgeted in her chair. She refused to look at Jake as he finished both his story and his beer. She still wasn't talking to him when the two of them left Carl's house. She kept her distance, staying a few steps ahead of the tired policeman as they walked to where he'd parked the car.

Now, in the silence of the night, Caroline wondered if Jake and Maddy, like Martin and Nikki, were destined to be casualties of the Hurst/Moore war.

"Now that we've settled the issue of your qualifications as a mother," said Carl, "how about we walk over to the auditorium and check out the bulls."

Caroline raised her eyebrows. Her own restlessness had apparently affected the professor.

"You think that's a good idea? Moore's men might think we're up to no good and take a potshot at us."

"I doubt they have guns, Cari. The most they can do is shoo us away."

"I don't know."

"Aw, come on. I haven't seen a bull up close and personal in ages."

Caroline gave in, too worried to argue. "If you insist. But after that, I'm going home. I'll take a sleeping pill if I have to, but one way or another, I'm going to get some sleep tonight."

"Stick to warm milk," advised Carl as he left the sidewalk and cut across the lawn fronting the gymnasium.

Caroline followed him down the narrow cement path between the gym and Hildy Hall. The lamp over the players' entrance was broken, leaving the gangway dark except for a glimmer of light near the rear of the auditorium. This faintest of glows came from an exit sign above the stage door, and it was weak to the point of uselessness. Caroline kept one hand on the auditorium wall as a guide and prayed she wouldn't trip.

"Somebody ought to light this path better," she complained as she picked her way over the crumbling cement. "They ought to repave it, too."

"Tell that to all the wealthy alumni who show up for the Homecoming game."

"Yeah, right," muttered Caroline. She stubbed her toe on the raised edge of a piece of broken pavement and stumbled hard against the professor. "Sorry about that," she said as she regained her balance. "This is the last time I navigate this path at night."

"It's not quite dark up ahead," said Carl. "It looks like someone turned on the floodlights at the back of the auditorium."

Someone *had* turned on the lights, and that someone was Gabriel Bruck. The youngest by thirty seconds of the triplet brothers, Gabe supervised the security department's night shift. Caroline saw him standing near one of the holding pens when she rounded the corner of Hildy Hall. His eyes were fixed on the bulls as he talked quietly on his cell phone. Next to him stood Ben Halloway. The cowboy's face was hidden by the brim of his stained Stetson, but his attention also seemed drawn to the animals in their wire enclosure.

Carl greeted the two men with his usual robust gusto. He started towards them, but stopped abruptly when Gabe raised one hand in traffic cop fashion.

"Don't come any nearer, Professor. We have a problem over here."

Caroline stepped out of the shadows and waved at Gabe. "Do you need any help?"

"Is that you, Mrs. Rhodes?"

Gabe shaded his eyes with his hand. A look of relief spread over his face when he identified the ER nurse standing in the wash of the floodlight. He hurried over to her.

"It looks like one of the students got trampled by a bull." Gabe motioned towards Halloway. "Ben was in his trailer when he heard the animals kicking up a ruckus out here. He came out to investigate and found the kid in the pen. We don't know if he's dead or alive."

"We've got to get him out of there," said Caroline.

"That'll be hard to do," replied Gabe with a slight shake of his head. "Ben says the bulls are disturbed by the smell of blood. All except one have moved away from the boy. That last bull is so upset it's liable to charge anyone who comes near it."

"Time is a critical factor here, Gabe. Somehow or another we have to restrain that animal." Caroline looked over at Halloway. "Ben! Can you throw a rope on the bull and pull it towards the back of the pen?"

"That's easier said than done," replied the cowboy. "But we can try."

He loped off to his trailer. He returned moments later with a long length of rope.

"I'll help Halloway while you two grab the kid," said Carl.

"We only need a few seconds," said Caroline as the professor hurried away. "Have you called 911, Gabe?"

"Yes. An ambulance is on its way. I told them not to use the siren. I don't want them stirring up the bulls any more than they are already."

"Good thinking. Remember to be careful with his neck and back. If the kid's alive, there's a chance of a fracture in one of those two places."

"I understand. We'll do it quickly but carefully."

Ben and Carl were now positioned a few feet apart behind the pen. The big bull had seen them and turned slowly in their direction. Agitated by the scent of human blood, it snorted and pawed at the ground near the boy's body. Ben motioned to Carl. The professor whistled shrilly, then waved his arms in the air. The animal's head came up, the whites of his eyes showing as he bellowed in anger and fright.

"Back up now!" cried Halloway. "Keep waving your hands!"

Carl did as he was told, and the bull moved forward in a mincing prance. Its eyes trained on the professor, it didn't see the lasso that whipped through the air and settled around its neck. It felt it tighten, though, as Halloway took in the slack. It immediately plunged backwards pulling Halloway off his feet.

"Help me!" Ben hollered.

Carl rushed forward and grabbed the loose end of the rope. He was older than Halloway by several decades, but he had two hundred pounds on the man. He planted his heels in the dirt and used all of his weight to draw the line taut.

Halloway regained his footing.

"It's now or never," he yelled as the bull strained against the rope.

Gabe ran to the pen and tore the lock off the gate. He swung it open wide enough for Caroline and him to slip through. The bull sensed their presence immediately. He lowered his head and kicked outward with his back feet. His left hoof grazed the security officer's back and sent him reeling to the ground.

"I'm okay," Gabe said shakily as he scrambled to his feet. "Let's get him out of here!"

The boy was facedown on the ground. Caroline quickly moved to his side and positioned one hand under his throat, her fingers supporting the jaw to stabilize his neck. She tucked her other hand under the young man's right arm. At the same time, Gabe grabbed the boy's belt and his left arm. Moving as smoothly as they could, they dragged him out of the pen.

Gabe slammed the gate shut and locked it.

"You can let go," he shouted to Halloway.

Ben motioned to Carl with his head and the two men released the rope at the same time. The bull continued to kick and buck until the noose loosened around its neck. After several minutes it calmed down and stood panting in the center of the pen, the lasso dangling between its feet.

Halloway and the professor rejoined the others as the ambulance careened to a stop near the corner of the auditorium. Caroline and Gabe had log-rolled the boy onto his back and were doing CPR. Caroline looked up into Carl's worried eyes as she pressed down on the boy's chest with overlapped hands.

"He's been dead for a while," she said. "We're only doing this until the paramedics can hook him up to a monitor and confirm asystole."

Ben's eyes registered shock at the emotional detachment in Caroline's voice. He backed off from the body, then turned and walked hurriedly towards his trailer.

Carl understood Caroline like few other people in Rhineburg did or ever could. Like her, he'd seen death in many forms over the years. He knew she wasn't being heartless, only truthful.

"I'd better call Garrison," he said with a sad shake of his head. "The President should hear about this before the media gets hold of the story."

He moved into the shadows and flipped open his cell phone as the paramedics took their place beside the body. Caroline stood up and let them get on with their work.

"You know the kid?" asked one of the paramedics as he attached the leads of the heart monitor to the boy's chest.

Caroline kept her eyes on the flat line wiggling across the screen.

"He played football here at Bruck. His name is Trace Golden."

FIFTEEN

CAROLINE WASN'T DUE to work on Halloween. When she finally hit the sack a little after 1 a.m., her plans for that day included a lunch hour rendezvous with Martin during which she intended to apologize for her part in their argument. An early morning phone call from Nikki changed all that. Instead of meeting Martin at noon at the university, she found herself talking with him at 9 a.m. in a small interrogation room at the Rhineburg police station.

"Jake can't possibly think you had anything to do with Trace's death."

Caroline's words sounded silly even to herself. Of course Jake Moeller thought her son was involved. He wouldn't have pulled him into the station if he hadn't believed Martin knew something about what Garrison Hurst was calling "an unfortunate incident."

"I swear, Mom. I had nothing to do with it. Trace was standing with the other guys during the argument last night, and sure, I wanted to punch him out when I saw him grinning at me like some damned Cheshire cat. But no, I didn't hit him then, and I sure as hell didn't push him into the pen with that bull."

"Then what's all this about?"

"I can answer that question," said Jake from the doorway. He glanced at Caroline, then walked across the room and handed Martin a cup of coffee. "Glad to see you could come, Cari. Your son doesn't think he needs a lawyer. He doesn't want Nikki here either. He did agree to your presence when I suggested it."

Jake straddled a chair at the end of the scarred wooden table that separated Caroline from Martin. He looked from mother to son before speaking.

"I want you to know that I hate with a passion what I have to do here this morning. I wouldn't have pulled you in, Martin, if it hadn't been for the circumstantial evidence against you."

"I don't know what you're talking about, Chief. Like I told my mother, there was no love lost between Trace and me, but I had nothing to do with his ending up in that cattle pen. The best I can figure is he wanted to cause some trouble for the rodeo by letting the bulls loose. A bull probably kicked him and he fell. Then…oh, I don't know. Maybe he couldn't get away from the animal once he was down on the ground."

"That sounds like a reasonable explanation, except for one thing. Trace was dead long before he went into that pen."

"I…I don't understand."

"I don't either, Martin, and that's why you're here."

Caroline didn't like what she was hearing. She reached over the table and took Martin's hand.

"I don't think you should say another word until there's a lawyer sitting next to you in this room."

"I don't need a lawyer, Mom. I didn't do anything!"

"I believe you're telling the truth, Martin. Unfortunately, the truth has cost a lot of men time in prison. If you can't afford one, I'll pay for a lawyer myself."

"No!" Martin stood up and began to pace the room. "I'm not some little kid that needs to be protected by his mother. Chief Moeller knows I'm no killer. I trust him to get to the bottom of this."

"Nobody's out to railroad you," said Jake. "I only want to know where you were last night and what you were doing."

Martin stopped pacing and stared at the Chief.

"It wouldn't matter what I told you because I was alone the entire time. I have no alibi that's provable."

"Provable or not, I'd still like to hear your story."

Martin hesitated, then walked slowly back to the table and sat down.

"I'll cooperate in every way possible if you agree to two things."

"And what might your demands be?" Jake cocked his head to one side as if seriously considering Martin's request.

"First, what I tell you has to be in the strictest confidence. I don't want a word of it getting back to Nikki or the university. Second, I want to know what kind of evidence you have against me."

Jake rocked back in his chair and scratched the back of his neck.

"Fair enough," he said with a shrug. "There are only three of us in this room. If your mother can keep quiet, so can I."

Martin shifted his gaze to Caroline.

"Can I trust you, Mom?"

"I swear, Martin, this time I'll keep my mouth shut." Caroline made an X on her chest with one finger. "Cross my heart."

"Okay. Fire away with your questions, Chief."

Jake pulled a notepad and pen from his shirt pocket. He opened the pad and wrote Martin's name across the top page in block letters.

"Start from the time you left Nikki in the street. That was a little after eight o'clock."

Martin took a deep breath and ran his fingers through his hair.

"I was pretty upset with my wife," he said in a low voice. "She'd just told me she was pregnant. It took me by surprise, and I needed to get away and think things out. I started walking, and then…"

"Which direction did you go?"

"East along Circle Road. I kind of wandered along until I came to the gym. Then I took the side path to the player's entrance and let myself into the locker room."

Martin hesitated, and Jake looked up from his notepad.

"What happened next?" the policeman asked.

"I…I didn't stay but a few minutes in the gym. It didn't feel right there, so I walked back outside and crossed over to Bruck Green. I found a bench back among the trees and sat down to think."

"How long were you there?"

"I don't know. Maybe half an hour or so. I don't think anyone saw me, though. Most of the students were down by Bruck Hall. After that, I walked over to the stadium."

"The stadium?" Jake raised one eyebrow. "What did you do there?"

"I let myself in by the construction entrance. There's a lock on the gate, but it's so cheesy anyone can pick it."

"I take it you've done this before."

"Once, with some of the guys from the team. We wanted to see the renovations. I went there last night because I needed to be alone. I needed time to think."

"About the baby."

"Yeah, that's right. About the baby."

"When did you arrive at the stadium? And how long did you stay there?"

"I'm not sure when I arrived. I must have fallen asleep in the stands because I don't remember being there all that long. Still, when I looked at my watch, it was after midnight. All I wanted to do then was go home and crawl into bed."

"And did you go home?"

"No," said Martin with a shake of his head. "I was ashamed of the way I'd treated Nikki. I figured she'd be sleeping and I didn't want to wake her. I went instead to Professor Atwater's office and let myself in through the window. I stretched out on his couch and fell asleep. When I woke up, the professor was standing over me with a cup of coffee in his hand."

"And what time was that?"

"About six-thirty. Professor Atwater is an early riser. He always shows up at the office by seven."

"Then what?"

"The professor told me about what happened to Trace. I drank a cup of coffee while we talked, then I called Nikki at the apartment around seven o'clock. That's when she told me you were looking for me. I cleaned up a bit in the office bathroom, and then I borrowed Professor Atwater's car and drove into town."

"Where's your car?" Jake asked.

"Nikki has it. She gave me a lift to the campus yesterday before going to work. I never left the grounds until this morning."

Caroline let the questions and answers burrow into her memory as the interrogation drew to a close. She shifted her eyes from Jake to Martin. Neither man had registered a great deal of emotion during the exchange. Nevertheless, the tension in the room had increased in a subtle and indefinable way.

Jake glanced down at his notes. Caroline felt a shiver of apprehension run down her spine when the big man looked up again, an expression of skepticism highlighting his face.

"All right, Martin," Chief Moeller said with a tight little smile. "Let's take it from the top again. And this time, why don't you tell me the truth."

SIXTEEN

ANNIE HOLTZBRINCK, JAKE'S efficient but nosy secretary, unwittingly saved Martin from a charge of murder when she chose that moment to rap on the tiny window set in the door of the interrogation room.

"Mayor's on the phone, Chief," she bellowed through the thin plate glass. "He's got his shorts in a knot over the Golden kid and wants to know when you're gonna make an arrest."

Jake rolled his eyes.

"If she weren't so damned good at her job, I'd fire that woman," he said in an exasperated tone of voice. He grunted as he pushed himself up from the chair. "This may take awhile, Martin. I'd advise you to use the time wisely by thinking over what you've told me. I have witnesses who will poke holes in your story if they're called to testify in court."

Martin looked defiant.

"I swear I had nothing to do with Trace's death."

"If that's so, then why are you lying?" Jake turned to Caroline. "Talk some sense into your son, Cari. I'd hate to have his baby grow up without a father."

Jake stalked out of the room. Caroline looked hard at Martin, her face giving away none of the fear she felt for his safety.

"I don't know what's going on inside your head," she said. "But you'd better get your priorities straightened out right now. Like it or not, your wife is pregnant. She and your unborn child deserve more from you than what you're giving them at the moment."

Martin pounded his fist on the table. "I'm doing my best to protect them!"

"From what, Martin? What could hurt them worse than if you're arrested?"

"I won't be arrested, Mom. I've told you a hundred times, I had nothing to do with what happened to Trace. I don't even know why the police think he was murdered."

"I don't either. But obviously, they have evidence that points in that direction. Why else would the mayor be calling Jake about an arrest?" Caroline drew a deep breath to calm herself. "The Chief is not a stupid man. He wouldn't have pulled you into the station if he didn't have something that linked you to Golden. Circumstantial or not, it could be enough to land you in prison."

Martin averted his eyes from his mother. "Maybe you'd better go check up on Nikki. She's probably been trying to reach me at the university."

"And what do you want me to tell her?"

"Say I'm all right. Tell her I'll be home for dinner."

Caroline leaned back in her chair and stared at Martin. She couldn't believe her normally sensible son was acting in such an irrational manner. What actually happened last night? Why was Martin being so secretive, and what was he holding back from the police?

"Please, Mom. Go talk to Nikki."

Martin looked so miserable that Caroline wanted to reach across the table and hug him. Instead, she stood up and walked to the door.

"I'll be back," she said grimly. "Think about what I said."

The post office where Nikki worked was only a few doors away from the police station. Caroline expected to find a few customers there when she arrived. What she hadn't counted on was the presence of Maddy Moeller behind the counter. Assisted by Agatha Hagendorf, Maddy was sorting and stamping mail.

"Where's Nikki?" she asked in alarm.

Maddy waggled her head in the direction of the back room.

"Bertha stopped by with a coffee cake hot out of the oven. She's under the assumption that pregnant women need a daily dose of pecans and gooey frosting."

"Sounds good to me," said Caroline, her trepidation eased somewhat by Maddy's casual tone of voice. The worry lines vanished from her face entirely when a smiling Bertha Meyer appeared in the doorway of the back room holding a steaming teakettle.

"As my Irish friends would say, we're enjoying a cuppa and a bit of nourishment. Will you join us?"

Bertha, a many times removed cousin of the long-dead poet Goethe, had not one drop of Irish blood in her. Today, though, she looked like a troll from the Emerald Isle with her elfin figure encased in a white baker's apron and splotches of flour dotting her shamrock green blouse. Her white chef's hat perched precariously atop her equally white curls, she hustled back to the table and sliced a large wedge of coffee cake, placed it on a paper plate, and handed it to Caroline.

"A cup of tea would be delightful," said Caroline as she sat down across from Nikki. She looked over at the girl. "How are you holding up?"

Nikki's shoulders jerked in what passed for a shrug. "I'm over being angry. Now I'm just plain worried. I don't understand why the police want to question Martin."

"Apparently he spent the night roaming about the campus. Jake thinks he might have seen something that could help them in their investigation of Trace Golden's death."

The lie worked to erase some of the tension in Nikki's face.

"He told me he fell asleep in Professor Atwater's office."

"Yes, Carl found him there this morning."

"I brought some clean clothes for him from the apartment. I figured he could change here in the post office before he goes back to school."

"Good idea, although I don't know how long he'll be at the station. Jake keeps getting called away. I think he's interviewing several people at the same time."

Lies were piling up on top of lies, but Caroline couldn't think of a better way to handle the situation. Her main concern at the moment was not Martin, but Nikki. It was important to keep her pregnant daughter-in-law as worry free as possible until Jake decided his next move.

"I need to call the hospital," said Caroline. "Do you mind if I use the phone upstairs?"

"Go right ahead," said Nikki, rising to her feet. "The coffee cake was delicious, Mrs. Meyer, but I should get back to work."

"I'm glad you liked it, dear. Now you tell Maddy and Agatha to come have a piece."

"Will do," said Nikki as she disappeared through the doorway.

Caroline pushed the plate with her half-eaten piece of coffee cake to the center of the table.

"My compliments to the baker," she said as she slipped out of her chair and walked over to the staircase on the far wall of the tiny room.

Bertha turned from the sink where she was refilling the teakettle. She placed a finger to her lips and shook her head so violently that strands of hair as soft as lamb's wool escaped the confines of her hat and tumbled over her forehead.

"Don't go yet," she whispered. "We need to talk."

Caroline looked over her shoulder at the empty doorway.

"Not here. Not if it's about Martin."

"You're right. We wouldn't want Nikki to overhear us." Bertha thought for a moment. "Make your phone call and then come over to the boarding house. I'll be waiting there with Maddy and Agatha."

Caroline hesitated. She had to get back to the police station soon. If Martin compromised himself with another foolish lie...

"It's important that you meet with us. We've heard things that could help your son."

Caroline knew the value of the local grapevine. She also knew that if anyone in town was tuned in to gossip, it was Bertha and her friends at the Rhineburg Boarding House and Home for Gentle Women.

"I'll be there as soon as I can."

She cast a grateful smile at Bertha before mounting the creaky wooden staircase that led to the most infamous site in all of Rhineburg.

SEVENTEEN

THE SECOND FLOOR of the post office had once been the exclusive domain of Emma Reiser. The former postmaster's murder earlier that year had sent shock waves through the little town of Rhineburg. Emma had manned the P.O. for longer than anyone remembered. A quiet and unassuming woman, she'd also run a lucrative side business from the safety of her well-wired upstairs apartment. Her funeral had drawn hundreds of mourners, most of them confirmed bettors on everything from horse racing to college basketball.

Life as a bookie had proved profitable for Emma. Her collection of antique furniture, tapestries, and rugs rivaled the museums of many small cities. Mayor Schoen had cried for joy when he discovered she'd left it all to the town in her will. The subsequent auction, handled by none other than antique maven Maddy Moeller, enriched the town coffers but left the second floor of the post office as bare as Mother Hubbard's cupboard.

Caroline opened the door to Emma's former office and recalled how it looked the first time she'd seen it. A row of sturdy cabinets had lined one wall. In front of the cabinets had stood a desk bearing three telephones, three answering machines, and a computer linked to a fax machine and printer. A metal shelf holding four sixteen-inch black and white TV sets had decorated the wall facing the desk.

An old copy of the Daily Racing form lay forgotten in one corner of the office. Outside of that, the only things remaining in the room were the metal shelf and a telephone. Why the phone hadn't been removed along with its companions was anyone's guess, but there it stood, still connected to the outside world.

Caroline lifted the receiver and dialed the direct line to St. Anne's Emergency Room.

"ER. Can I help you?"

"Is that you, Chan? What's a mighty doctor doing answering the phone?"

Chan Daley recognized her voice and laughed.

"It's a little slow around here today, Cari. I got so bored that I offered to play receptionist."

"A regular man of the people, aren't you," said Caroline wryly.

"I'm not above getting my hands dirty once in a while."

"I'll remember that the next time a patient asks for a bedpan."

"Don't push your luck, Mrs. Rhodes. Now enough of this silly patter. I suppose you've called for news on the Golden boy."

"You read my mind, Chan. I'm interested in the results of the autopsy."

Caroline heard the creak of Chan's chair as he rocked back in it.

"You and a million other people. Seems like everyone in town wants the dirt on Golden."

"I need it for a good reason, Chan. The police think my son had something to do with that boy's death."

The creaking stopped as Chan sat bolt upright again.

"Hey, I'm sorry to hear that. If there's anything I can do to help…"

"You can tell me what killed Trace Golden. I know you weren't in the ER when they brought the body in. Still, I was hoping curiosity got the better of you."

"Curiosity has nothing to do with it. Lack of sleep does. We got a wake-up call from Garrison Hurst early this morning. He wanted to notify Lian of Golden's death before she heard about it on the news."

"I'm almost beginning to feel sorry for Hurst. He hasn't been having a good week, has he?"

Chan snorted. "That man's got rocks for brains. If he hadn't hired that damned rodeo… But that's another story altogether, isn't it."

"What do you mean by 'that's another story'? Are you saying the rodeo isn't connected to Golden's death?"

Something Jake had said swam to the front of Caroline's brain, then just as quickly dived back into oblivion. She brushed the memory away as she concentrated on what Chan was saying.

"Not directly. Andy Zapp did the autopsy first thing today. I came in early to observe it."

"Because of Lian?"

"Of course. As a board member, she deserves to know the facts of the case before the newsboys start hounding her."

"I understand. And what did the pathologist find?"

"Dr. Zapp did a thorough exam of the body. There were a lot of old bruises and a couple of healed cuts, but there were also some new abrasions on the boy's hands and a minor laceration to the face. It looked like he scuffled with somebody shortly before his death."

"That might have happened when he fell in the pen."

"Zapp didn't think so. The blood had clotted on the laceration. There were specks of dirt ground into the abrasions, but the dirt on the face was layered on top of dried blood."

Caroline thought back to how she and Gabe had carried Trace out of the pen. They'd found him lying face down in the dirt. When they moved him, she'd supported his neck and head with one hand. His own hands, though, had dragged along the ground.

She told Chan about the rescue.

"Your description of events would fit in with Zapp's findings," said Chan. "The soil imbedded in the abrasions is probably due to his hands trailing alongside his body. You kept his head above ground, though, so the debris on the facial wound was there simply because he was lying facedown in the dirt."

The elusive memory groped its way back into Caroline's consciousness. She closed her eyes and tried to recall a remark Jake made early on in his questioning of Martin.

"There were no marks on the body to indicate the bull had stomped on the boy," Chan continued. "Those hoofs would have made quite an impression on the skin, if not downright torn it open. What did kill him was a crushed larynx."

Jake's words suddenly came back to Caroline. The Chief had said Trace was dead before he landed in the bulls' pen.

"You're sure an animal that big couldn't have crushed his windpipe if it stepped on him?"

"Oh, sure it could. But again, there was no mark on the throat to indicate an attack by a bull. Sorry, Cari, but it looks like somebody strangled the kid and then put him in the pen. Whoever did it probably hoped he'd stir up the animals. He figured they'd make such a mess of the body, nobody could tell they hadn't killed him."

"Ben Halloway said the scent of blood riled them up. When Carl and I got there, most of the bulls were standing in the far end of the pen. But there was one big fellow pawing the ground near Trace. It seemed on the verge of attacking."

"Gabe Bruck stopped by the ER before he went off duty

this morning. He told me how Halloway heard the bulls bellowing and left his trailer to check up on them. That cowboy probably got there only minutes after Trace was placed in the pen. His very presence may have prevented the bulls from charging the body."

"I don't know anything about bull psychology, Chan, but you may be right. I expect those animals are used to Ben. Maybe he had a calming influence on them."

"So how does Martin fit in the picture? Or shouldn't I ask?"

"Martin and Trace didn't get along very well. Actually, they didn't get along at all."

"I did a wound check on Martin yesterday. A facial laceration he said he received during a fight with another football player. That other player wouldn't have been Golden, would it?"

"Yes, it would. The two of them got into it after the game on Saturday. Trace made a disparaging remark about Nikki, and Martin felt duty bound to protect her honor."

"My kind of man," said Chan. "Look, Cari, if it'll help, I'll try to get you a copy of the autopsy report."

"Thanks, Chan. That would be great."

Caroline hung up feeling more depressed than ever. From what Chan had said, it was pretty obvious that Trace's death was a murder. He'd had a fight with someone between the hours of eight p.m., when he was last seen in the circle of people surrounding Martin and Nikki, and midnight, when he was pronounced dead at St. Anne's Hospital. Rigor mortis hadn't set in yet when Caroline and Gabe had dragged him out of the bulls' pen. That didn't mean much, though. Given Golden's athletic physique and the effect of the cold night air on the body, the murder could have occurred as early as eight-thirty.

Eight p.m. and midnight. The very hours during which

an angry Martin was roaming about the campus. Martin, who'd fought with Trace in front of dozens of witnesses on Saturday afternoon.

No wonder Jake had pulled her son into the station. Martin had to be his number one suspect.

EIGHTEEN

"I can't stay long," said Caroline when Agatha met her at the door of the Rhineburg Boarding House and Home for Gentle Women. "I have to get back to the police station."

"We know you're worried about your son," Agatha said as she took Caroline's jacket and hung it on a hook next to a half dozen other coats lining the foyer hall. She led her guest past the antique mirrored hallstand that Maddy had been lusting after for months and ushered her into the living room. "But there's no need to rush. Chief Moeller was called back to the university before he had a chance to get Martin's formal statement."

Caroline stared at the little mistress of the house. Agatha was clad in an azure blue ribbed turtleneck that extended below her knees to cover a baggy pair of purple pants. Over the shirt she wore a cinnamon and orange striped sweater patched at the elbows with bits of worn leather. Completing the outfit was a bright yellow scarf embroidered with sequins that she'd wound round her neck and tied in a bow. With her wrinkled face and blue rinsed curls, the woman looked like a badly painted lawn gnome brought inside for the winter.

Caroline was startled by Agatha's looks, but even more so by her words. News traveled fast in Rhineburg, but not at the speed of light. Either Agatha ranked high on the grapevine, or she had a direct link to someone at the police station.

Someone at the station.

But of course, thought Caroline, her brain recovering more quickly than her mouth, which at the moment hung open in dead fish surprise.

"Maddy. It had to be Maddy."

"What had to be Maddy?" said Madeleine Moeller, choosing that moment to walk into the living room. She carried a large bowl in each hand, the first one filled with popcorn balls and the second with tiny bags of candy corn. "What mischief have I been up to now?"

"Not mischief," said Caroline. "Sleuthing. You're the only one who could have found out what's going on at the station. You called Jake, didn't you?"

Maddy's brown eyes sparkled. "Not Jake," she said, shaking her head. "Annie Holtzbrinck. Jake may be the Chief of Police, but Annie's the power behind the throne. She knows everything that goes on at the station, and given a little incentive, she's more than willing to tell you about it."

"I didn't realize the two of you were such good friends."

"Annie can be a pain at times, but I've learned to overlook her faults. It doesn't do to make an enemy of your husband's secretary."

"It doesn't do to make an enemy of anyone," said Bertha Meyer as she entered the room. "Look what it did to Trace Golden."

Bertha's down-home wisdom was properly respected by the five elderly females, all residents of the boarding house, who followed in her wake. The quintuplet bobbed their heads in solemn agreement before approaching Caroline. Under the watchful eye of their leader, each woman first hugged her, then murmured a word of sympathy in her ear.

Caroline felt like she was at a wake, the hapless victim being her son. Unfortunately, it was difficult to keep a straight face when all the mourners resembled clowns.

At sixty-five, Emily O'Hara was the youngest of Agatha's boarders by a good ten years. Emily was a rosy-cheeked woman, short in stature but broad abeam, who served as the medical librarian at St. Anne's Hospital. She'd been widowed for several years. Preferring independence to a life with her children, she'd rented a room in Agatha's old Victorian shortly after her husband's death.

Like Agatha, Emily was dressed in a combination of outrageous colors. She wore a black knitted vest emblazoned with screaming orange pumpkins over a chartreuse and white polka dot blouse. Her slacks were emerald green, two sizes too large, and rolled and pinned at the bottoms. Four strings of Mardi Gras-style beads accented her short neck and double chins.

The normally austere Eleanor Naumann looked equally odd in a pair of tan riding breeches and an old tuxedo jacket the color of cooked beets. The jacket's lapels were overly wide and made of a creamy satin material now decorated with a variety of Halloween stickers. Beneath the jacket Eleanor wore a Bruck U. sweatshirt topped by a mauve and blue neckerchief knotted at the side of her throat.

Sarah Sonnenschein, Rhineburg's recently retired head librarian, looked anything but her usual quiet self, dressed in a yellow flowered Hawaiian muumuu over a pair of bright red flannel longjohns. In keeping with the theme, Sarah had chosen a plastic lei of faded pink flowers to complete her outfit.

Marie Moser and her sister Myrtle Jennings had obviously visited both the Salvation Army store and the Army Navy Resale Shop when purchasing their clothes. Marie wore a pair of desert fatigue pants under her pink and yellow checkered blouse and pink velvet jacket. Myrtle was clad in orange ski pants topped by a sweater the color of poppies, embroidered with three pheasants in flight. The tan wings of the pheasants matched the stains on her white Navy dress jacket, with its row of faded battle ribbons and tattered blue and gold epaulets.

Agatha and her boarders seemed unaware of the extraordinary appearance of their clothing. Maddy also appeared unfazed as she helped Bertha pour coffee at the sideboard. Watching the women as they settled into the overstuffed chairs scattered about the room, Caroline decided she was the one out of place in this crazy household.

"Thank you, ladies. I appreciate your concern for Martin's welfare."

"It's young Mrs. Rhodes we're concerned about," Miss Sonnenschein murmured in her whispery librarian's voice. "Someone in her delicate condition shouldn't be under such a strain."

"That's right," agreed Mrs. Meyer. "Your son ought to know better than to cause his wife such grief."

Bertha gave the words *your son* the same emphasis a prosecuting attorney might have employed when describing a serial killer to a jury. Caroline would have found it amusing if the situation hadn't been so grave.

"Despite any rumors to the contrary, Martin had nothing to do with Trace Golden's death. I have total faith in my son."

"Now don't go getting all huffy over a few misspoken words," said Maddy as she handed Caroline a cup of coffee. "Bertha didn't mean to imply that Martin was guilty of murder. Did you, dear?"

She scowled at Bertha who at least had the decency to blush.

"Of course not," said the baker's wife hurriedly. "We all know Martin's not capable of that."

"Which is precisely why we asked you to come here

this morning," added Emily O'Hara. "We think we can help prove his innocence."

"And how do you intend to do that?" Caroline asked warily. Past experience had taught her the dangers of intimate involvement with Agatha's merry band of boarders. The six ladies had caused a whole passel of problems during a previous murder case in Rhineburg after drawing Caroline smack dab into the middle of it.

"We'll act as your eyes and ears on campus," said Eleanor. "We'll ferret out the truth through stealth and cunning!"

"We'll be your spies!" added Agatha gleefully.

Spies? Oh, lord, thought Caroline with growing dismay. Now Martin really was in trouble.

"I don't think that's a good idea," she said, shaking her head. "Stealth and cunning aside, I don't think you ladies have the qualifications for police work."

"Oh, pooh!" Bertha wrinkled her nose in disdain. "With apologies to Mrs. Moeller, it doesn't take a genius to do police work in Rhineburg. Why, there's hardly a soul in town who doesn't know everybody else's business, including who hates who enough to take a swing at him. All you have to do is ask the right questions of the right people."

"Trace Golden wasn't the nicest boy in the world," said Eleanor as she refreshed her coffee cup from the pot on the sideboard. "Anyone with a lick of sense would know there were plenty of other people besides Martin who might have fought with him last night."

"And not all of them live on campus," said Emily. "Tom Walker was fit to be tied when he found out Trace told Sue about that little blond Tom was shacking up with down at the trailer camp."

"Annie Holtzbrinck was none too happy herself when Trace sideswiped her car outside the police station. That's when Trace got arrested for drunk driving," Bertha reminded them.

"Seeing as how she's been on crutches since the accident, I think we can eliminate Annie from the list of suspects," Maddy said dryly. "But the ladies are right, Cari. Trace made some enemies both on campus and in town. It wouldn't hurt to find out where they all were last night."

"Don't tell me you're in on this, too," exclaimed Caroline. "Come on, Maddy. Jake'll have a fit if he catches you interfering in the investigation."

"So let him be angry. What do I care?"

The little redhead lifted her chin and looked down her nose at Caroline. The stubborn glint in her eyes was proof enough that war was still being waged in the Moeller household.

"I read Jake's notes while he was shaving this morning. Like everyone else, he assumed Trace's death was an accident at first. He visited the Bruins' dormitory after the paramedics left with the body. Gabe dragged the entire team out of bed so Jake could question them."

This last piece of information sparked Caroline's interest.

"Did anyone know what Trace was doing behind the auditorium?"

Maddy shook her head. "Jake's first thought was that Golden wanted to cause trouble for the Moore sisters. Releasing the bulls on campus would have done that. He figured the animals got spooked and trampled Trace before he could back out of the pen. But the other players denied any knowledge of an attack on the rodeo."

"I doubt the team would have confessed to a plot even if there'd been one."

"According to Jake's notes, he agrees with you on that.

What bothered my husband last night, though, was the fact that the gate on the pen swung outward, not in."

"Meaning it couldn't have swung shut if Trace fell against it."

"Exactly," said Maddy. "In order for Trace Golden's death to be an accident, you'd have to believe that he opened the gate, went into the pen, and then shut the gate behind him. Now why would he do that if he intended to stampede the bulls? Surely he would have left the gate open."

"Maybe he wanted to harm the animals rather than set them free," said Eleanor Naumann.

Maddy shook her head again. "There was no weapon found on Golden's body or in the pen."

"Face it, ladies," said Caroline. "It doesn't make sense that Trace went into that pen of his own free will. Even if he'd been drinking, which he probably was, given his history and all the partying that was going on outside Bruck Hall, he still wouldn't have been crazy enough to duke it out singlehandedly with a herd of bulls."

"But we know all that already, don't we," said Bertha a bit impatiently. "I mean, we know Chief Moeller is interrogating…people." She tactfully omitted Martin's name. "That means the Chief thinks somebody killed Trace Golden."

"Yes, he does," said Maddy. "There was an autopsy performed early this morning. I heard Jake talking to a Dr. Zapp on the telephone before he left for the station. I don't know what the cause of death was, but I did hear Jake say, 'Then it's murder.'"

A shiver of excitement rippled through the room as the residents of the Rhineburg Boarding House and Home for Gentle Women exchanged knowing glances. Caroline decided not to raise their heart rates any higher by repeating what Chan had told her: Trace Golden had been strangled by someone powerful enough to crush his windpipe.

"Golden's teammates didn't know what he was up to," Maddy continued. "But some of the boys saw him trailing Martin down the street after the argument with Nikki."

"Jake mentioned some circumstantial evidence," said Caroline. "Is that all he has? A couple of witnesses who saw two men walk in the same direction?"

"Actually," said Maddy hesitantly, "there's something a bit more damning. One of the Bruins became concerned when he saw Trace take off after Martin. He was afraid the two of them would get into another fight over Nikki, so he followed them to the gym. He said both men entered the locker room. Martin came out about twenty minutes later, but Golden never showed his face again."

Caroline felt like someone had slammed her in the chest with a two by four. She'd known Martin was lying to Jake, but she didn't know why. Now she could guess at what he was hiding, and she was both angry and frightened.

She glanced around the room at the faces of her eight companions. Surprisingly, what she saw in their eyes was not doubt, but sympathy.

"Having heard the evidence against him, are you women still willing to help my son?"

"Lordy sakes alive!" said Bertha as she walked over to hug her. "Why else do you think we're all here?"

Caroline smiled her appreciation as Bertha's words were seconded in a chorus of gentle exclamations. When the last "but, of course!" and "you betcha!" died away, she lifted her coffee cup and extended it in a toast.

"All right, then, ladies. Here's to a successful venture in spying. *And* proving Jake Moeller wrong."

Maddy clinked her cup against Caroline's.

"Amen to that," she said with a grin.

NINETEEN

CAROLINE WAS TOO angry with Martin to return to the police station. Instead, she drove to the campus where she tracked down Professor Atwater in his office.

"I need your help," she said as she sunk down on a brown leather chair across from his desk. "The police are holding Martin on suspicion of murder. Jake thinks he killed Trace Golden."

"What!" Carl stared at her slack-jawed.

"Close your mouth before you swallow a fly."

The professor clamped his lips shut and glared at Caroline. "How can you make jokes at a time like this?"

"According to Lian Daley, joking is a way of coping with stress. I can't argue with her since it seems to be working for me at the moment."

Carl huffed and puffed through his mustache. His opinion of psychiatrists was not exactly high. He suffered Lian only because she was married to Chan Daley, his favorite ER doc.

"So why in the world would Jake arrest Martin?"

"Martin's actually been detained for questioning. I expect Jake will want a little more evidence before he formally charges him."

"Start from the beginning," demanded Carl.

Caroline did. She began with the police call to Nikki, progressed through Jake's interrogation of Martin and her subsequent conversation with Chan, then ended with an

abbreviated version of her visit to the Rhineburg Boarding House and Home for Gentle Women.

"Are you out of your mind?" Carl thundered when she
finished. "You can't get mixed up with those women again.
They're crazy, every one of them."

"They're a little on the peculiar side, but I wouldn't
call them crazy."

"Peculiar, crazy—it's all the same. I'm warning you,
Cari, keep away from them."

"I'm sorry you feel that way, especially since I told the
ladies you'd help them."

"What!" Carl's eyebrows practically shot off the top of
his head. "Now listen here, Cari. I'm willing to do whatever it takes to help Martin, but I won't work with those
women. No, that's where I put my foot down."

"Now relax and listen to me for a minute. You may find
this game plan more appealing than you think."

Carl snorted derisively, but he did keep quiet while Caroline outlined the women's strategy. By the time she finished, the professor was almost smiling.

"So, have you lifted that big foot of yours?"

"High enough to plant it on Jake's back," said the professor. "And I assume that's where you want me to keep it."

"Yes, we want you to hold him down until we have
proof of Martin's innocence. Feed him all the information
we can come up with on other suspects. Give him something to think about so he'll reconsider charging Martin."

"You're right when you say he'll never listen to Agatha's
bunch. They burned him once before, and he's never for-
given them. Me, though, he trusts."

"And that's why he'll take what you say seriously."

"So we're turning my office into the command center
for this little operation."

"Exactly. We'll all be carrying cell phones. We'll call

you whenever we learn something that might relate to the murder. You'll collect the facts, piece them together the best you can, and pass them on to Jake."

"Have you thought of the danger involved here, Cari? Trace was no Charles Atlas, but he certainly was a strong young man. Whoever strangled him was stronger still."

"We're all aware that, muscle wise, we're no match for the killer. That's why we'll work in pairs and never go anywhere without our phones. But we're hoping we're a little smarter than whoever put Trace in that pen. We're also hoping that inside knowledge of the people in this town will give us a bit of an advantage."

"So when do we start?"

"The others are already hard at work on their assignments. Right now I need to shake Gabe out of bed. I need the names of the players who saw Trace follow Martin to the gym."

"No need to wake him," said Carl as he lifted the receiver from the phone on his desk. "Michael's on day duty in the security office. I'm sure Gabe filled him in on everything that occurred during his shift."

Carl was right in assuming that the eldest Bruck brother could help them. Michael gave him a list of names, then referred him to other students he'd questioned that morning. The professor hung up the phone with a satisfied grunt.

"Three members of the team saw Trace head down the street after Martin, but it was Al Sperling who followed the two."

"Al Sperling? The field goal kicker?"

"He brought Martin his gym bag after the fight on Saturday."

"I remember him. He seemed like a good-hearted guy."

"Some people thought Al Capone was a good-hearted guy because he bankrolled a couple of soup lines during the Depression," Carl reminded her. "Sperling may have been truly worried about Martin. On the other hand, maybe Golden was making trouble for him, too. It could be our young field goal kicker saw a perfect opportunity to eliminate his problems last night. He may have killed Trace and then made up a story to implicate Martin." He ruffled through the department schedule list and pulled out a sheet of paper. "Ah! Mr. Sperling is taking American History this semester. He should be in Sue Chuey's class right now. Let's see if I can convince him to talk to us."

Caroline reached for the phone as Atwater clambered to his feet.

"I'm going to call the station. I want to know what's happening there."

"You better check on Nikki, too."

"Good idea."

Caroline dialed the non-emergency police number and waited through twelve rings before someone answered.

"Rhineburg Police," a female voice snapped. "Is this an emergency?"

"No, but I'd…"

"Hold, please."

Annie Holtzbrinck was notorious for screening Chief Moeller's visitors. Many a person had been turned away from his office, their complaint deemed too insignificant to draw the attention of the town's top cop. The blunt manner in which she dismissed minor crime offended its victims, but secretly pleased the Chief. Jake was more than willing to let his officers handle the small stuff while he reserved his strength for bigger cases.

Today, though, Annie sounded not only curt but also harried. Caroline wondered what new catastrophe had reduced the Chief's secretary to playing dispatcher.

"Yes, can I help you?"

"Hi, Annie. This is Caroline Rhodes. I was…"

"It's about time you called," Annie hissed in what amounted to little more than a whisper. "Have you found a lawyer yet for that idiot son of yours?"

A lawyer. That little problem had completely slipped Caroline's mind.

"I've done everything in my power to distract the Chief," Annie continued in the same low voice. "But I can't work miracles by myself."

"I'm sorry, Annie. I haven't called one yet, but…"

"Then write this down." She rattled off a phone number with a local exchange. "Nancy Kuhnkey over on Washington Street is a cousin of mine. You won't get Hank Matthews to represent Martin 'cause he's a hunting buddy of Golden Sr. Nancy can't stand either one of those guys, so she'll be happy to help."

As far as Caroline knew, Nancy Kuhnkey couldn't stand anyone. The crotchety old lawyer handled wills for some of the elderly residents of Rhineburg, but nobody under the age of eighty-five hired her any more. Her bad temper aside, Kuhnkey had quit reading up on legal precedents back in 1988 when she went into semi-retirement. Nowadays she spent most of her time either fishing for bluegills down at the river or gossip down at the beauty shop.

"Maybe I better discuss this with Nikki," Caroline said firmly. "After all, she is Martin's wife."

"Then hurry up and do it, 'cause the Chief's getting might unhappy with young Mr. Rhodes. That boy of yours doesn't have the sense of a hedgehog."

"What's he saying now?"

"It's what he's not saying that's the problem. The chief had a second go at him, but I managed to think up a crisis down at the bank that pulled him away before Martin made a bigger fool of himself."

"A crisis at the bank?"

"My sister's a teller over there," Annie whispered. "I had her hit the burglar alarm under her counter, then feign a panic attack when the Chief arrived."

"A panic attack?"

"My sister's going through menopause. She's been kind of weird since her estrogen dried up. Cries at the drop of a hat."

"Oh, dear."

"It took the Chief a good half hour to sort it all out. He couldn't tell if someone had actually tried to rob the bank, or if Betty's hormones were just acting up again. Got him real confused."

"Ah!" Caroline could sympathize with Jake. She herself was becoming more confused by the minute. Bank robbers? Burglar alarms? But why? Annie's next words answered that question.

"Maddy gave me a couple of other ideas for delaying Martin's arrest, but to my way of thinking, the best thing we can do for your son is get him a good lawyer."

"I guess you're right," Caroline said weakly. "Maybe I'd better call your cousin."

She wrote down the phone number Annie gave her, then hung up and dialed the post office. Nikki answered on the first ring.

"I'm worried, Mom. The police should have finished with Martin by now."

"I understand Jake was called away from the station due to a problem at the bank. Martin probably had to wait for his return." Caroline proceeded more cautiously. "You know, Nikki, it might be a good idea to have a lawyer present when Martin talks to Jake. He's not in any real trouble yet, but it looks like Trace Golden wasn't killed by that bull."

"You're telling me someone murdered him, aren't you? You're saying Chief Moeller thinks it was Martin."

"Jake's talking to a lot of people, dear. I think it wouldn't hurt, though, if Martin had counsel with him when he makes his statement."

There was a long silence on the other end of the line. Caroline chewed on her bottom lip, nervously waiting for Nikki to say something. The girl had to be in shock, not a good thing for a mother-to-be. Hopefully she would think of her unborn baby and at least try to stay calm.

Caroline was pleasantly surprised when Nikki came back on the line. Upset as she probably was, her voice was stronger than before.

"Martin has a temper, but he'd never let it get out of control to the point where he'd kill someone. It's ridiculous to think he'd murder Trace Golden."

"But you agree with me that he needs a lawyer."

"Of course he does. I don't want him saying something stupid to the police and then having to explain himself for hours on end."

"You're talking about the fight after the game on Saturday."

"What happened outside the gym is common knowledge by now. I'm sure the Chief will question Martin about it." Nikki hesitated. "The problem is, I don't know who to call to represent him."

Caroline told her about Annie's cousin.

"Hank Matthews is a friend of the Golden family, so your best bet is Nancy Kuhnkey. I know she's a bit over the hill, but she should be able to do the job for now. If it looks like Martin needs better representation later on…"

"Don't go there, Mom. Jake Moeller will catch whoever killed Trace, and then this will all be over."

Caroline wasn't as confident of that as her daughter-in-law, but she wisely refrained from saying so. She gave Nikki the number to Kuhnkey's home and told her to keep in touch.

"I'll be carrying my cell phone all day. Call me if you need me."

She glanced at her watch as she hung up the phone. According to the schedule worked out earlier, Maddy and Bertha Meyer should be deep in conversation with Alexsa Stromberg Morgan right about now. The other ladies would be carrying out their own assignments, Agatha and Eleanor at the Dip-N-Do Bath and Beauty Salon, Emily and Sarah at Kelly's Hardware, and Marie and Myrtle at the Sugar Bowl Café.

Caroline's own "to do" list included a visit to the *Rhineburg Rag,* the town's local newspaper. Her inquiries there would focus on Trace, but she also had questions about his father. As outlandish as it might seem, it was possible the young football player's death was somehow connected to the senior Golden's bank dealings. Bankers were known to make enemies. There was always the chance that some frustrated customer had taken revenge on Trace Sr. through his son.

Her interview with the *Rag*'s editor would have to wait, though. She needed more personal information on Trace, something she hoped his teammates could give her.

Caroline knew many of the Bruins due to her job as team nurse. Al Sperling, though, was one player whom she'd had little contact with. He'd never required care in the ER, nor had he appeared in any game she'd attended. She recalled having seen him at practices, but before Saturday, she hadn't even known his name.

She wondered what the boy was like and what he'd hoped to achieve when he transferred to Bruck. Had he thought his kicking skills would attract the attention of the NFL scouts? Or was he one of those rare young men who was actually using his athletic prowess to pursue an education?

Another more chilling thought suddenly struck Caroline. Was it possible that Al had been forced to switch schools? Perhaps he was trying to escape something in his past when he moved to Rhineburg, some indiscretion that, if known, would embarrass or even ruin him. If so, Trace could have discovered his secret and used it against him in some way.

Al's remarks to Martin on Saturday proved that he was no fan of Trace Golden. But did he hate the boy enough to kill him? Caroline could only guess at the answer.

Remembering what Carl had said about Al using Martin as an alibi, she decided to tread carefully when she questioned the student.

TWENTY

"I BET YOU never saw a black clown before."

Al Sperling flapped his oversized shoes on the floor of Carl's office in a mock tap dance. Dressed in a flame red T-shirt and baggy pants wired at the belt to extend several inches beyond his waist, he finished off his shuffle with a deep bow that exposed the bald spot on the crown of his curly orange wig.

"Actually, I've seen several. But they were all rodeo clowns."

Caroline tried to keep her irritation from showing, but the truth was, Sperling's antics rubbed her the wrong way. She hadn't expected an overwhelming display of grief from the boy. Still, this flippant bit of nonsense was surprising, to say the least. Al appeared strangely unaffected by his teammate's death, and she wondered why.

Her words triggered a flash of anger in the young man's eyes that he quickly hid with a brilliant but condescending smile.

"I was talking about circus clowns, Mrs. Rhodes."

"Sorry," said Caroline with a shrug of her shoulders. "I haven't been to the circus lately."

Al's smile dimmed only slightly. He glanced at the chair next to Caroline, then dropped down on the sofa where Martin had spent the night. His move forced Caroline to shift around in her seat.

"What's with the clown getup?" she asked, pointing to his clothing.

"You don't like it?" Al spread his arms and examined his outfit as if seeing it for the first time. "None of my teachers complained, but if the university has some kind of ban on celebrating Halloween…"

Caroline mentally kicked herself. With her mind on graver matters, she'd completely forgotten what day it was. Now she understood why Agatha and her friend were dressed so strangely.

"No ban that I know of," murmured Carl. He'd scooted behind his desk after ushering Sperling into the room and was now settled comfortably in the overstuffed armchair he'd appropriated years before from Bruck Hall. Saving Caroline from further embarrassment, he quickly changed the subject.

"I'm sorry I had to pull you out of class, Al. Unfortunately, the events of last night require you to answer a few more questions."

"No problem, Professor," Al said with a grin. "You did both me and Mrs. Chuey a favor."

"A favor?" Carl raised his eyebrows. "How's that?"

"Chuey…I mean *Mrs*. Chuey…was lecturing on the birth of the Klu Klux Klan. I think some of my comments on racism were a little too subjective for her liking." Al turned to Caroline. "You white folks wouldn't understand, but it's hard to be objective when your great-granddad was lynched by the KKK."

Caroline bristled at the implication that all white people were insensitive clods. She wasn't sure why Al had decided to play the racial card in this conversation, but she held her peace, refusing to react to the bait. Her need for information was too pressing to waste time on a foolish argument.

Apparently Carl had no compunctions in that area. Leaning forward in his chair, he pointed a finger at Sperling.

"You black folks don't understand, but it's hard to be

objective when your nephew was gunned down by a gang of African American thugs."

Al obviously hadn't expected a rebuttal. His eyes narrowed into mere slits and he stared uncertainly at the professor, the grin now gone from his face.

"I don't have to talk to you two," he said in a quavering voice. He scrambled up from the couch, a mixture of fear and anger on his face. "The cops questioned me along with the rest of the team. I told them everything I know about Trace Golden's movements last night."

"And they believed you," said Carl firmly. "We only want to hear the story in your own words."

"So you can twist it around and make me look like the bad guy here?" Al shook his head. "It's no good, Professor. I was no friend of Trace Golden, but I had nothing to do with him getting killed. I don't know why he went to the gym, and I sure as heck didn't know he was gonna mess with those bulls. If any of the other guys knew, they didn't tell me."

"Golden wasn't killed by any bull," said Caroline quietly. "He was strangled and then thrown in that pen to confuse the police."

Sperling spun on his heel. "You've got to be kidding. Trace was murdered?"

"That's right."

Sperling seemed genuinely surprised by the news, meaning he either knew absolutely nothing about the murder, or he was an extremely good actor. Caroline bet it was the former.

"Chief Moeller pulled Martin into the station this morning. He's being held for questioning."

"Martin? But why?"

Caroline pointed to the chair next to hers. "Why don't you sit down, Al. I know we didn't get off on the right foot here, but we do need your help. Please tell us what you saw last night."

"What I saw," Al repeated. A flurry of emotions passed over his face. He glanced at the professor before returning his gaze to Caroline. "It's because of what I said, isn't it? I mean, Chief Moeller arrested Marty because of what I told him."

"You weren't the only one who saw Trace follow Martin last night," said Carl. "Don't hold yourself responsible for his situation."

"But I do feel responsible," Al insisted. He sunk down on the edge of the chair and buried his head in his hands. "Marty's my friend. I wouldn't have said what I did if I'd known it was going to get him in trouble."

"Like the professor said, you aren't responsible for Martin's problems, Al. You told the truth as you saw it, right?"

Sperling raised his head. His eyes locked with Caroline's.

"I swear, Mrs. Rhodes, what I told the Chief was true. I wouldn't lie about Marty. But I didn't know Golden was murdered. I thought the bulls got him."

"Why don't you start at the beginning and tell us the whole story."

Sperling blew out a long breath. "I was worried about Marty when he walked away after the argument with his wife," he said slowly. "I knew something was bugging him last evening. Their fight only made it worse."

"He was upset before he saw Nikki?" asked Caroline.

"He was okay when we arrived at Bruck Hall. But then Golden started getting on his case."

"About what?"

"I don't exactly know. It had something to do with football, at least that's what Golden hinted." Al hesitated. "He was cracking jokes about Marty. He told the other guys

Marty wouldn't last out the season. I didn't think much of it in the beginning. Trace was always making himself out to be the big wheel on the team. I figured he was picking on Marty because of the fight on Saturday."

"Go on," said Carl.

"About a half hour before the women showed up on campus, Trace came over to where Marty and I and some of the other guys were standing. He muttered something under his breath as he passed us. Marty exploded. He said something like, 'I've had enough of this.' Then he took off after Trace. He caught up with him over by the corner of the building."

"He didn't hit Trace, did he?" Caroline asked anxiously.

Al shook his head. "They just talked, but Golden did most of the talking. He was laughing a lot. Marty looked too stunned to answer him."

Caroline glanced over at Carl. The professor was stroking his beard, a habit he cultivated when considering a particularly troublesome problem.

"Golden walked away after a minute or so," Al continued. "Marty just kept standing there in the shadows of the trees. The rest of us let him be. We figured whatever Trace had said, Marty was taking it hard."

"I saw him come out of the shadows when Nikki passed by in the picket line."

"That's the next time I saw him, Mrs. Rhodes. Like I said before, I consider Marty my friend. But we're not close like some guys are. I didn't think I had the right to ask him about Trace. After the argument with his wife, though, I was worried about him."

"So you followed him to the gym."

"Not at first, Professor. I wouldn't have followed him at all if I hadn't seen Golden trailing after him. I figured there might be trouble between the two of them. I wanted to be there if Marty needed help."

"Was there trouble?" asked Caroline.

"I don't know. Marty went into the gym. A minute or so later, Trace did the same. I thought about going after them, but I didn't." Al paused and looked down at his feet. "To tell you the truth, I chickened out."

Caroline exchanged glances with Carl. The professor lifted his shoulders in a "God-only-knows" gesture and continued to stroke his beard.

"Was Golden making trouble for you, too?" Caroline asked Al.

Sperling clenched both hands between his knees and ducked his head even lower.

"What's said in this room is strictly confidential. It needn't go any further unless it has something to do with Trace's murder."

"It doesn't, Mrs. Rhodes," Al murmured. "I swear, I had nothing to do with Golden's death."

"Then tell us about it. It might make you feel better to get it off your chest."

Sometimes seconds seem to last an eternity. It seemed this way to Caroline as she waited for Sperling to come to a decision. When he finally did, it wasn't the one she'd hoped for.

"I'm sorry, but I think it would be better if I just kept my mouth shut. Trace is dead. Whatever problems the two of us had are over now." Al stood up and faced the professor. "I saw Marty leave the gym about twenty minutes after he entered it. He crossed over to Bruck Green and sat down on a bench. He stayed maybe twenty, thirty minutes. Then he left. Where he went after that, I don't know. As for Golden, I never saw him again. He didn't come out of the gym. When Marty took off, so did I."

"Did you go back to the picket line?" asked Carl.

Al shook his head. "No. I went to the dorm and sacked out. The next thing I remember is being awakened by the security officer. That's when I learned Golden was dead."

"I guess that's it then." Carl glanced questioningly at Caroline, but she shook her head. "We won't keep you any longer, Mr. Sperling."

"Right." Al walked to the door. He hesitated, one hand on the knob, then turned to face Carl. "I'm sorry about your nephew, Professor. I guess we all have reasons to be prejudiced."

"Not reasons," said Carl. "Excuses. You didn't shoot my nephew, and I didn't lynch your great-grandfather. Let's judge each other on our own merits, not on the deeds of other people."

"That works for me," said Sperling. He looked over at Caroline. "Tell Marty to hang in there. I'll keep my ears open for any gossip about Golden. If I hear anything, I'll tell Professor Atwater."

Caroline waited until the door closed, then leaned forward and slammed her fist on the desk.

"Dammit, Carl. I *knew* Martin was hiding something!"

"It seems so, if we're to believe young Mr. Sperling."

"I think Al was telling the truth when he said he had nothing to do with Trace's murder. As for Martin..." Caroline stood up and walked to the door. "It's time that boy and I had another little chat."

"Stay cool," warned the professor. "Don't let your anger get the best of you."

"I have a right to be angry," growled Caroline. "He lied about what happened last night. Now he's going to admit the truth, even if I have to choke it out of him!"

She stormed out of the office with all the fury of a mother scorned.

TWENTY-ONE

CAROLINE'S FIRST IMPULSE was to drive directly to the police station and confront Martin with Al Sperling's story. She was midway to town before Carl's warning and her own common sense forced her to rethink the idea. Attacking Martin at this point in the game might only antagonize him further. There had to be a reason for his secretiveness. If she wanted to learn what it was, she would have to keep a tight rein on her emotions. Martin was not a violent man, but he could be as stubborn as a mule when challenged.

Easing up on the gas pedal, Caroline coasted off the highway at the Rhineburg exit, made a sharp right turn at the end of the ramp, and guided the Jeep off the asphalt and through a thicket of weeds blocking the entrance to an abandoned gas station. She parked next to a rusted Texaco pump, its red star faded a dull orange by the sun, and switched off the engine.

Cornfields bracketed the county road leading into town. The field nearest to the station ended at a hillock a few feet beyond the cracked pavement of the parking lot. Browned by the sun, the corn here had not yet been harvested. The withered stalks swayed in the wind, their leaves twisted and tan and their grip on the crumbly soil tentative at best. Except for the rustle of the wind through the dying plants, the countryside was bathed in silence.

Caroline leaned back against the cushioned car seat and drank in the quiet. A thousand thoughts crowded her brain, each one clamoring for attention even as she consciously pushed them aside. What she needed now was to empty herself of all feeling, all doubts, and immerse herself in the healing stillness of her surroundings until, renewed in body and spirit, she could return to the problem at hand with an open mind uncluttered by emotion.

She closed her eyes and dew in a series of deep, calming breaths that slowed her heartbeat and dulled the pounding in her forehead. Gradually, the tightness in her neck and back muscles began to ease. She let her arms fall lazily to her sides, her hands resting lightly on her thighs. Sensation seemed to slip away from her limbs until the touch of her fingertips was barely perceptible. As her breathing became more shallow and rhythmic, a feeling of complete weightlessness swept over her. It was as if her mind had separated itself from her body and was floating free of all earthly constraints.

Her peace was shattered by the rumble of an eighteen-wheeler pulling off the highway behind her. She straightened up in her seat, reality quickly setting back in, and glanced out the Jeep's side window. The truck passed by the gas station, gathering speed as it rolled up the road toward Rhineburg. Loaded with sleek new vehicles, it was a car carrier obviously bound for Bill Morgan's auto dealership.

Caroline recalled her conversation with Donna Moore the previous day. The feisty little woman had claimed that Bill Morgan was underwriting the publicity for the rodeo. Because of that, she and several contestants were slated to appear at his dealership on Wednesday. Moore had also arranged for a parade through town on Halloween evening. Caroline wondered if either event would go on as scheduled. Trace's death and the ongoing conflict with the university had thrown a monkey wrench into the rodeo contractor's plans.

At least Moore and her people could be counted out as suspects in Golden's murder. Crossing out extraneous names was helpful, thought Caroline, until she paused to reconsider the matter. One name that couldn't be crossed off the list was that of Ben Halloway.

Caroline rolled down the window and let the chilly air sweep the last of the cobwebs from her brain. She hunched her shoulders against the wind as she considered the matter of Mr. Halloway.

Ben had been in the crowd during the Bruins' protest on Sunday. He would have noticed that Trace Golden was the team's self-proclaimed leader. He'd ignored Golden when the boy approached him and Donna Moore in the Blue Cat Lounge later that evening, but Caroline couldn't state for a fact that Ben and Trace hadn't tangled during the melee that followed. Ben's injuries seemed severe for a man who'd tripped and fallen over a fence. The two broken ribs discovered on X-ray could well be the result of a nicely placed punch by a muscular football player.

And Trace was nothing if not muscular. Somehow Caroline couldn't envision Ben stepping back from a fight. If he and Trace had exchanged blows at the Blue Cat, a similar battle between the two might have occurred Monday night. Maybe Trace had attempted to free the bulls from their pen, and Ben had caught him at it. Ben may have strangled him in the ensuing struggle, then tossed the body into the bullpen in an effort to hide what he'd done.

But Ben hadn't exhibited the kind of nervousness one would expect from a murderer. He'd appeared relatively calm when she first saw him standing near the pens with Gabe, and he'd been more than helpful in recovering Trace's body

Despite all that, Halloway was still an unknown entity. Being good with horses and cattle didn't necessarily mean you were good with people. For all Caroline knew, the man could be a serial killer wanted for the murders of a dozen Iowa women.

But wouldn't Jake have investigated Moore's right hand man? Caroline had to admit the Chief was no slouch when it came to police work. Still, it took time to do a background check on someone from another state. Halloway could have a record as long as his arm, and Jake wasn't aware of it yet.

Annie Holtzbrinck would know if Jake was looking into Halloway's past. Caroline would ask her about the cowboy when she reached town.

Having left the campus before interviewing any of the other Bruins, Al Sperling remained her only suspect on the football team. Her gut feeling was that Al had nothing to do with the murder. Still, like Martin, Al was hiding something. Whatever it was, it might account for the underlying hostility in his opening remarks.

Al's references to racism had been pointed and personal. It was almost as if he'd attempted to create a diversion that he could later use against them if needed. By claiming she and Carl were racist in picking on him for questioning, he could raise a smokescreen that would bring into doubt any investigation of his role in the murder.

But Carl had refused to play Al's game, something the student hadn't reckoned on. And, Caroline thought, the young man had seemed genuinely surprised when told of Martin's situation. He'd come to Martin's defense, but in doing so, had only worsened matters for her son. The discrepancies between his and Martin's stories were all Jake needed to hold Martin in jail. Unless she could resolve those discrepancies to his liking, the Chief had every right to charge her son with murder.

She would have to find out what Al was withholding

from them. If Trace had learned something about Al's past and was using it to blackmail him, he could have been doing the same kind of thing to other people. Al may have put up with Trace's threats, but one of his other victims might have thought murder was a better way to handle the situation.

The only other person Caroline could consider as a suspect was Tom Walker. Trace had ratted on him to his wife, telling Sue about Tom's little fling with a blond bombshell down at the trailer park. Tom had appeared drunk Monday evening when he interjected himself into the argument between Martin and Nikki. But the man had been consuming a steady diet of alcohol for years. As Caroline well knew, the longer you drank, the more liquor it took to put you under. Tom may not have been as intoxicated as he looked. He could have simply been acting, covering his tracks while he waited for the right moment to take his revenge on Golden.

Tom Walker would make an attractive suspect, but only if he couldn't account for his whereabouts late Monday night. It was possible he'd gone home with Sue after the protest broke up. It was also possible that the beating by his wife had sent him scurrying to the arms of his lover. What Caroline hoped was that he had no alibi at all. She would have to rely on Maddy or one of the other ladies to learn more about the fickle Tom.

Caroline rolled up the window of the Jeep and switched on the ignition. Summarizing the list of possible suspects had helped to settle her. She felt ready now to face Martin. Before doing that, though, she would call Carl at his office and ask him to interview the other Bruin players. Then she would stop at the newspaper office as originally planned. She still wondered if Trace's death might have been connected to one of his father's business dealings. The senior

Golden was a powerful man in the community, and powerful men were known to make enemies. It was a long shot, for sure. Still, it wouldn't do to overlook any possibility.

Her emotions firmly in check, Caroline pulled out of the gas station and pointed the nose of the Jeep toward Rhineburg.

TWENTY-TWO

AMOS DALTON HAD the grizzled features one associated with an old-time, hard-nosed reporter. At sixty-seven his face was spider-webbed with age lines that curved like tiny half moons from his mouth to his cheekbones. The skin at the corner of his eyes crinkled in miniature pleats, and two deeper groves puckered the soft skin above the bridge of his nose. His forehead was high and furrowed beneath a thatch of unruly gray hair that badly needed a trimming. Steel rimmed glasses rode low on his nose, the brown eyes behind them dulled to the color of weak gravy by twin cataracts.

Dalton looked like a man who ate little and slept even less, but when he extended his hand to Caroline, his grip was firm.

"Figured you'd be stopping by," he drawled as he appropriated a chair from a neighboring cubicle and placed it next to his desk. "Have a seat while I get us some coffee. Or would you prefer tea?"

"A Coke would work better for me," said Caroline, eyeing the old fashioned Coca Cola cooler sitting in the corner of the office. "Unless that thing's only for decoration."

"It's old," said Dalton. "But still serviceable."

He opened the lid of the cooler and withdrew two stubby bottles decorated with the famous Coca Cola logo.

"I prefer drinking Coke this way," he said as he flipped the caps off the bottles. He handed one to Caroline. "Don't like the taste of it in plastic or cans. A little harder to find in the stores, but, in my humble opinion, well worth the search." He sat down and pushed a pile of photocopied news stories across the slick wooden surface of his desk. "I expect those are what you've come for."

Caroline put down her Coke and picked up the top paper on the pile. It was a copy of Trace's birth announcement as written up in the *Rhineburg Rag* eighteen years earlier. She flipped through the rest of the papers, then glanced over at Dalton.

"This is a complete file on Trace Golden, everything from the day he was born until the day he died."

"It's what you wanted, isn't it?"

"Yes," said Caroline slowly. "But how did you know? I didn't even call to say I was coming, much less ask to see this stuff."

Dalton leaned back in his chair and grinned.

"I've been a newspaper man for nigh onto fifty years now. I know what I'd go looking for if I was in your shoes." The grin slowly faded from his face. "I was sorry to hear about your son. The little I know of him, he seems like a nice guy. Not your typical candidate for the role of murderer."

"Chief Moeller might disagree with you there. Martin and Trace were both seen entering the gym last night. Only Martin was seen to leave."

Dalton lifted one bushy eyebrow. "So Jake has a witness, does he? Well, that puts a different light on the matter. I guess he didn't have any choice but to pull your boy in for questioning. Still, the apple doesn't fall far from the tree. My money's on Martin."

"I'm sure he would appreciate your vote of confidence."

"I have faith in you, too, Mrs. Rhodes. You were pretty sharp when it came to figuring out those other murders here in Rhineburg. You'll come up with something to help your son."

Caroline wished she were as confident as the *Rag*'s editor. The prospects for clearing Martin's name seemed pretty bleak to her at the moment.

"I feel I owe you one."

"You owe me? But why?"

The veteran newspaperman shrugged. "This was a pretty dead town news wise before you came to live here. I was starting to get bored writing stories about livestock fairs and high school dances. Oh, I covered an occasional Friday night dustup over at McGinty's, but never a murder as complicated as the one last winter."

He was referring to a bombing that had resulted in the deaths of several patients on the psych ward at St. Anne's. Caroline's role in the investigation and the subsequent capture of the killer had occupied the front page of the *Rhineburg Rag* for the entire week between Christmas and New Year.

"Things got even more interesting after our esteemed postmaster bit the dust back in May. I actually found myself looking forward to coming to work. My investigative juices started flowing again, just like in the old days." Dalton ran a hand through his unkempt hair. "'Course this town isn't half as exciting as Chicago was back when I started out as a cub reporter. But it was a nice place to retire to after my heart attack sidelined me two years ago. I got to play editor at the *Rag,* whip it into shape as a real newspaper. But even that got old after a while. Until you came along, that is."

Caroline didn't know what to say. She was aware that she was something of a celebrity in Rhineburg due to her involvement in three previous crimes, but now she was being credited with reinvigorating a man who was a legend in the newspaper business. Amos Dalton had won more awards for investigative reporting than all of his former comrades on the newspaper put together. The fact that he'd settled in Rhineburg was probably amazing to anyone who'd known him before his illness.

"But you came here to discuss Trace Golden, not me," said Dalton with a smile. He pointed to the photocopies. "I pulled those out of the file when I got the report on Golden's death. Then I heard about your son. I figured you'd be hotfooting it over here sooner or later, so I made a duplicate set for you."

"I appreciate that," said Caroline. "Do you know anything about the boy that's not in these reports? Something that might not have been fit to print?"

"You mean like some kind of scandal."

Dalton leaned back in his chair and scratched his chin. He hesitated long enough for Caroline to wonder why. For a brief moment she had the feeling he was hiding something. But his answer, when it came, seemed innocuous enough.

"It's pretty well known that Trace was into booze. I'd say he was well on his way to becoming an alcoholic, if he wasn't one already. They lifted his driver's license after that episode a couple of weeks ago."

"I heard he sideswiped Annie Holtzbrinck's car."

"Could have killed someone, his alcohol level was so high. 'Course I didn't print that in the paper. Golden Sr. would have stormed in here with his lawyer if I had."

"I wanted to ask you about Trace's father. Do you know anything about him that might indicate a link between his son's death and his banking business?"

"You're thinking the old man might have made some enemies, one of whom killed Trace."

"It was a thought," said Caroline. "Bankers make foreclosures on homes all the time. They also deny loans to people. Maybe Golden Sr. did something that sent some-body over the edge. Maybe that somebody took out his anger on Trace Jr."

"I suspect Golden isn't the most beloved of men—he's pretty hardnosed when it comes to business—but I don't recall hearing of any specific trouble between him and his customers. And no one's made open threats against him. Not that I know of, anyway."

"What about the bank itself? Is it solid?"

"Solid as the rock of Gibraltar. Golden may have been overly indulgent with his son, but no one could accuse him of that when it came to business. He's always been con-servative in how he invested the bank's money. He's also been conservative in how he spent it. His annual reports are picture perfect when it comes to gains versus losses. As long as I've been living here, the 1st National's funds have shown steady growth."

Dalton got to his feet.

"Can't tell you much more than that," he said as he walked Caroline to the door. "I'll check the past issues of the paper and see if anything shows up on Golden Sr. If I find something interesting, I'll give you a holler."

Caroline shook hands with the newspaperman and climbed into her car. Pulling away from the curb, she glanced back at the office through the rearview mirror. What she saw shocked her.

Amos Dalton was straddling the doorway of the *Rhine-burg Rag,* his eyes firmly fixed on the departing Jeep. A scowl had replaced the editor's previous jovial smile. He looked worried as hell, maybe even a little afraid, as he stood there chewing on his bottom lip.

If Caroline hadn't known better, she'd have thought he was glad to be rid of her.

TWENTY-THREE

NANCY KUHNKEY WAS making her presence known at the police station when Caroline walked through the door. The elderly lawyer stood in the center of the anteroom, her black orthopedic shoes planted toe to toe against the scuffed boots of Rhineburg's top cop. Bellowing out her demands in a no-nonsense voice, she had cowed even the loquacious Annie Holtzbrinck into silence.

"You'll either charge the boy or release him," Kuhnkey boomed in a raspy voice. Her massive breasts brushed against Jake's shirt as she leaned in closer and jabbed him in the chest with a pudgy index finger. "You haven't got a leg to stand on, Moeller, and you know it."

"I have a witness," Jake hollered back. "Martin Rhodes was seen at the gym with Golden."

"He entered the gym *before* Golden, not *with* him, you idiot! *No one* saw them together."

Jake looked absolutely apoplectic. His face was the color of an overripe tomato, and his normally neat hair was wildly ruffled. Caroline suspected he was ready to tear it out by the roots.

"Chief Moeller?" Caroline took a step forward. "May I speak with Martin?"

Jake swung on her like a tiger scenting a jackal come to feast on his kill. His eyes blazed in ill-contained anger.

"No, you may not! No one is seeing that young man again until he agrees to tell me what happened last night."

Nancy Kuhnkey's aquiline nose quivered in outrage. "I

hope you don't think you can deny my client counsel, Chief Moeller. If so, you're making one helluva big mistake."

Jake sputtered an epitaph that barely reached Caroline's ears. Recognizing a frustrated man when she saw one, she took pity on the Chief and held up one hand.

"I think I can talk some sense into Martin if you'll let me speak to him, Jake. With Miss Kuhnkey there to advise him—" she glanced at the lawyer and got a nod in response "—I believe he'll make a full and truthful statement to you shortly."

Jake looked from Caroline to Kuhnkey, then back to Caroline again. He blew out a long breath, then turned on his heel and walked toward his office.

"All right," he growled over his shoulder. "You've got ten minutes to convince him to talk. After that…"

"Comes the rubber hose treatment," mimicked Kuhnkey. She curled her lip and sniffed disapprovingly. "You've been watching too many movies, Chief. You make a lousy George Raft."

"And you make a lousy Perry Mason," Jake shot back. He stormed into his office, slamming the door behind him.

"Geez!" said Annie, coming around from behind her desk. "You laid it on awfully thick, Nancy. The Chief isn't used to being talked to that way."

"Well, he better get used to it," Kuhnkey said with a sly grin. "He's not dealing with that chump Hank Matthews, you know. I stand up for my clients, even if they are murderers."

"Martin is not a murderer," Caroline said sternly. "If you don't believe my son…"

"Don't get your knickers in a knot, Mrs. Rhodes." Kuhnkey peered at Caroline over the rim of her half glasses, her deep blue eyes twinkling merrily. "Just testing the waters to see your reaction. Now that I know where you stand, I can use you to get to your son." She motioned to Caroline to follow her. "Martin hasn't been very forthcoming with me," she said as she lumbered down the hallway leading to the cells. "I don't think he trusts me yet. You, with your implicit faith in his innocence, might convince him to talk. At least it's worth a try."

Kuhnkey signaled to a lanky gray-haired man slouched half asleep on a chair outside Martin's cell.

"This old coot is Frank Mustard," she said, patting the man on the shoulder. "He's a temporarily deputized member of the police force ordered to guard your notorious son." She grinned at Mustard. "Has he made any move to escape yet, Frank?"

The elderly gentleman shook his head. He rose slowly to his feet and ambled over to the cell door.

"Ain't done nothing but lay there on his cot and stare at the ceiling," he said as he produced a slightly tarnished key from his pocket. "A right full fellow, if you ask me."

He swung open the cell door, and Caroline and the lawyer stepped inside.

Martin had been dozing, but he sprang to his feet when he saw his mother. "How's Nikki?" he asked anxiously.

"She's holding up." Caroline examined her son. Still garbed in his uniform, he looked tired and disheveled. "But of course she's worried about you."

"She shouldn't be," Martin said with a grimace. "I've done nothing wrong."

"You've done a lot wrong," Caroline snapped. "You've lied to Jake about your movements last night. In doing so, you've made yourself a suspect in this case."

Martin's expression grew mulish, but Caroline didn't give him time to object.

"Al Sperling made a statement to the police early this morning. Jake knows that Trace followed you into the gym last night. He also knows that you had words with Trace shortly before your argument with Nikki."

Caroline outlined Al's story to Nancy Kuhnkey. When she finished, she turned to Martin.

"We're trying to help you, but you're tying our hands. We need to know the truth, and we need to know it now."

Martin slumped down on the cot and buried his face in his hands.

"I can't believe this is happening," he said quietly. "I never guessed anyone saw us."

Nancy Kuhnkey sat down on the opposite bunk and opened her battered briefcase. She took out a legal pad and a pen.

"Okay Martin. Tell us what occurred between you and Golden last night. And no lies this time."

Martin glanced first at his mother, then at the elderly lawyer. His face was considerably paler now and there was a hint of desperation in his eyes. When he spoke, his voice trembled.

"They say the truth will set you free. In my case, though, the truth could hang me."

TWENTY-FOUR

J ake M oeller had been invited to join them in Martin's cell. He opted instead for the interrogation room where a tray of sandwiches awaited them. After passing out the food, he called to Annie Holtzbrinck and asked her to bring a tape recorder and her steno pad.

"Annie will take down what you say in shorthand," he told Martin. "I'll compare her text to the tape before I ask you to sign a formal statement."

"Let's get on with it then. Where do you want me to start, Chief?"

"Start with yesterday afternoon. Tell me about the picket line and your first contact with Trace."

"I originally saw him in the gym before the picket line formed. Coach thought it would be best if we protested as a team, so we changed into uniforms in the locker room."

"Did anything happen between the two of you at that time?"

"Not then," said Martin with a shake of his head. "Trace was joking around with a couple of the other guys. I heard him mention my name, but I ignored him and went on dressing. I left the gym before he did."

"What happened next?"

"We marched around for a while outside Bruck Hall, then everyone sort of drifted onto the lawn. A bunch of fellows from Rhineburg arrived with beer coolers. They set up their chairs near to where Trace was standing talking with his buddies. The guys from town all seemed to know Trace. A couple of them took him aside and, I think, shared their beer with him. I can't be certain that's what happened, but he smelled like a brewery when he joined the team again."

"Is that when you and he had words?"

Martin shook his head again. "Trace was carrying on about one of the men who'd arrived with the beer coolers. The fellow was married, but Trace said he'd had an affair with a woman down at the trailer camp. I wasn't interested in the story, so I walked away. Trace saw me leave. He turned in my direction and made a crack about me not lasting much longer on the team.

"Like before, I let it go. I promised Nikki I wouldn't let Trace get under my skin again. I meant to keep that promise, so I kept on walking. Al Sperling was discussing the Homecoming game with some of the other Bruins over by the sidewalk. I joined that group and tried to tune out Trace's taunts."

Martin paused to take a bite of his sandwich. He chased down the food with a swallow of Coke, then continued with his story.

"Golden walked past us a few minutes later. He made a point of raising his voice so I'd be sure to hear him."

"What did he say?" asked Jake.

Martin frowned at the policeman. "He said I might as well stay home on Saturday because I wasn't going to play in the Homecoming game. He said the coach wouldn't let a cheat like me on the field."

"And that's when you went after him?"

"I didn't exactly go *after* him, Chief. Sure, I followed him because I was angry. I didn't know why he called me a cheat, but I wasn't going to let him get away with it."

"Understandable."

"I caught up with Trace and told him to cut it out, he was

going overboard on this silly vendetta of his. He laughed in my face." Martin glanced down at his hands. He'd been twisting his napkin into a tight knot and now he threw it down on the table. "Trace said he'd seen some papers from the NCAA on Coach Wilkins's desk. He claimed I was ineligible to play football at Bruck, had been ineligible all season. He accused me of knowing about it, but playing anyway."

"That's a pretty nasty charge," said Jake. "Something like that could affect your chances of landing a job at Bruck."

Martin lowered his head. "Everyone knows I want to work at the university after graduation. Nikki and I love Rhineburg. We'd hoped to stay here forever."

"I suppose it wouldn't look too good on your resume if you were found in violation of NCAA rules. People might not believe you didn't know about it."

Nancy Kuhnkey rapped on the table with her knuckles. "Hold it right there, Chief Moeller. Martin's making a statement, not a confession. I agreed to let him tell you his story, but I won't agree to the tactics you're taking. My client has the right to remain silent, and I'll tell him to do so if you interject one more leading comment into the conversation."

"Sorry, Counselor." Jake glanced from Kuhnkey to Caroline. "I'm not trying to railroad your son. I only want to understand what was going through his head at the time."

"It's not that hard to figure out," said Caroline mildly. "Think how you'd feel if you were hit with a bombshell like the one Trace laid on Martin."

"I'd be angry," answered Jake. "Maybe angry enough to take a swipe at the guy."

"I was more in shock than angry," said Martin. "Wilkins had assured me that even though I'd run track at Bruck back in my undergraduate days, I was still eligible to play football as a doctoral student. I trusted him to know the rules, so I never bothered to look into it myself. I filled out the forms he gave me and figured that was all there was to it."

"What happened next?"

"Like I said, I was in shock. Trace walked away laughing, but I felt like I was rooted to the ground. I couldn't move at all. Then I saw Al watching me. I figured he'd seen me talking to Trace, but I didn't want to answer any questions right then. I turned and slipped into the shadows over by the corner of Bruck Hall." Martin took a deep breath. "I needed to be alone to think things over. I knew I had to talk to Coach Wilkins, but I wasn't sure what I'd say. I was as angry with him as I was with Golden. If what Trace told me was true, then Wilkins had been playing me for a fool all along. He never used me in a game until Trace got suspended, but I thought that was because Garrison Hurst forced him to accept me on the team. I figured Wilkins resented the President's interference. His treatment of me was his way of getting back at Hurst."

"So you stayed where you were and didn't go after Trace."

"That's right," said Martin. "I must have stood there in the shadows ten, maybe fifteen minutes. Then I saw Nikki protesting with the other women. Something in me snapped when I saw the sign she was carrying. Things were bad enough without her turning against me." Martin swiveled around to face Caroline. "I know I was wrong to think that way, but I felt like the world had turned upside down. I needed Nikki to be on *my* side, not marching for the rodeo."

Caroline reached over the table and squeezed Martin's hand. Now that she knew the whole story, she couldn't help feeling sorry for him. If what Trace said was true, Martin would be branded a cheater despite the fact he'd done nothing intentionally wrong. Wilkins would cover his own tail, for sure. He was that kind of a man, concerned first and foremost with himself. He'd keep his job somehow. Martin, on the other hand, would be lucky if he graduated. Garrison Hurst was a stickler for propriety. He wouldn't relish a scandal involving the Bruins, especially when he was using the team to reel in donations from alumni. Rather than broaden the scandal by expelling Martin, he might suggest that her son finish his studies elsewhere.

But Martin was only a few months away from receiving his Ph.D. Hurst could decide to simply ignore his presence at the university in hopes that once graduated, he would slink off quietly into the sunset.

Whichever way it went, the odds of Martin getting a teaching position at Bruck were practically nil. He'd be lucky to get a job at any college with the title of "cheater" hanging over his head.

Of course, the title of "murderer" was much worse.

Caroline shook off visions of her son in prison stripes and forced herself to concentrate on what Martin was saying. He was past the part about the argument with Nikki and was telling Jake how he'd set off for the gym to confront his coach.

"I didn't know Trace was following me. I went in the locker room entrance and walked down the hall to Coach Wilkins's office. I was about to knock on his door when I heard him talking to someone inside. I thought maybe he was on the phone, but then I heard a woman answer him. I decided their conversation was none of my business. I walked back to the locker room, figuring I'd wait there until the woman left. Unfortunately, Trace was at his locker when I arrived."

Martin straightened his shoulders.

"I won't lie to you, Chief. I stopped dead when I saw Trace sitting there grinning at me like some damned ghoul. Something broke inside of me. I wanted nothing more than to wipe that smile off Golden's face. I swung at him, swung hard. My punch connected, and Trace went down like a sack of potatoes. He wasn't out, but he was hurting real good. He swore at me as I walked out the door."

"Did he follow you?" Jake asked.

Martin shook his head. "I swear on my father's grave, I never saw him again. I don't know why he didn't come after me. I expected he'd want to continue the fight, and that's why I parked myself on that bench on Bruck Green. To tell you the truth, I wanted another go at him. I was so frustrated that I wanted to hit something, anything, and he would have made a perfect target."

"But you say he never came out of the gym."

"Not while I sat there. I waited a good half an hour, but he didn't show. I figured he was licking his wounds in the coach's office."

"Did anyone come out of the gym? The woman you heard talking to the coach, or the coach himself?"

"I didn't see either one of them, but I might have missed them in the crowd. There were a lot of students walking back and forth between the dorms and Bruck Hall. I was watching for Trace and no one else."

"And you're sure Trace never left the gym."

"Like I said, he didn't leave while I was sitting on the bench. He might have walked out after I left the Green."

"Where did you go next?"

"I went to the stadium like I told you before. The rest of my original statement is true. I didn't lie about that."

Jake drummed a tattoo on the tabletop with his fingertips. His eyes never left Martin, but when he spoke, it was to Nancy Kuhnkey.

"Your client's not in the clear yet, Miss Kuhnkey, but I don't have enough evidence to hold him."

"You're damned right about that, Chief Moeller." Kuhnkey rose to her feet. "I take it Mr. Rhodes is free to leave now."

"With the usual warning to stick around town. Annie will piece together his statement. He can come by later to read and sign it."

"Thank you, Chief." Martin held out his hand. "I hope you'll forgive my lack of cooperation earlier today. It was foolish of me."

"Yes," said Jake with a sigh. "It was very foolish of you. I wasted valuable time trying to back up your alibi."

Martin gazed at the policeman in surprise.

"You mean, you actually believed me?"

"I'm not a fool, Martin. I didn't fall for everything you said, but I believed enough of it. I've gotten to know quite a bit about you over the past year. Somehow I don't think you're the kind of man who would strangle a teammate and then throw his body into a bullpen."

Jake stood up and walked to the door. He opened it, then turned back to face Martin. His mouth was set in a grim line, but the look in his eyes was one of unaccountable sadness.

"For the sake of Nikki and your mother, I hope I'm right."

TWENTY-FIVE

"I'M GOING OVER to the gym to talk with Coach Wilkins," Martin said as they left the police station. "I want to ask him about my eligibility."

"I don't think that's a good idea," said Caroline. "Jake will want to talk to Wilkins about that NCAA letter. If you get to him first, he'll have time to destroy it."

"And if the Chief gets to him first, I may never learn the truth. Any papers he has will be impounded, and I'll be left hanging without any answers."

"He can't impound them without a search warrant," said Kuhnkey as she lit up a cigarette. "Unless, that is, Wilkins willingly gives them up. I doubt he'll do that, though. Any hanky-panky involving the NCAA could cost him his job."

"How long would it take to get a search warrant?" Caroline asked. She watched with envy as the lawyer took a long drag on her cigarette. Giving up smoking was one of the hardest things she'd ever done. The smell of burning tobacco still caused her to have cravings.

"Not long in this case." Kuhnkey took another drag on the cigarette, exhaled slowly, and blew a ring of smoke into the air. "Hank Matthews is acting as point man for the Golden family. Golden Sr. wants an arrest ASAP, and what Golden Sr. wants, Golden Sr. gets. Matthews will see to it that Jake Moeller gets all the search warrants he needs."

"Matthews must be a powerful man."

Kuhnkey snorted. "Matthews is a hack. Golden Sr. is the one with the power."

"I'm going to run over to the post office before I go back to Bruck," said Martin, looking impatiently at his watch. "I want Nikki to know I'm okay."

"Now wait a minute, young man," Kuhnkey hollered as the boy loped off. "We still have matters to discuss."

"Later!"

Martin waved over his shoulder at the two women before disappearing into the post office. Nancy Kuhnkey was not at all pleased.

"Obnoxious little pup," she growled. "Was he as bull-headed as a child as he is now?"

"He came by it naturally. His father was born stubborn."

"Makes me glad I never married. One man would be bad enough, but the thought of bearing a child like Martin would drive me to drink."

"He's actually quite a likable fellow," said Caroline. "You're just seeing him at his worst."

"Most of my clients are at their worst when I see them. If they're not dying, they're on their way to jail. Wills and drunk driving cases. That's about all that's thrown my way nowadays."

"Then you haven't handled many murder cases."

"Not a one," Kuhnkey replied solemnly. "But I've read every Perry Mason book in the library."

Caroline's heart tap-danced against her ribs in a wild "this-can't-be-happening-to-me" kind of beat. She clutched at Kuhnkey's arm and pulled the woman towards her.

"We are not some characters in a damned mystery novel!" she snapped. "This is a real murder, and my son is a real suspect."

Kuhnkey gazed at Caroline over the top of her glasses. Then she threw back her head and let out a loud guffaw.

"No need to have a heart attack, Mrs. Rhodes. I was only kidding."

Caroline flushed a bright pink. "I'm sorry," she said as she backed off a step. "I guess I'm a little on edge at the moment."

"Understandable. It isn't every day that your son's accused of murder."

"I guess there's a first time for everything. But I'm glad to hear you've represented people in situations similar to Martin's."

"Actually, I haven't."

"Now, wait a minute. You said…"

"No, I didn't," said Kuhnkey, shaking her head. "I told you the truth when I said I've never worked a murder case. The part I was kidding about was reading all the Perry Mason books. But take heart," she said as Caroline's jaw dropped. "I have watched Court TV."

TWENTY-SIX

"A WOMAN? THERE was no woman here last night."

Wade Wilkins leaned back in his desk chair, his right hand tightening on the padded armrest. Caroline sensed his unease as his hooded eyes flicked from her face to Nancy Kuhnkey's before settling on the worried features of her son.

"I was listening to a talk show on the radio." The coach's shoulders rose in a slight shrug. "That's probably the sound you heard."

"It wasn't a radio program," Martin insisted vehemently. "There was someone in this office, a woman, and you were talking with her. I'd know your voice anywhere."

Wilkins's eyes hardened. "Think what you want, Rhodes, but I'm telling you, there was no one here but myself."

A muscle twitched in Martin's jaw. Caroline caught hold of his arm and tugged on it. He glared at her, but she shot him a look that brooked no argument. Ignoring his angry frown, she turned to face Wilkins.

"What about the letter Trace saw on your desk?"

"Letter?" Wilkins feigned a puzzled expression. "What letter are you talking about, Mrs. Rhodes?"

"The one from the NCAA." Nancy Kuhnkey positioned herself next to Caroline, effectively blocking her client's attempt to edge past his mother. "The letter addressing Martin's eligibility status. We want to know…"

"If you folks don't mind, I'd like to be the one asking the questions here."

Caroline spun around as Jake Moeller strode into the room. Their eyes met and he glared at her, obviously displeased that she and her son had gotten to the coach before him.

"I wouldn't want to accuse you three of obstructing justice," Jake said, his voice dripping with sarcasm. "But I will if you continue to meddle in this case."

"My client has a right to see any communication that deals with his status on the team," said Kuhnkey. She swept Martin aside with a broad forearm and planted herself under Jake's nose. "As his lawyer..."

"As his lawyer, you ought to know better," Jake growled. "That letter is possible evidence in a death investigation." He dismissed Kuhnkey with a wave of his hand and turned to Wade Wilkins. "I'd appreciate it if you'd hand it over to me."

"I would if I could," Wilkins replied in a bored tone of voice. "But I can't. Let me tell you something about Trace, Chief Moeller. The 'Golden Boy' was a born liar. He was angry that Rhodes beat him up last Saturday, so he concocted a story to upset him."

"You're saying that letter doesn't exist."

"That's exactly what I'm saying. Golden was taunting Rhodes, nothing more. And now, if you're done with your questions, I'd like to get back to work."

Wilkins reached for a manila folder lying on the desk, but Jake was quicker than the coach. The big policeman picked up the folder and tossed it on a nearby chair.

"That'll have to wait. We need to talk a little more about Martin's standing on the team. But first, I'd like to hear about your movements last night."

"Oh, come now," Wilkins sneered. "You think I put

Golden up to that stunt with the bulls? Knowing his past history, the boy was probably drunk when he fell into that pen. You'd be better off looking for the local yokels who fed him the liquor last night than wasting your time questioning me."

"Trace Golden didn't fall into the bullpen, Mr. Wilkins. He was placed there after he died."

Wilkins looked surprised. "You mean he was murdered?"

"That's right," said Jake. "Somebody put an arm around the boy's neck and crushed his windpipe. Then that same somebody tossed his body in with the bulls to make it look like an accident."

"That's a nasty way to kill a guy." Wilkins swiveled around in his chair. He grinned at Martin. "Now I know the real reason you came storming in here with your lawyer. The cops think you murdered Golden, and you're looking to me for an alibi."

"I don't need an alibi," Martin said angrily. "I didn't kill Trace Golden."

"Oh, of course not." Wilkins turned to Chief Moeller. "I was here in my office from seven o'clock until nearly eleven. I was alone the entire time working on the game plan for Saturday. When I finished, I locked up the gym and went home. I never saw Rhodes or Golden after they changed into their uniforms earlier in the evening. I had no idea Trace was dead until President Hurst called me with the news early this morning."

"Is there anyone who can corroborate your story?"

"Like I said, I was alone the entire time."

"That's not true," said Martin. "I don't know why you're lying, but you are."

Wilkins shot out of his chair. He leaned across the desk and swiped a finger across his throat.

"I've had it up to here with you and your stories, Mr. Rhodes. You're a pain in the butt, but I've put up with you because you're Hurst's little darling. Well, I don't have to put up with you any more." He glanced at Moeller while pointing to Martin. "Rhodes fought with Trace Golden on Saturday and again last night. If you ask me, this son of a bitch strangled my star player."

"Why, you…"

Martin lunged forward, his hands outstretched. Caroline made a desperate effort to grab his sleeve, but he slipped from her grasp and launched his body across the desk. He came up short as Wilkins took a quick step backward. A smile tweaked the corners of the coach's lips as Jake tackled the young man from behind.

"That's enough!" Moeller roared. He spun Martin around and pushed him towards his mother. "Get him out of here, Caroline. Take him home and make him stay there."

Tight-lipped with fury, Caroline linked hands with Nancy Kuhnkey and dragged a loudly protesting Martin out of the office. They were barely a yard down the corridor when a voice called out behind them.

"Hey, Rhodes!"

Martin spun around, pulling Caroline and Kuhnkey with him. Wilkins was standing in the doorway. A wicked grin creased the coach's face.

"Don't bother to come back for practice, boy. We don't want any murderers on the team."

Martin took only one step toward Wilkins before he was shoved to the floor, his arms pinned tightly behind him.

TWENTY-SEVEN

A LATE MORNING wind shift brought the scent of approaching rain to Rhineburg. By noon, the sun had vanished behind a gaggle of humpbacked clouds that sprawled, black and menacing, across the sky. An hour passed in silent anticipation. Then, like giant crows spreading their wings in flight, the clouds dipped low over town and stripped the buildings of color. Gray shadows disappeared as day turned into night, cold, dark, and ominous. Thunder pounded the air, and lightning spider-webbed the sky in staccato bursts of bright white heat. The storm had arrived, and it promised to be a bad one.

Caroline ignored the weather as she hurried down the sidewalk bordering Wilhelm Road. Maddy's phone call had come as she was leaving the post office after depositing Martin in Nikki's care. The message was brief but explicit. Caroline was to drop everything and hotfoot it over to the Sugar Bowl Café where the ladies of the Rhineburg Boarding House and Home for Gentle Women were gathered in conference. Their sleuthing had gone well, but they needed to consult with Caroline before launching part two of their plan.

Caroline stepped into the restaurant as the first drops of rain hit the plate glass door. It was a little after one-thirty, and the lunch hour crowd was mostly gone. A few stragglers, retired farmers dressed in worn overalls and John Deere caps, sat at the L-shaped counter in the back of the room. They seemed content to sit out the storm over cups of coffee, ignoring, for the most part, the elderly women huddled around a large oval table in the front of the café.

"How'd it go with Alexsa?" Caroline asked as she slipped into a chair next to Maddy.

"You won't believe it, Cari, but she knew we were coming." Maddy glanced down the table to where Bertha Meyer was regaling the other women with vivid descriptions of Alexsa's palatial estate. "Bertha thought it was simply a coincidence that there were three places set for tea in the garden room."

"Nothing's a coincidence when it comes to Alexsa," said Caroline dryly. "That woman has more spies at her service than the CIA."

"She doesn't need spies as long as she has Bricole."

Maddy gave Caroline one of those knowing looks that said more than words ever could.

"Now you're guessing," Caroline retorted.

Bricole Gregori was Alexsa's ten-year-old ward. Orphaned by the simultaneous death of both parents in a car crash, Bricole had for years roamed the fortune-telling circuit with her gypsy grandmother. A longstanding debt of honor had caused Alexsa to claim the child after Maria Gregori's untimely death in May.

Despite her advanced age and the disapproval of the child welfare agency, she'd come out a winner when Bricole's fate was decided in court. A high priced Chicago lawyer had pleaded Mrs. Morgan's case most eloquently, later claiming it was one of his best efforts. Of course, it hadn't hurt that Alexsa was an old and dear friend of the presiding judge who had contributed heavily to each of his reelection campaigns.

Regardless of how it had been accomplished, the fact remained that Bricole was now a beloved member of the Morgan family. Alexsa's teenage great-granddaughters treated the girl like a little sister, and Alexsa herself was absolutely smitten by the child. Bricole was bright and charming and blessed with skills beyond those of most ten-year-olds.

One of those skills was an uncanny ability to occasionally foresee the future.

A Rom by breeding and birth, Bricole possessed what her grandmother had called "second sight." This "gift" gave her an awareness of things beyond even her own understanding, enabling her to sometimes sense what was going to happen before it occurred.

Caroline had seen Bricole in action several times. She'd learned not to doubt the child's word when she spoke of one of her "feelings." Still, she doubted Bricole had foreseen Maddy's and Bertha's arrival. It was more likely that Elvira Harding, the Morgans' housekeeper, had learned of the women's plans via the ever-active Rhineburg grapevine and had warned Alexsa beforehand. Alexsa, being the gracious hostess that she was, would have readied the garden room in preparation for the visit.

"Call it guessing if you will, but Bricole was the one who greeted us at the door. She acted like she was expecting us. She took us directly to the garden room where Alexsa had begun to pour the tea."

Caroline found this latest revelation by Maddy a bit more intriguing. Still, she tried to find a logical reason for Alexsa's behavior.

"Maybe she was pouring for herself, Bricole, and Elvira. It could be the three of them were sitting down for a cup of tea when you arrived."

Maddy shook her head. "We passed Elvira in the driveway as we drove up. She was in her car headed for town, probably to do the week's shopping. As for Bricole, she scooted out of the room as soon as we were seated. No,

Cari. Something very weird was definitely going on in that house today."

"What do you mean, weird?"

"Weird, like in strange, nutty, offbeat. You ask Bertha. She noticed it, too, but she didn't connect it to Bricole."

Of course not, thought Caroline. Alexsa had gone to great lengths to shield Bricole from the public eye. Outside of the Morgans, only Caroline, Carl Atwater, Maddy and Jake Moeller, and Elvira Harding knew about the child's "gift".

"How's Martin doing?"

"Jake released him an hour ago," said Caroline. "He immediately got into more trouble."

Maddy clucked her tongue. "Now what's he done?"

"He tried to attack Coach Wilkins. He would have succeeded, too, if three Bruins hadn't tackled him from behind. Now he has a lump on his head to match his other war wounds."

"Ladies!" Bertha called for attention by rapping a spoon against the side of her water glass. The maneuver effectively silenced everyone at the table. "Now that Mrs. Rhodes has arrived—" she bobbed her white head in Caroline's direction "—we can begin our reports. Agatha, you and Eleanor were assigned to scout out the action at the Dip-N-Do Bath and Beauty Salon. We'll hear from you first."

Agatha Hagendorf glanced nervously around the table. "I hope I can remember it all," she said in a tremulous voice. "I wanted to take a notebook to write down what everyone said. But Eleanor wouldn't let me. She said that would give us away."

"I'm afraid it would have," Caroline said gently. "No one expects you to recall every bit of conversation, Agatha. Try to recall if you heard anything out of the ordinary. Sometimes it's the unusual that matters most."

"Well, I did hear Sue Walker say Tom never came home last night."

"He didn't? I wonder where he was."

"Not with his girlfriend, that's for sure."

Caroline's eyebrows soared. "Don't tell me Sue went looking for him."

"I wouldn't have bothered," sniffed Agatha. "But Sue said she was madder than a wet hen when midnight arrived and Tom hadn't shown up yet. She got in her car and drove down to the trailer camp. Just about tore the place apart before she found Hailey Wills's trailer—Hailey Wills is the blonde Tom's been seeing—but then Tom wasn't there." Agatha gave the other women a conspiratorial wink. "Hailey was tucked up in bed with some college kid. She was none too happy when Sue came bursting through the door. According to Sue, Hailey nearly killed her when she threw an ashtray at her. Hit her smack in the head. She's got a big bruise on her forehead to prove it."

"Did she ever find Tom?" asked Maddy.

"She quit looking for him after that. As far as Sue's concerned, Tom needn't bother coming home. She says she's divorcing him."

"I find that hard to believe," said Bertha, looking Agatha straight in the eye. "Sue sure did seem like a different woman when she went after Tom with that signboard yesterday. But people don't change their personalities overnight. Sue's been a dyed-in-the-wool doormat all her life. Now, all of a sudden, she's acting like little Miss Independence."

"It does seem odd," agreed Eleanor. "But Agatha's telling it like it happened. Sue let everyone in the shop know she was done with Tom."

"I wonder where Tom Walker spent the night," said Caroline. "He had as good a reason to kill Trace Golden as anyone else in town what with Trace telling Sue about his girlfriend."

"I can't imagine Tom was too pleased," said Maddy wryly. She added, "He might have gone home with one of his drinking buddies. Maybe Carl could look into that for us."

"First we should contact Annie over at the police station and find out if Jake's thought to question Tom."

"Good idea," said Maddy, reaching for her cell phone. "Keep going with your reports, ladies. I'll be right back."

Maddy slipped out of her chair and walked a few feet away to make the call. As she dialed, a monstrous clap of thunder shook the windows of the café. Shafts of lightning danced among the trees on the square, illuminating the restaurant in brilliant white light. The nine women jumped as one as the lightning pierced a huge oak directly across the street. The tree split in two and crashed to the ground, its upper branches landing inches from the Sugar Bowl's front door.

"Lordy sakes alive!" Marie Moser clutched her throat with one hand and her coffee cup with the other. Coffee sloshed on her pink velvet jacket as the poor woman struggled to regain her composure.

"It's all right, dear," said Myrtle Jennings, giving her sister a quick little hug while keeping her eyes on the windows. "The tree didn't hit the power lines, so we're okay."

The words were barely out of her mouth when the overhead lights first flickered, then abruptly shut down.

"At least, we were okay," Myrtle muttered as the restaurant plunged into darkness.

Caroline pushed herself up from the table. "They must have a stash of candles hidden away somewhere in the back," she said as she turned to look for the waitress. The woman was nowhere in sight, but the crash of falling crockery coming from the kitchen told her where to look. "I'll be back in a minute. Everyone stay calm."

The men at the counter had flicked on their cigarette lighters and were acting like nothing out of the ordinary had happened. They watched in stony silence as Caroline swept past them. She nudged open the swinging door leading to the working section of the restaurant and disappeared into the kitchen. A moment later she returned holding three empty Chianti bottles covered in hardened wax. A bright orange candle protruded from the neck of each of the bottles.

"Here's one for you," she said, setting a bottle on the counter in front of the men. "Beth's coming with a couple more."

Having lit her own candles from one of the men's lighters, she carried two bottles to the front of the café and placed them on the oval table.

"Let there be light," she said with a smile.

The tension in the room dissipated as the glow from the candles softened the darkness. It vanished entirely when Bertha pulled a package of marshmallows from the shopping bag next to her feet and tore open the plastic wrap.

"I was going to make those marshmallow rice cakes for the trick-or-treaters," she said, handing the open package to Eleanor. "But I think we could all use a little sugar right now."

Caroline watched in amused silence as, one by one, each woman stabbed a marshmallow with her fork and began toasting it over a flame. Still smiling, she glanced up at Maddy who'd returned to the table, her cell phone still plastered to her ear. The police chief's wife waggled her eyebrows at Caroline.

"I'm waiting for Carl to pick up," the redhead whispered. She covered the phone's tiny speaker with one hand. "Annie said Jake's been too busy to worry about Tom, so I thought I'd ask the professor to look for him."

"Good."

Caroline stared over Maddy's shoulder at the rain streaming down the café window. The squall line was passing, but the wind still howled outside. Branches of the fallen oak tree beat against the glass, smudging the window with wet leaves and obscuring her view of the town square. Something dark and furry moved into her line of sight. It crouched outside the window and seemed to peer in at her from the street. She leaned forward to get a better look, but whatever had been there abruptly vanished.

Returning her attention to Maddy, Caroline dismissed the strange object in the window as nothing more than a figment of her imagination. Then the door of the café slammed open. Into the room stumbled a stocky creature that appeared to be part man and part animal.

The figure was dressed in human clothing, but its face was covered by a mass of shaggy gray hair that fell in layers from the top of its head to the tips of its sloping shoulders. Crowning the head was a pair of chiseled ears resembling those of a dog. The ears tipped forward above jutting brows that arched over eyes the color of coal dust. Below the eyes, an elongated snout protruded from the face. The jaws were open exposing a pink tongue nestled between neat rows of wicked-looking teeth.

The creature covered the distance from the door to the table in two easy strides. It stared at the shocked faces of the women sitting there, then signaled its agitation with a roar that shook the very floorboards of the room.

It didn't take a genius to see that this was one very disturbed werewolf.

TWENTY-EIGHT

"GOOD GRIEF, CARL! Calm down and quit shouting. And please, take off that silly disguise."

"I am calm!" came a muffled cry from beneath the werewolf mask. "And I'm not shouting! Now help me get this damned thing off!"

Caroline sighed as she rose from her chair and gripped the mask by its ears. Three good tugs later a disheveled Professor Atwater stood before her, rain dripping from his clothes and his bushy white hair standing on end.

"Why in the world were you wearing that thing?" Caroline pulled another chair over to the table and motioned Carl to sit. "You looked ridiculous."

"I lost my hat in the wind," Carl grumbled. "I didn't want my head to get soaked, so I put on the Halloween mask I bought to scare the kids with." Halfway out of his jacket, he stopped to eyeball the nine women huddled around the table. They were staring at him as if he'd gone completely mad. "Hey! I'm not the only crazy one around here," he bellowed, gesturing at the outfits they were wearing. "Take a look at yourselves in the mirror. At least I had a good reason to look foolish."

"Now, Carl, simmer down. You're going to send your blood pressure soaring through the roof."

Atwater turned on Caroline like a sheepdog on a wolf.

"My blood pressure would be fine if I didn't have to worry about you all the time! Where have you been, Cari? And why haven't you answered my calls?"

"Your calls? You've been phoning me?" Caroline suddenly felt like Alice in Wonderland, confused and tongue-tied.

"For hours," raged the professor. He ran a wet hand through his mussed hair. "Didn't you have the damned thing turned on?"

"There's no need to swear," Bertha huffed as she hauled herself to her feet. "We're all upset enough as it is with this storm. We don't need you hollering at us." She pointed to the empty chair next to Caroline's. "Now sit yourself down and behave. I'll go get us some coffee and then we can continue with our reports."

Carl shot a quizzical look at Caroline. "Reports?"

"We've been discussing the murder and what's being said in town. Agatha was telling us what she'd heard about Sue and Tom Walker," said Caroline.

"Before we were so rudely interrupted," added Eleanor, looking rather pointedly at the professor.

Carl's eyes narrowed, but he settled for a snort rather than a rebuke. He tossed his werewolf mask and wet jacket on a nearby table and took a seat next to Caroline.

"Check your cell phone," he growled.

Caroline rolled her eyes, but did as he asked. Sure enough, the phone was turned off.

"I'm sorry, Carl. I must have hit the off button when I put the phone in my pocket. Why were you trying to contact me?"

"You called me earlier and asked me to talk to some of the other football players. Well, I did. I wanted to tell you about it." Carl glanced over at Maddy Moeller. "Your husband had already quizzed most of them."

Maddy had been suppressing a fit of giggles ever since Carl walked through the door. She now found it impossible to meet his eyes.

"If you'll excuse me," she said, covering her amusement with a fake cough and a hand over her mouth, "I think I need a glass of water."

The pert little redhead scrambled from her chair and made a beeline for the kitchen. She nearly crashed into Bertha as the baker's wife came through the swinging door carrying a pot of coffee in one hand and a plate of cookies in the other.

"That woman's nuts," Carl muttered with a shake of his head.

Caroline nudged him in the ribs. "Hush up and behave."

Bertha did the honors with the coffeepot after passing the cookies to Agatha. Her duties over, she signaled the group for silence.

"I think we've heard all we need to about Sue Walker. Eleanor, do you have anything of interest to add to Agatha's statement?"

"I do have one bit of information," said Eleanor. She turned her head slightly to glare at Agatha who was slurping her coffee with something akin to religious fervor. "I only hope you can hear me above all this noise."

Bertha showered Mrs. Hagendorf with one of her rare frowns. "Agatha, dear. We could do without the background music."

"Hmm?" Agatha surfaced from her coffee cup long enough to glance blankly around the room. "I'm not sure they have a radio here, Bertha, but if you want me to ask them for music…"

"Oh, forget it!" Eleanor growled. Turning her back on her former comrade, she drew in a deep breath and silently composed her horse-like face into less of a scowl.

"I can tell you one thing for sure," she said with a meaningful dip of her head. "Brighty Pfister thinks mighty highly of Otto's two nieces. It seems those Iowa girls have been through a lot in the last few years, but they keeping plugging along."

"You're talking about the Moore sisters," said Caroline.

"Well, of course," said Eleanor, a hint of impatience in her voice. "Who else would I be talking about? Otto doesn't have any other nieces in Iowa."

Carl nudged Caroline's ankle with his foot and gave her a "don't-you-dare" look. She covered her amusement with a pathetic grimace.

"I'm so sorry. I guess I wasn't paying attention."

Eleanor looked down her nose at Caroline. "Pull yourself together, Mrs. Rhodes. This is serious business." Turning to Bertha, she continued her report. "First it was their father's death and all that debt on the land. Then Allison had a failed romance with a jock she met in college. It almost killed her when he broke off their engagement."

"That's the problem with young people today," piped up Agatha. "They can't make commitments. Now you take my nephew…"

"But he couldn't stand life on the farm," said Eleanor hurriedly, her voice raised to drown out Agatha. "So he up and left town. Allison saw her duty to her sister and stayed put in Iowa. Donna's the stronger of the two, the real brains behind the operation. Brighty says she's ready to go to court if Hurst refuses to honor their contract."

This was old news to Caroline who'd heard the same thing from Donna herself. It seemed like the only ones who'd profit from the current mess were the lawyers.

"I don't think we can consider the Moore sisters as suspects," she said. "But I'd like to know more about that foreman of theirs, Ben Halloway."

"Annie told me that Jake's running a background check on him," said Maddy, returning to the table red-faced but in better control of herself. Her lips twitched when she caught sight of the professor, and she quickly averted her eyes, concentrating instead on Caroline. "It's standard police procedure to investigate whoever finds the body."

"Makes sense," said Carl. "You only have Ben's word for it that he wasn't the one who killed Golden."

Bertha gave Eleanor a sharp look. "You think Brighty knows anything about this Halloway person?"

"She didn't mention his name, but that won't prevent me from asking. I'll call her after we're done here."

"Good." Bertha turned to Emily O'Hara and Sarah Sonnenschein. "What about you two? Did you hear anything useful over at the hardware store?"

"Not much," said Emily disgustedly. "The crowd over at Kelly's treated us like we were spies. They were pretty closemouthed about the murder."

"I think the men were making plans for a rally at the university," said Sarah. Then she added, "At least, that's what it sounded like."

"A rally?" Carl scratched his head. "But it's Halloween!"

"So we noticed," murmured Eleanor innocently.

Carl shot her a look that said, watch it, lady!

"It's hard to believe they'd be picketing again so soon after the murder," said Caroline. "You'd think Trace's death would have sobered them up some."

"From the way they were talking, it's only strengthened their resolve. It's like they owe it to him to continue the fight."

"Emily's right," said Sarah. The retired librarian tugged nervously at the plastic lei wound around her neck. "They were using duct tape to form the number thirty-two on the backs of their jackets. One of the men said that was Trace Golden's uniform number."

"And that's not all," said Emily. "While we were pok-

ing around the aisles pretending we were shopping, Bill
Morgan arrived with a box full of football helmets. Young
Peter Kelly came out of the back room with a half dozen
cans of spray paint, and then all the men trooped outside."

"They painted the helmets to match the ones worn by
the Bruins," said Sarah in her whispery voice. She glanced
over at Bertha. "Your husband got spray paint all over his
apron."

Bertha's eyebrows flew up in horror. "John was there?
My John?"

"None other," said Emily with a wicked little smile. "It
looks like you've lost control of him, Bertha."

Bertha lifted her double chins and looked down her
nose at Emily. "I do not control my husband," she fumed.
"We don't always agree on things, but I've never told him
what he could or couldn't do."

This lie brought a chorus of snickers from the other
women at the table that was quickly squelched by Madeleine Moeller.

"I suggest we stick to the matter at hand, that being
Martin's possible incarceration for the murder of Trace
Golden. If we want to help Caroline, and her son, we need
to come up with more than rumors and innuendo."

Marie Moser raised her hand.

"I think my sister and I may have something more sub-
stantial to report."

"That's right," chimed in Myrtle. "Half the town was
here for lunch today. We talked to a lot of people, and they
were all willing to discuss the murder."

"Go on," commanded Bertha, cutting in before Maddy
could speak. As unofficial chairman of the meeting, she
was not about to relinquish her role to the police chief's
wife.

"First of all," said Marie, "there wasn't a lot of grief

over Trace's death. People were a little stunned by the idea of another murder here in Rhineburg, but they're getting used to such things since Caroline arrived in town." Marie dipped her eyes in Caroline's direction. "Sorry about that, dear, but it does seem like you attract trouble."

"No offense taken," said Caroline with a sigh.

"Anyway, as I was saying, Trace's death was a hot topic of conversation here at the Sugar Bowl. It seems that while the men admired him as a football player, not one of them was eager to have his daughter date the boy."

"Golden had a bad reputation with women," said Myrtle. "Love 'em and leave 'em, that was his motto."

"Or love 'em and leave 'em with a baby," retorted Marie. "There's more than one girl in these parts who wishes she'd never met Trace Golden."

Now this was more like it, thought Caroline. "Do you know of anyone recently pregnant whose father might have wanted to strangle Trace?"

The two sisters exchanged glances.

"We sure do," Myrtle piped up, speaking for them both. "The Walker's daughter gave birth last month. Jennifer and her baby are living with Sue and Tom now."

"That's right," said Carl, snapping his fingers. "I remember Shiloh telling me he hired Jennie to work at the Blue Cat Lounge. She was our waitress Sunday night."

The night of the fight between the football players and the other students from Bruck. The fight that Ben Halloway might have taken part in.

"Was Jennie hurt in that melee?" asked Caroline.

"Don't know for sure," said Carl. "Shiloh said a couple of the waitstaff got roughed up trying to stop the fight, but I assumed they were all men. I can ask him about Jennie."

"Do that, Carl. I don't recall seeing a chart with her

name on it, but it was so busy in the ER that evening that I might have missed it."

"So," said Maddy, beginning to wrap up on what they'd heard so far, "Tom Walker might be the man we're looking for. First Jennie gets pregnant by Trace, then Trace tells Sue about Tom's affair. Seems to me that would give Tom a mighty good motive for murder."

"And Tom went missing last night after Sue bopped him on the head with her sign board."

"Right, Cari. He didn't go home, and he wasn't with his lover. So where was he?"

Maddy looked at the others at the table like she expected an answer to her question.

"Tom's as possessive of his daughter as he is of his wife," said Bertha. "He regards them both as his property. If Jennie got hurt during the fight at the Blue Cat, Tom would have taken it personally."

"You mean it might have given him another reason to hate Trace."

Bertha shrugged. "I don't imagine he was real happy when his daughter came home pregnant. It's amazing to me that he didn't throw her out on her ear."

"And now he's gone missing," said Caroline. She turned to Carl. "You have to talk to Jake, get him looking for Tom. He's our best suspect so far. Outside of Martin, that is."

Carl reached out and patted Caroline's hand. "Don't sound so glum, Cari. We'll figure this one out."

Caroline blew out a long breath. She wanted to agree with the professor, but something told her they were still a long way from the truth.

TWENTY-NINE

"AT LEAST IT'S stopped raining."

Maddy Moeller had accompanied Caroline and Carl to the police station where the professor was now deep in conversation with Jake. Waiting outside with Caroline, the chief's wife scanned the heavens for signs of another storm.

"I always feel sorry for the kids when it rains on Halloween."

Caroline checked her watch. "They should be getting out of school right about now. In another half hour, a hoard of trick-or-treaters will be hitting the streets."

"The rodeo parade is scheduled for five o'clock. Do you think Donna will go on with it?"

"Knowing her, I'd say yes."

"I heard that all of the animals but the bulls are quartered at the Pfister farm. Otto and Brighty are playing host to some of the contestants as well."

"Otto runs a farm as well as the feed store?"

"He's got three sons. One of them works in the store with Otto while the other two manage the farm. I want to be here for the parade. It's suppose to wind around the square before heading to the university."

"Donna's looking for trouble if she thinks she'll be gladly received at Bruck."

"You never know," said Maddy. "A lot of the female students have gone over to her side. She might get a rousing welcome from them."

"The Archangels must be tearing out their hair by now."

"They'll probably have every man on the force out on patrol tonight. Jake's doing that here in town."

Caroline glanced at her friend. "Jake won't be happy when he finds out you've been snooping around on this case."

"I'd be snooping even if you hadn't asked for my help, Cari. You came through for me when Emma Reiser died and that awful FBI agent nearly cost Jake his job. Now it's my turn to help you. And I don't care what my husband thinks about it."

"I don't want to cause trouble between the two of you."

Maddy pooh-poohed that notion quickly enough.

"Jake and I have been through a lot together. It would take more than Trace Golden getting murdered to tear us apart. Now tell me, what did you think of Alexsa's little time bomb?"

"You mean what she said about Trace's father and the university? Well, I wasn't surprised that she knew about it. After all, she is a trustee. What startled me was the amount of information she was willing to disclose. Alexsa guards her knowledge like the Treasury Department guards the U.S. Mint."

"Maybe better," Maddy chuckled. "But she wasn't being very secretive today. I got the feeling she wanted the news to leak."

"You may be right. I don't think Alexsa and President Hurst are always on the same page. Tell me again what she said about Golden calling in the bank loan on the stadium. I want to make sure I've got all the facts right."

Maddy pulled a tiny notebook out her pocket and flipped through the pages.

"I wrote it all down so I wouldn't forget anything important. Let's see now. Alexsa began by telling us how sorry

she was to hear of Martin's arrest. I assured her he was
only called in for questioning and would be released in no
time flat. Of course she didn't believe me. 'You wouldn't
be here if Caroline hadn't sent you,' she said. 'And Caroline wouldn't send you unless Martin needed help.'"

"You'll never pull the wool over Alexsa's eyes," said
Caroline. "She's too sharp to believe in fairy tales."

"Well, she certainly didn't believe we were there to
visit. And like I told you before, she knew we were coming. She was ready and waiting when we walked through
the door. That Bricole…"

"Please, Maddy." Caroline cut in before her friend could
go off on her hobbyhorse again. "Time's at a premium,
and right now I need to know more about this deal Hurst
cut with the bank."

Maddy had the good grace to blush.

"Sorry, Cari. Sometimes I get carried away." She
ducked her head and frowned at her notes. "Alexsa told
us that Golden Sr. signed off on a loan to the university
for the construction work on the stadium. He gave the
school some generous terms, apparently on the unspoken condition that Golden Jr. would be named the Bruins' number one receiver. He also insisted on choosing
the team's coach."

"And Hurst agreed to that?"

"Like I said, the terms of the loan were generous. Hurst
doesn't know anything about football, but Golden Sr. does.
Hurst was more than willing to let the banker strut his
stuff."

"So it's true what I heard. Mr. Golden was the one who
brought Wade Wilkins to Rhineburg."

"Alexsa said Wilkins coached high school football before he came here. Golden met him when the Rhineburg
Maniacs played Wilkins's team in the state tournament.

I guess Wilkins saw the move to Bruck as a step up the ladder. He had no problem with playing Trace in a top position."

"Carl said Trace was a popular player back in high school, but the Division One colleges bypassed him due to his off-the-field antics."

"About the only thing the kid was good at was football. Jake was on his case all the time, either for speeding or drinking. And Trace wasn't what you'd call a hard worker in school. It's a miracle he even graduated what with all the D's he got."

"Daddy's influence again?"

"Of course. Golden's bank holds the mortgage on practically every house in town. It wouldn't be wise for a teacher to flunk his only son."

Caroline rolled her eyes. "So Golden Sr. foisted Trace off on Bruck in exchange for the construction loan."

"And when it looked like the rodeo was going to disrupt the Homecoming game, he called in his markers. Hurst owed him big time, and Golden let him know it. He brought the loan paperwork to the Board meeting on Sunday, and guess what? There was a bit of legalese tacked on at the end that would have allowed Golden to cancel the loan at his discretion. God only knows how it got past the university lawyers, but it did. Hurst was as surprised as everyone else, even though he supposedly read the agreement before signing it."

"So Golden had Hurst and the Board over a barrel."

"You could say that. Hurst capitulated pretty quickly, but then Moore dragged her lawyer into the mess. A lawsuit, even if won, would have cost the university big money. More importantly, a judge could have signed an injunction stopping the Homecoming game until the matter was settled."

"Golden would have been furious if Trace lost his opportunity to show off in front of the alumni. Hurst would have felt the same way if his potential donors arrived in town only to find that the game was canceled."

"Donna Moore sure has stirred up a hornet's nest."

"None of this is Donna's fault," Caroline said brusquely. "Hurst should have known better when he told her she could use the stadium."

"Alexsa would agree with you about that. She was highly critical of Garrison Hurst and his role in this fiasco. Most of all, though, she was angry that Golden has tried to blackmail the Board."

"Did she tell you anything about Golden's private life? Did he have any enemies among his clients at the bank?"

Maddy shook her head. "Alexsa doesn't deal in rumors. Oh, she listens to them, no doubt about it. But whatever she tells you is backed by fact. She doesn't move in the same circles as the Golden family, so what she knows about is based purely on local gossip. She did hint at a problem with one of the bank's clients, though. She kind of let it out accidentally."

"I've never known Alexsa to do anything accidentally," Caroline remarked. "She's always careful to be one step ahead of the game."

"I think she dropped the ball this time," said Maddy. "It was after she'd told us about the wording of the loan. I said something about how Amos Dalton would love to get his hands on that story. Alexsa shook her head and stared at me with that pitiful little look she reserves for lesser mortals. Of course I immediately knew I'd said something stupid."

"Something about Amos? Or about letting out the story?"

"Definitely Amos. Alexsa said, 'Mr. Dalton wouldn't

dare print a word of what I've told you. You should know he's owned by the bank.'"

"Owned by the bank? What does that mean?"

Maddy shrugged. "You've got me. I tried to question Alexsa about it, but she clamped her mouth shut and wouldn't say another word on the subject. Bertha and I left the house shortly after that."

"Another in a growing list of mysteries." Caroline sighed dispiritedly. "Every time I think we're getting somewhere, another question mark pops up. Amos gave me a file on Trace when I visited him at the *Rhineburg Rag* today. Now I have to wonder if that file's complete. If Amos is in debt to Golden Sr., he may have stripped it of anything useful."

"Nancy Kuhnkey could help us here. She'd know how to find title and mortgage info on the *Rag*. Those records should tell us if Dalton's the legal owner and how much he owes to the bank."

"Make a note of that, Watson," said Caroline, pointing to Maddy's notebook. She smiled ruefully at her friend. "There have been times today when my emotions have completely overwhelmed my common sense. Thankfully, I have you and Carl to keep me on track."

Maddy put an arm around Caroline's shoulders and hugged her.

"You're frightened for your son, and what mother wouldn't be. Martin's a murder suspect. It's only natural that you're going to have moments when everything looks its blackest."

"But I have to be the strong one here. Martin can't help himself, and Nikki's in no condition to do anything but worry."

"So Superwoman rises from the grave."

The two women turned to see Professor Atwater standing in the doorway of the police station. He was looking straight at Caroline and shaking his head.

"I thought we killed her off last winter. Do we have to stab her through the heart with a wooden stake to keep her dead?"

"You do that to a vampire, Carl, not Superwoman." Caroline held up both hands to ward off further criticism. "Okay. I get the message. I have to remember that I can't solve all my children's problems."

"Right," said Carl as he joined Caroline and Maddy on the sidewalk. "You help where you can, and you let your friends help, too."

"Speaking of help," interrupted Maddy, "did Jake hear you out about Tom Walker?"

"Yes, he did. And he told me a few things you women-folk weren't able to find out. About Tom, that is."

"What? Come on, Carl. Out with it!"

"Not so fast, Cari. My stomach thinks my throat's been cut. I haven't eaten since lunch and I'm starved."

"You've got to be joking," fumed Caroline. "You're going to put food before…"

"Okay, kids. Let's not fight." Maddy linked one arm around Carl's elbow and the other around Caroline's. "There's only one solution to this problem. Sugar Bowl Café, here we come!"

THIRTY

"TOM WALKER'S MISSING."

Carl made this pronouncement between mouthfuls of cold chicken salad on rye. Thanks to the electric company, the power was back on in the Sugar Bowl and the staff was hard at work preparing for the dinnertime crowd. No one paid much attention to the three friends talking quietly in a corner booth.

"We knew that already," said Maddy. "Sue said he didn't come home last night."

"I don't mean missing from home," said Carl. "I mean missing like in vanished, disappeared, skedaddled."

Caroline frowned. "Are the police looking for him?"

"Oh, yeah. Annie Holtzbrinck put a bug in Jake's ear about Tom and that woman down at the trailer camp. She also told him about Trace Golden's conversation with Sue. Jake's thinking twice about who his main suspect should be."

"So Annie got to my husband before us. I should have known," said Maddy with a sigh.

"Jake sent one of his men out to the Walker place, but Tom wasn't there. He wasn't at work, either. Now the entire force is out searching for him. It seems no one's seen hide nor hair of the man since the demonstration—or should I call it the battle of the sexes—outside Bruck Hall."

"Maybe Tom did kill Trace," said Maddy. "Maybe it happened by accident and then he panicked and left town."

"And maybe it was no accident at all." Carl paused to

take a swallow of beer. "Walker had a reason to hate Trace. Add motive to opportunity and you come up with a pretty incriminating picture."

"Hold on a minute," said Caroline. "Trace was an athlete, used to lifting weights. From what I've heard, the only thing Tom Walker ever lifted was a glass of beer."

"You're saying Walker isn't strong enough to kill someone as young and fit as Trace Golden."

"Well, is he, Carl? The Tom Walker I saw last night was all beer belly. I don't believe he'd have lasted five minutes in a fight with a kid like Trace."

"It's true Tom isn't in the best shape," said Carl. "But he's been cutting stone down at the quarry all his working life. He's tougher than you think. And he was drinking last night. From what I hear, he can be one mean son of a gun when he's under the influence of alcohol."

"And if he didn't do it, why did he disappear?" asked Maddy.

"It could be Tom saw something he shouldn't have seen," said Caroline. "Maybe he witnessed the murder, and now he's running scared."

"You think he's gone into hiding," said Carl.

Caroline shrugged. "It's a possibility, especially if the murderer knows Tom saw him. On the other hand, his vanishing act may have nothing whatsoever to do with Golden's death. Maybe he simply walked out on Sue. She could be shielding her pride by saying she's the one who dumped him."

"This case is getting way too complicated," Maddy said with a sigh. She glanced at her watch. "The rodeo parade will start in another hour. Are you going to stay in town to watch it, Cari?"

"I don't know. I want to check in with Martin and Nikki,

then talk to Nancy Kuhnkey again. Carl, don't forget to call Shiloh and ask him about Jennifer Walker."

"Perhaps I should pay Jennie a visit." Lost in thought, Carl stroked his beard. "I doubt she was Trace Golden's biggest fan. After all, he got her pregnant and then dumped her. Maybe she knows who his enemies were."

"Why don't I go along with you," said Maddy. "Being a woman, and a new mother, Jennie may feel more comfortable talking to me rather than you."

"That's fine with me. If we need an excuse to get inside the house, I'll say I was worried about Jennie after the fight at the Blue Cat Lounge. Once we're past the door, I'll leave the girl to you while I tackle Sue. It could be that woman knows more about Tom's whereabouts than she's saying."

Carl paid for his meal, then he and Maddy headed off for the Walker house in Maddy's van. Caroline watched them pull away from the curb before walking dejectedly toward the post office.

What Maddy had said was true. This case was altogether too complicated. Jake was concentrating on Martin as the murderer, but Tom Walker could have been the one who killed Trace. As for Al Sperling, he wasn't out of the running either. Al was definitely hiding something. Until she learned what it was, Caroline refused to discount him as a suspect.

Then there was the matter of Wade Wilkins and the NCAA paperwork. Was Trace lying about the papers, or was Wilkins also hiding something? If Martin had been ineligible to play, and Wilkins knew it, it could mean the end of the coach's career at Bruck. Was that motive enough for murder?

No, thought Caroline. Trace needed Wilkins more than the coach needed Trace. Golden wanted recognition on the field in order to move up the ladder to a Division I school.

For that to happen, he'd have to play football on a regular basis. That meant staying in Wilkins's good graces. Trace wouldn't dare blackmail his coach over something as unimportant to his own career as Martin's eligibility.

Caroline's spirits needed a boost before she faced Martin and Nikki. She decided to call Eleanor Naumann. Maybe by now her friend had learned something about Donna Moore's right hand man.

"Ben Halloway's made quite an impression on the Pfisters," said Eleanor when she answered her cell phone. "Brighty says he's a real gentleman, and a hard worker, to boot."

"I take it there's nothing sinister about the man."

"Sorry, Cari, but according to Brighty, he's as straight as an arrow."

"What about his past? How long has he been with the Moore sisters?"

"Brighty said he was a rodeo clown who met the Moores while working the circuit. They offered him a permanent job on their ranch after Allison's fiancé walked out. Remember how I told you she fell for some boy she met in college? Well, apparently he went to work for the Moores after graduation doing detail jobs for the rodeo. Things didn't work out between him and Allison, and he up and left."

Caroline had little interest in Allison Moore's love life, but she tried not to show her impatience.

"I recall you telling us that earlier today. Getting back to Halloway, did Brighty say if he ever mentioned Trace Golden? Maybe talk about the fight at the Blue Cat Lounge?"

"Brighty hasn't seen Ben since yesterday morning, but she said he didn't mention anything specific about Trace at breakfast. Donna told them about the fight and how Ben fell over the fence and hurt his ribs. Donna wanted him to stay at Brighty's and rest up, but Ben insisted he had to check on the arrangements for the stock. Apparently he was gone all day. Then last night he and Donna drove out to escort Allison and the trucks into town. Guess they were a little worried about what kind of reception they'd get at the university."

"I thought Ben was living in a trailer next to the bullpens."

"He is now. He and Donna were staying at Brighty's place, but when Allison arrived yesterday, she took his room. Ben drove his trailer over to Bruck and parked it where he could keep an eye on the stock."

"And you're sure Ben's never been in any kind of trouble before."

"Not that Brighty knows of. She says Donna thinks highly of Ben. She treats him like family." Eleanor's voice went dreamy. "Apparently he's keen on marrying Allison, which is maybe why he quit rodeo and took the job at the ranch."

Caroline cut in before Miss Naumann could expound further on her romantic notions.

"Thanks for calling Brighty, Eleanor. I appreciate everything you're doing to help Martin."

"Don't mention it, Cari. See you at the rally tonight."

She hung up before Caroline could protest. In Rhineburg, beer accompanied almost every male activity. This "rally" that John Meyer and the others had cooked up could turn nasty if, like on Monday, the men relied on alcohol to spike their fervor.

Caroline decided there was only one way to prevent further trouble on campus. Shaking her head in disgust, she turned on her heel and walked back to the police station.

THIRTY-ONE

I⊤ TOOK LESS than five minutes for Caroline to explain the situation to Jake and for the chief to spring into action. He was understandably furious at the news, the Rhineburg police force being too understaffed to handle more than one major incident at a time. He immediately radioed the nearest car in the area. In less than dulcet tones, he told his senior officer to doubletime it over to Kelly's Hardware and tell those fools to cool it. He then called Michael Bruck at the university security office. From the sound of the conversation, Caroline could tell that Michael shared Jake's feelings. She scooted out of the station while the phone lines were still sizzling and before Jake could question her as to the source of her information.

Neither wind nor rain could keep the trick-or-treaters from their appointed rounds. They were out in force when Caroline left the police station, their mission to clean out the stores along Wilhelm Road. Picking her way through a swarm of witches, ghouls, and assorted hobgoblins, she collided with two miniature Wookies and an even shorter version of Darth Vader in the doorway of the post office. She stepped aside, bowing to the fact that Star Wars lived on in the heartland of America.

"Kind of cute, aren't they?"

Caroline turned to see Nancy Kuhnkey emerging from the post office.

"Cute, but formidable. One swing of those candy sacks and you're a goner."

"That's why I only hand out popcorn balls," said the lawyer. "They weigh less as lethal weapons." She thumbed over her shoulder. "Wouldn't bother going in there, if I were you. Our young lovebirds are in the process of making up after a heated discussion on the issue of trust in a marriage."

"I take it Nikki wasn't pleased that Martin kept the news of his ineligibility from her."

"That's putting it mildly. But Martin made all the right noises, and Nikki calmed down after awhile."

"That's good. At least everything's out in the open now."

"So tell me," said Kuhnkey as she steered Caroline away from the post office and toward her parked car. "Did your little band of merrymakers come up with anything I can use for Martin's defense?"

"You know about Bertha and the other ladies?"

"Annie Holtzbrinck told me what was going on. Agatha and her nutty boarders seem unlikely candidates to play detective. But then, you never know. Everyone thinks they're a harmless bunch of screwballs. Why not satisfy their curiosity?"

"I wouldn't call them screwballs," protested Caroline. "They're a little unique…"

"Trust me," said Kuhnkey with a hearty laugh. "I've known these women longer than you have. They're definitely surfing in a flat sea." She glanced at her watch. "Almost five o'clock. That damned parade will be starting soon. If I don't get my car out of here now, I never will."

"Why don't I follow you to your office and we can talk there."

"I work out of my home. If you don't mind a few dozen cats and the smell of cigarette smoke, you're welcome to come."

"I can manage with both. Lead on, MacDuff."

Caroline traipsed the half block to her own vehicle and pulled away from the curb only seconds after Kuhnkey. The lawyer was driving an ancient Cadillac, the kind with tail fins and a bumper that could definitely spell trouble for a tailgater. Caroline had no trouble following her as she coasted north on Wilhelm at a sedate twenty-five miles per hour.

Kuhnkey's home stood on a half acre of land a mile or so outside of town in a wooded area near the river. A two-story frame building sporting a wrap-around porch, the house was painted pale blue with white trim around its arched windows and glass-paneled front door. The door itself was a deeper blue, as was the porch and the sloping shingle roof that extended several inches beyond the railing.

Flower gardens now covered in mulch bordered the house and the long gravel driveway that ran from the street to the back of the property. At the end of the drive stood a dilapidated coach house that Kuhnkey had converted to a garage. The wide wooden doors were flung open and sagged precariously on their hinges. Kuhnkey gave the left door a glancing blow with her fender as she nosed the old Caddy into the darkened interior. The entire structure shuddered, and it was a wonder it didn't collapse on the car.

Caroline parked her Jeep closer to the house and waited for the lawyer to emerge from the garage. When she did, she was carrying a battered briefcase in one hand and a bag of groceries in the other.

"Can I help you with that?"

Caroline reached for the bag, but Kuhnkey shook her head. She strode toward the back of the house, leaving Caroline in her wake.

"I can manage. Go get the door."

Caroline sprinted ahead and climbed the steps to the porch. The back door to the kitchen was unlocked.

"Make yourself at home," said Kuhnkey as she brushed past her guest. She dropped her briefcase on the oak table in the center of the room. Plopping the groceries on the counter next to the sink, she stripped off her coat and began to unload the bag.

"There's beer in the fridge. I think we could both use one after the day we've had."

Caroline was in full agreement with the lawyer. Leaving her jacket draped over a kitchen chair, she popped the caps off two bottles of Sam Adams, handed one to Kuhnkey, then sat down at the table with her own. She took a long pull of the icy cold brew and let it trickle slowly down the back of her throat.

"Tastes good, doesn't it," said Kuhnkey. She held up a package of wieners. "It'll taste even better washing down a couple of chili dogs. Tell me what you and your friends were doing today while I cook up our dinner."

Caroline filled her in on everything that had happened since her early morning visit to the police station. She told her about Sue Walker and her missing husband, Al Sperling's secret problem, and the odd things Alexsa had said about Amos Dalton.

"So Alexsa thinks Amos is owned by Trace's father. Well, it makes sense. Golden's bank lent Amos the money to buy the *Rag*. I don't imagine the paper makes much of a profit, if any."

"But Golden Sr. couldn't pull the plug on Dalton's loan, could he? Amos must have a legally binding agreement with the bank."

Kuhnkey shrugged her shoulders. "Maybe he's behind on his payments. Golden would have phrased the contract to stipulate foreclosure on the property if Amos was late on a regular basis."

"I hadn't thought of that." Caroline leaned forward to take the plate Kuhnkey offered her. The scent of steaming hot dogs smothered in chili reminded her how hungry she was. She dug in eagerly after coating the dogs with a thick layer of ketchup and onions.

"Amos has been very kind to the Golden family in his newspaper," said Kuhnkey as she settled herself across from her guest. "He reported Trace's most recent accident, but he left out all mention of alcohol."

"The way I hear it, Trace was loaded to the gills when he sideswiped Annie Holtzbrinck's car."

"Hank Matthews got him out of that mess with little more than a slap on the wrist from the judge. And that wasn't young Golden's first accident. He was a regular customer at the local body shop."

"His father has a lot of influence in this town."

"You're darned right, he does. He holds the mortgages on most of the homes in this area. That's pretty powerful stuff, when you consider it."

"Maddy said something to the same effect earlier today. We were talking about the construction loan the university received for the stadium. Maddy found out that Golden Sr. used his son as a bargaining chip when brokering the loan. Bruck got the money on the condition that Trace was placed in a starring position on the football team."

"Sounds like something Golden Sr. would do. I'll be frank with you, Mrs. Rhodes."

"Please. Call me Caroline, or Cari."

"All right. And since we're foregoing all formality, you might as well call me Nancy." She took a bite of her hot dog before continuing. "As I was saying, you might as well know that I'm no fan of Trace Golden Sr. or his late son. The father wields much too much power in this town, and the son took advantage of that. Trace Jr. was a sneaky little bastard who belonged in jail instead of in college."

"Don't hold back," murmured Caroline. Kuhnkey eyed her over the top of her glasses, and she hurried to amend her statement. "I only said that because I've heard the same sentiment—phrased in gentler terms—from other people today. Personally, I didn't know much about the boy before Saturday."

"You're lucky then." Kuhnkey polished off her beer and rose to get another from the fridge. Without asking, she handed a second Sam Adams to Caroline. "I'm sure you noticed the unfortunate condition of my garage," she said, thumbing over her shoulder at the window that looked out onto the big backyard.

"It does appear to be a bit on the wobbly side."

"Wobbly, my eye. The whole darned thing is ready to fall down." Kuhnkey sank into her chair and stared at Caroline. "My grandfather built that coach house seventy-five years ago. He used strong timbers to support the roof and only the best wood for the walls. I had it converted to a garage when I inherited this place."

"It's stood for a long time then."

"And it would have stood for many a year to come if I hadn't been in Chicago two years ago today."

Caroline thought she knew where this was heading. "Tell me what happened."

"I was away visiting a friend when Trace and his hooligan friends arrived here that Halloween night. Apparently they were sore that they'd traveled this far out of town only to come up empty handed in the treats department. They decided to pay me back with a trick."

"They rammed your garage with their car."

Kuhnkey's eyebrows rose. "Now I know why Carl Atwater thinks so highly of you. You've got a brain in that head of yours, don't you?"

"It wasn't so hard to figure out," said Caroline with a smile. "You said that Trace treated the body shop like a home away from home. I take it he was pretty wild with the car Daddy gave him."

"Wild isn't the word. And it wasn't a car, it was a pickup truck. Trace Golden was a downright destructive young man. The insurance adjuster said to do that kind of damage, Trace must have rammed the side supports five or six times. The timbers cracked and the walls buckled in under the pressure."

"But you haven't torn the garage down."

"I haven't, and I won't. At least, I won't until Trace's father pays for the damages."

"Trace denied he was at fault."

"He could hardly deny it when he left one of his license plates imbedded in the garage wall. It must have caught in the wood during one of the hits. Of course, Golden Sr. said the garage was so old, it needed ripping down. He acted like young Trace had done me a favor."

"And he refused to pay for repairs."

"I wanted a whole new garage. Mr. Banker said that wasn't necessary. We've been fighting it out in court ever since."

"The more I hear about Trace, the more I dislike him."

"It's a sad thing to say, but Rhineburg is better off without the boy."

"From what I hear, there are quite a few fathers in town who would agree with you. Apparently Trace was quite the ladies' man."

"He was named in two paternity suits in the past three years. Both times his father settled the matter out of court."

"Was one of those suits instituted by the Walker family?"

"The Walkers?" Kuhnkey appeared momentarily flustered. "Why would you ask that?"

"I've been told that Trace was the father of Jennie Walker's baby. If that's true and Tom knew about it, he would have had a perfect motive for murder."

Kuhnkey stood up and started clearing the table.

"You're barking up the wrong tree," she said as she placed the plates in the sink. "Tom pushed his wife around all their married life, but he didn't have the guts to take on another man."

"Carl said Tom could be pretty mean when he was drinking."

"There are various kinds of meanness. Tom specialized in only one kind."

Caroline was about to ask what Kuhnkey meant by that when her cell phone rang. She grabbed it from her jacket pocket and flipped open the cover.

"Hello?"

"Where are you, Cari?"

Carl's voice sounded tinny, but his agitation came through loud and clear.

"I'm at Nancy Kuhnkey's house," said Caroline. "What's wrong, Carl?"

"All hell's broken loose at the university. Donna Moore led her rodeo parade through town as promised, but then they headed for Bruck. The Bruins and their supporters were out in force to meet them. Now the women have arrived, and...ouch! Watch who you're hitting, young lady!"

"Carl! Are you all right?"

"Battered, but still alive," grumbled the professor. "You'd better get over here, Cari."

"Why me? There's nothing I can do to stop the women from demonstrating."

"It's not the women I'm worried about, it's Martin."

"Martin?" Alarm bells went off in Caroline's brain. "But he's home with Nikki. At least, they should be home by now. The post office closed at five, and the two of them..."

"Cari, listen to me. Martin's not at the post office and he's not at home. More importantly, he's not with his wife."

Caroline waited in silence for the other shoe to drop.

"He was standing on the sidewalk outside his apartment watching the rodeo parade with Nikki. All of a sudden, he slipped away. He simply dropped out of sight, Cari. Right now, nobody knows where he is." Carl's voice grew quieter. "Or what he's up to."

THIRTY-TWO

Nancy Kuhnkey elected to remain at home rather than accompany Caroline to the university.

"I have a friend in Chicago who's a private investigator. He mainly does divorce work, but he knows how to access various kinds of electronic records. I'm going to ask him to look into Martin's eligibility status."

"Couldn't Martin call the NCAA office tomorrow and get that information?"

"He could, but it might alert Wade Wilkins to the fact that we're checking up on him. There's something fishy about that man's story, and I aim to find out what it is."

Caroline couldn't see how investigating Martin's eligibility to play football was going to help him. It didn't matter if Trace had been lying about those NCAA papers or telling the truth. The fact remained that Martin believed what he'd been told. A smart prosecutor would claim her son had been stunned by the information, then lost his temper and lashed out at Trace, killing him in the process.

She didn't bother explaining all that to Nancy Kuhnkey. The elderly lawyer was already walking her to the door as if eager to usher her into the darkness outside. It was the second time that day that Caroline had felt unwanted.

"First it was Amos Dalton. Now it's Kuhnkey," muttered Caroline as she walked down the driveway to her car. She got into the Jeep, switched on the ignition and the headlights, and backed down the drive to the main road. Banishing both the lawyer and the newspaperman from her thoughts, she concentrated on getting to Bruck as quickly as possible.

It was half past six, but there were still a few trick-or-treaters out making the rounds on Wilhelm Road and the adjoining streets. Caroline slowed down as she passed through town, then pulled out all the stops when she hit the highway. She made it to the university in less than fifteen minutes.

Circle Road was practically impassable when she arrived at the campus. Students dressed in Halloween garb mobbed the route from Bruck Hall to the gymnasium. Chanting and waving signs, they spilled over onto the sweeping lawns, an undulating mass of humanity that swarmed over the grass like locusts at an autumn harvest.

Mixed in with the students were older alumni and even older residents of the community. Caroline recognized several of the senior citizens, including Bertha Meyer and her sidekick, Eleanor. Carl was nowhere to be seen, nor were Martin and Nikki.

Caroline pulled into the nearest cul-de-sac and parked where the faint glow of a Victorian-style lamppost washed the street of shadows. She trotted back toward the campus, her breath escaping in ragged puffs that hung mistlike in the frosty air. The night had turned cold, but not as cold as the fear that gripped her heart.

From the moment she'd heard Martin was missing, she'd known there was trouble ahead. Call it a premonition, or simply a feeling of dread. Whatever it was, it was real and deep and frightening. She tried to shake it off now as she plunged into the crowd outside Bruck Hall, looking from side to side, searching for a familiar face.

"Caroline! Over here!"

She turned and saw Carl Atwater standing beneath the portico in front of the Hall's massive doors. She pushed her way through the mob, calling out to the professor as she mounted the staircase.

"Did you find Martin?"

"Not yet."

Carl reached down and offered her his hand. She took it, more out of need for human contact than for help, and scrambled up the last step. She stared into the professor's eyes, looking for some sign that all was not as bad as she thought.

"We've searched everywhere," Carl said grimly. "God only knows where he's gone off to."

"Did he take the car?"

"Yes."

"Then he may not be on campus."

"We thought of that, too. Jake has an APB out on him. So far, nobody's sighted him on the road."

Caroline's fear was quickly turning to anger.

"Why the hell would he do this? He knows he was supposed to stay in his apartment. He wasn't to go on campus or anywhere else." She eyed the crowd on the street. "Where's Nikki?"

"She's with Maddy over at my place. Martin took his cell phone with him. She's trying to reach him on it. So far, he's not answering."

"And he didn't tell her where he was going."

"Not a word. Nikki said they were watching the parade when all of a sudden Martin snapped his fingers and said, 'That's it.' She was only half listening to him at the time. Donna and Allison Moore had begun some kind of demonstration in the middle of the street—rope twirling, I think it was. Their act lasted a couple of minutes. When it was over, Nikki turned to say something to Martin. That's when she discovered he was gone."

"This is simply unbelievable. Martin knows better than to up and disappear like this."

"Maddy and I ran into Nikki on our way back from the Walker place. When she told us what happened, my first thought was that Martin had returned to Bruck. The three of us drove over here to search the campus. But with this crowd..." He gestured at the people milling in the street.

"All you could do was try." Caroline could sense Carl's frustration. She reached out and squeezed his arm. "I'm sure Nikki appreciates your help."

"I wish I could have done more. The problem is, it's Halloween. A lot of students are partying in the street. Plus, you've got all these demonstrators."

"And it's a dark night." Caroline pointed to the vast expanse of Bruck Green. "Martin could be standing under any one of those trees, and we'd never see him."

"At least it's brighter here on this side of the road. Michael Bruck insisted we leave the shades pulled up and the lights on in all the classrooms. The extra light will make it easier for his men to keep tabs on the demonstrators."

Caroline let her gaze wander the length of the street. From her perch at the top of the staircase she could see all the way to Hildy Hall. She noted that the Bruins had set up camp in front of the gym.

"Do they have a fire going down there? It looks like something is burning."

"It's been a tradition on Halloween for the students to build a bonfire behind the auditorium. The kids party until midnight. For a grand finale, they gather up all the scarecrows and throw them on the fire."

"That's something I missed last year."

"And you'll miss it again tonight. Michael Bruck won't allow a bonfire anywhere near those bulls. He told the students they could set up gas grills outside the dorms. The Bruins must have set up theirs in front of the gym."

"You don't get exactly the same ambiance from a gas grill as you do from a bonfire," said Caroline. "Still, it's better than nothing for keeping warm."

The professor's cell phone came alive with the most famous bars of Tchaikovsky's 1812 Overture. He pulled the tiny instrument from his pocket, flipped open the cover, and hit the talk key. A second later, he smiled.

"It's Maddy," he said, covering the bottom of the phone with his hand. "They've found Martin. He's on his way home."

Caroline said a silent prayer of thanks, then waited impatiently as Carl yes-ed and no-ed his way through a too-long-for-her-liking conversation. She breathed a sigh of relief when he at last hung up.

"So where was he? And why didn't he answer his phone?"

"He forgot to turn it on," said Carl with a grin. "I guess he takes after his mother."

"Very funny. Now tell me what he was up to tonight."

"He drove to Newberry to use the computer in their library. He said he needed to do some research."

Caroline exploded. "Research? On what? Has that boy completely lost his mind?"

"Now, calm down, Cari. It's not going to help for you to get all stirred up over this."

"I'll get stirred up if I want to," growled Caroline. "Answer my question, Carl. What kind of research was Martin doing?"

"I don't know," the professor said with a shrug. "Maddy told me he called from his car to say he was on the way home and Nikki shouldn't worry about him. I guess Nikki was so relieved to hear his voice that she didn't ask any questions."

"Is Maddy going to drive Nikki back to the apartment?"

"No. Martin's on his way to my place. He'll pick up Nikki there."

"And Maddy?"

"She says she's coming over here. She thinks it would be better if she wasn't around when Martin arrived. Also, she wants to talk to you about Jennie Walker."

"I almost forgot about Jennie and her mother. Did Sue say anything that could lead us to Tom?"

"Not really. Why don't we wait for Maddy to arrive before we discuss the Walkers."

Caroline stuffed her hands in her pockets. "I hope she hurries. I'm getting cold standing here."

"Let's take a walk and go visit the Bruins. We can warm our hands over their grill."

"And maybe pick up some useful gossip on Trace at the same time. I would like to know what the other players think of his murder."

Caroline and Carl descended the steps of Bruck Hall. Keeping to the grass, they edged past the revelers in the street, most of them wearing Halloween costumes of one kind or another. The crowd was largest down by the auditorium where a jerry-rigged sound system blared out rock and roll from the bed of a pick-up truck stationed in the parking lot.

"This is quite a party," said Caroline as she and Carl approached the Bruin's camp. "I wonder how that music's going to affect the bulls."

As if in answer to her question, Donna Moore suddenly appeared at the end of the sidewalk that stretched between the gym and the auditorium. She stood stock still in the shadows of the two buildings, a look of fury on her face as

she stared at the loud speakers in the back of the pick-up.
Ignoring the students dancing to the music in the parking
lot, she sprinted toward the truck and jumped up on the
running board. She leaned over the side and, before anyone could stop her, yanked out the wires connecting the
sound system to its generator. The music stopped with a
suddenness that took even Caroline by surprise.

"Are you people crazy?" yelled Moore. She jumped
down from the truck, waving her arms and shifting her
head from side to side. "Who's in charge here anyway?"

A young man stepped away from his dance partner
and jogged over to the pick-up. He glanced at the wires
lying twisted and torn in the truck bed, then turned angrily to Moore.

"Who the hell do you think you are? That's private
property!"

"And so are my bulls, you idiot! That noise has them all
stirred up. They're about ready to tear down their pens."

"Hold on, everybody!"

Gabriel Bruck pushed his way through the crowd and
walked over to Moore.

"What's going on here?" he demanded in a voice that
carried over the loud grumbling of the students.

"These fools are spooking my stock," said Moore. "Unless you want a stampede on your hands, you'll keep that
damned music turned off."

"Now wait a minute!" stormed the boy. "Who gave her
the right to break up our party!"

Gabe held up both hands for silence.

"Listen to me, everyone! There's been trouble enough
on campus this week. Let's not have more of it. You kids
move that pick-up over to the parking lot by the dorms.
You can play your music, but keep it down."

"Aw, Gabe, you're spoilin' these kids' fun," called an

elderly man sitting on a lawn chair near the gym wall. Dressed in a tattered jersey with the number thirty-two plastered across the front in duct tape and wearing a silver and blue painted football helmet, he waved his cane in a friendly salute to the head of security.

Gabe stared slack-jawed. "Grandpa? Is that you?"

The old man's creased face split into a wide grin. "None other," he chortled, waving his cane more vigorously.

Gabe spun on his heel, his face beet red, and grabbed the walkie-talkie clipped to his belt. Caroline saw him mutter something into it. A moment later a troupe of security officers moved in on the crowd and began moving them off the parking lot.

"Oh, oh," Caroline whispered in Carl's ear. "I think there's going to be trouble."

Gabe had abandoned Donna Moore and was marching toward the Bruin camp, his eyes riveted on his grandfather. A small knot of men standing near the grill roused themselves and moved to block his way.

"He's got a right to be here," insisted one fellow whose football helmet was much too large for his head. Pushing up on the chin guard, the man flipped the helmet back to reveal his identity. It was John Meyer, Bertha's baker husband.

"Get out of my way, John," snarled the overwrought Gabe. "This is between me and my grandfather."

"'Taint so," said a man who Caroline recognized as Pete Kelly of Kelly's Hardware. "We're here to support our team, which we got a full right to do."

"Yeah!" called out another Bruin backer. "You can't push us around like you do those kids."

By now, half the students in the parking lot had escaped Gabe's reinforcements and were pushing forward to watch the action outside the gym. Gabe grabbed his walkie-talkie a second time, but not before one of the townsmen threw a popcorn ball at his chest. This latest indignity caused the security chief to lose his temper completely.

"You men are on private property, and if you don't ske-daddle immediately, I'll have every one of you arrested!"

"We'll be glad to help you do that," came a female voice from the sidelines. Bertha Meyer extricated herself from the crowd and strode over to Gabe.

"Good grief!" said Carl, pulling Caroline behind two Bruins and back against the wall of the gym. "She's got a gun!"

Bertha did have a gun, but it was the plastic kind made in Japan. Tucked in a holster buckled around her ample waist, it provided the perfect accent to her buckskin skirt and fringed jacket. The cowboy hat riding gloriously atop her head was slanted sideways to conceal her brow while exposing a batch of white curls that cuddled the left side of her face. The effect was dramatic, Bertha not only appearing sinister, but sounding that way, too.

"Let me at him," she hissed. She raised her hand and twirled a clothesline lariat above her head.

Gabe jumped between Bertha and John, both hands extended in front of him.

"Stand back, Mrs. Meyer, and drop your weapon!"

"You ought to be ashamed of yourself, young fella," snapped Eleanor Naumann from behind Bertha's back. She pointed a bony finger at John Meyer. "You're aiding and abetting a crazy man!"

"A crazy man, am I?" Meyer pushed Gabe aside and pulled the lariat from Bertha's hands. He waved it in the air at his companions. "Now you see what rodeo does to women! It makes 'em want to hog-tie their menfolk and send 'em off to the slaughterhouse!"

"Down with the rodeo!" shouted Pete Kelly.

"Down with football!" countered Eleanor.

"Oh, dear," said Caroline in dismay. Dueling chants echoed off the walls of the gym as other protesters joined in the argument. The verbal volleys became louder and more demanding, each side championing its cause with evangelistic fervor. Then someone shoved Bertha, and she shoved back. One of the clumsier Bruins tripped over his own feet in his haste to get out of her way. The young man tumbled to the grass, taking a rather comely cheerleader with him. The coed's date for the night treated this faux pas as a personal insult. Unable to get at the fallen boy, he lashed out and whacked the nearest football player he could find on the evident belief that one Bruin was as good as another. This, of course, resulted in himself being whacked, which in turn led to a general flurry of fists among the male portion of the student body present outside the gym.

With the younger members of the crowd engaged in fist-icuffs and the older members still shouting at each other, it occurred to Caroline that this was not the place to be at the moment. She edged backward toward the science building, pulling at Carl's sleeve to force him to follow. The two of them managed to make it halfway there before a merry band of inebriated alumni pushed them back into the thick of the fight.

One of the drunks draped his arm around Caroline's shoulders. His hundred-proof alcohol breath nearly overwhelmed her.

"Wass goin' on, lady? Havin' a party?"

Caroline disentangled herself from the man's grasp.

"It's a local cult meeting," she said with mock solemnity. She thumbed over her shoulder at the crowd. "They like to get in a few rounds of boxing before the midnight sacrifice."

The drunk's eyebrows soared. He swayed to the left, bumped into the professor, then reeled back toward Caroline.

"An' whad dey gonna sassifice, lady?"

"Drunken alumni."

The man reeled backwards against his buddies, his glazed eyes growing wide.

"Don'd soun like fun ta me. Less go, guys."

Carl grinned at Caroline as the drunks staggered off. "They've got the right idea. Let's get out of here while we still can."

This time they hurried, making it all the way to the entrance of the science building before meeting their next obstacle. It was Maddy, and she was plainly eager to see what all the excitement was about down by the gym.

Caroline grabbed her friend's arm. "Forget it, Maddy. We're not going back there."

"But what's happening? Another demonstration?"

"Not like the one that was going on when we arrived earlier this evening," said Carl. He grinned at Caroline. "It got pretty wild when the parade hit campus. The football players were waiting to protest, as were your lady friends."

"Bertha talked a bunch of the female students into marching with them," said Maddy. "Boy! Did that rile up the team!"

"But Pete Kelly and his gang were here, too," said Carl. "It took most of the security officers to keep those two groups apart."

"They must have been going at it when you called me at Nancy Kuhnkey's house. If I remember correctly, I think you got hit by somebody while we were talking on the phone."

Carl grimaced. His hand strayed to the back of his scalp.

"Some girl dressed up like a witch whacked me on the

head with her broom. I've got a nice little bump where the pole made contact with my skull."

"You'll live," said Maddy, impatiently brushing off the professor's injuries. "Now tell me. What's going on by the gym?"

"Donna Moore got into an argument with one of the male students," said Caroline. She recounted the events of the past half hour. "I don't know where Donna went to, but it looks like the others are still arguing."

"They're doing more than arguing," said Carl. He pointed to the flames leaping high above the Bruins' gas grill. "It looks like the Bruins have started burning their scarecrows. There are more fires over by the dorms."

Sure enough, flames could be seen rising from the grills set up outside the two dormitory buildings. The smoke from the fires was blowing directly towards the security office, and from there, in the direction of the gym.

"If those bulls weren't spooked by the noise, they surely will be by the smoke," said Caroline. "I'm beginning to get a little nervous about this."

The three of them watched as the smoke billowed higher into the air. It covered the parking lot by Hildegard Hall, wafting past the far side of the auditorium and slipping down the narrow walkway between Hildy and the gym. In the distance, they could hear the bellowing of the rodeo bulls mixed with the shouts of the crowd.

"I hope Ben Halloway's keeping a close eye on his animals," said Carl nervously. "It would be a catastrophe if they got loose on campus."

Caroline didn't want to even consider that possibility. She gazed back at the area by the gym where the sounds of verbal battle continued. It was difficult to see through the thick gray haze from the fiery grills, but it appeared that the crowd was thinning out and moving toward the dorms. The sound of sirens drifted to her ears, police or fire vehicles speeding south from Rhineburg. She glanced over her shoulder in time to see the flashing lights of a black-and-white as it turned onto Circle Road.

"Gabe must have called in reinforcements."

A stream of police cars sped toward them followed by an ambulance and a pumper truck emblazoned on the side with the logo of the Rhineburg Fire Department. The lead cruiser pulled over, letting the column pass by. The squeal of its brakes echoed off the walls of the science building as the car jerked to a halt at the curb. Caroline wasn't surprised when the window slid down and Jake stuck his head out the opening.

"Come on!" the police chief shouted. "I'm going to need your help!"

The three of them ran toward the cruiser, Carl bringing up the rear due to his less than athletic figure. They climbed into the car, Caroline and Maddy in the backseat and Carl up front. When they were safely belted in, Jake turned to look at them.

"Bertha Meyer and the other ladies have locked themselves in the security building. The menfolk are standing around outside threatening to tear the place down if they don't come out. Meanwhile, we've got two old geezers, supposedly protesters supporting the football team, down on the ground suffering from smoke inhalation. We've also got students fighting all over the place and a bunch of drunken alumni roaming the halls in the women's dorm."

Jake paused as if to make sure his message was sinking in.

"To top it off, it appears that some of the Big Bad Bruins think all their troubles will disappear if Donna Moore's bulls do the same thing. Right now, Ben Halloway is the only one standing between those animals and their freedom."

Caroline looked at Maddy. They both looked at Carl. Not one of them said a word.

"You three started this mess," growled Jake. "And now you're going to help us clean it up."

He threw the car into drive, pressed the gas pedal to the floor, then quickly slammed on the brakes.

"Son of a…!"

"Whoa!" murmured Carl, bracing himself against the dashboard with both hands. "Now that's what I'd call a big one!"

"What's a big one?"

Caroline freed herself from Maddy's arms where she'd landed after the sudden stop. Struggling upright, she leaned forward to peer over the professor's shoulder. The huge head and curling horns visible through the windshield sent her scrambling for her seat belt.

"Hang on, Maddy! I think we're going for a ride."

The words were barely out of her mouth when the thousand-pound bucking bull outlined in the headlights lowered its head and charged. The first blow sent the cruiser rocking backwards toward the curb. The second blow pushed it up on the sidewalk. Apparently not satisfied with its efforts, the bull then hooked its horns under the front fender and gave a mighty heave.

The next thing Caroline saw through the windshield was the pale orb of the harvest moon.

THIRTY-THREE

"I DON'T REMEMBER another Halloween this bad," remarked Carl as he drained a can of beer in the living room of his home two hours later. "Garrison Hurst is going to have a fit when he hears what happened."

"So will the Board of Directors," said Caroline. She closed her eyes and let her head sink back onto the soft pillows bunched at one end of Carl's sofa. Shoes off, she'd kicked back on the couch immediately upon entering the house. Her own beer sat on the floor next to her drooping left hand, the can half empty. "It was a miracle Ben got those bulls back in their corral."

"Halloway knows his business. And the Moore sisters aren't exactly what you'd call slouches when it comes to hard work."

"They're strong women. We're lucky they stayed behind on campus after the parade ended."

"With Ben and Allison on horseback and Donna coordinating the police cars, the operation went more smoothly than I thought it would."

Caroline giggled. "It was kind of fun watching Jake herd cattle with his cruiser. That must be a first for him."

"I wonder what his insurance company will say when he tells them his car was beat up by a bull."

"Seeing as how this is farm country, they'll probably believe him." Caroline turned on her side. "I imagine the damage to the security office will be harder to explain."

"Your lady friends sure picked a fine time to surrender."

"Come on, Carl. Give them a break. They simply got curious when all the men suddenly up and vanished. They didn't know there was a bull standing right outside the building."

"They should have looked out a window before they opened the door."

"In case you forgot, the security office windows are set high up on the walls to discourage break-ins. All they knew was that the men had stopped pounding on the door and hollering at them to come out."

Carl gave in grudgingly. "I suppose it wasn't their fault. Still, that damned bull sure made a mess of the place when he charged into the office."

"Gabe was practically in tears. Michael and Rafe weren't too happy either when they saw all their computers lying shattered on the floor."

"That animal put the Archangels out of business, at least for the time being. It'll take days to repair the damage to the walls and get new equipment set up in there."

"You never did tell me what happened out at the Walker place," said Caroline, changing the subject. "Did Sue say anything that could help us?"

"Not much. I used the pretext of being worried about Jennie after the fight Sunday night to get into the house. Sue seemed to accept that excuse. She let us talk to her daughter, but she stayed in the room the entire time. Then Maddy asked to see the baby. I said I had a little cold and didn't want to infect the child. Jennie took Maddy upstairs while Sue and I stayed behind in the kitchen."

"You're turning into a perfect liar, Carl. Pretty soon even I won't be able to trust you."

"I appreciate your vote of confidence."

"So what happened when you were alone with Sue? Didn't she say anything about Tom?"

"She was pretty glib with her answers when I first asked her where he was. She mentioned kicking him out of the house and how they were getting a divorce. It all seemed rehearsed to me, though, like she'd been practicing her lines all day."

"You have to remember, she regaled half the town with that story at the beauty shop this morning. She was probably sick of repeating it."

"Maybe. But Maddy said Jennie told her the same story almost word for word when they were alone upstairs. I think the two of them put their heads together and made up that tale."

"Then you think Tom's in hiding somewhere and they're protecting him."

"I didn't agree with you when you first mentioned that possibility. Now, though, I think you may be right. I pushed Sue a little harder after listening to her spiel. She wasn't comfortable with my questions, especially when I asked if Tom held a grudge against Trace because of the baby. She definitely paled at the idea that Tom could have killed the boy."

"I don't suppose it's easy to think of your husband as a killer, even if you don't love him any more."

"Jennie seemed equally nervous when Maddy questioned her about Trace. At first she denied he was the father of her child. Then, all of a sudden, she changed her story. She told Maddy that Trace would have married her except his father wouldn't let him. Maddy asked if she'd considered filing a paternity suit, especially since she didn't have much means of support."

Caroline remembered Nancy Kuhnkey's strange reaction when she'd asked if the Walkers were one of the two families who'd brought suit against Trace. Kuhnkey had

seemed astounded by the idea, if not downright uncomfortable with it.

"What did Jennie say?"

"She got pretty flustered, according to Maddy. She said
she couldn't do that. Not 'wouldn't', but 'couldn't' do it."

"You're sure of that."

"Oh, yes. Maddy caught the difference in the wording right away and pressed the girl about it. She said Jennie clammed up and refused to say anything more on the
subject."

"Very strange," said Caroline. She sat up and swung
her feet off the couch. "I'm too tired to discuss this any
further tonight, but I think you and I and Maddy should
talk some more in the morning. Tom Walker's disappear-
ance is simply too much of a coincidence coming as it did
right after Trace's murder."

"I feel the same way," said Carl. "Maybe after a good
night's sleep we'll have the energy to figure out if and how
the two events are linked."

The professor flipped his recliner into a sitting position
and heaved himself out of the chair. He walked Caroline
to the door.

"Are you working tomorrow?"

"In the afternoon," said Caroline. "I'll call you some
time in the morning, after I talk to Martin. I want to know
what kind of research he was doing in Newberry tonight.
That's a thirty mile drive, not something you do on the
spur of the moment."

"It must have been important, Cari, or he wouldn't have
run off like that. Don't be too hard on the boy."

"Don't worry," said Caroline as she walked down the
sidewalk to her car. "I'll leave my rubber hose at home."

Circle Road was deserted, a curfew having been instituted by the Archangels immediately after the melee at

the university. The open road called for speed, but Caroline drove slowly, in no hurry to return to her apartment. Tired as she was, she was too edgy to fall asleep. Rather than toss and turn in bed, she pulled over to the curb and parked the Jeep near the driveway leading to the nursing school dorm.

She got out of the car and stretched her arms in the cool night air. To her right lay St. Anne's with its sprawling lawns and three-story parking lot. To her left were the cul-de-sacs with their rows of faculty bungalows. This latter section claimed her attention, a host of Jack-o-lanterns having joined the Fred Astaire scarecrows dancing across the lawns. The pumpkins varied in size and shape, but each one sported an evil grin as it sat in the glow of a late evening porch light.

The sight of the pumpkins triggered memories for Caroline. She recalled the days when carving Jack-o-lanterns was a major event in her household. A much younger Martin had drawn face after face on paper before choosing the perfect one for his masterpiece. His sister Krista had etched gargoyle grins on her pumpkins and added pointed ears and clawed feet. The baby of the family, Kerry, had opted for a simpler approach. Triangle eyes and toothy smiles characterized her Jack-o-lanterns, the advantage being that she was always done long before the others.

Those days ended when, one by one, the children went off to college. Martin had married soon after graduation. He and Nikki had stayed in Rhineburg, moving into an apartment above Kelly's Hardware Store on Wilhelm Street. Krista lived in the Chicago suburb of Evanston where she taught art at a local high school. Kerry, a theater major, was finishing her education at an Illinois state university.

Alone after the death of her husband, Caroline had

moved to Rhineburg the previous year. She missed the companionship of her daughters, but she was content with her new life. She now had a circle of friends that included the irrepressible Maddy Moeller and her long-suffering husband, Jake. Her closest and dearest friend remained Professor Carl Atwater.

She thought of Carl now as she crossed the street and stepped onto Bruck Green. She'd forgotten to tell him about her conversation with Nancy Kuhnkey. Nancy's opinion of Tom Walker differed only slightly from the professor's. Both agreed that Tom could be mean when drunk, but Nancy saw him more as a threat to women than to men. In her words, he was a bully and a coward, but probably not a killer.

Winding cobbled walks criss-crossed the huge expanse of Bruck Green. Caroline took the nearest northbound trail and immediately plunged into a heavily wooded area. The wind-ravaged branches of a dozen towering oaks combined with shoulder high bushes to cut off the light from the road's Victorian-style street lamps. She slowed her steps, allowing her eyes to adjust to the darkness.

Through the trees she could see Bruck Hall awash in the glow of ground level spotlights. Mullioned windows lined the stone walls and bracketed the whitewashed portico. From perches high above the windows, ancient gargoyles sneered down on anyone who dared approach the entrance. The building was imposing, as it should be since it was, in truth, the heart of the university. It was here that plans were laid, decisions made, and careers won or lost.

And it was here that Garrison Hurst would meet with his Board of Directors on the day after Halloween.

Caroline could only guess what the results of that meeting would be. If Hurst was half as smart as she thought he was, he'd use tonight's disaster to push for the cancellation of the rodeo. Donna Moore could hardly dispute the danger involved with quartering her bulls on university grounds. They'd practically destroyed the security office after wreaking havoc on Jake's cruiser. More importantly, their rampage across campus had presented a clear threat to both students and older demonstrators. Even its most rabid supporters would have difficulty making a case for the rodeo after tonight.

Caroline cut onto a less wooded trail that led east toward the gym before circling back in the direction of St. Anne's. She decided to leave the Jeep where she'd parked it and, after a brisk walk across the Green, check in at the ER before heading up to her apartment in the nursing dorm.

The night was clear and cool with only a hint of a breeze to ruffle the barren treetops. The scent of burnt wood still lingered in the air, a byproduct of the students' smoky grills. To Caroline it seemed a pleasant odor in tune with the season. She took a deep breath, letting the smells of autumn chase the tension from her body.

Less on edge now, she picked up her pace, skirting the path that led to the gym and turning instead toward the hospital. A block of hundred-year-old oak trees stood between her and the street, their branches intertwined to form a thick canopy that shut out the moonlight. She hurried through the patch of woods, being careful to dodge the many branches that dangled dangerously close to her face.

Looking straight ahead, she almost missed seeing the scarecrow sitting propped against a tree alongside the trail. It was doubled over, head to its knees, its arms hanging loosely at its sides and its legs at odd angles to its body. One foot protruded into the path, and it was this that finally caught her attention. She stumbled over the scarecrow's gym shoe and staggered sideways, avoiding a fall only by grabbing on to the trunk of a dying oak. Scrambling upright again, she kicked at the offending foot.

Her toe hit not straw, but something harder and unyielding to the touch. Puzzled, she moved closer for a better look.

THIRTY-FOUR

"QUIT ASKING QUESTIONS, Carl, and get over here!"

Caroline practically shouted the order into her cell phone as she stood beneath the trees looking down at the dead body of Wade Wilkins. Unsure of where Gabe was now that the security office lay in ruins, her first call had been to Michael Bruck at his home in Rhineburg. Her second call went out to Jake Moeller at the police station. She'd stuck to the facts, reciting her story quickly but leaving nothing to the Chief's imagination. Jake had listened without interrupting her even once.

Talking to Carl was an entirely different matter. Barely awake, the professor had first asked her if she was kidding.

"I don't kid about murder," Caroline had snapped. "Now get up and get dressed. You need to see this before Jake ropes off the entire area."

Carl wasn't content with a mini version of events, but Caroline cut him off with a curt "good-bye" and slipped her cell phone back into the pocket of her coat. She hunched down to inspect the body more closely.

Her initial examination had confirmed what she instinctively knew when she first saw Wilkins propped against the tree. Bruck's football coach was beyond help, the blood already dry on the back of his shirt where a gaping wound could be seen through the tattered material. Nevertheless, she'd gone through the motions of CPR, checking for breathing and feeling for a carotid pulse while being careful not to touch the body more than was necessary.

Wilkins had not died a natural death. Whether his life had ended through murder or by accident—and she very much doubted the latter —her duty was to preserve any evidence on or near the corpse that could aid the police in their investigation.

Now, as she waited for help to arrive, she squatted on the ground a few feet from Wilkins and let her eyes take in as much detail as possible. The coach was dressed in his usual polo shirt and Dockers. A light jacket, open in the front, covered the upper part of his torso. On his head he wore a Bruck baseball cap, and on his feet, dirty gym shoes.

Caroline couldn't get a good look at Wilkins's features. His forehead rested on his knees, his chin concealed by the collar of his shirt. There appeared to be no blood on his pants legs. From that she assumed he'd suffered no major lacerations to the face. Still, there might be minor scratches present, or bruising of the skin. Either one could indicate his death had been preceded by a struggle.

She shifted her position to get a better view of the coach's hands. They also appeared free of blood with no abrasions or bruises visible on the knuckles. The only real wound seemed to be the one on the left side of the coach's back slightly below the shoulder blade.

Twin beams of light pierced the darkness to Caroline's left. She rocked back on her heels and waved both hands in the air.

"Over here, Gabe! This way!"

Rising to her feet, Caroline moved back another pace from the corpse.

"I called Jake," she said as Gabe Bruck trotted down the path toward her, his flashlight bobbing in his hand. He bent down to examine the body.

"It doesn't look like there's much we can do for him now."

"No," said Caroline. "I'd say he's been dead for quite a while."

"This is Buck Mallo, one of our security officers." Gabe thumbed over his shoulder at the man standing behind him. "He's new with us this year."

"Nice to meet you, Buck," said Caroline, extending her hand to Gabe's companion. The young man in the gray guard's uniform couldn't have been more than twenty years old. Even in the darkness, she could tell he was a little green around the gills. "It's been a pretty bad night, hasn't it?"

"Sure has," the boy mumbled. His eyes were riveted on the body leaning against the tree. "Never saw a dead man before, least not like this."

"It's not a common sight on campus," said Gabe. He turned and motioned to their surroundings. "Pull out that tape we brought and string it from tree to tree. Start back a good three, four yards from where we're standing. I want a nice wide area left here in the center."

Mallo looked relieved to be given a job some distance away from the corpse. He touched his forehead in a two-finger salute before taking off up the trail.

"These killings keep up and I'm gonna lose every new officer I've hired," grumbled Gabe as he watched the boy hurry about his task. He turned and aimed his flashlight at Wilkins. "How'd you know it was me out there?"

"It couldn't have been Jake," said Caroline. "He would have arrived with his siren blaring. And Michael couldn't have made it here that quickly. The only one left was you."

"Highly deductive reasoning." Gabe did what Caroline had done earlier and squatted down to take a better look at the body. "Have you deduced anything about our friend here?"

"Looks like the wound on his back was what killed him. I can't tell if he was knocked out before he was stabbed. That cap covers most of his head."

"We won't touch him till Jake and the coroner get here." Gabe got to his feet. He moved the flashlight from side to side, sweeping the ground near the corpse. "If there's a weapon here, I don't see it."

"I didn't either," replied Caroline. "Whoever killed him either threw the knife some distance into the bushes or took it away with him when he left the scene."

"You're assuming our murderer was a man."

"Not really. It seems only natural to refer to a killer as 'he' or 'him.' It could have been a woman who stabbed the coach."

"Lord knows, there have been some mighty angry women on campus lately."

"You'd be hard pressed to come up with a motive if you're talking about Bertha Meyer and her friends. They may be a little screwball, but they're not dangerous."

"It depends on how you define dangerous," said Gabe, his voice tinged with a hint of annoyance.

"I'm sure the ladies are sorry about what happened to your office tonight."

"Sorry won't pay the repair bill. But I know you're right. None of those woman have it in them to murder somebody. I'm not so sure, though, about Donna Moore."

"What motive would she have," asked Caroline in surprise. "I might agree with you if this was Garrison Hurst lying at our feet, but killing Wilkins makes no sense. As far as I know, he wasn't at any of the meetings with Moore at Bruck Hall. Trace Golden Sr. was Wilkins's mentor on the Board. He pressed the case for canceling the rodeo."

"Still, she might have blamed Wilkins for all the trouble."

"So she set up a meeting with him here on the Green, and came armed with a knife. That theory would suggest premeditated murder, Gabe. Again, I don't see that the rodeo is motive enough for Donna to kill anyone, least of all Wilkins."

The security officer shrugged. "Then we have to assume Wilkins had an enemy here on campus, someone on the staff or among the students."

A chill ran down Caroline's spine as she thought of the argument between Martin and the coach earlier that day. Hopefully, her son had arrived home long before the time of the murder.

Gabe's two-way radio crackled to life. He lifted it to his lips, said a few words, then turned his flashlight in the direction of the road to highlight their position.

"Michael's arrived. Jake and his men are behind him. It might be better if you waited back a ways on the trail, Mrs. Rhodes."

Gabe's sudden formality struck Caroline as a bad sign. He'd probably heard about the argument in the gym and was already considering Martin a suspect. If so, then Jake most likely was thinking the same way.

She turned on her heel and walked north to where Buck Mallo stood waiting at the edge of the now roped off area.

"I'll be over there on the lawn if anyone wants to speak to me," she said, pointing to a bench a few feet beyond the trees.

Carl still hadn't arrived, and Caroline wondered why. Living so close to the Green, he should have been at her side by now. The professor was curious by nature. A murder scene was one thing he'd never purposely miss. His absence was strange, to say the least.

She glanced up at the sky, now speckled with a thousand brilliant stars. The wind had picked up, and pale clouds tickled the moon before sweeping over and under it like broad bands of ragged lace. Behind her, branches rustled in the dark.

Jake and the others had parked near Bruck Hall. Caroline saw two policemen unload what she assumed to be crime scene equipment from their cars. They followed the Chief across the Green, their pace not as hurried as she would have expected. Apparently the Rhineburg Police Department was becoming accustomed to murder in their town.

Jake led his men down the path without once glancing in her direction. She was relieved that he passed her by. Off in the distance she could see Carl hotfooting it across the grass. She wanted to talk to him before she was quizzed by Jake. She let out a shrill whistle, and Carl responded with a wave of his hand.

"What took you so long?"

Carl huffed and puffed to a halt, out of breath after trekking across the lawn at a speed greater than usual for him. He sunk down on the bench next to Caroline and held up one hand for silence.

"Don't say it," he wheezed. "I know. I have to lose weight."

"We can discuss your health another time," said Caroline. "Tell me what held you up."

Carl released a long breath, then sat up straighter on the bench.

"Maddy called me the minute Jake left the house. I was almost out the door myself, but I'm glad I stopped to answer the phone."

"Why? What did Maddy have to say?"

"She told me about Wilkins, but of course, I already knew he was dead. She said Jake was making noises about

Martin and the fight he'd had with the coach. He sent one of his men to check if Martin was at home."

"I'm assuming he and Nikki were either in bed or on their way there."

Carl looked uncomfortable, and Caroline grabbed his arm.

"What is it, Carl? What's happened?"

"Now don't get excited, Cari," said the professor, closing his huge paw over her much smaller hand. "I called Martin to warn him, and Nikki picked up the phone. Martin arrived at my place like he promised. He took Nikki home, but then he said he had something else he needed to do. He packed a bag with some clean clothes and left about a half an hour later."

"What time was that?"

Carl looked at his watch. "It's almost eleven now. Martin took Nikki home around seven. He must have left the apartment between seven-thirty and eight o'clock."

"And he took a bag with him."

"He told Nikki he'd be back sometime late tomorrow evening. I asked where he was going, but if she knew, Nikki wasn't telling."

"You think she was being evasive with you?"

"She sure didn't seem upset by his absence. I got the feeling the two of them had cooked up some kind of plan to clear Martin's name. I think your son has gone off to do a bit of sleuthing."

Caroline rolled her eyes. "I hope he talked to Nancy Kuhnkey first. She has a P.I. friend in Chicago she planned to bring in on the case to investigate the NCAA charge. She wanted it done quietly so as not to alarm Wade Wilkins."

"Looks like we don't have to worry about that now."

"What we do have to worry about is Martin. He tried to

attack Wilkins today. Jake saw the whole thing. If Martin doesn't have an iron-clad alibi for the past few hours, he's sure to be a suspect in the coach's murder."

THIRTY-FIVE

CAROLINE GOT OUT of bed the next morning feeling like
a drunk after a two day binge. A lack-of-sleep induced
headache radiated from the back of her neck to her forehead. Every muscle in her body seemed in spasm as she
hobbled from her bedroom to the bathroom. She looked
in the mirror at her red-rimmed eyes.

"You'll never pass for Sleeping Beauty," she told herself as she pulled a bottle of aspirin from the cabinet. She
shook two tablets from the bottle and swallowed them with
a chaser of water. A few minutes later, semi-awake after a
hot shower, Caroline emerged from the bathroom in time
to catch the six o'clock news.

"The body of Wade Wilkins, football coach at Bruck
University, was discovered late last night in a wooded area
on the college campus. Wilkins was pronounced dead by
coroner Harold Schmidt who said an investigation is under
way into what apparently was a murder."

Apparently? Caroline shook her head. Unless Wilkins
had reached over his shoulder and stabbed himself, which
was highly improbable and almost impossible to do, the
coach had most certainly been murdered. "Apparently"
was not a word that fit the situation.

"A graduate of the University of Iowa, Wilkins had
coached high school football in southern Illinois before
being recruited by President Garrison Hurst to lead the
Bruck Bruins. Contacted at his home, Hurst expressed sor-
row at the sudden death of a man he called 'a great coach.'"

Hurst said the Homecoming game will go on as planned, but other activities planned for the weekend might be canceled out of respect for the late Mr. Wilkins.

"In other news, the Mad Maniacs of Rhineburg High School will…"

Caroline switched off the radio. She dressed quickly and left the apartment, heading downstairs for the underground corridor that connected the nursing dorm to the hospital. Ten minutes later she emerged from the hospital cafeteria carrying a cup of hot chocolate and a Styrofoam container filled with scrambled eggs, bacon, and two slices of wheat toast.

"What are you doing here," called out Chan Daley as Caroline walked into the ER. "I thought you had a couple of days off."

The little doctor was straddling a stool next to a cart on which sat John Meyer. The white-haired baker had his left shoe off and his leg extended.

"I couldn't resist the gourmet breakfast being served in the cafeteria," said Caroline, placing her container on the desk. She walked over to the side of the cart, sipping her hot chocolate. "What happened to your foot, Mr. Meyer?"

John Meyer glanced up sheepishly. "I think I broke my toe last night. It's all swollen up."

"How'd it happen?" asked Caroline. Knowing that Meyer was too embarrassed to meet her eyes, she kept them glued on Chan's fingers as he probed the skin around the baker's little toe.

"I must have tripped on something," said Meyer with a shrug.

"Right!" said Chan, grinning. "I heard about that little standoff over at the security building last night. I'll bet you kicked the door, didn't you?"

Meyer shrugged again. "I might have. Then again, I could have tripped."

Chan stood up and slapped the old man on the shoulder. "It's off to X-ray with you. Now behave yourself in there and don't kick any doors."

Meyer's face reddened. Fortunately, Ellen Healy appeared at that point with a wheelchair and saved her patient from any further embarrassment.

Chan walked over to the desk and sat down. He leaned back in his chair, folded his hands over his midriff, and gazed up at Caroline quizzically.

"So, what are you really doing here this morning?"

"I've come to find out when the autopsy will be done on Wade Wilkins." Caroline took another sip of chocolate. "I'm the one who found him, you know."

"So I heard. You seem to have some kind of affinity for the dead lately. First Golden, now Wilkins."

"I don't stumble over bodies by choice. Somehow I always manage to be in the wrong place at the wrong time."

"Excuses, excuses." Chan waved to the chair next to his. "Take a load off and tell Dr. Daley all about it."

Caroline did. By the time she finished with her story, Chan's mouth was hanging open.

"Hustled by drunks, attacked by a bull. Then, to top off the evening, you practically fall over a corpse on the Green. What other kind of trouble can you get into, Cari?"

"I'm not the one who's in trouble. It's my son again."

Caroline told Chan about Martin's disappearing act.

"Jake sent an officer over to his apartment after I called to tell him about Wilkins. He wasn't pleased at all that Martin had flown the coop."

"You've got to admit, if the boy was anyone other than your son, you'd be suspicious, too."

"You're right; I would be. I'm going to visit Nikki this

morning. I have a feeling she knows where Martin is. Before I leave for the post office, though, I need to know when the autopsy will be done. I'm hoping Andy Zapp will allow me to watch."

"You're too late, my dear. The estimable Dr. Zapp worked his magic long before the cock crowed today. He's leaving on a hunting trip this morning, so Jake called him at home and dragged him out of bed. The autopsy was over by 2 a.m."

"And you were working the night shift."

"Me and Miss Healy, per usual. Fortunately, this place was empty," said Chan, letting his eyes roam over the ER. "I left Ellen to hold down the fort while I played assistant to Andy."

"What did he find?"

"A stab wound in the back between the third and fourth ribs. The knife sliced straight into the heart, so death couldn't have taken long. The wound was messed up, though."

"Messed up? What do you mean?"

"The entrance wound had been widened somehow. Whoever killed Wilkins must have drawn the knife halfway out and then wiggled it around to create a larger area of damage to the back muscles. Don't ask me why it was done, but it didn't fool old Zapp. The knife penetrated the heart in a nice clean line."

Caroline stared at Chan. "Does Jake know about this?"

"Sure. He was waiting in Zapp's office and heard the report right away."

"Then he probably has it figured out already."

"And I suppose you do, too," grinned Chan.

"Well of course," said Caroline. "The killer wanted to make Wilkins's death look like an accident. He knew the rodeo bulls had been loose on campus earlier in the evening. They were everywhere, including on the Green. A wound like that could be mistaken for the work of a bull."

"You mean the killer wanted us to think Wilkins was gored by a bull's horns."

"Exactly. Whoever murdered the coach didn't count on Dr. Zapp's experience as a pathologist. Living out here in farm country, he's seen all kinds of work related deaths, including, I'm sure, the occasional death by animal attack."

"Being a city boy myself, I wouldn't have caught onto that. But Zapp knew something was weird about the wound. If he hadn't been in such a hurry to get out of here, he probably would have come up with the same theory."

"Jake's smart enough to figure it out for himself." Caroline stood up and threw her empty cup into the wastebasket under the desk. "Time's a-wastin', Chan. I have to get going."

"Hold on!" called Chan as she walked toward the ER exit. "You forgot your food."

"You can have it," Caroline said with a wave of her hand. "I think I'll eat breakfast at the Sugar Bowl Café."

THIRTY-SIX

"So you see," said Caroline between bites of an English muffin, "whoever killed Wilkins wanted it to look like an accident. He…"

"Or she," countered Carl.

"Or she," Caroline conceded. "He or she used the stampede to his or her advantage."

"But it didn't work for him or her."

"Oh, please!" said Nancy Kuhnkey grumpily. She threw down her napkin and glared at the two people sitting across from her at the table. "Quit all this personal pronoun business and call whoever did it 'the murderer.'"

"Fine with me." Caroline looked up from her breakfast as the door to the restaurant swung open. Maddy Moeller made an impressive entrance dressed in thigh high boots over black tights, a black skirt that barely skimmed her knees, and a close-fitting black leather jacket. The pert little redhead wore aviator type sunglasses and bright red lipstick. A Bruck U. book bag was slung over her shoulder.

"How do you like it?" she said as she pirouetted coyly before them.

Carl eyed her over his coffee cup. "Halloween was yesterday."

"I wasn't asking you," said Maddy, thumping the professor on the shoulder. "What do men know about clothes, anyway?"

"Maddy, dear, why do you look like you just climbed off a motorcycle?"

Caroline couldn't keep the laughter out of her voice. For once, Maddy had outdone herself in the clothes department.

"Et tu, Brute?" Maddy let the book bag slip to the floor and seated herself in the booth next to Martin's lawyer. "I'm supposed to look like a college student, not a biker chick."

Kuhnkey lowered her nose and glanced at the Chief's wife over the rims of her half-glasses.

"Few and far between are the times that I've agreed with a man, Mrs. Moeller. Today, however, Professor Atwater's opinion mirrors my own."

Maddy glared at her three companions. "I'll have you know, I worked hard on this costume. I have to look the part if I want to infiltrate the enemy camp unobserved."

"What enemy camp?" asked Carl. "And unobserved by who?"

"I'm talking about Bruck University. Jake and the Archangels have quarantined the place. Nobody goes on campus, nobody goes off without their permission."

"And I take it, you want to go on campus."

"That's right, Cari. I've been thinking about Jennie Walker and her baby. Jennie would have been a student at Bruck this semester if she hadn't gotten pregnant in her senior year of high school. Most of her former classmates are at Bruck. I want to talk to them, especially the girls. Jennie must have confided in someone as to the identity of the baby's father."

"Then you don't think it was Trace," said Caroline.

"Jennie denied he was involved when I first asked her about the baby. Then she turned around and gave me this big song and dance about Trace wanting to marry her. She said his father found out and refused to allow it."

"Sounds like something Trace Sr. would do," said

Kuhnkey. "I really don't see that it matters who the baby's father is. Jennie Walker couldn't have killed Trace."

"But her father might have," said Carl. "We're looking for motive here. Tom would have had reason to attack Golden if the boy had gotten his daughter pregnant and then abandoned her."

Kuhnkey continued to play devil's advocate. "But why would Walker have stabbed Wade Wilkins? Unless you think we have two murderers wandering the streets of Rhineburg, you'll have to prove Tom did that killing, too."

"She's right, you know," said Caroline. "Unless we can come up with something that links Tom to Wade Wilkins, we have no case."

"The question remains, why did Tom disappear if he wasn't involved in the first murder?" Carl looked from face to face to see if the others were following his train of thought. "Could it be, as Cari suggested, Tom witnessed Trace's death and ran off because he was afraid?"

"Maybe Wilkins killed Trace," said Maddy. "Maybe Tom tried to blackmail the coach last night and they ended up in a fight. Maybe Tom killed Wilkins in the struggle."

"That's an awful lot of maybes," said Kuhnkey. "I think we should stick to the facts as we know them and concentrate on Martin. What would really help is if we could find people who would support his alibi for Monday night."

"That's almost impossible to do," protested Caroline. "Martin said he broke into the stadium and sat there until midnight before going off to Carl's office. We'd have to find someone else who was scouting out the field at the same time Martin was there."

"Then do it," said the lawyer. "If Martin could pick that lock, then so could others. I'll bet half the kids in the school look on that stadium as their personal lovers' lane."

"That's a thought," said Carl. "I could ask around

among the students, spread the word, so to say. Maybe someone will come forward to support Martin's story."

"But that won't be enough," insisted Caroline. "There are too many time gaps, too many holes in his alibi. We need to find someone who saw Trace Golden alive after Martin left the gym." She sighed in disgust. "If only Wilkins had admitted to having a woman in his office that night. She would have had to see Trace when she left the gym. The locker room entrance was the only door open at that time of night."

"My P.I. friend in Chicago is looking into Wilkins's background," said Kuhnkey. "He's also checking to see if Martin violated any NCAA rules when he played football. Wilkins said that Golden's claim about Martin's eligibility was a hoax. If so, that knocks out any motive for murder on Martin's part."

"Even if it was hoax, Martin didn't know that Monday night." Caroline was finding it difficult to contain her growing irritation with the lawyer. Kuhnkey seemed unable to understand that the only way to clear Martin was to find the real killer.

"It's all about doubt, Mrs. Rhodes. Put enough doubt in the mind of a jury and they'll never go for a conviction." Kuhnkey elbowed Maddy out of the booth. She got to her feet and absently brushed a few crumbs off the front of her blouse. "I have to get back to my office. I'll be home most of the day. If you hear from Martin, tell him to call me."

"I don't care what she says," grumbled Maddy as the lawyer walked out the door. "I'm still going to sneak onto the campus and try to hunt down some of Jennie's friends. Tom Walker fits into this case somehow or another, and his wife and daughter are being totally weird about it."

Caroline only half heard what Maddy said. She was watching Kuhnkey through the big glass window at the front of the café. The lawyer had climbed into her car and made a U-turn on Wilhelm Road.

"She's not going home."

"Hmm? What are you talking about, Cari?"

"Nancy Kuhnkey. She's not going home like she said, Carl." Caroline craned her neck to get a better view out the window. "She's turning west on Kaiser."

Carl glanced over at Maddy. "That's the route we took when we drove to the Walker place yesterday."

"But why would she want to visit Sue Walker?" asked Maddy. "She pooh-poohed the whole idea of Tom being a suspect in the murder."

"Maybe she's not going to the Walker house," said Caroline, settling back once more in the booth. "There are plenty of other homes out that way, plus the strip mall. Maybe I'm imagining things."

Carl's eyes narrowed. "Imagining what, Cari?"

"I don't know," said Caroline with a wave of her hand. "But every time Tom Walker's name is mentioned, Nancy tries to draw our attention in another direction. I get the feeling she knows more about the Walker family than she's letting on."

"I don't think she's particularly close friends with Sue," said Carl.

"Until this week, Sue wasn't particularly close friends with anyone," Maddy said with a knowing look in her eyes. "Outside of the weekly square dance, Tom never let her go anywhere. I was as surprised as everyone else when she showed up at the demonstration Monday evening."

An idea starting cooking in Caroline's brain.

"I think I'll take a ride out to Alexsa's place. If anyone does, she'd have the lowdown on the Walkers."

"And I'm going over to the campus," said Maddy. She reached down at her feet and pulled something out of her bag. It was the latest yearbook from Rhineburg High. "Jake gets one of these books every year when the current crop of seniors graduate. It helps him place names to faces when he's trying to track down a kid."

Carl pointed to the book. "Jennie Walker's picture must be in there. Trace Golden's, too."

"Along with all of their friends. With your help, Carl, I hope to track down some of these kids in their classes. I'm going to tell them I'm an exchange student visiting for the week. Hopefully, I can worm my way into their confidence and find out how close Trace and Jennie really were."

Carl rolled his eyes. "They'll think you're from Transylvania University dressed in those clothes."

"I can wear my vampire teeth, if that'll make you happier," Maddy said sweetly. "Oh, come on, Carl! Help me out on this one."

"Jake'll have my head if he finds out about this," said Carl, rising to his feet. "But I'll talk to some of the teachers and see what I can do. I'll also try to track down any student who might have been at the stadium Monday night."

Carl paid for his and Caroline's breakfast, then left with Maddy Moeller. Caroline thought about visiting Nikki, but decided the girl was too stubborn to tell her anything of value. Jake had probably grilled her by now as to Martin's whereabouts. Annie Holtzbrinck would have called her or Maddy if Nikki had cracked under the Chief's questioning.

She checked her cell phone to make sure it was turned on, then walked briskly to her Jeep parked at the end of the block. Getting into the car, she thought of calling Alexsa. She decided against it and slipped the phone back into her pocket. Arriving unannounced had its advantages. It gave Alexsa no time to prepare her answers.

Not that Mrs. Morgan had any reason to lie to her. Alexsa had seemed more than willing to confide in Maddy and Bertha on Halloween. But it was always a gamble as to how much dirt Rhineburg's matriarch was willing to dish out on her neighbors.

Caroline could only hope that Alexsa was in a talkative mood.

THIRTY-SEVEN

THE WELCOME MAT had already been laid out for her when she arrived at the Morgan house a few minutes later.

"I knew you'd come," said Bricole as she led Caroline down the long hallway to the garden room. "I told Alexsa that you'd need her help." She stood aside in the doorway, smiling gravely up at the ER nurse. "She's waiting for you over in the cutting area."

"Thank you."

Caroline watched Bricole skip off down the hallway. The little girl never failed to amaze her. Today, though, she felt uneasy about the child. It was nothing she could put her finger on, just a disquieting sensation deep in her bones she tried to shake before turning to scan the glass-walled garden room. Alexsa was standing hunched over a wooden bench some thirty feet away potting cuttings from a single geranium. She looked up when Caroline approached.

"Bricole was right again," the old woman sighed as she wiped her hands on a rag. She waved at the table and wicker lawn furniture set off in one corner of the room. "We might as well sit down and wait for the child to bring our tea. She always makes the strongest tea when I have visitors. Seems to be a tradition she learned from her grandmother."

"Why isn't she in school today?" Caroline asked as she settled herself in a chair.

"Trace Golden's murder upset her. I think it reminded

her too much of last spring and her grandmother's death. She stayed home yesterday, even refusing to go out trick-or-treating with the other children. Then this business with Wade Wilkins was all over the radio this morning." Alexsa shrugged. "I could hardly refuse her request to stay home here with me."

"Maybe you should talk to Lian Daley. She's worked with children in her practice. She might be able to advise you on the best way to handle the situation."

"It wouldn't hurt. I'll speak with her later today." Alexsa's eyes strayed to the doorway. "Perhaps we should discuss your troubles before Bricole returns. I assume you've come here because of Martin."

"He's a suspect in the murders. While he had the motive and opportunity to commit both crimes, he didn't kill either Golden or Wilkins."

"I didn't think that he had. The problem, as I see it, is one of suspects. There don't seem to be too many other people who tangled with both men in such a short span of time."

"Then you know all the facts of the case."

"Elvira keeps me apprised of what's happening on campus. Her grandson is a freshman at Bruck this year. He didn't make the football team, but Kurt Zumwald, the trainer, took him on as his assistant."

Caroline looked surprised. "Would that be Jerry Harding? I met him last winter when he came to St. Anne's with Elvira."

"That's the boy. He's probably grown some since you last saw him. He helps out here on the weekends with some of the outdoor chores."

Bricole chose that moment to enter the room carrying a tray holding a plate of cookies, a china teapot, and two matching cups and saucers. She placed the tray on the table between the two women.

"I know you'd rather talk without me here," she said solemnly. "If it's all right with you, Alexsa, I thought maybe I could go to the car lot with Bill. Some of the rodeo people are stopping by this morning with their horses. I was hoping I could draw them."

Back in the spring, Bricole had watched with utter fascination as a portrait artist drew a sketch of Carl at Bruck University's Renaissance Faire. Seeing her interest, Alexsa had arranged for Bricole to take art classes. The little girl's talent was apparent immediately. Her pen and ink drawings now decorated one wall in the hallway, replacing older pictures of Alexsa's long dead relatives with scenes of Rhineburg.

"Are you sure you won't be afraid?" asked Alexsa.

Bricole shook her head. "I feel better now that Mrs. Rhodes has come. And Bill said he wouldn't mind my company at the car lot."

Alexsa laughed. "You've given him a good excuse to stop off for ice cream on his way to work. Make sure he only orders two scoops, not three." She drew the girl to her and hugged her closely. "Tomorrow, it's back to school for you!"

Bricole broke away with a smile. She waved to Caroline before running out of the room.

"I almost forgot that the Moore sisters were making an appearance at Bill's place today," said Caroline. "I wonder if Donna is holding out any hope for continuing with the rodeo."

"There's a Board meeting scheduled for eleven o'clock to discuss that very matter."

Caroline looked at her watch. It wasn't yet nine-thirty,

but she knew Alexsa would need time to prepare for the meeting.

"I won't stay long," she said as she watched Mrs. Morgan pour the tea. "I only wanted to ask you a few questions about Tom and Sue Walker."

"Tom's disappeared, you know."

"Yes, I heard that yesterday."

"Strange for him to up and leave town that way."

"I thought so, too." Caroline took the cup Alexsa offered her. "Professor Atwater and I have a couple of theories as to why he vanished so soon after Trace Golden's death."

She explained their reasoning to this point. Alexsa kept silent, but she wore a look of skepticism.

"It would certainly help Martin if Tom showed up and confessed to both murders," said Caroline. "But I don't think that will happen."

"I don't either." Alexsa fixed Caroline with a hard stare. "And you know why."

"I think I do. Tom's dead, isn't he?"

THIRTY-EIGHT

CAROLINE PARKED IN front of the post office and pulled out her cell phone. She dialed Nancy Kuhnkey's number, waiting through a number of rings until the answering machine picked up.

"This is Caroline Rhodes. You and I need to talk, Miss Kuhnkey. I know about Jennie Walker. I know why Tom disappeared. Call me before noon. After that, I'll go to the police."

She flipped the cover down on the phone and slipped it back into her pocket. Climbing out of the Jeep, she walked to the post office, stepping aside at the door to let a woman with a baby stroller pass through ahead of her.

The lobby was empty of customers except for the young mother and her child. Caroline stood off to one side, waiting impatiently as the woman inquired about shipping rates. Nikki glanced at her once or twice while answering questions, but Caroline resisted making eye contact. She was irritated with the girl and had visions of an unpleasant conversation ahead.

Apparently satisfied that Nikki was not going to charge her an arm and a leg for a one pound package, the woman with the stroller finally left. Nikki unlatched the gate in the counter and beckoned to Caroline.

"Would you like to come in the back and have a cup of coffee?"

"No coffee, thanks." Caroline brushed past Nikki and entered the tiny room that served as a kitchen for the staff.

"I had tea with Alexsa a little while ago. Before that, I had breakfast with Carl and Maddy. And with Nancy Kuhnkey," she added. "Nancy had no idea that Martin had left town."

Nikki walked over to the sink.

"It was a spur of the moment thing," she said, not looking up as she fixed a new pot of coffee. "He'll be back tonight."

"Where is he, Nikki? What's he up to?"

"He had some things he had to do, nothing important."

Caroline slammed her hand, palm down, on the table.

"Where is he?" she demanded loudly.

White-faced with fear, Nikki turned to face her mother-in-law. They stared at each other in silence. Then Nikki broke down in tears.

"We didn't know Wade Wilkins was going to get killed!" she sobbed. "Martin wouldn't have gone off like he did if he'd known he needed an alibi."

"Sit down and stop crying," Caroline said sternly. She picked up a napkin from the table and handed it to Nikki. "You both knew it was a mistake for Martin to leave town. He's a suspect in a murder, damn it!"

Nikki cringed at the anger in Caroline's voice.

"Martin discovered something when he went to Newberry. He had to follow up on it."

"I don't have a lot of time to waste here, Nikki. I want the whole story, from the time Martin left you at the parade yesterday afternoon until he took off again last night. It's important that you tell me the truth, and tell it quickly."

Nikki wiped her eyes and sat down at the table. Caroline took the chair opposite her.

"We were standing on the town square watching the end of the parade. Donna and Allison Moore were the last two riders, and Allison was carrying a bullhorn. She started talking through the bullhorn, inviting everyone to the rodeo Friday night.

"Martin was behind me. I heard him say 'That's it' when Allison finished her spiel. I thought he meant, that's the end of the parade. But then Allison handed the bullhorn to one of the cowboys, and she and Donna started doing rope tricks with their lariats. I watched them for a while, then I turned to say something to Martin. That's when I discovered he'd left."

"And he didn't say where he was going?"

Nikki shook her head. "I was looking for him when the professor and Mrs. Moeller drove up. We went to the university, thinking he might have gone there. Then the professor called you while Mrs. Moeller and I walked to his house. We waited there until Martin called, then Mrs. Moeller walked back to Bruck. Martin picked me up about twenty minutes later, and we drove home."

"What reason did he give for going to Newberry?"

"Martin thought he recognized Allison Moore's voice. He said it was the same voice he heard coming from Coach Wilkins's office the night Trace Golden was killed."

Caroline rocked back in her chair and stared at Nikki. "He's sure it was the same voice?"

"Positive. Allison has a high pitched, nasal kind of voice, very distinctive. It's the sort of voice you don't forget once you've heard it."

"But Martin was standing in the hallway. He couldn't have heard the woman all that well."

"Oh, yes, he could. Think of the layout in the gym, Mom. The other coaches' offices are behind the basketball court. When Wilkins arrived here last summer, there was no place to put him. The maintenance men carved an office for him out of a storage area across from the shower room. They added a cheap plywood wall and hung an old door that looks like it came from a flea market. That door was warped when they hung it. It's warped even more now due to the steam coming from the shower room. When it rains, or the humidity's high, the wood swells to a point where it's almost impossible to close the door."

"It rained pretty heavily on Saturday."

"Yes. And on Monday, Wade Wilkins didn't bother to fight with the door. Martin said it was open at least a half an inch. He could hear every word that was being said inside."

Caroline sat up straighter.

"Do you mean to say, Martin overheard a conversation between Wilkins and Allison Moore, and he never even mentioned it to Jake?"

"He didn't know it was Moore when Chief Moeller questioned him," protested Nikki. "But he did say he'd heard a woman talking to the coach. Wilkins denied it, and the Chief believed him, not Martin."

"Don't you understand, Nikki? The only thing Martin said was that he heard a woman's voice in the office. He never told us he could repeat the conversation word for word. If he had, Jake would have pressed Wilkins harder and forced him to tell the truth."

"I never thought of it that way," said Nikki miserably.

"Obviously, Martin didn't either." Caroline drummed her fingertips on the table. "Well, that's water under the bridge. Did Martin tell you anything else about this little tête-à-tête?"

"He heard Allison tell Wilkins he'd changed since college. She said something about liking him better when he was hairy."

"Hairy? You mean, like with a beard?"

"Or a mustache. Wilkins had a mustache when he first came to Bruck, but he shaved it off before the first game of the season. Anyway, Allison sounded angry. Martin didn't want to be caught eavesdropping, so he walked back to the locker room. That's when he ran into Trace."

"Hmm."

"Martin thought Chief Moeller might be more inclined to believe the rest of his story if Allison Moore confessed to being the woman in Coach Wilkins's office."

"Allison must have seen Trace when she left the gym."

"That's right. The locker room door was the only entrance open at that time of night. She would have had to go out that way."

"But Al Sperling didn't see her. He also didn't see Trace."

"I called Al at the dorm this morning and asked him about that. He told me he was watching from behind some bushes on the front lawn. He never actually saw the locker room entrance because that's on the side of the building."

"Of course!" said Caroline. "Allison must have followed the sidewalk to the rear of the building instead of to the front. Trace could have done the same thing."

"That's what I was thinking. I've been waiting for Martin to call me so I could tell him."

"Jake should be on this by now. He's probably questioning Allison even as we speak."

Nikki ducked her head and said nothing. Watching her, Caroline felt her heart sink.

"Oh, Nikki. Don't tell me you've kept all this from Jake."

"He didn't ask me about it when he came to the apartment this morning," Nikki said defensively. "He only wanted to know where Martin was, and I told him the honest truth: Martin didn't say where he was going last night."

Caroline exploded. "Don't treat me like I'm some kind of fool! You know perfectly well where your husband is. Not only that, you could have told Jake about Allison Moore, but you probably promised Martin you'd keep your mouth shut until he got home. Why, Nikki? Why?"

Nikki got up from the table and walked to the sink. She splashed a handful of cold water on her face, letting it dribble down her neck as she stood for a long minute with her eyes closed. More composed, she turned to face Caroline.

"Martin feels like his whole world is crashing down around him. Trace's accusation was bad enough, but now everyone thinks he's a murderer. He needs to get back in control, take charge of his future. He doesn't want to rely on his mother to get him out of this jam."

"So it's a matter of pride."

"It may seem silly to you, but it's important to him."

"Martin's been managing his own life for years, Nikki. In my opinion, he's made good decisions up until now. This is not the time to prove his manhood."

"That's not how he feels."

Frustration showed on Caroline's face. "Like it or not, Martin can't go it alone. He needs to talk to Jake and Nancy Kuhnkey."

Nikki said nothing. Caroline let it be and reverted to the previous subject.

"Tell me more about Martin's trip to Newberry."

"Martin wanted to use the internet to research Wade Wilkins's background. He was hoping to find some kind of connection between the coach and Allison Moore."

"That would have reinforced his claim that he'd heard the two of them talking in the office."

"Exactly. Unfortunately, our computer is in the shop for repairs. Martin knew there'd be trouble if he went back to the campus, so he drove to Newberry to use the computer in their library."

"And what did he find?"

"Absolutely nothing."

"What do you mean, nothing? Wilkins coached high school football before he came to Bruck. His name should have shown up on some school website."

Nikki shook her head. "Martin did two different searches and came up with zip. He did find a few people with the same name, but none of them had anything to do with football."

The tiny bell over the front door of the post office jingled as a customer entered the building.

"Be right with you!" Nikki hollered. Lowering her voice, she said, "I have to get back to work, Mom. I promise I'll call you as soon as I hear from Martin."

"Wait a minute, Nikki. Before you go, tell me where he is."

Nikki hesitated. "You won't tell Chief Moeller, will you? I'm afraid he'll send someone after Martin to arrest him."

"I won't say a word unless it's absolutely necessary. That's the best I can promise, Nikki."

"That'll have to do, I guess." Nikki glanced through the doorway into the main part of the post office. Her customer was busy filling out forms for several packages and appeared in no hurry to be served. "Martin went to Iowa," she said, turning to face Caroline. "He drove to the town where the Moore Sisters' Rodeo is headquartered. He took a team picture with him."

"He thinks someone there will recognize Wade Wilkins from his photo."

"That's what he's hoping for. He has to find some way to connect Wilkins to Allison Moore. What better way than through an eyewitness?"

"Not a bad idea," said Caroline. She put an arm around

her daughter-in-law's shoulders and hugged her. "Don't worry, Nikki. We'll get through this."

"I hope so," said Nikki. She placed her hand on her still flat abdomen. "I'd rather Martin wasn't in jail when this baby arrives."

"He won't be," said Caroline grimly. "I'll see to that."

THIRTY-NINE

"YOU CAN CALL off Maddy," Caroline told Carl when she phoned him from her Jeep a few minutes later. "Tell her the Walker scheme is a washout."

"You've dropped him as a suspect?"

"Yeah." Caroline watched the door of the post office close on Nancy Kuhnkey's back. "I don't have time to explain. Tell Maddy to get over to Bill Morgan's car lot as fast as she can. The Moore sisters are making an appearance there today. I want her to keep an eye on them, watch for any suspicious behavior. In particular, I want her to find out when Allison Moore arrived in town."

"She came with the stock trucks late Monday evening, didn't she? Long after the blowup between Martin and Nikki."

"That's what we all assumed. But I had a talk with Nikki. According to my son, Allison was the woman in Wilkins's office that night."

There was silence on the other end of the line. Caroline imagined Carl tucked behind his desk, one hand stroking his beard as he considered this latest bombshell.

"If you remember, we were at your house watching the football game when Jake turned up at the door with Maddy. He said the rodeo people had arrived on campus and all hell was breaking loose."

"That was an hour or more after Martin stalked off to the gymnasium."

"You're right. According to Martin's timetable, he'd already left the locker room and was either sitting on a bench on Bruck Green or walking toward the stadium. His times are a little fuzzy, but any way you look at it, he was nowhere near the gym when the trucks pulled onto campus."

"I wonder why Wilkins didn't want us to know about Allison Moore."

"And I wonder why Miss Moore didn't come forward when she heard of Trace's death. She must have seen him in the locker room. She had to pass through there on her way out of the gym."

"I'll hunt down Maddy and tell her what's happened."

"I have another job for you, Carl. Find Al Sperling and ask him exactly where on the lawn he positioned himself when he followed Martin to the gym. I need to know if he could see the players' entrance from where he stood. It's possible that both Allison and Trace took the sidewalk to the rear of the building instead of to the front."

"I'll not only ask him, I'll also take him to the gym and have him show me the spot."

"Good. I have more to tell you, but it will have to wait. Nancy Kuhnkey just stepped out of the post office. I need to talk to her."

"Stay in touch."

"I will." Caroline hit the off button on her cell phone and reached for the door handle. She was out of the Jeep before Kuhnkey could reach her car. "Nancy! Wait up a minute!"

She could tell by the look on her face that the lawyer wasn't pleased to see her. Kuhnkey glanced furtively up and down the street before motioning Caroline into her ancient Cadillac.

"I got your message. Let's go somewhere private and talk about it."

Caroline shook her head. "No. Let's talk right here. I

have an appointment with Amos Dalton in a few minutes. I told him I might have a good story for him."

"Don't do that," said Kuhnkey with a worried look. She shifted around to face Caroline. "Sue Walker deserves a fair shake. She won't get it if Amos gets wind of what's happened and runs off to Jake Moeller."

"Jake's going to find out sooner or later. You know I can't keep this from him."

"You can for a while. At least until I can persuade Sue to turn herself in."

"And what if she leaves town?"

"She won't. She doesn't have any money, and she won't leave Jennie."

"Was Jennie in on it?"

"No. It was an accident, Caroline. It really was."

Caroline looked skeptical. "But you suspected what had happened all along, and you never said a word. You let Martin believe you were free to defend him."

"I didn't know for sure until today when I talked to Sue. I swear on my mother's grave, there's no conflict of interest here. I can represent both Sue Walker and your son, and do both jobs well."

"I wonder about that."

Kuhnkey waved off the remark. "I spoke with my P.I. friend a little while ago. He dragged some information out of the folks at the NCAA headquarters this morning. Trace Golden wasn't lying about that letter. They sent one to Wilkins back in September telling him Martin was ineligible to play on the team. It has something to do with his status as a post-graduate student and the fact that he ran track for four years as an undergraduate. I don't have all the details, but as Martin's lawyer, I can get a copy of the letter."

"Then I take it Jake didn't find the original letter in the coach's files."

"According to Chief Moeller, his men went over Wilkins's office with a fine tooth comb. The letter wasn't there."

"Wilkins must have destroyed it. Martin shouldn't have been on the field Saturday afternoon. Wilkins knew it, which is why he made him wear Trace Golden's number. Golden was listed in the program, not Martin."

"It's a safe bet that with the weather conditions being what they were on Saturday, no one on the sidelines noticed the switch."

"Martin's teammates knew he was replacing Golden."

"Sure, but what did they care what number he wore? All that mattered was that he could play the position." Kuhnkey reached into the pocket of her coat and pulled out a pack of cigarettes. She offered one to Caroline who declined it with a shake of her head.

"I quit a while back. At times like this, though, I really yearn for a smoke."

"I've quit a hundred times, but I always go back," said Kuhnkey. "At my age, what the heck does it matter? Getting back to the substitution on Saturday, I called Bruck after I heard from my friend. It took a while, but I tracked down the kid who did the announcing for the game. He didn't know about Golden's suspension, and he had no idea Martin was playing in his place."

"It doesn't say much for the coach's character, does it?"

"No, but that's a point in our favor. Like I explained to Nikki a few minutes ago, the real victim here is her husband."

Caroline glanced over at the post office. "I hope Nikki told you everything she told me."

"I know about Allison Moore, if that's what you mean.

I'm going over to the police station now. I'm going to set up a time for Nikki to meet with Chief Moeller. She's agreed to tell him the whole story."

"I'm glad to hear that. Jake will want to question Allison."

"It would help Martin a lot if that woman admits to being in the gym Monday night. By the way, I understand your son couldn't find anything on the internet about Wilkins. Neither could my friend in Chicago."

"That's because both of them were looking for information under the wrong name," said Caroline. "Tell your P.I. to do a search for Harry Wilkins or Harry Wade."

"Is this a hunch, or do you know something I don't?" asked Kuhnkey.

"Right now I'm only guessing, but I think it's a good bet Wilkins was living here under an assumed name. Ask Nikki to repeat word for word the conversation Martin overheard in the gym Monday night. Listen hard and you'll come to the same conclusion I did."

Kuhnkey grunted. Reaching into her purse, she pulled out a notebook and pen and jotted down the two names.

"Any other ideas on what he should look for?"

"Ask him to check with the University of Iowa. The radio report this morning said Wilkins graduated from there. While he's at it, have your friend look into Allison Moore's background. Martin said she mentioned knowing Wilkins in college. Maybe they both went to Iowa."

Kuhnkey scribbled another note on the pad. "I'll have him get on this right away. I'll also give the information to Jake Moeller."

"Jake might be able to learn something from the authorities in Iowa. The Moores come from a small town. I'm sure the chief of police there knows them. He may also know Wilkins."

"You have a good head on your shoulders, Mrs. Rhodes. I can see why folks think so highly of you as a detective."

"I'm no detective," said Caroline. "But nursing has taught me to take note of the little details as well as the big ones. Sometimes it's the less obvious signs and symptoms that lead to a diagnosis in the ER."

"That policy seems to work equally well with crime." Kuhnkey slipped the notebook back into her purse. She peered at Caroline over the rims of her glasses, her blue eyes twinkling. "It looks like we have our killer, doesn't it?"

"Only one of them," said Caroline, opening the door of the Caddie.

Kuhnkey reached out and grabbed Caroline's arm. The smile had faded from her face and was replaced by a look of worry. "Are you still going to give Amos that story?"

"Only if I have to. Like I said, though, I'll go to Jake first."

"Give me a little time. Wait until this evening."

Caroline glanced at her watch. "I'll give you until five o'clock, Nancy. This business with the Walkers is complicating my son's case. Jake still has men out looking for Tom."

"I know. But I've got to wait until Jennie gets home from work. There's the baby to think of. And I want to do this with the least amount of hoopla from the press. We're less likely to draw Dalton's attention if we wait until dinnertime."

Caroline stared at Nancy Kuhnkey for a long minute. Sue Walker's guilt was undeniable. But after everything she'd been through, the woman deserved a break. She also deserved a lawyer who cared, and Kuhnkey obviously cared.

"Call me when you and the Walker women reach the

police station. I'll make sure Amos is out of the loop." She climbed out of the car, then paused to look back at Kuhn-key. "I hope I don't live to regret this."

"It's been a helluva week so far," said Kuhnkey, shaking her head. "But I have a feeling our troubles are coming to an end. I think we'll all rest easier tonight."

Caroline stood aside to allow the lawyer room to maneuver the Caddie out of its parking spot. She wished with all her heart that some of the woman's confidence could rub off on her.

Unfortunately, knowing what she did, that feat was impossible.

FORTY

Amos Dalton was standing behind his desk, staring out the huge plate glass window of the *Rhineburg Rag,* when Caroline walked into his office a few minutes later.

"Did you read over that file I gave you?" he asked without looking away from the traffic on Wilhelm Road.

"The one on Trace Golden? No, I didn't bother."

Amos bobbed his head, his back still turned to his visitor. "It probably wouldn't have helped any."

"Not after you'd sanitized it." Caroline walked over to the cooler in the corner of the room. She pulled out a bottle of Coke and flipped the cap on the cooler's rusted opener. "You want one?"

"No thanks. I'm more in a mood for tea today." Amos moved away from the window and circled his desk. He waved at the few chairs scattered about the room. "Make yourself comfortable. I'll be back in a minute."

He disappeared behind a curtain screening a doorway at the back of the room. Caroline checked her annoyance as she watched the curtain fall into place. Pulling a chair up to the desk, she sat down to wait, wondering as she did if the editor had skipped out on her. Dalton's minute stretched into five, then ten. She was about to go search for him when the editor of the *Rag* reentered the room carrying two bulky envelopes under his arm.

"Sorry to keep you waiting," Dalton said, tossing the envelopes on his desk. "I store most of my personal files in the safe downstairs. It took longer than I thought to make copies of everything."

"Copies of what?"

Dalton pointed to the envelopes. "That top one contains a complete dossier on Trace Golden and his father. In the other is every scrap of information I have on Wade Wilkins. They're yours, if you want them."

Caroline picked up the first envelope. It was considerably heavier than the file Amos had previously given her.

"What made you change your mind?"

"I'd like to say my conscience was bothering me," Dalton said as he sat down across from Caroline. "But that's not entirely true. Expediency had a part to play in my decision."

"Giving me the complete file wasn't to your advantage yesterday. Today, it is."

"Something like that." Dalton glanced down at the envelopes, then up at Caroline. "I got a call from a friend in the county records office this morning. It seems someone's interested in the *Rag*, who owns it, what the mortgage is on the building, stuff like that. The fellow asking was a private detective."

Maddy must have remembered to pass on Alexsa's remark about Dalton to Nancy Kuhnkey. The old lawyer's Chicago connection was certainly paying off, thought Caroline.

"It wasn't difficult to figure out who wanted that information," the editor continued. "I guess I was a little too energetic in my defense of Trace Golden, Sr."

"Some people think he owns you. If that's true, it would be foolish of me to believe anything you say."

Dalton rocked back in his chair and pursed his lips as if considering what to say next. He stared at Caroline for several seconds, then his eyes strayed to the wall flanking his desk. It was covered with framed citations and wooden plaques, a tangible record of his many accomplishments as a reporter.

"You see those awards hanging up there, Mrs. Rhodes? I earned every one of them, fair and square."

"I don't doubt it," said Caroline. "But that was then, and this is now."

"And none of us are the same people we used to be. I'm sure your P.I. friend has already given you his version of my life story. Now let me give you mine."

Caroline fought to keep her expression neutral. If Amos wanted to think she knew more than she did, so be it. Maybe in baring his soul to her, he'd reveal something of value to the investigation.

"When I was younger," Dalton said, "I didn't mind working my butt off to expose some two-bit politician or crooked businessman for the scum he really was. Back then, I thought truth mattered. I thought it led to justice. Over the years, though, I learned differently. My reporting earned me awards from my peers, but it didn't put guys behind bars. I was bucking a system built on wealth and power, and the system was stronger than I was. No matter how many times I cried foul, the politicos and the rich guys went right on screwing the public. What I wrote never really changed anything for the better. What it did change was me."

Dalton got up from his chair and walked to the window. "It took me a long time," he said, his back turned to Caroline. "But I finally wised up to how the real world runs. After years of knocking myself out to write the best story possible, I figured, what the hell. Why bother when nobody really cares."

He turned to face her. "We had interns on the paper by then, college kids who came in bright eyed and bushy tailed thinking they were going be the next Bob Woodward. I started using those kids like a queen bee uses her worker bees. I had them running their legs off doing grunt work for my articles. I took what they gave me, filled in the blanks, and left it to my editor to decide if the story was good enough to print. Half the time, it wasn't.

"The last kid assigned to me had a lot of ambition but a lousy work ethic. One day I sent him to interview a doctor for a story I was writing on politics and medicine. I was behind schedule, and I used what the kid gave me without checking the doctor's statements. A week later, my editor called me into his office. He told me the paper was being sued for defamation of character. Turns out my intern spent only five minutes talking to this doc. Then he went to the beach to catch some rays with his girlfriend. Before he came back to the paper, he wrote up a bunch of garbage based on what he thought the guy said."

"And you were in big trouble."

"I'd gotten lazy, burned out. I deserved to be fired."

Dalton returned to his chair. He leaned back and gazed up at the awards on the wall.

"I couldn't get a job after that. The newspaper I worked for settled with the doctor out of court. They let me go very quietly, but the story got around. Nobody trusted my work any more." He shook his head, a shadow of a smile playing on his lips. "So there I was, too young to collect Social Security and too old to start over in a new career. I lived off my savings and the charity of friends for two years. Then I heard that the *Rag* was for sale."

"And you bought it."

"In a New York minute. The newspaper business is the only life I know. I couldn't give it up."

"People in town think you retired due to a heart attack."

"That was my cover story. It seemed to go over well

enough with people outside my profession. I even used it when I applied to the bank for a loan to buy this place."

"Is that when you first met Mr. Golden?"

"Yeah. He personally drew up my paperwork, said he was glad to see the *Rag* back in business again. He was sympathetic to my financial problems and gave me a generous loan at a pretty good rate."

"And what did he want in exchange?"

"You're nobody's fool, are you, Mrs. Rhodes?" Dalton said, smiling ruefully. "I have to admit, I let my guard down when I moved here. Coming from the city, I had this view of Rhineburg as a bucolic little town where everyone played bingo on Friday night and went to church on Sunday."

"And never was heard a discouraging word."

"You got it. Clear skies, roaming buffalo, home on the range updated by a hundred years. It was a stupid mistake on my part." Dalton glanced at Caroline's now empty Coke bottle. "I never did make that cup of tea. Guess I'll join you in one of those."

He stood up and walked over to the cooler, opened two new bottles of Coke, and handed one to Caroline.

"I put out my first edition of the *Rag* on a Thursday in September two years ago. Golden came to see me the next morning. He told me his son played football for Rhineburg High School. He said there was a game that night. He wanted me to write a story about it, mentioning his son as one of the team's outstanding players."

"That took a bit of nerve, didn't it?"

"Oh, he has plenty of that," said Dalton. A sad little smile tugged at his lips. "I told Golden I'd attend the game, but I couldn't promise to include his son in the coverage. He stared at me with those cold eyes of his and said, 'Oh yes, you'll include him.' He told me he expected more than a mention of Trace. He wanted me to frame the story around Trace's success on the field.

"I was dumbfounded, to say the least. I protested, but he was in no mood for an argument. He made a remark about how I didn't have an intern to rely on any more. He told me I'd better get my facts straight if I wanted to stay in business."

"So he knew about your past."

"Apparently. If I hadn't had a heart attack before I came here, I was close to having one then. It was like Golden stuck a knife in my gut and twisted it. I told him one mistake didn't condemn a man for life. He laughed in my face. Then I told him I'd sell the newspaper before I lied to the public again. He thought that was even funnier."

"I bet he wrote some kind of clause into your contract that would have bankrupted you if you tried to sell."

"I would have lost my entire investment. But how did you know?"

"He loaned the money to the university for the stadium repairs. He put a similar clause in their contract, and now he's blackmailing President Hurst with it."

Dalton's wrinkled face took on more lines as he frowned at her.

"He's a regular bastard, isn't he?"

"I've never personally met Trace Golden Sr. But from what I hear, that's a pretty good assessment of the man. So, tell me, Amos. How did you handle the threat?"

"The only way I could. I gave Trace Jr. all the publicity his daddy wanted."

"You also made sure he didn't get the publicity his daddy wouldn't want."

"Yes, I did. I deliberately avoided reporting anything that would hurt the boy's reputation. His car accidents, his acts of vandalism, and especially his sexual flings."

Caroline sat waiting quietly while Dalton took a long pull on his Coke. Wiping his mouth with the back of his hand, he set the bottle aside and glanced up at her. He had the hard look of a man in whom hatred simmered just below the surface.

"I came here to reestablish my reputation as an honest reporter, Mrs. Rhodes. Golden ruined all that when he walked into this office two years ago. Now I'm getting my revenge."

FORTY-ONE

"SOUNDS LIKE AMOS DALTON was ready to make a confession," said Professor Atwater when Caroline told him about the editor's remark. They were sitting in Carl's office at Bruck, munching on cheese and crackers left over from the Board meeting while waiting for Maddy Moeller to arrive.

Caroline hadn't eaten since breakfast, and it was now almost five o'clock. She popped another piece of cheese in her mouth to calm the rumblings in her stomach, then withdrew a file from the envelope marked "Trace Golden."

"He was only leading up to the rest of his story," she said, handing the papers to Carl. "Amos hates Golden Sr., but there's no reason to think he murdered Trace. He's been plotting a perfectly legal means of revenge for almost two years. This file contains everything he needs to bring the banker to his knees."

Carl flipped through the pages, glancing only briefly at the typewritten forms. "What is all this?"

"A month by month record of Trace Jr.'s mischief making along with witness documentation, copies of court records, and affidavits from injured parties. Amos built up enough evidence to ruin the boy if his father ever tried to call in the bank loan. Dalton also gathered information on Golden Sr."

"I'll bet it was harder to dig up dirt on him."

Caroline pointed to the file. "Amos collected sworn statements from elderly residents of the county who lost their homes to the Rhineburg 1st National Bank. The statements alone aren't proof positive of deception, but they do indicate a pattern of questionable activity on the part of the bank. Amos has enough info to write a whole series of articles on the 1st National's lending practices."

"Dalton has a way with words. He'd phrase his accusations in such a way that the bank's legal eagles couldn't touch him. Still, there'd be no doubt in anyone's mind as to Golden's guilt."

"As they say, the pen is mightier than the sword."

"Which is why you're discounting the *Rag*'s editor as a suspect."

"Yes. While the file on Trace is interesting, it doesn't intrigue me as much as the one in the other envelope. Apparently Amos was keeping tabs on Wade Wilkins from the moment he arrived in town."

Carl picked up the second envelope. He pulled out a file almost as thick as the first one and opened it. Several pictures fell out and landed on the desk.

"Looks like Dalton's as handy with a camera as he is with a pencil. These are nice, clear shots."

He examined a 5x7 photo of Wilkins speaking with Golden, Sr. outside the gym. Wilkins appeared angry while Golden was all smiles.

"Interesting picture," said Carl. "I'd love to know what they were talking about."

"Can't you guess? Golden brought Wilkins on board at Bruck. Given what we know of the banker, I'd say he's reminding Wilkins of that and demanding special favors for his son."

"You're probably right. Still, there's no reason Wilkins had to bend to the request. Golden may have sponsored him for the coaching job, but he couldn't affect Wilkins's status once he was hired. The man had a legal contract with the university."

"He had a contract, but I'm not sure how legal it was. Take a look at the other pictures. Wilkins is wearing a mustache in that first photo with Golden, but he's clean shaven in the other two."

"He looks much younger here," said Carl, holding up a thumbnail shot of the coach in a football uniform. "When was it taken?"

"About ten years ago. Dalton got that out of a yearbook from a college in Iowa. Look at the writing on the back."

The professor turned the photo over in his hand. His bushy eyebrows immediately merged into a frown.

"Harry Wade? You mean, Wilkins wasn't the man's real name?"

"Nope. He assumed that name sometime after he left school."

"You don't seem surprised by that," said Carl, his eyes now firmly fixed on Caroline. "Why do I get the impression you knew about this before your visit with Dalton?"

Caroline grinned. "Nikki provided me with a clue earlier today." She told Carl about the conversation Martin had overheard in the gym. "Wilkins sported a mustache when he arrived at Bruck. Martin assumed Allison was referring to that when she said, 'I liked you better when you were hairy'. But 'hairy' isn't a word you'd normally use to describe a mustache. It made more sense to me that Allison was calling Wilkins by a previous name. 'I liked you better when you were Harry.'"

"A remark like that would indicate some degree of intimacy between Wilkins and Miss Moore."

"Definitely. I can't believe the two of them were strangers meeting for the first time. Backing up my theory was the fact that Martin couldn't find any information about Wilkins on the internet. Nancy Kuhnkey's friend in Chicago had the same problem. I suggested the detective do a search for the name Harry Wilkins or Harry Wade."

"Why Harry Wade?"

"I once read that people who assume new identifies often incorporate part of their old name into their new one. With the coach, it could have been either Wade or Wilkins."

"You continue to amaze me," said Carl, shaking his head. He glanced back at the file on Wilkins. "You've obviously checked through these papers already. Why don't you spare me the effort and tell me what else is in here."

Caroline reached for another piece of cheese. Two chews and a swallow later, she did as the professor asked.

"Amos honestly believed that none of the information he'd collected on Trace would help the police. That's why he didn't show Jake his files after the murder. Then he heard Martin had been taken in for questioning. Knowing I'd get involved in the case, he prepared a sanitized version of the files and simply waited for me to show up at his office. Everything was going well until I asked him about Trace's father. At that point, he began to suspect I knew his secret."

"Dalton was originally from Chicago. So were you. He might have thought you'd heard about the scandal before you moved here."

"Possibly. What really threw him was the fact that Nancy's Chicago connection was looking into his financial records. Alexsa's comment to Maddy that Amos was owned by the bank put everything he said into doubt. I thought it was important to know how far I could trust his word."

"He probably wouldn't have come clean with you except for that phone call from his buddy in the county records office."

"I think you're right about that. But I believed him

when he said Wilkins's death changed his mind about
going to the police. He showed me the files he prepared
for Jake. He left out the paperwork on the bank dealings—
that was solely for my benefit to prove he wasn't 'owned'
by Golden—but he included everything you see here on
Wilkins and Trace, Jr."

"So Jake now knows what we know."

"I should think so. Amos dialed the police station as
I was leaving. I assume he was setting up a meeting for
four-thirty this afternoon with Jake."

A rap on the door preceded Maddy Moeller's grand entrance. Carrying a large boxed pizza and a two-liter bottle
of Coke, she waltzed into the room, did a nifty pirouette,
and then bowed from the waist.

"Your dinner, madam," she said as she slid the box onto
the desk. "And for you, sir, champagne."

"That's a weird color for champagne," grumbled Carl.
"A weird bottle, too."

"Use your imagination," said Maddy. "We'll toast with
the real stuff later tonight when Jake can join us."

"And what will we be celebrating?" asked Caroline.

Maddy looked at her in surprise. "Why, Martin's vin-
dication, of course. Haven't you heard? Sue Walker's over
at the station making a confession. I was there when she
arrived with Jennie and Nancy Kuhnkey. Tom didn't kill
Trace after all. It was Sue!"

FORTY-TWO

"Hot diggedy dog!" Carl rubbed his hands together in glee. "Martin's off the hook."

"Of course I don't have all the details," said Maddy as she opened the box and pulled out a slice of pizza. "Jake hustled the three of them into his office the minute they arrived. But Sue was carrying on about making a confession, and Jennie looked white as a ghost."

"Hold on a minute," said Caroline. "It wasn't…"

"Annie didn't know a thing about it, which is strange because she's usually on top of everything that goes on at the station." Maddy handed the pizza to Carl and dived back in the box for a second slice. "I rushed over here as soon as I could."

"Maddy…"

"But I had to stop for something to eat. As Jake would say, no celebration's complete without pizza!"

Caroline waved both hands in the air in a desperate attempt to draw Maddy's attention. She felt like a railroad flagman standing in the middle of the track trying foolishly to halt a runaway train.

"I would have called first if I'd known you hadn't heard," said Maddy, pushing a piece of pizza into Caroline's outstretched hand. "But I figured Nancy Kuhnkey would have…"

"Stop!" cried Caroline, pushing her friend's hand aside. "You've got it all wrong, Maddy. Sue didn't kill Trace. She killed her husband!"

Speechless with surprise, Maddy stumbled backwards and flopped into a chair. Across the desk from her, Carl froze like a statue, the pizza he held to his lips dangling between his open jaws like an oversized tongue.

"I'm sorry, but it's true," said Caroline, shrugging her shoulders apologetically. "Sue was too busy trying to dispose of Tom's body Monday night to have anything to do with Trace Golden's murder. As for Wilkins, she didn't even know the man."

Carl and Maddy erupted into speech simultaneously.

"How do you know that?"

"When did you find out?"

"Why didn't you tell me?"

This last comment came from the professor, who by now was looking quite put out over the entire matter. Caroline hastened to put things right again.

"I didn't know Maddy was stopping by the police station before coming here, Carl. If I had, I would have told you about Sue. As it was, I was saving that bit of news for when we were all here together."

"You could have warned me," Carl grumbled. "Given me a hint of what was to come."

"Don't be childish," said Maddy, taking the high road on the issue. Having recovered the use of her vocal cords, she put them to work chastising the professor. "Caroline's been through a lot today what with her son running away and her daughter-in-law acting crazy. We have to forgive her if she couldn't find time to communicate with her friends. Perhaps she forgot to turn on her cell phone again."

Caroline took the dig as gracefully as possible. Instead of throttling her friend, she merely punched the little redhead on the arm.

"Give it up, Maddy. A sweet young thing like you shouldn't pout."

Maddy glared narrow eyed at Caroline, then relented with a long drawn out sigh. "Ruins my image, doesn't it," she said, breaking into a grin. "I guess I'm better at Lucille Ball than Bette Davis."

"Ladies, please!" said Carl, grumpily. "Enough with the small talk. I want to know what happened to Tom Walker."

"He's dead," said Caroline. "Sue killed him Monday night."

"You said that already," growled the professor. "Now tell me how she did it and why."

"How, I don't know. We'll have to wait for Jake to fill us in on that. As to why she did it, that's simple. Tom was abusing Sue and Jennie. If I'm not mistaken, he was the father of Jennie's baby."

"What?" gasped Maddy. "I don't believe it! Jennie told me Trace fathered her child."

"Only after you suggested it. Remember, Maddy, you told us she denied it at first. Then she spilled out some story about Trace Golden Sr. refusing to allow a marriage between his son and her. It was a story no one could contradict. Trace was dead and, given the circumstances, who would believe anything his father said?"

Caroline grabbed a slice of pizza and bit off a piece while the other two mulled over what she'd said. Carl finally broke the silence with a question.

"Where's the proof?"

"I have no proof, at least not yet. Again, we'll have to wait until we hear more from Jake. But think about the kind of man Tom Walker was. Everyone I've spoken to has had negative things to say about him. Jake called him a control freak, and Bertha Meyer said he treated both Sue and Jennie like property. Nancy Kuhnkey told me that Tom pushed his wife around all their married life. She made a remark about various kinds of meanness. She said Tom specialized in only one kind."

"She was implying Tom was an abuser."

"That was my impression. She unintentionally gave me another clue while we were talking. I suggested the Walkers might have been involved in a paternity suit against Trace Golden. Nancy became flustered and blew me off. She obviously didn't want to discuss Jennie's baby."

"She knew Trace wasn't the father," said Maddy.

"I'm think Nancy was counseling Sue and Jennie. I think she suspected they'd done away with Tom when he disappeared. She used the past tense yesterday whenever she mentioned his name. It was as if he didn't exist any more."

"That's why she kept trying to get us off the subject of Tom at the café this morning. And why she drove off in the direction of Sue's house." Maddy's anger flared. "How could she sit there and listen to us talk about him when all the time she knew he was dead!"

"Don't be too hard on her, Maddy. I don't think Nancy knew for sure until she confronted Sue this morning. I talked with her this afternoon. She assured me there's no conflict of interest in her representing both Martin and Sue. She's as upset about this as we are."

"So you think Sue killed Tom sometime after the demonstration Monday night."

"Yes, Carl. I think Trace told Sue more than we thought he did. The knowledge that her husband was camping out with a trailer court tramp wouldn't have stirred an abused woman to the kind of anger Sue displayed at the demonstration Monday night."

"I can only imagine what I'd feel if someone told me my husband raped my daughter," Maddy said slowly. "No matter how afraid of him I was, I'd kill him without a second thought."

"The proverbial straw that broke the camel's back," said Carl. "Jennie had to be involved in this, though. She must have broken down and told Sue the truth about her pregnancy, probably after Trace let the cat out of the bag."

"We'll know for sure when all becomes public, as it certainly will." Caroline glanced at her watch. "It's almost six-thirty. I imagine Sue's in custody by now, and Jake has men out looking for Allison Moore."

"Allison? What does she have to do with all this?"

Caroline looked up at a mystified Maddy before realizing how little the woman knew of the whole story. She told her about the conversation Martin had overheard between Allison and Wade Wilkins.

"Martin's in Iowa trying to prove a connection between the two of them. Nancy's P.I. in Chicago is doing the same thing."

"And you think Allison killed Wilkins?"

"Yesterday in the café, Eleanor Naumann said Alison had a failed romance with an ex-jock she'd met in college. I think that jock was Wade Wilkins."

"I don't remember…"

"I think you'd gone off to get a glass of water," said Caroline with a meaningful nod of her head.

"Oh, right!" said Maddy, glancing over at the professor and giggling again. "Carl had arrived in that silly costume."

"And you had a coughing fit," Carl supplied sourly. "Don't think I didn't know you were laughing at me, Maddy."

"That's why I asked Jake to tell you to keep an eye on the Moore sisters today," said Caroline. "You did drive over to Bill Morgan's place, didn't you?"

"Me and everybody else in town," replied Maddy with a grimace. "Talk about parking! The dealership was so crowded, I almost missed seeing little Bricole there." She reached into her purse and pulled out a folded sheet of paper. "Bricole was sketching pictures of the cowgirls and their horses. She asked me to give you this one."

Caroline took the paper and slipped it in the pocket of her jacket.

"I'll look at it later when I'm in the mood to appreciate art. Right now, I'd like to hear your take on Allison Moore. I think I have a fix on Donna's personality, but I've never met Allison."

"From what I saw last night, I'd say she's pretty handy with a horse," said Carl. "Outside of that, I don't know a thing about the woman."

"She's younger than Donna," said Maddy. "Prettier, too. She's probably in her late twenties, blond with a natural wave. She doesn't seem as tough as her sister, but she's as good with a lariat as Donna. They put on a mini Wild West show for Bill's customers. There was a roping demonstration, and Donna threw knives at a target, and…"

"Forget about that," cut in Caroline. "Tell me more about Allison. Did she seem nervous today? Ill at ease?"

"Not particularly." Maddy pursed her lips and looked down at the floor. "Now that you mention it, though, she walked out of the showroom a little before the others. Bill came out of his office and went over to talk with Allison and Donna. I heard him mention Wilkins's name, and I figured he was telling them about the murder. Donna seemed to take it in stride, but Allison looked upset. Ben Halloway said something to her and the two of them walked out of the building."

"Did you ever find out the results of Jake's background check on Ben?"

"I asked Annie about that when I stopped by the station. So far, Ben's come up clean. No prior arrests, no complaints on file. Apparently he's exactly what he says he is: a cowboy who retired from the rodeo to work for the Moores."

"I wonder if he's interested in one of them. Romantically, I mean."

"He sure seemed concerned about Allison when I saw them at the dealership. He had his arm around her shoulders when they left the place."

"If Ben is in love with Allison, it could be he killed Wilkins," said Carl.

"You're losing me again," said Maddy. "You forget, I don't know everything you know."

"What I meant was," said Carl, "Ben could have been jealous if he found out Allison had gone to see her old boyfriend. Jealous men have been known to kill their rivals."

"Over one conversation? No," said Caroline. "I don't think so. This was no crime of passion. Chan Daley told me the wound in Wilkins back had been enlarged after death. Whoever killed the coach went to great lengths to make it look like a bull gored him."

Frustrated, she shook her head.

"After my meeting with Amos, I drove down to the river and sat there trying to sort out my thoughts. This case is so puzzling, and frankly, I haven't been able to think clearly what with worrying about Martin and Nikki. I know I'm missing something, but for the life of me I can't figure out what it is."

"You've done your best, Cari. Now let it go," said Carl. "Thanks to you, Jake's in possession of Dalton's files. He'll get to the bottom of this mess before long."

Maddy raised her hand sheepishly. "Forgive me for asking, but what's all this about Amos Dalton?"

"Amos collected a file of information on Wade Wilkins. The file could help catch the coach's killer," said Caroline. "Amos was meeting with Jake at four-thirty today to hand it over."

Maddy stared at Caroline, her brows scrunched up in a frown.

"I got to the police station at four o'clock, and I didn't leave until after five. I can tell you right now, Amos Dalton never met with Jake today."

Caroline sat up straighter in her chair.

"Are you sure of that?"

"I'm positive," insisted Maddy. "I spoke with Jake for a few minutes when I first arrived. Then I stepped outside and called Bertha on my cell phone. We talked about the demonstration scheduled for tonight, whether we should honor the curfew imposed by the Archangels or go on with the picketing as planned. After that, I spent nearly an hour talking with Annie. There's no way Amos could have slipped in the building without my noticing him."

Caroline reached for the phone on Carl's desk.

"I'm going to call the *Rag*. Without that file, Jake's still working in the dark."

She dialed the newspaper's phone number and sat waiting through a half dozen rings. The answering machine picked up and she left a short message along with her cell phone number.

"I don't understand," she said, hanging up the receiver. "I heard Amos set up that appointment with Jake. I wonder why he didn't show."

"Maybe he had second thoughts," said Carl. "Maybe his sense of integrity isn't as strong as you thought."

Caroline shook her head. "I don't believe that. Something else must have happened after I left. Something important enough to make him break the appointment."

"I could call Annie and ask her about it," said Maddy. "She'd know if he canceled."

Caroline waited impatiently as Maddy dialed the police station. Her frustration grew deeper when the Chief's wife hung up the phone.

"Annie's gone to dinner, and Jake's too busy to talk."

Carl rose from his chair and reached for his briefcase.

"I apologize to both of you ladies, but I have a meeting to attend. President Hurst met with the Board again today. He's called a special faculty meeting for seven o'clock to discuss Wilkins's death and its impact on the coming weekend."

"Is he canceling the Homecoming game?" asked Maddy.

"I doubt it," said Carl. "But I think the Board came to a final decision on the rodeo. The Moore sisters were asked to attend the second half of tonight's meeting, presumably so they could hear the worst. I've been told the Board members will be there, too."

"The eagles gather," muttered Caroline. She stood up and closed the now empty pizza box. "You go on, Carl. Maddy and I will clean up this mess."

"Actually, I have to leave, too," said Maddy, rising to her feet. "I was supposed to meet Bertha and the others outside Bruck Hall ten minutes ago." She waved at the box and napkins on the desk. "You can take care of this by yourself, can't you?"

Caroline waved them both to the door. "Go on, you two. This won't take a minute. I'll make sure the door is locked when I leave, Carl."

The professor grunted his assent and ushered Maddy out of the office. Caroline watched them go, then turned quickly to her work. Three minutes later she was walking down the hallway to the building's lobby. Two minutes after that, she was in her Jeep headed for Rhineburg, her destination, the *Rhineburg Rag*.

FORTY-THREE

CAROLINE STOOD OUTSIDE the *Rhineburg Rag* and peered in through the plate glass window. Dalton's desk was visible a few feet away, but the rest of the room was buried in angular shadows that blended into total blackness at the back of the room. In the far corner of the office, a thin strip of pale yellow light scored the floor beneath what Caroline knew to be a drape. She stared at the doorway through which Amos had disappeared only hours before. Was he there now, in that room behind the curtain?

She tried the door, expecting it to be locked. Instead, the knob turned easily in her hand. She stepped into the darkened hallway leading to the printing press room on the right and the large open office on the left.

"Mr. Dalton? Are you here?"

Somewhere in the rear of the building, a radio was playing soft music. Caroline felt along the wall and found a light switch opposite the main office. She flipped the switch, flooding the hallway with light.

"Amos? Are you in here?"

Again, there was no response. Caroline entered the office area, flipping switches as she found them until the entire room was bathed in brightness.

Amos's chair stood at an angle to his desk, pushed back until it touched the window. Outside of that, nothing seemed out of place in the office. Caroline hesitated, then walked across the room to the curtain and pulled it aside.

The doorway led into to a windowless room that had

probably been used for storage prior to its conversion to a kitchen cum lounge. Its only furnishings were a worn leather couch stacked with throw pillows, a short, squat coffee table fashioned from cement blocks covered with plywood, and a tiny sink with a counter and built in cabinet. Half a dozen mugs rested on the counter next to an automatic coffeepot. Next to them sat a portable radio tuned to classical music.

To the left of the doorway was an enclosed staircase leading down to what Caroline presumed to be the basement. A bare bulb protruded from a wall socket illuminating the steep wooden steps.

"Amos? Are you down there?"

Caroline gripped the banister and cautiously descended the stairs. The basement lights were turned on revealing long rows of filing cabinets positioned behind a wide wooden counter on the left side of the room. The surface of the counter was bare, while beneath it, protected by glass doors, were shelves lined with dated ledgers. To the right of the staircase was a smaller counter similar in design to the first. This one held a copying machine, several reams of paper, and a shredder. A dozen feet behind the counter stood a floor-to-ceiling shelving unit filled with cardboard boxes.

The musty odor of old newspapers clung to the place despite the whirring sounds of a dehumidifier and two ceiling fans. Another scent lingered in the air, one that made the hairs rise on the back of Caroline's neck. She took a step forward, searching the room with her eyes for the source of the smell. Circling the counter to her right, she found it.

Amos Dalton lay facedown, spread-eagled on the floor. The back of his head was a mass of clotted blood.

FORTY-FOUR

CAROLINE KNELT DOWN and ran her fingertips up the editor's neck. His carotid pulse was thready and barely palpable, but it was there, and that was a miracle in itself. Reaching for her cell phone with one hand, she slid the other under Dalton's nose and mouth. She felt a hint of warm breath on her fingers and said a silent prayer of thanks.

"I need an ambulance at the *Rhineburg Rag,*" she said when the 911 dispatcher came on the line. "And the police. Amos Dalton's been attacked. He's unconscious with a head injury."

She stayed on the line, giving information to the dispatcher even as she continued to examine Amos. Running her fingers down Dalton's limbs, she checked for obvious broken bones and found none. Her eyes strayed to a piece of cream-colored stationery clutched in his right hand. She slipped it from his grasp, glanced at the writing, then tucked it into her jacket pocket.

Shielded by the thick basement walls, Caroline didn't hear the wail of the approaching ambulance. It was the sound of booted feet running across the floor above her that alerted her to the presence of the paramedics.

"Down here!" she shouted. "In the basement!"

She stood up as the crew moved in with their gear. Jake was right behind them and motioned to her as she stepped aside.

"What happened?" he asked.

Caroline shrugged her shoulders. "I don't know. I came

looking for Amos when I heard he didn't keep his appointment with you this afternoon. All the lights were off in the building, but the door was unlocked. I came in and heard the radio playing in that little room upstairs. The light was on in there and on the staircase. I called for Amos, but there was no answer. Then I came down here and found him lying on the floor. Somebody smashed him in the back of the head."

"You don't think he fell?"

"No way," said Caroline, shaking her head. "Look around you. There's nothing here that could have caused that kind of damage to his skull."

Jake let his eyes rove over the counter. "No blood on the corners of that thing?"

"None that I saw. You can check it out for yourself once the paramedics have moved him."

"I certainly will," said Jake. He gazed down at Dalton. "Any idea why someone would want to hurt him?"

"It may have something to do with his files."

"What files?"

Caroline told him about the records Amos had amassed on Trace Golden and his father. "He also looked into Wade Wilkins's background. He had proof that Wilkins wasn't the man he claimed to be. The coach's real name was Harry Wade."

"You seem to know a lot more about Wilkins than I do," grumbled Jake. "How come Amos told you what he had, but didn't bother to contact me?"

"But he did, Jake. That's why he set up that four-thirty appointment with you. He was going to hand over the information he'd collected."

"He didn't say that when he called. I was under the impression he wanted an update on the murders."

The paramedics had finished their survey of Dalton's

wounds, started an IV, and hooked him up to a heart monitor. One of the men handed Jake the editor's wallet and car keys. Then he and his partner lifted the stretcher and started towards the stairs.

"He's in a pretty bad way," the medic said grimly. "I don't think he'll be talking to you soon, if ever."

Jake motioned to the uniformed cops waiting near the stairs.

"Treat it as a crime scene, boys. I want the works, prints, photos, everything. Got it?" He turned to Caroline. "Any idea where he kept those files you mentioned?"

"He said they were in a safe somewhere down here. He gave me copies, and I assumed the package meant for you contained copies also. The originals should be here, unless whoever hit him stole them."

"Then it's a safe we're looking for. Murphy! Get over here!"

Jake said a few words to one of the uniforms. The man grunted in reply and walked off toward the far side of the room, his hand resting lightly on his gun.

"Let's take a look at this end, Cari. If it's a wall safe, it may be hidden behind those cartons."

Jake circled the spot where Amos had fallen. Caroline followed, and the two of them began removing boxes from the shelving unit. Five minutes later, the Chief clapped Caroline on the shoulder and pointed to a spot on the wall where a thin band of metal showed at the edge of one carton. He pushed the carton aside and smiled.

"Found it! Okay, Harry. I need you to dust this door for prints before I open it."

One of Jake's men hurried over with a brush and powder. He performed his magic on the safe, then moved away as his boss took over.

Jake held up a slip of paper he'd removed from Dalton's wallet and read off a series of numbers.

"Five will get you ten, this is the combination."

Caroline looked on as Jake fiddled with the lock. Sure enough, the tumblers soon clicked into place. The door swung open, revealing nothing but empty space.

"Damn!"

Jake slammed the door shut and shouted for Murphy who came running on the double.

"I'm going upstairs, Murph. Seal off this area until the coroner gets here, then assign each officer to a section of the room. We're looking for two files, one on Trace Golden and the other on Wade Wilkins. I want to know one way or another if those papers are still in this building." Jake turned and walked to the staircase. "Come on upstairs with me, Cari."

"You can have my copies," Caroline said as she climbed the steps behind the big policeman. "I'm pretty sure Amos gave me everything he had on both men."

"That'll help," grunted Jake. "But I'd like to get my hands on the originals. Let's check out Dalton's office. Maybe we'll get lucky and find those files locked up in his desk."

But they weren't lucky. The desk held nothing but the usual items found in any office plus a few hand-written notes dealing with coming events in Rhineburg. Jake searched Dalton's filing cabinet next. It, too, was empty of any incriminating evidence.

"I can't waste any more time here," said Jake as he closed the last drawer in the cabinet. "Murphy can work on this room next if he doesn't find anything downstairs."

"I'll get you the files Amos copied for me," said Caroline. "They're out in my car."

She walked outside to the Jeep, acutely aware of the

need for haste now that the killer had struck again. She thumbed the remote control device on her key chain and watched the interior light flash on in the Jeep. Pulling open the passenger side door, she reached in to grab the envelopes lying on the front seat. Her hand froze in mid-air. She rocked back on her heels, a tingle of fear running down her spine.

The files were gone.

FORTY-FIVE

CAROLINE RELEASED THE gas pedal and flipped on the Jeep's turn signal. Tapping the brake, she nosed the SUV off the highway at the Bruck University exit. Misty rain washed the windshield and glistened on the blacktop road leading to the college. Watching the wipers do their work, Caroline thought the weather perfectly matched her mood, gray and depressing.

The attack on Amos weighed heavily on her mind. Measuring her own actions against the results, she found them wanting. In hindsight, she should have insisted that Amos go straight to Jake with his files. Waiting may well have cost him his life.

But she hadn't known then the extent of the information in those papers. It was only after skimming through the files that she'd been able to link Wade Wilkins to Allison Moore.

Allison, the elusive Allison. Younger than Donna, and prettier, too. She'd gone to see Wilkins the night of Trace Golden's murder. Wilkins, the man she'd almost married, the man who'd abandoned her for a coaching career. Allison had been angry, had remarked that she'd liked him better when he was Harry Wade. Wilkins must have said something nasty to warrant that kind of response from his former lover. But then Wilkins was a nasty man, egotistical and cold-hearted.

Had Trace, like Martin, overheard their conversation? Had he followed Allison when she left the gym, so angry over the possibility of a rodeo destroying his chance to impress the scouts that he confronted Moore outside the bullpen?

Allison was physically strong. Caroline had seen that the previous night when the bulls escaped on campus. Riding with Ben Halloway, she'd risked life and limb rounding up the animals. She could have killed Trace in a moment of fury, then done the same to her ex-lover, Wade Wilkins.

Caroline needed to know more about Allison, needed more proof of a link between her and Wilkins. If only Martin would call. She'd tried to reach him once on his cell phone, but he'd turned it off, probably to prevent a possible trace on his calls by the police. There was one other person who could help her, though, and that was Brighty Pfister.

Pulling off to the side of the road, Caroline pulled out her cell phone and dialed Brighty's number. Mrs. Pfister answered on the second ring.

"Brighty, this is Caroline Rhodes. I was wondering if you could answer a question for me about your niece, Allison."

"What kind of question?" Brighty asked suspiciously. "You're not in cahoots with that slimeball Hurst, are you?"

"Me?" Caroline laughed. "Oh, no. He's the last person I'd be in cahoots with, Brighty. Personally, I can't stand the man. I called to ask where Allison attended college. I have a nephew interested in rodeo. I thought maybe Allison's school had a collegiate rodeo team."

"Truth be told, I don't know about that," said Brighty, her voice taking on a friendlier tone. "I suppose your nephew could call the University of Iowa, though, and ask somebody there. That's where Allison went to college."

"I'll have him do that," said Caroline. "Thanks for the help, Brighty."

She rang off, satisfied that her little white lie had

worked. If the radio account that morning was correct, Wilkins had graduated from the U. of I. It was a sure bet Allison had met him there.

She thought of the letter she'd taken from Amos Dalton's hand and smiled grimly. Thanks to Brighty Pfister, Allison was not going to succeed at framing Martin.

Caroline dropped the cell phone on the passenger seat and drove the rest of the way to the campus. The street in front of Bruck Hall bristled with parked cars when she arrived there. Bill Morgan's shiny new Cadillac led the pack, indicating he'd chauffeured Alexsa to the meeting. Lian Daley's red Volkswagen sat nose to bumper with the Caddie followed by a black Chevy pickup truck with the words "Moore Sisters, Rodeo Contractors" emblazoned on the door.

It looked to Caroline like the entire Board had shown up for the meeting along with all the university lawyers and those faculty members who lived in town. The line of vehicles stretched from the administration building to Hildy Hall, forcing her to park in the lot next to the auditorium. Locking the car, she walked hurriedly through the rain toward Bruck Hall. She'd gone only a few yards when she remembered the cell phone lying on the passenger seat.

"Damn!"

She jogged back to the Jeep, reached into her pocket, and pulled out a folded sheet of paper along with her keys. The paper fluttered to the ground.

"Double damn!"

She bent to retrieve it, punching the remote control on the key chain at the same time. The Jeep's roof lamp flashed on as the locks clicked open. Illuminated by the dim light, a scribbled message showed on one corner of the now damp paper.

Caroline opened the car door and smoothed out the folds

on the picture Bricole Gregori had entrusted to Maddy earlier that afternoon. It was a drawing of two women dressed in fringed jackets and buckskin skirts.

One woman was etched against a background of three long-horned cattle. She appeared despondent, standing with head bent low and hands covering her face. Her companion was drawn in bolder strokes in the forefront of the picture. This woman's upper features were shadowed by the broad brim of a cowboy hat, only her mouth showing clearly. Her lips were open, her smile wide as she danced arm in arm with a ragged scarecrow.

Caroline turned the drawing over and glanced at the words "be careful!" penned in red letters on one edge of the cream-colored paper.

"Don't worry, Bricole," she murmured. "I already know how dangerous Allison can be."

She tossed the picture on the passenger seat. Grabbing her phone, she locked the car door and hurried off toward Bruck Hall.

Frosted glass globes jutted from the brick walls on either side of the Hall's massive doors. Caroline paused in the lamplight to shake the rain from her jacket, undecided as to what excuse she'd give for barging in on the meeting. She needed to find Carl, but she didn't want Allison Moore alerted to her presence in the building.

"Nothing works like the truth," she muttered as she entered the Hall's spacious lobby. "Or a reasonable facsimile thereof."

She was greeted by the grim faces of six previous university presidents who glared down at her from their framed homes high on the lobby's walls. She gave the oil paintings a cursory glance before her attention was drawn to the long corridor leading to the rear of Bruck Hall.

A door midway down on the left had been flung open

and people were swarming into the hallway. Caroline recognized several of the male professors she'd met at the previous year's Christmas party. Of the women present in the group, one in particular stood out from the others. Tall, blond, and willowy, Sue Chuey was dressed in a conservative gray suit that did little to hide her curvaceous figure. A splash of red dotted her neck where the collar of her silk blouse bloomed into overlaying ruffles that spilled over the narrow lapels of her jacket. The effect was both feminine and regal, and Sue clearly knew it. Head held high, the history professor ignored the admiring glances of the men around her and waved languidly in Caroline's direction.

"Mrs. Rhodes! How nice to see you again."

Veering away from the others, Sue approached Caroline, gripped her by the elbow, and casually steered her towards a reception room off the lobby.

"I'd like to speak to you, if you have a moment," she said quietly. "I'd rather the others not hear us."

"I'm afraid I don't have time to talk right now," said Caroline, darting a glance over Sue's shoulder. "I need to find Professor Atwater before he leaves the building. I mistakenly left a package in his office today. I'd like to retrieve it before it gets tossed in with the outgoing mail."

"Carl's deep in conversation with Mrs. Morgan and probably will be for quite a while. Don't worry. You won't miss him." Sue kept her hand on Caroline's arm and drew her deeper into the room. "I want to talk to you about Al Sperling. What I have to say is rather important."

Caroline's reluctance must have shown because Sue hurriedly added, "I promise I won't keep you long. Please, Mrs. Rhodes. Hear me out."

Caroline relented with a sigh. "I don't have more than a minute or two. I need to find Carl."

"Yes, I know. I also know you believe Al may have murdered Trace Golden."

"Do you think he did it?"

"Of course not." Sue shook her head impatiently. "Al can be difficult at times, but he has a good heart. He's gentle and quite bright."

"Bright people make the best murderers. It's the dumb ones who get caught."

"You're probably right about that. But Al doesn't have it in him to kill someone."

"Given the right circumstances," said Caroline, "almost anyone could kill."

"Again, you're probably right." Chuey looked back nervously at the open door. "I could get fired if what I'm about to say became public knowledge. But I have to take that risk. I'm hoping that what I tell you will deflect suspicion away from Al."

"The only person I want to deflect suspicion away from is my son, Miss Chuey. I'm not about to lead the police astray. Not to save Al Sperling's skin. Or yours, if it comes to that."

"I'm not asking you to lie. I'm only asking that you try to understand my position."

"And what is your position," asked Caroline, angry now because she could guess what was coming.

"I'm…I'm fond of the young man," said Chuey, blushing. "I know it sounds ridiculous. I'm old enough to be Al's mother. But Al is rather special. He's…"

"I don't have time for this. If you know something about Golden's murder, spit it out. If not…"

Chuey grabbed Caroline's arm as she turned to walk away.

"Please, listen to me! I was with Al at the gym Monday evening. I can vouch for what he told you."

"You were at the demonstration?" Caroline looked at Chuey in surprise. "I wouldn't have thought you'd risk being seen together."

"I wasn't dressed like this," said Chuey with a rueful little smile. "It's amazing how you can blend into a crowd when you're wearing jeans and a Bruck sweatshirt. A baseball cap helps, too."

"I guess it does. So you were with Al when he trailed Martin to the gym."

"Actually, I followed him there."

"It must have been a regular procession. First Martin, then Trace, then Al, with you bringing up the rear. It's a wonder no one else chose to tag along."

"But there was someone else near the gym that night. I don't think Al noticed—he was too busy worrying about Martin—but I saw her standing in the shadows near the entrance to Hildy Hall."

"Who was it?" Caroline asked sharply. "Who did you see?"

Chuey stole another glance at the doorway, her nervousness even more apparent now.

"I hate to pull another innocent person into this mess. I'm only telling you what I saw because this woman could confirm that Al left the gym with me. He had nothing to do with Trace's death."

"But don't you see, Sue? She could also confirm Martin's innocence!" Caroline threw up her hands in disgust. "I know you want to keep your relationship with Al a secret, but if you don't tell me who it was, I'll go straight to Jake with your story."

"And I'll deny I ever told you one word of it!"

"Don't be stubborn, Sue! Trace had a lot of girlfriends. If this was one of them, she might have been waiting for him to come out of the gym. She might have met up with him long after Martin left."

Sue shook her head. "I'm afraid you're barking up the wrong tree. This woman was definitely not an admirer of Trace Golden. When she stepped out of the darkness, I saw her face. I recognized her right away."

"I thought I heard voices in here."

Caroline and Sue turned simultaneously to see Donna Moore standing in the doorway. A grim smile played on Donna's lips as she peered into the darkened room.

"I was looking for the ladies' room, but I guess this isn't it. Would one of you mind showing me the way?"

"I had the same problem myself the first time I visited Bruck Hall," said Caroline. She moved past Chuey to intercept the older of the two Moore sisters. "But you've been here before, haven't you, Donna? In fact, you've attended several meetings in this building."

Moore shrugged. "I never had to use the ladies' room before."

"I see. Well, let me show you where it is." Caroline shot Chuey a warning look. "Thanks, for your encouragement, Sue. I'm so worried about Martin, I can hardly think straight any more. It's nice to know you believe in his innocence."

Sue played along.

"I'm not the only person who believes in Martin. The faculty is behind your son a hundred percent. We're sure this entire mess will be cleared up soon."

"I hope so," Caroline said glumly. She turned and motioned to Donna to follow her. "I can't believe how many things have gone wrong in the past week. I hope the news was better for you and your sister tonight than it was for me."

"The fight goes on," Moore said offhandedly. "At least

Allison didn't have to witness this latest battle. She hates all this fighting."

"Your sister wasn't at the meeting?"

"She and Ben are off checking up on the stock. We have them quartered at a couple of different farms in the area. Someone has to keep an eye on their care."

"That's understandable."

So Allison had missed the meeting. That meant she had no alibi for the attack on Amos Dalton. Another point in Martin's favor, thought Caroline. But how had Allison learned of the file on Wade Wilkins? Had Amos somehow tipped his hand when he was investigating Wilkins's background?

That was hard to believe. Amos was a wily old reporter with years of experience under his belt. But he didn't know that Allison had once been close to Wilkins. At least, she'd seen nothing in the file that indicated he knew. He'd covered the past week's mayhem, though. It could be he'd interviewed the two sisters and said something that aroused Allison's suspicions.

Loose lips sink ships, thought Caroline, remembering the old World War II adage. It would be a shame if Amos had unwittingly caused this night's attack.

Caroline tried to make light conversation until she could rid herself of Donna. She moved quickly down the hallway, avoiding the small groups huddled in conversation along the way.

"I suppose you and Allison divvy up the work when it comes to the contracting business."

"I take care of the promotion and publicity end of the business, plus problems like the ones we're having here. Allison handles the stock and transportation issues. Ben's our ranch manager."

"Hmm."

"See those guys?" Donna gestured at three men talking quietly outside President Hurst's office. Dressed in Armani suits, all three carried heavy briefcases. "They think they have me cornered. But what do lawyers know? They're so lost in legalese, they can't see the forest for the trees."

Caroline stopped dead in her tracks. Can't see the forest for the trees. Of course, she thought. How stupid of me!

"The ladies' room is right over there," she said, indicating a door off to their left. "If you'll excuse me, Donna, I need to find someone."

She turned on her heel and walked briskly back down the corridor. Her eyes searched the thinning crowd for a glimpse of Carl. The chairman of the history department was nowhere to be seen, nor was Alexsa with whom he'd supposedly been talking. When she reached the meeting room at the end of the hallway, it was empty.

"Rats! He has to be here somewhere."

"Talking to yourself again?"

Caroline spun around and came face to face with Lian Daley. Lian's dark eyes glistened merrily.

"That's a bad sign, you know," said the petite psychiatrist with a grin. "It's even worse if you start answering yourself."

Ignoring Lian's playful banter, Caroline said, "I've got to find Carl. Have you seen him anywhere?"

Lian frowned. "I think he said he was going back to his office. What's wrong, Caroline? You look like the devil's on your heels."

"Not the devil, Lian. A killer."

She swept by the other woman and out of the room. The corridor was practically deserted with only a few stragglers lagging behind. Donna Moore was nowhere in sight.

"Gotta find Carl," muttered Caroline as she dashed to the door. She threw it open and ran down the wet stairs, cutting across the lawn toward the social studies building. Her first thought on finding the files missing from the Jeep had been that they were stolen. Then she remembered she hadn't brought them with her. Carl had been examining the pictures of Wade Wilkins when Maddy arrived with the pizza. In the ensuing excitement over Sue Walker, the files had been pushed aside and forgotten.

If the killer hadn't gotten to them first, they were still lying on the desk in Carl's office.

FORTY-SIX

A SECURITY LIGHT burned brightly over the entrance to the social studies building. Passage into the building was blocked by a door that refused to budge when Caroline pulled on it. Locked for the night, the door was one more obstacle standing between her and the files.

The windows on either side of the entrance were shuttered, as were those of the first floor classrooms. Caroline backed away from the door and sprinted around the east corner to the rear of the building where the history department's headquarters overlooked the north end of the campus.

The rain had ended, but the lawn was soggy with water. The wet grass lapped at her ankles, soaking her blue denim gym shoes. Her feet were sodden by the time she reached what she guessed to be Carl's office.

Unlike the front windows, shades covered the ones here. If Carl was inside, he hadn't turned on a lamp. No light penetrated the shade or outlined its edges.

I've missed him, thought Caroline. She pounded the windowsill in frustration before remembering how easily Martin had gained access to the building Monday night. Carl was notoriously absent-minded when it came to the more mundane things in life, like locking office windows. Maybe, just maybe, he'd forgotten to do so tonight.

She pushed up on the wooden window frame. Sure enough, it eased open with the barest of creaks. Climbing over the sill, she entered the darkened office.

The files were lying on the far corner of Carl's desk. Caroline padded across the carpet and scooped up the envelopes. She checked their contents by the light of the moon shining through the open window. Everything was as she'd left it.

Breathing more easily, she threw one leg back over the sill. She was halfway out when she saw Donna Moore standing less than a foot away in the grass. Donna was holding a Bowie knife, its point aimed straight at Caroline's chest.

"Keep on coming," Donna hissed. "And do it quietly."

Caroline considered diving back into the office, but the knife was too close for comfort. Knowing she had no other option, she slid her other leg over the sill and dropped to the ground, the envelopes gripped to her chest.

"I'll take those," said Donna, extending her hand. "Close the window."

Caroline did as she was told. Moore slid a backpack off her shoulder and dropped to one knee. Her eyes never wavered from Caroline's face as she slipped the files into the bag. She zipped it closed and stood up.

"Now we're going to take a walk." She motioned with the knife toward the auditorium. "That way."

Caroline peered through the darkness to where the rodeo bulls were quartered in their pens.

"Planning another accident? How quaint."

"Shut up and move."

Moore stepped behind her and nudged her in the back with the knife. Caroline felt the blade against her spine.

"No need to ruin the jacket," she said dryly.

Her initial shock had given way to anger and a surge of adrenaline. She moved forward at a brisk pace, her thoughts racing as she considered various means of escape. The science building loomed ahead on the right, followed by the gym and Hildy Hall. A quick turn at the corner of one of them and she'd have a fair chance to out-run her captor.

Moore must have read her mind. She placed the tip of the knife against Caroline's neck.

"Move away from the wall. Do it now!"

"We'll be seen out there in the open field. You're tak-ing a risk moving out of the shadows."

"I've been taking risks all my life, Mrs. Rhodes. So far, they've paid off." Donna put pressure on the knife and drew blood. "Now, do as I say."

Caroline stepped away from the wall. The back of her neck tingled with pain. She hunched her shoulders, draw-ing her coat collar up against the wound. The nick was su-perficial, but Donna's willingness to use the knife sent a quiver of fear through her.

She steadied her nerves with a deep breath of cold night air, then lengthened her stride, unwilling to die before she saw her first grandchild born.

"I had it all wrong, didn't I? I thought Allison was the dangerous member of the family."

"She's much too sentimental to be dangerous."

"Yes, I realize that now. But, as you said earlier, some-times you can't see the forest for the trees."

Donna said nothing. Caroline kept up her patter as they passed the science building.

"You're the practical sister, aren't you? The one in charge of damage control. I should have realized from the way you handled President Hurst that you don't take kindly to threats."

Donna remained silent. Caroline tried to draw her out with a little embellishment on the truth.

"Chief Moeller knows about the relationship between

your sister and Wade Wilkins. He knows she was in his office Monday night."

"Allison was nowhere near the gym."

"It's a little late for denial, Donna. Allison went to see Wilkins—or should I call him Harry Wade?—and you followed her. Someone saw you outside the gym." Sue Chuey, to be exact. But she wasn't telling Donna that. No use putting Sue in danger, too. Perhaps another fib would help shatter Miss Moore's confidence. "You were seen entering the gym by the side door. What happened after that, Donna? Did you run into Trace Golden in the locker room? Did he threaten to make trouble for the rodeo?"

"I had nothing to do with Golden's death. Neither did my sister."

"Oh, come one! You killed Trace, and Wilkins saw you. You killed him to cover up the first murder."

"You've still got it wrong, Mrs. Rhodes. Even if I had gone into the gym like you say I did, I wouldn't have been the only person there. You forget Wade Wilkins was in the building." Donna tapped Caroline on the back with the knife. "Now, shut up and keep walking. Go that way, toward the auditorium."

Caroline veered to the right. The temporary corral was a mere dozen yards away.

"You'll never finger Martin as the killer if you toss my body in with the bulls. Jake's too smart to fall for it again."

"You talk too damned much," said Donna, her voice tight with anger. "I ought to slip this knife between your ribs right here and now."

"Blame it on my nerves. I tend to babble when I'm scared."

Better to let her think I'm afraid, thought Caroline as she stepped up her pace. Maybe she'll relax and let down her guard.

Donna wasn't taken in by the ploy. She shoved the knife between Caroline's shoulder blades, splitting the fabric of her jacket.

"Don't try anything funny or I'll drive this blade into your back."

"I'll behave," said Caroline, raising both hands waist high. "Just tell me where to go."

"Take the path between the auditorium and the gym. We're going to your car."

"I didn't drive tonight. I walked to the Hall."

"You're a poor liar, Mrs. Rhodes. I've been trailing you ever since you left the school this evening. You drove to Rhineburg, to the newspaper office. Then you drove back here. You parked in the auditorium lot."

"I thought you were at the meeting."

"Allison went in my place. I told her I wasn't feeling well."

Caroline was feeling none too well herself. Her hope of escape was fading fast as they passed the gym and approached the rear of Hildy Hall. The cracked walkway leading to the parking lot was narrow and poorly illuminated, certainly not conducive to a sprint in the dark. According to Maddy, who had seen a demonstration of her skill at Bill Morgan's dealership, Donna knew how to handle a knife. She wouldn't hesitate to throw it if Caroline bolted down the path.

Delaying tactics were definitely in order.

"Whoa!" Caroline faked a stumble and rolled to the ground. She grabbed her right leg. "I twisted my knee," she groaned. "Damn, that hurts! Help me up, Donna."

Donna took a step backwards as Caroline reached for her hand.

"Aw, come on. Help me."

"Get up," Donna hissed. "Now!"

Caroline shook her head. "I can't stand by myself. I think I tore a ligament, or maybe a tendon."

Donna sucked her bottom lip between her teeth. She scowled down at Caroline, a nervous twitch contorting one side of her face.

"I don't care if you walk or crawl, Mrs. Rhodes. One way or another, you're going to make it to your car."

She doesn't want to kill me here, thought Caroline. I wonder why.

She heard a scuffling noise off to the right and turned her head. Six feet away, a bucking bull stood wide-eyed in its pen, its head lowered and staring at her. Flared nostrils signaled its agitation. It rumbled a deep-throated bellow and pawed the ground.

"You don't want to upset them," said Donna, pointing to the bulls. "They can be mean when they smell fear."

Caroline hobbled to her feet. "I'll take your word for it."

She limped toward the walkway, dragging her right leg and wincing in mock pain. At the same time she glanced over her shoulder to where a light had gone on in Ben Halloway's trailer.

"Why were you following me tonight?"

"I saw you leave the *Rhineburg Rag* this afternoon. You were carrying a package."

"So?"

"I went there to discuss publicity for the rodeo. Dalton was on the phone making an appointment with Jake Moeller when I walked into the office."

"You saw the files he'd collected on Trace and Wade Wilkins."

"They were lying on his desk. He made me wait while he put them away."

"You followed him downstairs."

"Of course. I had to know if he'd found out about

Wilkins and my sister. I watched him put the files in the safe. Then I noticed he'd been running the copying machine."

"Ah!"

"It didn't take me long to put two and two together. You'd gone to him for help, and he'd given you all the information he had. I couldn't allow that to fall into the hands of the police."

"So you knocked Amos on the head, then came searching for me."

"I didn't see your car in town, so I took a chance you'd gone to the university. Uncle Otto told me you and Professor Atwater were working together to clear your son's name."

"While you were working to ruin it."

"Nothing personal, Mrs. Rhodes. It's just that prison doesn't much appeal to me." Donna closed the gap between them. "That's right. Turn here and keep moving."

Still dragging her leg, Caroline entered the shadowed recess between the gym and the auditorium. The sidewalk stretched before her, a black strip of cement bracketed by high walls. The electric exit sign over the players' entrance was dark.

"That exit lamp was lit last Saturday," said Caroline, stopping and pointing to the sign. "It was broken when Carl and I walked this way on Monday night. Did you smash the bulb before you dragged Trace's body out of the gym?"

"Look at me, Mrs. Rhodes. Do you really think I'm tall enough to reach that light?"

Caroline turned to face Moore. Her eyes locked with Donna's. In that moment, she knew the truth.

"Coach Wilkins killed Trace, didn't he?"

Donna nodded. "It's beginning to make sense to you now, isn't it?"

"Golden either saw or overheard your sister talking to Wilkins," Caroline said slowly. "They must have been discussing their past, the years when Wade Wilkins was Harry Wade." She paused, the look on Donna's face telling her she was right. "Wilkins must have had a good reason to change his name."

Moore cocked her head to one side, her lip curling in disgust.

"He sure did. Good old Harry got caught with his pants down in a high school locker room. He was the football coach, and he was screwing one of his players."

Donna's gaze wandered to a spot on the gymnasium wall. The hand holding the knife drifted downward.

"I told Allison from the start that Harry was no good. She thought she was in love with him, though. She wouldn't listen to a word I said."

Caroline bowed her head in feigned sympathy. She slid her eyes to the right. A foot behind her was the side entrance to Hildy Hall. She glanced down at the thin block of wood wedged between the fire door and the jam.

"It nearly broke her heart when he skipped town. It was even worse when the cops showed her pictures of Harry with that boy."

Caroline edged sideways toward Hildy Hall. She inched her arm down behind her back, her hand twisting outward.

"Then I saw him standing in the middle of the Emergency Room shouting at those boys. I couldn't believe he'd have the nerve to start over so near to home."

Donna shook herself. Her eyes shifted to Caroline's outstretched hand. Her own hand flew up, the knife extended and aimed at Caroline's throat.

"Urg!"

Donna lunged forward. Caroline ducked her head and rolled to the right. She crashed into the wall, slid backwards, and grabbed the edge of the door. Flinging it open, she used it as both shield and weapon, first deflecting the downward slash of the knife, then smashing the door full force into Donna's face. Moore ricocheted to the ground, blood pouring from her nose.

FORTY-SEVEN

DONNA WAS STILL on the ground when Caroline slipped through the doorway and into Hildy Hall. Guided only by the dim light from the exit sign, she sprinted down the carpeted aisle toward the stage. The staircase leading up to the apron was next to the orchestra pit. She rounded the pit at full speed and took the steps two at a time.

The outer curtain was drawn, hiding the main body of the stage. Unlike the last time she'd been in the building, she made no effort to circle the heavy velvet drape. Instead, she dropped to the floor and rolled under it.

Scrambling to her feet on the other side, she paused to get her bearings. As she did, she heard the side door slam.

Donna was in the building.

"The prop room," Caroline muttered, and swerved left toward where she thought was the door leading to the work area. In her haste on Saturday, she'd paid no attention to its exact location on the back wall. Now she wished she had. With the curtain closed, it was even darker here than in the rest of the theater. She could only hope she was headed in the right direction.

She'd taken only a few steps when her knee hit the edge of a sofa left behind from some past production. She stumbled against the armrest. The sofa shifted under her weight, scraping the floor as it moved. The scritch-scratch of wood on wood was barely audible, but it was enough to give her away.

"I hear you, Mrs. Rhodes. It's no use hiding from me."

Donna's voice echoed in the empty theater. It seemed to come from a distance, as if Moore had headed first to the lobby and was now walking slowly down the center aisle. Caroline guessed she had less than thirty seconds before the rodeo contractor reached the stage.

Moving quickly but cautiously, she continued her search for the prop room door. Her eyes were adjusting to the darkness now. She could make out the faint shapes of objects scattered about the stage, including two large crates standing directly in her path. She veered to the left to avoid them and stumbled into a second curtain, this one drawn back and gathered in tight folds against its rope pulley.

A booted foot scraped the floor of the apron. Caroline jerked her eyes to the right and saw the front curtain sway on its hangers.

Donna was searching for the center separation.

Time, thought Caroline. I need time!

She looked around her for something she could use as a weapon. Outside of the crates and a few pieces of furniture, the stage was bare. Her gaze settled on the rope tethered to the side curtain, and she had an idea. She edged around the crates, grabbed the rope, and pulled.

The pulley worked smoothly, but the metal runner attached to the ceiling screeched in protest as she hauled hand over hand on the thick cord. Mindless of the noise, she yanked on the rope until the second set of drapes swung shut a few feet behind the first.

Hoping this tactic would delay Donna another few seconds, she released the rope and sprinted across the stage. The doorway was where she remembered it, cut into the wall next to the edge of the backdrop. She grabbed the handle and pulled.

The door opened silently on well-oiled hinges.

"Damn!" she murmured as she slipped into the prop

room. The door's interior side was fitted with a push plate, but no handle or lock. There was no way she could prevent Donna from entering the room.

The way Caroline saw it, she had only one option: she had to get out of the building before Moore arrived.

Moonlight filtered through the windows set high in the walls on either side of the prop room. Caroline had no trouble making out the two lines of floats awaiting Saturday's Homecoming parade. She dashed between the rows to the tall double doors that opened onto the field behind the auditorium.

Her hope fell when she saw the padlocked chain wound through the vertical handles of the wooden doors. She turned to the smaller door set into one of the larger ones. It too was locked, this time with a key.

"Double damn!"

Caroline glanced up at the windows set in the east wall. A workbench stood beneath one of them, and next to it, an extension ladder rested against the wall.

"If I can find some way to break the window..."

The surface of the workbench was surprisingly free of equipment. Beneath it, though, was a cabinet with what looked like a simple latch lock. Caroline squatted down on her heels and slipped the latch to the right. The door swung open, exposing two shelves littered with an assortment of carpentry supplies. She chose a claw hammer from among the tools and hefted it in her hand.

"This should do."

She was about to rise when she heard the floorboards creak behind her. She twisted on the balls of her feet and glanced quickly around the room. Standing in the shadowed doorway was Donna Moore.

Caroline lowered her body to the floor and slithered snake-like toward the nearest float. It was one she'd seen being built on Saturday, a flatbed padded and painted to resemble a football. A ten-foot tall skeleton made of papier-mâché sat precariously on top of the ball with its legs dangling on either side. A dozen medium-sized pumpkins secured the skeleton's feet to the flatbed floor.

Caroline braced herself against the float and got to her knees. She raised her head high enough to peer over the pumpkins. What she saw didn't please her one bit.

Donna was fumbling with something on the wall near the doorway. Caroline guessed it was the light switch. She ducked her head and quickly looked around for a better place to hide.

"Where are you, Mrs. Rhodes?"

A dozen overhead lamps illuminated the prop room as Donna flipped the light switch.

"Come out, come out, wherever you are!"

Caroline shivered at the sound of Donna's voice. There was a singsong quality to it that made her question Moore's sanity. Had desperation forced Donna over the edge? If so, there was no telling to what lengths she would go to silence Caroline.

Matching wits with a cold-hearted killer was one thing. Competing against a crazy woman was quite another.

Caroline put down the hammer and edged toward the front of the float. Donna had moved away from the door, but not far enough to afford her prey a decent shot at escape. It was time for Caroline to make another tactical move.

Choosing the nearest pumpkin, she plucked it off the float and heaved it at the workbench. It hit the cabinet door with a thud that immediately drew Donna's attention. Caroline watched Moore's face contort with anger as a gooey mass of orange and ivory splattered across the floor.

She sent a second pumpkin sailing toward the double

doors, then a third between the two rows of floats. The results were the same as before, only this time Donna couldn't contain her rage. She charged down the center of the room with the knife raised above her head.

"You stupid woman! Don't you know he wasn't worth it?"

Caroline stepped away from the float and aimed a fourth pumpkin directly at Moore. It fell short, landing a foot in front of her. The shell broke into a dozen pieces sending a squishy concoction of fruit and seeds skittering across Donna's path.

Moore couldn't stop fast enough to avoid a fall. Her feet did a tap dance as she slid across the wet floor. She fought to stay upright, twisting her body and lunging sideways toward one of the floats. The effort to save herself failed. Arms flailing the air like the wings of a crow, she tumbled forward into the plywood legs of a scarecrow. A second later, she collapsed on the floor.

FORTY-EIGHT

"I DIDN'T MEAN to kill her," Caroline said as she sat in the stands Saturday afternoon watching the Big Bad Bruins fumble another ball. The score was 35-zip in the second quarter with the Bruins on the zip side. "I guess I hit her a little too hard with the stage door."

"It was you or her," said Professor Atwater. "You did what you had to."

Since Carl's eyes were firmly riveted on the Bruins, Caroline wasn't sure if the grimness in his voice was due to concern for her mental health or disgust for the football team. She decided to give him the benefit of the doubt.

"I felt the same way at the time."

"So it was the original fall that did her in?" asked Nikki from a seat one row below her mother-in-law.

Caroline glanced down at the girl happily entwined in the arms of her husband.

"According to the autopsy report, Donna developed an acute bleed in the brain when she cracked her head on the sidewalk."

"It would kill her that fast?"

This question came from Martin who had quit nuzzling Nikki's neck long enough to show some interest in Moore's demise.

"Allison said her sister was diagnosed with high blood pressure last winter. She'd been suffering from headaches for months and finally went to a doctor. He put her on medication, but she was lax in taking it. She relied instead on aspirin—lots of aspirin—to relieve her pain."

"So?"

"Aspirin's a blood thinner, Martin. It affects the clotting process. Taken in low doses, it helps prevent heart attacks. But Donna was taking too much of it too often. She tore a blood vessel in her brain when she fell. Because of the aspirin, her body couldn't react sufficiently to stop it."

"Wouldn't her blood pressure affect how fast she bled?" asked Nikki.

"Oh, yes," said Caroline. "The higher the pressure, the more force exerted on the vessels. The more force, the greater the possibility the tear would increase in size. And one thing I can guarantee: Donna's blood pressure was sky high Wednesday night. She was under a lot of stress what with her discovery of the files on Wade Wilkins. She acted on impulse when she attacked Amos Dalton. Then she had no choice but to come after me."

"She'd worked herself into a corner," said Carl.

"And all over a misunderstanding," added Caroline.

Her thoughts drifted back to the scene at Hildy Hall. Allison and Ben Halloway had arrived hard on the heels of the ambulance. The younger Moore sister had been near hysteria when she saw Donna lying on the floor amid the ruined pumpkins. Fortunately, Ben was made of sterner stuff. He'd gathered Allison in his arms and pulled her away, allowing the paramedics to get on with their work.

Later, in the hospital, Allison had confessed her part in the tragedies that had befallen the university.

"Donna called me at the ranch early Monday morning," Allison said in response to Chief Moeller's first question. "She told me Harry was living here under the name Wade Wilkins."

"Is that the first you knew of it?" asked Jake.

"Yes," replied Allison. "Donna thought it would be best if I stayed home and let one of the ranch hands bring the stock to Rhineburg. She thought seeing Harry again would upset me."

"But you came anyway."

"I wasn't about to let an old romance interfere with my present life. Ben and I had become close. Donna didn't know it, but Ben asked me to marry him last week."

Allison massaged the back of her neck with one hand.

"Harry skipped town without even saying good-bye. I was devastated when I learned what he'd done. Later, I became angry. People talked about me behind my back. Some of them thought I was a fool to have fallen for Harry. Others suspected I knew all along what he was doing with that football player."

She raised her eyes and glared at Jake.

"I might have been a fool, but I'd never condone something so ugly."

"You don't seem like the kind of woman who would," said Jake. "What happened after the phone call from your sister?"

"I decided I had to confront Harry. I left a couple of our ranch hands with the stock and slipped into town earlier than expected. I hadn't told Donna what I planned to do—I knew she'd be against it—but she was on campus when I arrived. She saw me park my car in the lot next to the auditorium."

"I have a witness who will swear Donna was lurking outside the gym Monday night."

"She followed me there. I never should have gone to see Harry," added Allison miserably. "I told him I was going to turn him in to the police back home. He just laughed in my face. He said he'd swear I was part of the affair."

"Why would anyone believe him?"

"The cops had found photographs of Harry with that boy. He'd rigged the camera himself, but he was going to claim I was the one who took the pictures."

Jake waited while Allison dug through her pockets for a tissue. He phrased his next question after she'd had time to compose herself.

"Did you see Trace Golden in the locker room?"

"I didn't know his name at the time, but I passed him in the hallway when I left the gym. He was standing outside Harry's office."

"What happened next?"

"I ran out of the building and back to my car. Later that night, Donna told me she'd waited until I drove away, then she went in to see Harry. He told her I'd come by because I wanted to get back together with him. It was a lie, but she believed it."

"Did Donna see Trace in the gym?"

"I asked her that same question when I saw the boy's picture in the newspaper. She told me she interrupted a conversation between him and Harry when she walked into the office. He left when she arrived, and she never saw him again."

"Did you suspect your sister killed Wilkins?"

It was at this point that Allison broke down completely.

"I knew she'd done it," the young woman sobbed. "She wouldn't believe me when I said it was over long ago between Harry and me. She was convinced I was going to leave the ranch and run off with him."

Jake's expression was stern, but his voice gentle.

"So she told you she'd killed him."

Allison shook her head. "She didn't have to tell me. I knew there was something wrong when the bulls got loose Tuesday night. Ben had padlocked the gates to the pens after the incident with Trace Golden. Only he and

Donna had keys to the locks, and Ben was with me the entire evening."

"You mean only Donna could have opened the gates and let the bulls out."

"She did it to cover up the murder. I think she called Harry and asked him to meet her somewhere private. She probably offered him money to stay away from me."

"And Wilkins chose to meet on Bruck Green."

"Donna could have picked the spot. It's a wooded area not all that far from the pens. We rounded up two of the bulls near to where Harry's body was found." Allison paused, her voice catching in her throat. "Donna couldn't run the ranch by herself. She would have lost the land and the business if I left."

Which gave her a pretty good motive for murder, Caroline thought as she rehashed the conversation in her mind.

"Hey, Cari! Pay attention!"

"Hmm?" Caroline turned to see Atwater staring at her. "Oh! Sorry about that, Carl. I was thinking about what happened at the hospital Wednesday night."

"It was a pretty bad scene. Chan Daley had his hands full between Amos Dalton and Donna Moore."

"I'm glad Amos pulled through. He's not out of the woods yet, but at least he's in stable condition. As for Donna, Allison made a wise decision when she agreed to terminate life support. To my mind, it was an act of mercy." Caroline shifted her gaze to the field. "I should have guessed something was physically wrong with her when she began acting so oddly in the prop room. I thought she was cracking up mentally. Instead, her brain was flooding with blood."

"It's hard to make a proper diagnosis when you're fighting for your life. Of course, it would have helped if you'd had your cell phone turned on. You might have been able to answer my calls, and then we would have found you faster."

"I never even thought of my phone until after Donna went down." Caroline sighed. "I made too many mistakes, Carl. I was too emotionally involved in this case to think straight."

"Aw, come on, Cari. You're beating yourself up again."

"No, I'm not. I'm only speaking the truth. I suspected everyone but Donna. I counted her out way too early."

"She didn't seem to have a motive."

"Not in Trace Golden's death. And that's what really confused the issue."

"We were hunting for two murderers instead of one."

"Actually, there were three murderers, if you want to include Sue Walker."

"She's claiming she killed Tom in self-defense."

"I know. I talked with Nancy Kuhnkey yesterday. She's handing over Sue's case to a criminal lawyer in Chicago."

"The way I heard it, Kuhnkey plans to be the prime witness for the defense."

"It seems Nancy was the only real friend Sue ever had. She knew how abusive Tom was; she'd seen Sue's bruises over the years. She also knew Tom fathered his daughter's baby."

"Is it true Sue was planning to divorce Tom?"

"Nancy was working on the papers when Tom died. Apparently he came home drunk Monday night and heard Sue talking to Nancy on the phone. He was already angry with Sue because of the scene she'd caused at the demonstration. Finding out about the divorce only worsened matters."

"So you believe Sue when she says she was protecting herself."

"Yes, I think it was a case of self-defense. It was a bad move on Sue's part to stuff the body in the basement freezer, but given the situation, I can understand she'd be rattled. I guess she hoped people would accept the story about Tom walking out on her."

"It would have helped Martin if we'd known the truth earlier."

Caroline glanced down at the two lovebirds sitting in front of her. At the moment, their eyes were on the field instead of on each other.

"I should have paid more attention to what Maddy said Wednesday in the café."

"What's that?" asked Carl with a frown.

"She suggested Wilkins had killed Trace Golden and was caught in the act by Tom Walker. She thought Tom was in hiding because he was afraid of Wilkins."

"Well, we know that part of it wasn't true."

"Yes, but she also thought Tom might be blackmailing the coach."

"So?"

"Don't you see, Carl. Maddy had the right idea, only she had the wrong people. Trace was doing the blackmailing, and that's what caused his death."

"He overheard Allison call Wilkins by his real name."

"Yes. And I'll bet that's why Donna saw him in the office talking with Wilkins. He was telling the coach he knew about his past. He left the office when Donna arrived, but he didn't leave the gym."

"And I have a witness who will testify to that."

Caroline and Carl looked up in surprise at the sound of Jake Moeller's voice. Jake clapped Carl on the shoulder as he and Maddy slipped into two seats behind their friends.

"Sorry we're late. Have we missed much?"

"Not if you're talking about the game," grumbled the professor. "The Freebies are giving another one away."

"It figures," said Jake. "These guys can't tell one end

of the field from the other. I can't believe I'm wasting a beautiful day watching them fumble the ball."

"You are such a liar, Jake Moeller," said Maddy, slapping her husband on the arm. She leaned forward, winked at Caroline, and added conspiratorially, "He wouldn't have missed this game for the world. It gives him a chance to poke fun at President Hurst."

"Have you seen the portable johns?" asked Carl. "They make a stunning addition to the landscape."

"I can't believe Hurst only ordered three of them," laughed Jake. "We saw a line of people half a block long waiting to use them."

"Forget the johns," exclaimed Maddy. "Let's talk about something more interesting, like murder."

"That's exactly what we were discussing when you arrived," said Carl. "Cari was saying Trace never left the gym Monday night."

"That's what Sue Chuey claims," said Jake. "She saw both Martin and Allison leave the building, and Donna Moore go in. A few minutes later, Donna walked out alone. Sue swears she never saw Trace set foot outside."

"How long was she there?" asked Caroline.

"She left a few minutes after Donna. That's good enough for me, though. It establishes the presence of both Trace and Wade Wilkins in the gym at the same time."

"Meaning Wilkins had the opportunity to kill Golden."

"I don't doubt he did it, Cari," said Jake. "Martin came back from Iowa with some pretty nasty stories about the coach. The Iowa police corroborated those tales, plus they had a few of their own to tell. Wilkins—or should I say, Harry Wade—was a real piece of work." Jake shook his head in disgust. "I think young Mr. Golden overheard more than he should have Monday night. Knowing Trace, he would have tried to benefit from that information."

"Nothing like a little blackmail," said Maddy with a meaningful nod of her head.

"For which he ended up dead," added Jake.

"You're fortunate to have a witness as reliable as Sue Chuey," said Carl.

"She took her time coming forward, but when she did, she supported Al Sperling's story."

"Al was in a belligerent mood when Cari and I questioned him. He clammed up when we asked him about his relationship with Trace."

"According to the people who know him, there was no relationship," said Jake. "Al didn't hang out with the Golden gang. It appears his only contact with Trace was on the field and in the locker room. Even then, I was told, Trace mostly ignored him."

"So you didn't consider him to be a suspect."

"He was one of the last people to see Trace alive, which naturally made him a suspect in my mind. As far as I could tell, though, he didn't have a motive for the killing." Jake shook his head in disgust. "I wish I'd known Miss Chuey was with him outside the gym that night."

"Al's in one of her classes," said Carl.

He's also in her bed, thought Caroline. Which is why *he* refused to answer our questions and *she* didn't come forward sooner.

"We could have cleared things up much earlier, maybe even prevented the attack on Amos, if she'd told me what she'd seen," said Jake.

Carl shrugged his shoulders. He was obviously struggling between loyalty to a friend and loyalty to a fellow faculty member. It showed in the way he phrased his reply.

"In Sue's defense, only two days passed between Trace's murder and Donna Moore's death. Sue probably didn't realize what she'd witnessed until it was too late."

Caroline averted her eyes from the two men, uncomfortable with keeping the truth from them. The affair between Al Sperling and Sue grated on her conscience. She was almost positive Trace Golden had sniffed it out and was blackmailing either one or both of them. What she thought and what she could prove were two different things, though. Without anything stronger than a hunch to go on, it was better if she kept her suspicions to herself.

"Never did find that letter Wilkins allegedly received from the NCAA," said Jake as he stared down at Martin two rows below him. "I guess your son's still in limbo when it comes to football."

"He looks happy enough where he is," said Maddy with a playful laugh. "And I'm sure the grandmother-to-be is relieved her son's not in uniform."

Caroline blushed. "I have a confession to make," she said as she reached into her pocket and pulled out two crumpled sheets of paper. She separated the pair, twisted around on the stadium bench, and handed one page to Jake. "This is what you've been looking for. I found it clutched in Amos's hand Wednesday night."

Jake glanced at the paper. His eyebrows soared when he saw the NCAA logo. He looked over at Caroline, and for a moment, she thought he was going to explode.

"Don't be angry," she pleaded. "Donna planted that letter on Amos. She knew Martin was a suspect in both of the previous murders. She tried to pin this attack on him, too."

"I know," said Jake, his voice registering a modicum of understanding along with undisguised exasperation. He folded the letter and tucked it in the inside breast pocket of his jacket. "I'll have to keep the original until the case is officially closed, but I'll make Martin a copy of the letter."

Maddy patted her husband's arm.

"You're a good man, Jake Moeller."

"That's what all the women say," growled Jake. He pointed to the other piece of paper in Caroline's hand. "I hope that's a signed affidavit promising you'll never again withhold evidence from the police."

"Not quite," said Caroline with a smile. "It's a picture by Bricole Gregori showing two women dressed in western clothing. She drew it on Wednesday at Bill Morgan's dealership and gave it to Maddy to give to me." Caroline handed the drawing to Carl. "You can't see either of the women's faces, but you can tell by their body language that one is despondent while the other is quite gleeful. The gleeful one is dancing with a scarecrow."

"Bricole was sending you a warning," cried Maddy. "She knew Donna was up to no good."

"I doubt she 'knew' what Donna was doing," said Caroline. "I think Bricole is simply more sensitive to the people around her than most children her age. She probably picked up on the emotional currents swirling around Allison and Donna, then translated what she saw and felt to paper. Unfortunately, I mistook the gleeful figure for Allison and the sad figure for Donna. In reality, it was vice versa."

"Why did she draw Donna with her arms around a scarecrow?" asked Carl as he passed the picture on to Jake.

"That's easy," said Maddy. "Caroline thought Wilkins was a scarecrow when she first came across his body on Bruck Green. What better way to warn her than to show Donna dancing with death?"

"I know you think Bricole is gifted," said Jake. "But you're pushing it now, don't you think?"

Maddy pointed to the scarecrow. "Take a closer look, then tell me that's not Wade Wilkins."

Caroline, Carl, and Jake put their heads together and examined the picture more closely. Caroline was the first to look away.

"I can't believe I didn't notice it before," said Carl. "Look at the head. It's long and narrow, not round like most hay-stuffed scarecrows."

"Wilkins had those same facial features," said Caroline slowly.

"And there's hair showing under the scarecrow's hat, short on the sides and long in the back," added Jake. "The coach wore his hair that way."

"Look at the heavy eyelids and the brows jutting out from the forehead," said Maddy. "Again, just like Wilkins."

"Not the typical face of a scarecrow," said Carl. He looked up at Caroline. "What do you think, Cari?"

"I think…" Caroline hesitated. In her mind she saw again the cobra-like eyes of Wade Wilkins. Seaweed green with flecks of amber, they'd sent a chill down her back when she'd looked into their depths last Saturday. Now she felt that chill again.

She glanced down at Martin sitting with his arm around Nikki. She thought of her unborn grandchild, and the chill slowly subsided.

"I think it's over," she said firmly. "And that's all that matters."

She took the picture from Carl and tore it into a dozen small scraps that caught in the breeze when she tossed them in the air. Satisfied, she watched as they fluttered toward the field and disappeared, ground into the dirt by the cleats of eleven Big Bad Bruins.

* * * * *

REQUEST YOUR FREE BOOKS!

2 FREE NOVELS
PLUS 2 FREE GIFTS!

WORLDWIDE LIBRARY®
Your Partner in Crime

YES! Please send me 2 FREE novels from the Worldwide Library® series and my 2 FREE gifts (gifts are worth about $10). After receiving them, if I don't wish to receive any more books, I can return the shipping statement marked "cancel." If I don't cancel, I will receive 4 brand-new novels every month and be billed just $5.49 per book in the U.S. or $6.24 per book in Canada. That's a savings of at least 31% off the cover price. It's quite a bargain! Shipping and handling is just 50¢ per book in the U.S. and 75¢ per book in Canada.* I understand that accepting the 2 free books and gifts places me under no obligation to buy anything. I can always return a shipment and cancel at any time. Even if I never buy another book, the two free books and gifts are mine to keep forever.

414/424 WDN F4WY

Name	(PLEASE PRINT)
Address	Apt. #
City State/Prov.	Zip/Postal Code

Signature (if under 18, a parent or guardian must sign)

Mail to the Harlequin® Reader Service:
IN U.S.A.: P.O. Box 1867, Buffalo, NY 14240-1867
IN CANADA: P.O. Box 609, Fort Erie, Ontario L2A 5X3

Want to try two free books from another line?
Call 1-800-873-8635 or visit www.ReaderService.com.

* Terms and prices subject to change without notice. Prices do not include applicable taxes. Sales tax applicable in N.Y. Canadian residents will be charged applicable taxes. Offer not valid in Quebec. This offer is limited to one order per household. Not valid for current subscribers to the Worldwide Library series. All orders subject to credit approval. Credit or debit balances in a customer's account(s) may be offset by any other outstanding balance owed by or to the customer. Please allow 4 to 6 weeks for delivery. Offer available while quantities last.

Your Privacy—The Harlequin® Reader Service is committed to protecting your privacy. Our Privacy Policy is available online at www.ReaderService.com or upon request from the Harlequin Reader Service.

We make a portion of our mailing list available to reputable third parties that offer products we believe may interest you. If you prefer that we not exchange your name with third parties, or if you wish to clarify or modify your communication preferences, please visit us at www.ReaderService.com/consumerschoice or write to us at Harlequin Reader Service Preference Service, P.O. Box 9062, Buffalo, NY 14269. Include your complete name and address.

WWLi3R

ReaderService.com

Manage your account online!

- Review your order history
- Manage your payments
- Update your address

> *We've designed*
> *the Harlequin® Reader Service*
> *website just for you.*

Enjoy all the features!

- Reader excerpts from any series
- Respond to mailings and
  special monthly offers
- Discover new series available to you
- Browse the Bonus Bucks catalog
- Share your feedback

Visit us at:

ReaderService.com